T0356955

OBELISTS
EN ROUTE

C. Daly King (1895-1963) was an American psychologist and detective story writer. He was born in New York City and educated at Yale University. After fighting in World War I, he worked in textiles and in advertising before returning to school at Columbia to study psychology, with a particular focus on sleep and consciousness. In the 1930s, King published nine books that quickly established him as a master of the Golden Age mystery, but ceased writing fiction with the advent of World War II.

Otto Penzler, the creator of American Mystery Classics, is also the founder of the Mysterious Press (1975); Mysterious-Press.com (2011), an electronic-book publishing company; and New York City's Mysterious Bookshop (1979). He has won a Raven, the Ellery Queen Award, two Edgars (for the *Encyclopedia of Mystery and Detection*, 1977, and *The Lineup*, 2010), and lifetime achievement awards from NoirCon and *The Strand Magazine*. He has edited more than 70 anthologies and written extensively about mystery fiction.

OBELISTS
EN ROUTE

C. DALY
KING

Introduction by
OTTO
PENZLER

AMERICAN
MYSTERY
CLASSICS

Penzler Publishers
New York

Published in 2025 by Penzler Publishers
58 Warren Street, New York, NY 10007
penzlerpublishers.com

Distributed by W. W. Norton

Cover image: Andy Ross
Cover design: Mauricio Diaz

Paperback ISBN 978-1-61316-619-2
Hardcover ISBN 978-1-61316-620-8
eBook ISBN 978-1-61316-621-5

Library of Congress Control Number: 2024918841

Printed in the United States of America

9 8 7 6 5 4 3 2 1

INTRODUCTION

Right from the start, readers will know that they are in for a pleasurable ride with C(harles) Daly King as "The Transcontinental" pulls out of Grand Central Station on a three-day, non stop trip to San Francisco.

The humor is omnipresent, a bit situationally but mostly tonally, as the author's voice indicates that he is pleasantly bemused by everything and everyone that he observes.

A prominent banker, Sabot Hodges, eager to board the train but equally desirous of avoiding publicity by giving an interview, was "motioning surreptitiously to the porters; it was obvious that he cherished hopes of escape. He nearly made it."

Dr. L. Rees Pons, one of the psychologists selected for the celebrity-laden voyage, wondered why he had been invited for the trip because "lately his contributions had been widely spaced." He "had a family and his family ate food." To earn a living he had taken to writing popular novels, earning the disdain of his colleagues, so he reckoned that the publicist in charge of the guest list "must have consulted a *Who's Who* of previous years."

For a bit of wordplay, perhaps mainly to amuse himself, Daly names the very efficient secretary Entwerk. His full name is Xavier Lewis Entwerk. Which can be reduced to X.L. Entwerk. Get it? Excellent work.

As was true of Daly's earlier novel *Obelists at Sea*, there are psychologists on board, each a practitioner of a different school of thought. Making a repeat appearance in the present book from King's first novel is Dr. Pons, perhaps the most likable of the pedants whose intellectual duels helped to slow down the progress of the investigation. Also returning is King's young series protagonist, Lieutenant Michael Lord of the New York City Police Department, this time with a larger role.

For those of us who occasionally think that life would have been better in the simpler times before World War II (forgetting dentistry for the moment), the description of the train and its amenities is irresistible. In addition to the luxury staterooms and dining car, the coast-to-coast train has a "recreation room" for bridge, ping pong, and dancing, as well as a headline-making swimming pool that nicely serves as the murder venue.

Hodge is the perfect victim because no one seems to mind that he's dead. He had enemies in business and quickly found a way to make another one on board. When Hodge is fished out of the pool, the ship's doctor cannot immediately determine the cause of death so an autopsy informs one and all that he didn't drown and there are no poisons in his system. Discovering how he died, as well as the identity of the person who abetted the process, falls into the capable hands of Lt. Lord.

Although he had a very modest number of mystery novels to his name (seven, though only six were published), King has been (rightly) recognized as being among the most clever and original plotters in the golden age of the detective story, even mastering its most challenging sub-genre, the locked room mystery. Two of his novels are outstanding examples.

In *Careless Corpse* (1937), victims are poisoned in well-guarded areas where it would be impossible to administer.

In *Arrogant Alibi* (1938) the victim is stabbed to death in a locked room that appears to be impenetrable; there are nine suspects, all with airtight alibis.

Most remarkably, each of the stories in *The Curious Mr. Tarrant* (1935) is a masterpiece of the form, with such incredible episodes as crews abandoning a ship every time it sails, none surviving; a closely watched road on which headless torsos are discovered with no sign of the perpetrator—or of the heads; and the murder of a woman in a confined area accompanied by two men, neither of whom killed her.

It was the intent of classic detective story writers during its golden age to be fair to readers, slipping clues into the narrative that the observant reader could use to build a case against the murderer. A handful of authors were so scrupulous about the notion of fairness that their detectives would point to objects, statements, or moments to which the characters (and, by extension, readers) should pay special attention.

None were as meticulous about inserting clues as King, going so far as to include an Appendix at the back of the book called "The Clue Finder," in which hints are catalogued as they relate to the weapon, the method, a motive, etc. The Clue Finder is preceded by a warning: *Do not open until you have finished the story*, adding: *To cheat others is dishonorable; to cheat oneself is merely ridiculous.* The Clue Finder appears at the back of all three "obelist" titles but not in his other books.

By the way, in the first edition of *Obelists at Sea* (1932), King defined an obelist (a word he invented) as "a person of little or no worth." When it was published in America the following year, he changed the meaning to "one who views with suspicion," the same definition he used in *Obelists en Route* and, later, *Obelists Fly High*.

Fair warning: If you read King's first book, you will have noticed that its sprightly pace was interrupted on several occasions as the four psychologists trying to solve the murder expounded on their preferred practices. In the present volume, Noah Hall, an unpleasantly argumentative technocrat, engages Hodge in a debate on economics that endures for more than six pages. Worse, Lt. Lord, an otherwise attractive character, inexplicably brings the action to a screeching halt with a *non sequitur* lecture on a different branch of economics at even greater length. Feel free to skip both of those sections as they have absolutely nothing to do with the story and do not contain clues or, indeed, anything of relevance. Or, for that matter, interest. Whatever King could have been thinking when he intruded these sections in an otherwise delightful novel eludes me. Equally, one has to wonder if his editor was sane or sober when he allowed them to remain.

King was born in New York City in 1895 and was educated at Yale, where he graduated as a Phi Beta Kappa. After serving as a second lieutenant in the field artillery during World War I, he received a commission as a captain in the Reserves, which he resigned in 1926.

Deciding to return to school, he received his master's degree in psychology from Columbia in 1928 and a Ph.D. from Yale for an electromagnetic study of sleep. He divided his time between Summit, New Jersey, and Bermuda, where he wrote his detective novels. When World War II broke out, he stopped writing fiction but continued practicing psychology and wrote five books on various elements of the subject until his death in 1963.

One of the books, *Integrative Psychology* (1931), was cowritten with W. M. Marston and Elizabeth H. Marston, the couple credited with having invented an early version of the lie detector. King became close friends with his colleagues and you may have noticed that *Obelists en Route* was dedicated to William Moulton Marston.

Marston had another claim to fame: he went on to create perhaps the most famous female fictional character of all time—Wonder Woman.

OTTO PENZLER
May 2024

OBELISTS
EN ROUTE

For
WILLIAM MOULTON MARSTON
A.B., LL.B., Ph.D.

CONTENTS
PART ONE
ANONYMOUS: BEHAVIOUR

NEW YORK, Saturday, 10.30 p.m   3

HARMON, Saturday, 11.20 p.m.   10

ALBANY, Sunday, 1.11 a.m.   28

UTICA, Sunday, 2.43 a.m.   31

SYRACUSE, Sunday, 3.40 a.m.   33

ROCHESTER, Sunday, 4.55 a.m.   34

BUFFALO, Sunday, 6.12 a.m.   37

PART TWO
DR. MABON RAQUETTE: DEATH INSTINCTS

TOLEDO, Sunday, 10.33 a.m.   43

ELKHART, Sunday, 12.18 p.m.   70

ENGLEWOOD, Sunday, 2.05 p.m.   81

CHICAGO (ar.), Sunday, 2.30 p.m.   86

CHICAGO (lv.), Sunday, 2.37 p.m.   88

PART THREE
PROF. DR. GOTTLIEB IRRTUM: PATTERNS

OMAHA (ar.), Monday, 2.07 a.m.   95

OMAHA (lv.), Monday, 2.14 a.m.   116

FREMONT, Monday, 3.06 a.m.   119

PART FOUR
DR. IVA POPPAS: HORMIC URGES

COLUMBUS, Monday, 3.48 a.m.   135

GRAND ISLAND, Monday, 5.18 a.m.   149

KEARNEY, Monday, 6.07 a.m.   153

NORTH PLATTE (ar.), Monday, 8.04 a.m.   168

NORTH PLATTE (lv.), Monday, 7.11 a.m.   172

CHEYENNE, Monday, 12.29 p.m.   190

PART FIVE
Dr. L. Rees Pons: Appetite as Love

Laramie, Monday, 2.04 p.m.   197
Rawlins, Monday, 4.31 p.m.   205
Rock Springs, Monday, 7.00 p.m.   209
Green River, Monday, 7.45 p.m.   223
Evanston, Monday, 9.48 p.m.   233
Ogden (ar.), Tuesday, 12.24 a.m.   253
Ogden (lv.), Monday, 11.31 p.m.   256

PART SIX
Lieut. Michael Lord: Intrextroversion

Reno, Tuesday, 1.17 p.m.   275
Truckee, Tuesday, 2.32 p.m.   289
Sacramento, Tuesday, 7.20 p.m.   305
Oakland, Tuesday, 9.47 p.m.   330
San Francisco, Tuesday, 10.30 p.m.   337

APPENDICES

A. Bibliography of References   339
B. The Clue Finder   341

CHARACTERS OF THE BOOK

SABOT HODGES, Chairman of the Board, International Cities Bank.

EDVANNE HODGES, his daughter.

XAVIER LEWIS ENTWERK, his secretary.

HOPPING, his valet.

HANS SUMMERLADD, Publicity Director of "The Transcontinental."

NOAH HALL, an industrial engineer; likewise a technocrat.

DR. MABON RAQUETTE, a psychoanalyst, accompanying Hodges.

DR. IVA POPPAS, a Hormic psychologist.

PROF. DR. GOTTLIEB IRRTUM, a Gestalt psychologist.

DR. L. REES PONS, an Integrative psychologist.

LIEUT. MICHAEL LORD, of the New York City Police Department.

DR. LORESS BLACK, a medical examiner of the Chicago Police Department.

TITUS NUTT, conductor of "The Transcontinental."

DIAGRAMS

I. Route of The Transcontinental Limited xvi

II. The Transcontinental... xvii

III. Transcontinental Limited, Club Car xviii

IV. Transcontinental Limited, Refrigeration Car.................. xviii

V. Transcontinental Limited, Recreation Car xix

VI. Transcontinental Limited, Swimming Pool Car................53

VII. Transcontinental Limited, First Stateroom Car.............124

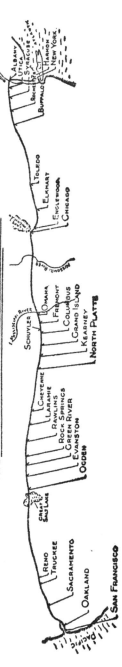

ROUTE OF THE TRANSCONTINENTAL LIMITED

XVI

THE TRANSCONTINENTAL LIMITED

Labels on train cars: RECREATION, STATEROOM, STATEROOM, DINING, STATEROOM, STATEROOM, POOL, CLUB, REFRIGERATION

XVII

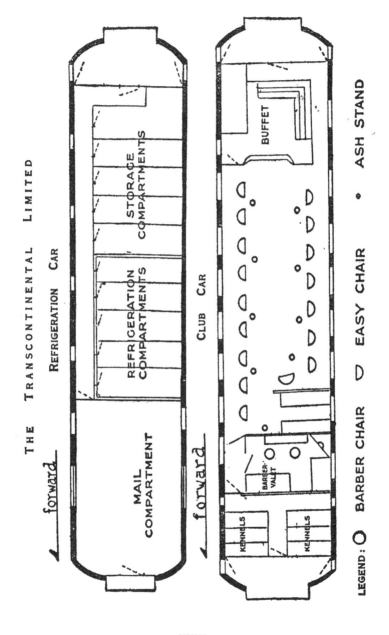

THE TRANSCONTINENTAL LIMITED

REFRIGERATION CAR

forward

MAIL COMPARTMENT

REFRIGERATION COMPARTMENTS

STORAGE COMPARTMENTS

CLUB CAR

forward

BUFFET

BARBER VALET

KENNELS

KENNELS

LEGEND: ○ BARBER CHAIR   ⊅ EASY CHAIR   • ASH STAND

XVIII

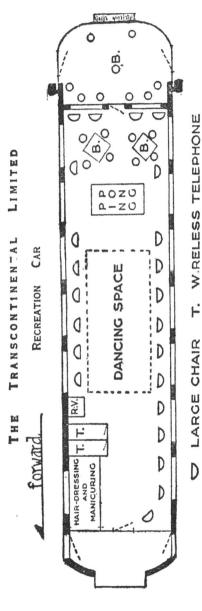

THE TRANSCONTINENTAL LIMITED
RECREATION CAR

forward

OB.

B.

B.

P
R
O
N

P
I
N
G

DANCING SPACE

R:V.

T. T.

HAIR-DRESSING
AND
MANICURING

LEGEND

D LARGE CHAIR   T. WIRELESS TELEPHONE

O SMALL CHAIR   R:V. RADIO~VICTROLA

B. BRIDGE TABLE OB. OBSERVATION PLATFORM

XIX

ACKNOWLEDGEMENTS

The author wishes here, in no wise inappropriately, to acknowledge the valuable assistance rendered him in the preparation of the following pages and to pay his thanks, thus individually, to

> his wife, Mildred Sisson King, for help in plot construction and editorial minutiae;

> his friend and physician, Dr. Charles W. Scranton, for medical advice of a technical character, as well as notable improvements in the schedules of the Twentieth Century Limited and the Overland Limited;

> his pedagogue, Dr. William M. Marston, for rescue from certain psychological haphazards.

PART ONE

Anonymous: Behaviour

NEW YORK
Saturday, 10.30 *p.m.*

". . . In the feat about to be witnessed, the first uninterrupted run across the continent, there is food for thought. Records are broken. Technological civilisation once again smashes space and time. We live in a different age, and we must employ new standards, new methods. As a representative of Technocracy, I greet you."

"Thank you, Mr. Hall, thank you." Hans Summerladd, Publicity Director of the very new Transcontinental Limited, gently pried loose the unexpectedly strong grip from the microphone standard. It was not his intention that any one should use it for more than five minutes.

He wiped his forehead, as Mr. Hall departed lingeringly. Then he started forward as there approached across the concourse of the Grand Central Terminal an imposing group. Sabot Hodges, Chairman of the Board of the International Cities Bank, accompanied by his daughter, his secretary, his valet and three laden porters, would have been glad to escape attention and reach his accommodations unnoticed; but in the circumstances he could scarcely hope to do so.

3

"Good-evening, Mr. Hodges." Summerladd placed himself squarely in the path of the financier, so that the whole party was halted perforce and another member of it, a stout, well-fed gentleman with a careful Van Dyke, caught it up.

"Summerladd," said Hodges, and indicated the new arrival. "Dr. Raquette, psychoanalyst. Going out with me."

While Summerladd was acknowledging the introduction, he took care to edge around toward the girl. "How is it going off, Hans?" she asked. "It certainly looks like Christmas or Old Home Week or something. I like your orchestra."

"No idea," he admitted. "I've been so busy right here, I haven't seen anything else at all. Glad you like the tunes; but you're the finishing touch, you know. You promised to be on the observation platform for the pictures; you won't forget?"

Edvanne Hodges laughed, a laugh of pure enjoyment. She was delighted with the excitement and ballyhoo. "I meant it," she promised, and added in a lower tone, "And thanks for the flowers, Hans. I love them."

Her father was motioning surreptitiously to the porters; it was obvious that he cherished hopes of escape. He nearly made it.

"Oh, Mr. Hodges." Summerladd caught his arm at the last moment. "Just a word over the air to our patrons," he pleaded. "If you will. Nothing much, just a couple of sentences."

The financier saw no way out. He took the microphone grumblingly.

"Ladies and gentlemen," he cried in a loud voice. "Hr-rmph. Pleasure to speak to you. We are about to leave on the first trip of a great train. Railroad has been good enough to invite me as well as others for the run. Take this opportunity to express my thanks publicly. Thank you.

"Now, Summerladd, do let us get on," he added, relinquishing the standard.

Summerladd grinned and Edvanne squeezed his arm, as the Hodges procession got under way. "Poor dad," she smiled, "he can't take it."

The publicity man wiped his forehead again and looked about. The scene was certainly animated, although by this time it was approaching ten o'clock and the Terminal would ordinarily have been but little filled. Now it was jammed. Across the floor from the Vanderbilt Avenue steps a wide passageway had been roped off, leading to the entrance to Track 26 where "The Transcontinental" awaited its first guests in all its splendour. Near the entrance a popular orchestra sat amid its traps and instruments, enlivening the hour with music, and some distance away the microphone had been set up, with Summerladd in attendance to capture the celebrities for the purposes of the air. The western balcony, decorated for the occasion, (as indeed was the whole station), and the broad spaces of the concourse itself were covered by the idle, the curious and the up-to-date who came, many of them in evening clothes and top hats, to witness the departure of the most famous, at any rate the most publicised, train in the world. Noise, commotion, music, commotion, noise.

Not without effort and imagination had "The Transcontinental" come into existence. It was the railroad's answer to the challenge of air travel. Extra luxury against extra speed. It was really an adaptation of the "land cruise" trains of 1928, with its recreation car possessing observation platform, radio-victrola, dance floor, two wireless telephone booths, games and ladies' hairdresser; its club car with valet and barber service, public stenographer, buffet and six kennels in a separate compartment; and its stateroom suite cars with accommodations for valets and maids in the rear. Each suite comprised a bedroom with twin beds and two easy chairs, a lavatory and a baggage compartment to hold three trunks and hand luggage. An innovation was the swimming pool car, including bath and showers. The pool itself was no canvas tank improvised in an ordinary car, such as had been carried before on western runs; it was a real tiled plunge, built into a car specially designed and constructed in the Pullman workshops. It had not, as a matter of fact, been unusually difficult to construct, but it was a new thing and, when the train was opened for inspection, commanded by far the greatest interest. The Transcontinental Limited made no passenger stops across the continent; it was to leave Grand Central Terminal in New York for its first run at 10.30 p.m., Saturday, May 13th, making its journey in three days flat and arriving in San Francisco 10.30 p.m. the following Tuesday.

Summerladd, appointed its Publicity Director, was largely responsible for the atmosphere of the first run. He had arranged the days of public inspection, the ceremonies at the Terminal, the microphone, the flashlights, the orchestra, the dedication. He had also suggested that on its maiden trip this pet train should carry as passengers only invited guests, a list of whom was taken bodily from *Who's Who* and included prominent business and professional men, scientists, artists and other notorious persons.

Now, with a moment's breathing space, he watched the initial development of his plans. A tall, cheerful-looking German boy, with an infectious grin and a pleasant face, he glanced about over the heads of the throng, while the noise continued unabated and behind him the orchestra broke into the lilting melody of the moment.

Then he raised his wrist and regarded his watch. Ten minutes past ten. The President must now have begun his dedication speech beside the train, in the glare of the news-reel cameramen. When he had finished, there would only remain to be taken the pictures of the observation platform as it receded along the track and slipped forth to the west. He meant to be on that platform with Edvanne; no reason why that Entwerk fellow, old Hodges' secretary, should get more of her time than could be helped.

First, however, he looked down the now empty passageway in search of late arrivals. Sure enough, down the steps came a large, heavy man, fanning his flushed face and grey hair with a white felt hat of generous proportions. His companion, slight, darker, with an alert and questing manner, seemed as cool as the other was overheated. Dr. Pons, perspiring profusely, approached Summerladd.

"Evening, doctor," the latter greeted. "You're just in time; I was about to make a farewell speech and go in to the train."

"Hello, Summerladd. Ah—it's hot, isn't it? Lots of doings. Ah—uh—by the way, do you know Michael Lord?" The two young men shook hands. "He's a detective," Pons added, *sotto voce*. "Younghusband to me, Lord to you."

Summerladd looked confused and Lord smiled. "First time I've seen Dr. Pons since we crossed on the *Meganaut* last year," he explained. "I was on a case then and went by the name of Younghusband. I'm assigned for your trip, by a request to the Commissioner, just in case any crooks or cranks smuggle themselves aboard, but there's no reason why I need any name but my own. Lord it is."

"Lord it is," Summerladd responded. "I wouldn't mention the detective part too widely, though. It's safe with me. Now, doctor," turning to Pons, "the uses of publicity——"

"Are sweet indeed," Pons finished, stepping up to the microphone with little hesitation. He spoke briefly and well, as one used to such occasions. Lights flashed, his picture was recorded for the morning papers. As he handed back the instrument, he remarked, "You ought to call it 'The Hollywood,' Summerladd; if I ever saw an M.G.M. opening, this is it."

"We strive to please, with circuses, if not with bread. If you'll wait a moment, I'll go along with you." Summerladd pulled a paper from his pocket, read his concluding speech over the air and putting the microphone in charge of a pair of studio men hovering nearby, turned away with Lord and Dr. Pons.

·　　　　·　　　　·

Everything in the relatively small space at the stationward end of the track was distinctly élite. Here there were only silk hats and evening gowns. Booths had been roped off and chairs placed in rows; some hundred of the elect reclined in them, while Sherry's servitors handed around trays of small sandwiches and what might have been champagne. The New York Central was having a time.

The President, his speech concluded, stood beside the last car, dedicatory bottle in hand. Titus Nutt, conductor of "The Transcontinental," was savouring the proudest moment of his life at the car's entrance.

Ten-thirty.

Titus Nutt snapped his watch shut, and blew a shrill blast on his whistle. Instantly the train began to move; he stepped aboard. Crash! went the President's bottle against the car's side, his words drowned out in the applause.

Cameras clicked, their lights flashed, friends shouted last farewells to friends over the clapping and tumult. Edvanne was pressed against the rail of the observation platform quite oblivious to the fact that Summerladd, who had pushed his way through the crowd until he stood close behind her looking over her shoulder, was holding her hand. She smiled and waved with the other hand; she cried out something that was lost in the noise.

The President, standing beside the empty track with the broken neck of the bottle still in his hand, looked just a little foolish.

"The Transcontinental" was off.

HARMON
Saturday, 11.20 *p.m.*

"THE TRANSCONTINENTAL" slid to a smooth stop at Harmon. The electric locomotive was quickly uncoupled; it pulled away rapidly, shunting leftward over switches into the maze of green, red and yellow lights that spangled the dark tracks. A minute later a darker mass loomed up out of the blackness ahead; it bore down on the stationary cars, slowed, crept up to them. A slight jog ran through the train, and there came the low hiss of released brakes. Then a little forward jerk. The platform lights started slowly gliding past.

By this time the excitement of departure had abated. In the recreation car two games of contract were in progress, but for the most part the passengers were still engaged in settling their quarters or, quietly appreciative of their new easy chairs, in glancing through the magazines with which most had provided themselves. Some had even begun to retire, but for the majority the unusual send-off had left them thoroughly awake; they were still exploring their novel quarters, opening and closing the trunks in their private luggage compartments, wandering through the train.

Dr. Pons, who had a stateroom suite to himself, had sat down in it shortly after leaving New York to look through the latest number of *Psychological Abstracts*.* His two large valises, his only luggage, still reposed on one of the twin beds where they had been placed when he first came aboard. He had passed from "407. Lindley, S. B. A rotary electric switch. *J. Gen. Psychol.*, 1932, 6, 221-222" through "489. Ingram W. R. & Ransom, S. W. Postural reactions in cats following the destruction of both red nuclei. *Proc. Soc. Exper. Biol. & Med.*, 1932, 29, 1089" and "502. Cheney, R. H. Buffer influence upon response of striated muscle to caffeine stimulation in fatigue studies. *Proc. Soc. Exper. & Med.*, 1932, 30, 3-7," to "732. Freistadt-Lederer, A. Das Dumme Kind. 1st Dummhcit heilbar? *Psychol. Rundschau*, 1932, 4, 128-130." At this point he had tired of the perusal and his thoughts wandered off into a reverie centering about the question as to how he happened to find himself en route to San Francisco, a luxuriously tended guest of the railroad company.

Publicity accounted for the unusual run of the train, of course; the doctor, no amateur himself as concerned that matter, was favourably impressed with Summerladd's accomplishment. But he was still a little puzzled about his own inclusion. Now Professor Irrtum, he thought, was understandable. A visiting celebrity from the University of Berlin, the latter had already received considerable attention from the press and was certainly one of the momentary notables, if it came to a question of scientists. Moreover, the professor was a leading, if not

---

* *Psychological Abstracts* is a monthly publication of the American Psychological Association; it contains non-critical *precises* of articles and books dealing with professional psychology that have appeared throughout the world during the period of issue.

the leading, exponent of the *Gestalt* school of psychology,* a movement that had recently succeeded in making a substantial stir. Dr. Pons promised himself a chat with this professor during the trip; it was possible, he considered, that there might be something more in the *Gestalt* ideas than appeared in the *Gestalt* literature.

But himself. Pons came back to his own problem. And, for the matter of that, what could one make of the case of Dr. Iva Poppas, the female Hormic† psychologist from Vassar, whose name Pons had noticed on the passenger list handsomely printed and carefully laid on each twin bed by the railroad? Dr. Pons knew Dr. Poppas casually, and she was certainly no celebrity. She was doubtless a competent teacher (which was, after all, her job) but she had not made any elaborate researches upon rats nor had she published those innumerable tracts, articles and/or books whose contents almost instantly vanish from memory but with which the academic reputation is inflated. Pons shook his head and decided that some of the original invitations had been unavoidably declined; obviously the question of alternates had arisen.

His perplexity over his own solicitation was not a matter of

---

* Gestalt (best English equivalent is "configuration") psychology: a school of psychology that emphasises the whole pattern of an event or activity or function as the determining factor therein. The present name, and even some of the more tedious expressions used, are modern; but the body of ideas receives periodic reformalising fairly regularly throughout the history of human thought under characteristic conditions, (1) when other evanescent fads are flourishing, (2) when there is little else to talk about.

† Hormic psychology: a subdivision of the purposivist school of psychology. The whole emphasis here is upon the "goal-seeking" tendency alleged to exist in animals and men; teleological conceptions are rampant; it is the defeatist school par excellence of psychology and is closely linked to the defeatest schools in physics and biology—the last stand of religion within the body of science proper.

And of course every M'Whale must have its Poppas.

modesty. He was well aware that he had made a name for himself with his experiments in the field of the emotions; and he knew that his inception and construction of Integrative Psychology, as a result of those experiments, was no temporary over-emphasis of some viewpoint or other but a comprehensive framework within which the complete science could develop.

But lately his contributions had been widely spaced. Dr. Pons had a family and his family ate food. To provide it the doctor had been writing popular novels and syndicated articles which his colleagues regarded with the more disdain the more practical their results turned out to be. Underneath his genial exterior and the obvious rationalisations that applied to the case, Dr. Pons undoubtedly indulged the academic implication to a slight degree. Sufficiently, at any rate, to make him conclude that Summerladd must have consulted a *Who's Who* of previous years.

"Ah, me," sighed the doctor; and went back to "770, Horst, P., The chance element in the multiple choice test item. *J. Gen. Psychol.*, 1932, 6, 209-211."

·   ·   ·

Michael Lord, meantime, had quickly arranged his quarters to his satisfaction and betaken himself to the recreation car at the end of the train where many of the passengers lingered for some time after "The Transcontinental" had pulled out of the Grand Central. It was his intention, now that he had the opportunity, to make a thorough inspection of the train. And not only of the train, but of the passengers as well. He was on board for a purpose; and, in the case of an event involving as much ballyhoo as the current one, he realised as well as did his hosts, that his presence was not exactly far-fetched.

However, there were no criminals, so far as he could observe, in the gay throng that stayed on in the recreation car. He remained until most of them had departed forward, when he began a leisurely progress through the train. First he encountered two stateroom suite cars. The doors of most of the staterooms were open and he looked casually into all that thus offered themselves for inspection. He noticed Dr. Pons, apparently engaged with his reading, and passed along without disturbing him.

The diner came next. Here the lights had been dimmed; no waiters were in sight but there seemed to be activity in the kitchen at the rear end. Then two more stateroom suite cars, in all respects like the previous ones, and he stepped into the swimming pool car.

Lord observed it with interest, not having seen it before. To begin with, one ascended three steps just after passing the vestibule; this made the roof rather low, since the car's height was the same as those of its companions, but accommodated the relatively large tanks with which it was equipped, underneath the flooring, where they were protected from the sun's heat. Ahead of him there then stretched a narrow passageway, to the right of which was the entrance to the men's dressing room and showers; to the left was a series of compartments for ladies, containing showers and lavatories, together with the single compartment that boasted a life-size bathtub in place of the shower.

Emerging from the passage, Lord came to the swimming pool itself. Its sides were raised about three feet from the floor level, below which it protruded to an extent of five feet, giving it a reasonable depth at one end, a depth that sloped up to a mere three and a half feet at the other end. It was narrow, admittedly, since it had been necessary to leave a two-and-a-half foot passage beside it; the broad windows along both sides were dark now, but he could see that it would be sunny and cheerful in the daytime. At the farther end, opposite his entrance, he perceived a considerable space left for the occupance of several small tables, some wicker chairs and a number of cigarette stands.

He could scarcely fail, either, to notice the girl who stood in her striking red, white and black bathing suit at the edge of the pool opposite him. The modern one-piece bathing suit has rapidly attained the point where it might better be described as consisting of one piecelet; it leaves little to the imagination. For many, such a suit would have been a distinct disadvantage, but this girl undoubtedly donned it without the slightest qualm. She had long, slender legs, goldenly tanned; for the rest, contrary to the doubtful fad of not so long ago, she possessed definite curves in very definite places. She had, in fact, a femininely lovely body.

It was certainly a tribute to her face that men, confronted by all her physical beauty, could with difficulty look away from it. It combined the piquant with the beautiful in some unusual way. Delicate brows over long-lashed dark eyes, a short, straight nose just a trifle tip-tilted, lovely lips that were really, rather than artificially, curved and a small, firmly rounded chin with an actual little dimple in it. Michael Lord, who was not especially susceptible, found himself very nearly staring.

The girl, who had not noticed his arrival, laughed gleefully at her companion in the pool. Edvanne Hodges had not enjoyed herself so much for a long time. Accustomed to most of the dance floors of New York, as well as to those of London, Paris, Berlin and Rome, she had skated at Tuxedo, sailed at Newport, golfed from Florida to California, tobagganed at Placid; these things begin to get monotonous after a time. But "The Transcontinental" was a brand new plaything; it was really novel to her experience and she gloried in it. Characteristically, she had seen the swimming pool and decided to try it now, not to-morrow.

As Lord watched, she entered the steps leading into the pool, flung herself forward in a shallow dive. Underneath the water, one stroke brought her to the end at his feet, where she turned, still under water, and with a strong push of her small feet sped back toward the other end. Three times she came the length of the pool and returned, then, rising in the shallow water, shook the rivulets from her bathing cap and drew long breaths of air. Her gracefulness made her companion, a strongly built, dark-haired young man, appear almost awkward.

Lord walked forward, glancing down as he passed. The girl smiled up at him. "Better try it," she invited. "It's not cold, really."

He smiled back. "To-morrow," he responded, and passed on. He was not exactly naive, but the manners of young ladies continued to surprise him. He had not the faintest notion who this remarkably good-looking girl was. He hardly blamed the man at her side for the slight scowl that had appeared on his face.

Now he stood at the entrance to the club car, beside the buffet at its rear end. Considering the hour, it was comfortably filled. Half-way up the car a distinguished-looking, lean and hawk-faced gentleman was noticeable, glancing through a late edition of the *Post*. Nearly opposite sat a lanky individual who frequently ran his left hand through the unkempt, sandy-red mop on his head. He was talking to a woman who sat beside him, who seemed somehow just a little dowdy as a passenger on this slick and elegant train but who was listening to him, at any rate, with a flattering attention.

With a smooth acceleration "The Transcontinental" was just pulling out of Harmon.

Lord advanced up the car and took a chair next to the lanky man.

The latter turned about in his seat at once and regarded him with a curiously blank expression. "Are you a scientist?" he asked.

"I'm afraid not." The abruptness of the inquiry had startled the detective.

"Oh. I was just explaining to Miss Poppas here that, if anything is to be done about it, the scientists must band together and do it."

Lord leaned forward, as did the lady also. They exchanged names; it was indicated that the lanky man was called Hall.

"I am in the dark," the newcomer confessed. "If we are to do what about what?"

"Civilisation," said Hall, shortly.

Miss Poppas leaned forward once more. "We were speaking of technocracy," she informed Lord. "Mr. Hall is a technocrat, I understand."

"Are you interested?"

"Somewhat," Lord acknowledged. "I have ideas on economics myself."

With scant ceremony Mr. Hall retorted, "It's not a matter of ideas; it has become a matter of facts. The facts, if you know them, speak for themselves. The Energy Survey of North America is not a theory."

"I believe, however, that there is some dispute concerning the accuracy of the figures." The statement was almost a question.

"Paugh!"

"At any rate," Lord conceded, "I'd like to hear it discussed with authority. So much that we hear is denied afterwards as being unauthorised. But why not," he added, "if we're to have a discussion, include Mr. Hodges, right opposite? He's an important banker. Between you, the question ought to be well opened up."

"We never argue," Hall stated belligerently. "We never answer criticisms."

Miss Poppas intervened. "But you won't object, will you, Mr. Hall? I agree that it would be interesting to hear the two points of view."

"It is useless to——" Hall began. But Sabot Hodges, who had heard his name mentioned across the aisle, was looking in their direction. Lord got up immediately.

"You are not acquainted with me, Mr. Hodges," he said, "but I know you by reputation. Mr. Hall, here, is about to discuss technocracy with us and I wondered if you would care to join? It has a bearing on banking, I believe."

"Hr-rmph," replied Hodges. "Don't abject. Poppycock, though," he added into Lord's ear for the latter's benefit alone. He drew his chair into the centre of the aisle and introductions were made.

"We state facts," said Hall at once. "We don't argue. Earthquakes don't argue and neither do the tides. Some of the facts you probably know. Up to the year 1800 no civilisation on the earth was able to utilise more than 2000 kilogram-calories of energy consumption per capita per day; to-day in America we consume 150,000 kilogram-calories of energy per capita per day. Most of this increase has occurred since 1900. It results not from machines but from the competent use of machines, which is technology. Now we have not only machines that improve the use of hand tools, but machines that oversee and operate other machines, hundreds of them sometimes."

"Sam Butler mentioned that. Machines almost a novelty then." Hodges chuckled.

"Facts," snapped the technocrat. "Not frivolous theories."

He continued. "The Energy Survey of North America has

shown that we have a continent here still supplied with every necessary resource, with a technological equipment for its use and trained men to operate that equipment. All previous history is that of a static social state because, despite outer differences of custom, dress and other nonessentials, it was based upon an unvarying energy degradation ultimately referable to the transformation-abilities of the human machine. We have turbines now that multiply the human energy conversion per twenty-four hours by 9,000,000. We have achieved a fundamental social change, we have a society of a different order of magnitude than ever before, just because the order of magnitude of any society depends ultimately upon its energy conversion rate. This change is susceptible of measurement in scientific units."

Dr. Poppas was heard endeavouring to break into the flow, and Hall hesitated momentarily. "But human nature remains the same after all," she contributed.

"Human nature, what's that? Can you measure it? Value has no metrical equivalent; we disregard it. The way men live depends on the mensuration of their energy conversions. And on nothing else. What you can measure you know about and what you can't, is merely nonsensical. For the first time in history we have the equipment, plant and services, to organise a civilisation on a continental scale that can easily supply every necessity and even luxury. Why doesn't it?"

Hodges' voice was definite. "Unemployment."

"Unemployment, my God!" cried Hall shrilly. "Don't you know that unemployment will increase anyhow? In two and a half years there will be 20,000,000 unemployed, under the very best conditions. Even with a return to those of the last artificial 'boom.' Not anything else but machines are putting men out of work and that has only begun. The Gaussian curve shows it distinctly as the next most probable social state."

"Hr-rmph."

"Just a minute," Lord interrupted. "What makes you think so. I've heard otherwise."

"You're thinking of new industries," Hall answered more calmly. "There's nothing in that. Under present conditions new industries reach their peak of employment even before their peak of production, and thereafter employment is reduced rapidly. And mere repair work won't employ more than a small fraction."

"But after all everybody doesn't work in a factory."

"It's the same everywhere. In farming certainly; man-hours per cultivation-area have gone down as rapidly as anything else. The salesman with his Ford sells ten times as much in a day as he used to on foot. No, unemployment is here to stay and you might as well face it. The problem has nothing to do with it anyway; the problem is that of the quantitatively balanced load, the problem of production and distribution as a single, uninterrupted process. And for that problem no sociological nonsense put forward now will suffice, not capitalism, not communism, not fascism. All of them depend on an antiquated and superstitious price system that technocracy has smashed. How could you look to a set of scalawags like politicians and bankers, anyhow? Scientists have produced technology, not bankers."

"Hr-rmph, what do you mean, sir—scalawags."

"I mean what I say. What have these incredible 'prices' got to do with anything? There is no article in the land that cannot be accurately measured in ergs or joules. That is its equivalent, not some fictitious designation that fluctuates from day to day. No one in his senses would use a variable as a measuring rod. It's plain enough why financiers cling to a 'gold standard,' though.

It's a racket they've got, hanging like leeches on the shanks of technology and rigging their ridiculous 'values' to their own ends."

Sabot Hodges' face had taken on a slight flush. "I object to your language, sir," he remonstrated. "Bankers are not leeches; they are reputable men who have much to do with the very production you are talking about."

"Who produces automobiles?" Hall demanded impatiently.

"Among others, the bankers who supply the capital."

"Paugh! Bankers have never supplied anything but debts. Their whole racket is built on debt creation and they have never created anything else. Fictitious fol-de-rol. What has debt to do with production? No one expects the debt claims of this civilisation to be paid, ever; in another ten minutes the 'interest' alone will be more than the national income. I would no more concern myself with a banker's criticism than I would with his piddle about plant being 'worth' so many billions one day and half as much the next."

The Chairman of the International Cities Bank made as if to rise. "I'm afraid you'll have to excuse——"

"No, you can excuse me," cried Hall, on his feet first. "I thought I was discussing matters with fellow scientists and I have no intention of wasting my time with outmoded dunderheads. I'd like to meet a few of you bankers on a good dark night. Paugh!"

He turned and before any one could say a word, strode out of the now almost deserted car. At the rear end Titus Nutt, sitting pleasantly with his dreams of glory, glanced up curiously as he passed.

For a space of some minutes there was silence in the forward half of the club car, where so much noise had been. Lord turned in his chair and peered through the dark window behind him. Across the river a few scattered lights twinkled, but that was all. "The Transcontinental" was roaring up the Hudson shore at some seventy miles an hour, but the tiny lights beyond the black waters told Lord nothing of its position.

As he turned back he smiled somewhat ruefully. "I'm sorry, Mr. Hodges. I've never seen the fellow before. I'd no idea he would become abusive, when I asked you over."

"Not your fault," the banker acknowledged, the flush on his high cheekbones gradually ebbing away. "Preposterous ass, with his mensurations and conversions and what-not. If that's a scientist, they're better out of affairs of business."

"But he's not!" Dr. Poppas' tone was nearly a wail. "That man isn't anything like a scientist. Science welcomes criticism; it doesn't refuse to entertain it. All scientific theories pass through one critique after another before they are accepted. But such force he had, such a terrific striving behind that purpose; he could be dangerous if his incentives pile up high enough. He—he—oh, he gave me a headache with all his drive. Really, he tired me all out. I think I'll go to bed if you gentlemen will excuse me."

"Too bad," Hodges grunted. "Damned shame. Don't see how he got on the train."

As Miss Poppas rose, Lord got to his feet. Good-nights were said and she trailed down the car; even her back looked weary, as she vanished into the passage beside the buffet counter.

Lord sat down again and stretched. "You know," he remarked, "it may have tired her out but it woke me up. I'm not a bit sleepy now."

"Unanimous. Never wider awake. Talk some more if you care to."

The financier pulled out two long, vicious-looking cigars. "Strong—good," he announced. "Made for me in Cuba. Have one?"

Lord declined the offer, but produced some Piedmonts from his coat pocket.

"What's your real opinion, Mr. Hodges," he inquired, "of the economic mess we've gotten into? You wouldn't deny that we *are* in a mess, would you?"

Hodges said, "Bad mess. Damned bad mess. But not the first; not last, either. Had 'em before, have 'em again. This one's worse because it's wider, more complicated. Foreign trade mixed up in it, international commerce, war debts. Bad, those debts; had a lot to do with bringing it on."

"You think, then, it's simply the usual thing on a broader scale?"

"No question about it. World's pretty small now, nations close together compared to thirty or forty years ago. Finance linked up internationally. Of course we've had a bigger depression; bigger stage for it. Bigger prosperity too, in the end."

"I'm not so sure," said Lord reflectively, "that under our present arrangements there will ever be a real prosperity again. At most we may achieve a final gasp of inflation before the last crash."

The banker leaned forward and tapped him friendlily on the knee. "Look here, young man," he adjured, "don't get silly about it. World wasn't built in a day. All kinds of fads and poppycock get started when things go wrong. Half a dozen cranks under every bush. Don't be fooled by plausible nonsense. Readjustment periods very healthy now and then. Disagreeable. Don't think I haven't lost money."

"You take it calmly, I'll admit." The detective smiled. "And I'll admit, too, that it's possible that a series of lucky circumstances could bring back one more artificial boom. But I do think the depression we've had, has shown, once and for all, that if we want to keep going as we have in the past, it's absolutely necessary for us to make some very definite changes."

"What changes?" Hodges asked. "Wouldn't put everything in charge of magnified works-managers, as they call 'em in England, would you? That's what that jackanapes who just left wanted. Fine mess we'd have then."

Lord smiled. "No," he said, "I wouldn't. As a matter of fact, in my opinion technocracy is looking more for a nice, fat job than for a solution. And it's afraid of criticism probably just because it needs it so badly. Some of their statements are certainly on the edge of the ridiculous. The tremendous population increase they postulate on the earth during the last hundred years or so, for example. There's a phantasy that's hardly scientific; to suppose that the planet can alter one of its most essential characteristics in a millionth of a split second of its existence . . . But I would do something."

"Well, what?"

"Well, what would you do?" Lord smiled back.

"I do? Just what was being done before all these silly codes and N.R.A. nonsense came along. Monetary deflation always comes about in depressions. Big factor, necessary to oppose it. Cheap money schemes fallacious. Thing to do is inflate credit—nine-tenths of our monetary system, anyhow. When credit is cheap and abundant, always comes a point when enterprise reorganises and takes advantage of it for renewed activity, people employed, prices rise, back comes prosperity. Unless this N.R.A. greenback inflation, or dollar cheapening, same thing, upsets the whole applecart. Might be necessary to cut down a few debts.

Some mortgage obligations. R.F.C.'s the best remedial measure possible."

"But not all mortgages, eh? No general moratorioum or cancellation of debts?"

Hodges snorted. "Pshaw! Wild ass nonsense out of the prairies. Banks supposed to be the villains. Want to cancel all the mortgages and other obligations to the banks; willing to cancel all depositors' claims against the banks, too? Anarchy, that's all. Never recover from it."

"I agree with you, as a matter of fact."

"Thought you didn't. Something in your mind. What is it?"

"Oh, I believe a change has got to be made, all right. I was in England last year and I met a chap named Douglas in London. Major Douglas. An engineer, I believe, who got interested in economics during the war. He's got a theory of the necessary correction to make capitalism work out under mass production conditions. The real solution, I think. It's a little hard on bankers, maybe, but I think they would gain more in the end than they'd lose by it. Ever heard of the A-over-A-plus-B Theorem?"

"Never have. Sounds like a crank scheme. Half a hundred of 'em around now."

"It's a scheme to be judged on its merits, certainly. But the necessity for some kind of corrective factor seems perfectly plain to me. We have a plant that is capable of producing at capacity $100,000,000.00 of goods per annum, perhaps more. We are distributing a little less than half that amount in purchasing power per annum. Isn't it obvious that our effective demand is about 50% of our actual demand, for the fact remains that we could, and wish to, use everything that can yet be produced when our plant is really operating?"

"But you can't raise salaries and pay extra dividends until demand comes back first. That's the fallacy of the whole Recovery Programme. When you do, you are operating at a loss. Answer to that is bankrupt plant."

"Yes, I know. Capitalistic plant has to operate at a profit. Which it's not doing now, by the way. Well, that's just where the Douglas scheme comes in; it's a device whereby the proprietor or the company makes its usual profit and nevertheless a sufficient demand is effectively instrumented to be able to purchase the product at a profitable price. As a———"

Lord looked up, to see the girl of the swimming pool car, now clothed in a smartly tailored travel suit, at his side. Behind her loomed the tall figure of her escort.

Sabot Hodges got leisurely out of his chair, flicking away the absurdly long ash on the end of his cigar.

"Sounds fishy," he remarked. "Hear the rest of it sometime, though. My daughter, Edvanne, Mr. Lord. Mr. Entwerk, Mr. Lord. Entwerk's my secretary."

Lord, on his feet, bowed to the girl and extended his hand to Entwerk. "I see you've finished the swim, Miss Hodges. I envied you; you seemed to be enjoying it."

"Yes." Edvanne's voice was abstracted and so was her expression. Gone entirely was the former gleefulness and the bright brilliance of her smile. As she pushed back a stray brown lock beneath the brim of her tight little hat her face looked almost sullen.

The train swept onto a bridge and across the expanse of the dark river below. Through the heavy, plate glass windows a string of bordering lights appeared, shining emptily above the bare stretch of embanked wharves to one side of the stream. Then the car swung into a curve to the right; and there came the low grinding of brake pressure.

They were all thrown off balance for a moment and Lord put out his arm to support the girl. She leaned against it heavily for some seconds, then straightened herself with a jerk, almost defiantly. She said nothing.

Lord, stooping to peer through the window against which he had nearly fallen, recognised the dismal reaches of the Albany train shed, just as "The Transcontinental" came to a full stop.

"I'M GOING to bed," said Edvanne abruptly. "Good-night, dad." She leaned forward and kissed her father on his cheek. "No, don't come with me; I'll go alone," she added, as Entwerk made to accompany her. She turned and passed down the motionless car, her small high heels sounding on its floor in the quiet that had descended with the cessation of the rumbling undertone of the train's passage.

"I'm damned," Hodges said. "Hasn't kissed me in months." He shrugged, as if to dismiss the implied query.

"She's a little tired, I think," Entwerk volunteered. "All the excitement at the station. That publicity fellow wanted her in the middle of everything. And she overdid the swimming a bit, too."

Hodges' expression evidenced his agreement, but Lord wondered. He wondered if she were a moody person, for there had certainly seemed a complete change in her demeanour. But tired? No, he didn't think so; he had seldom been so impressed with any one's vitality. Embarrassed perhaps, at meeting the man she had casually accosted in the pool car, with her father so soon afterwards. Hardly embarrassed, either; her attitude had hinted somehow at defiance. A damn pretty girl. Well, he gave it up, but he was glad she was aboard, anyhow. Lord was young and he preferred at least one good-looking girl to enliven the journey.

"I believe I'll turn in, too," Hodges was saying, depositing the remains of his Cuban cigar in a nearby ashstand. "Coming back with me?"

Lord nodded, and the three men began making their way through the train. As they mounted the pool car steps, there came the slight jerk announcing departure from the station.

"Don't waste much time, do they?" the banker grunted.

Entwerk said, "They can't. Seventeen hours to Chicago is pretty fast running. They change engines here and there; that's about all, I guess."

Just beyond the pool car Hodges halted and held out his hand to Lord. "My quarters here. First in the car, right over the wheels. Won't bother me; sleep sound, up early. Good-night, young man, we'll talk again. Night, Entwerk. Send Hopping up to me, will you?"

Lord and the secretary continued down the car.

"A pleasant man, Mr. Hodges," the detective ventured.

Entwerk agreed heartily. "A fine man," he said. "Big man, too. It's real pleasure to work for him. It's more like working with him than for him. I admire him tremendously. . . . Well, here's my place. Oh, yes, I must tell the valet."

Entwerk's stateroom was the last suite in the car, and beyond it were the smaller compartments for the body servants of the travellers. At the third of these he knocked; the door opened and a wiry little man, still in the attire of a highly-paid valet, looked out. A noticeable odour of whisky floated into the aisle.

Hopping's voice, however, was steady and his eyes clear. "Right away, sir." He stepped out and started forward.

"Good-night to you," said Lord. "I'll see you again."

"I hope so. Yes. Good-night."

Entwerk disappeared into his stateroom and Lord made his way back through the train to his own quarters three cars behind. Here he quickly undressed and as quickly arranged his clothes to his satisfaction. Plenty of time to settle down permanently to-morrow, he thought. I'm weary. I suppose I might have had one more look at the observation car, at that. Probably empty by now, anyhow; must be half-past one.

Ten minutes later he was asleep.

UTICA
Sunday, 2.43 a.m.

"The Transcontinental," after slowing somewhat through the city, was picking up speed again just beyond it. The quickening putt-puff, chug-chug of its powerful locomotive was faintly audible over the dull rumbling of the wheels and the occasional clank of a brake rod beneath the cars.

Sam, the porter of the first stateroom car, sat on a small seat in the last of the servant's compartments. Before him was the berth, partially made up but without sheets. A blanket lay at one end, an uncased pillow at the other. Here, presently, he meant to stretch out and doze. The call bell was just opposite on the wall across the aisle and with the door open he could easily hear a summons.

Meantime there now reposed on the mattress opposite him six pairs of shoes, some of them contributed by the porter of the next car to the rear; not all of the passengers travelled with valets. "Why ev'body al'ays wait till they get on train to brush 'emselves up?" he muttered. "They yalla shoes there ain' seen no shine f' six weeks, I bet."

Slowly he stretched out a dark hand and raised one of the

offending pair. "Haigh' weeks." Very leisurely, he commenced to remedy the defect.

The low rumble of the train sank into his consciousness. Now the engine was inaudible; they were descending a slight gradient and the brakes ground a little as they swept around a long curve. Then again the faint puff-puff puff-puff as they straightened out on a level track. Sam's head dipped forward ever so little, and he dozed. . . . Click!

Like many of his race, Sam's hearing was acute. His head jerked up and he looked across the aisle at the indicator. But he knew what he had heard was a click, not a bell. His curly poll protruded around the door, but the aisle of the car stretched empty and dim to the ell at the forward end.

"Soun' like a do' close," he mumbled. "They people cain' be p'radin' roun' this time o' night. Ev'thin' they need in they rooms anyway."

He surveyed the line of closed doors sleepily. Nearer at hand one was slightly open and he thought of getting up and closing it against the swaying of the train, until he remembered that these new doors were equipped with inside latches to hold them an inch or so open, if desired. He watched the door for a moment; it was perfectly steady and did not swing. Latched.

"Musta bin anotha come unlatch' an' swung to." Sam's head withdrew and he applied himself to the shoes.

SYRACUSE
Sunday, 3.40 *a.m.*

THREE-QUARTERS OF an hour later, after intermittent labours, Sam emerged, the freshly shined and gleaming footwear in his hands. The car was as deserted as before and he passed silently up the aisle, lifting the wall flaps at the baseboards of the proper staterooms and depositing the shoes in their respective boxes, from the inner ends of which their owners would retrieve them in the morning.

Back in his own compartment, he stretched out on the berth and pulled the blanket over his legs.

"Ain' likely be no calls in thisyea' ca'."

Five minutes.

The light gleamed down on his polished, ebony face and over the subdued roar of the train there was superposed the occasional ghost of a snore. . . .

ROCHESTER
Sunday, 4.55 a.m.

Dawn comes early in May, especially early when one is still on Standard Time. The false dawn was grey over Rochester as "The Transcontinental" tore through the town, clicking over the switches with little abatement of speed. The echoes of its passage, resounding from building to building in its wake, died away and, out in the country again, the track ahead took form in the lifting greyness, and wan clumps of trees with an occasional house in the distance hinted their presence. The arms and shapes of the block signals along the line solidified behind their succession of bright green lights and suddenly the brilliant beam of the head-light, still cutting through the air before the train, was dimmed to a mere glow.

At five-thirty promptly, beside the bunk in the barber-valet's compartment at the forward end of the club car, an alarm clock tinkled. The man rolled over and sat up, automatically shutting off the bell. He ran one hand through his touselled hair and without more ado got up and began dousing his face with water at the stand beyond the barber's chair.

It was half an hour later when he had finished shaving him-

34

self, got into his white-coated uniform and pressed the one suit of clothes that had come in late the night before. Three others had been delivered earlier; these he had pressed during the evening and he now gathered up all four suits and prepared to consign them to the designated porters.

The night lights still shone dimly in the swimming pool car, vieing with the brightness from the windows, as he passed through, holding the clothes-hangers aloft from the floor with his right hand. As he entered the narrow passageway leading past the pool, the train struck a curve, sending the water with a sharp slap against the wall next him and sprinkling his coat with the splash. The barber involuntarily glanced over the low barrier and into the pool.

He stopped short, as if suddenly stung, and his gasp could be heard the length of the car. Through the clear water he saw, prone at the bottom of the tank, the figure of a man in a bathing suit. The man did not move; but as the car straightened out from the curve, his body rolled slightly over until it was exactly face downwards.

For a moment the barber stood transfixed. Then, galvanised into action, he dropped the clothes to his feet and, just as he was, vaulted over the barrier and splashed into the water.

The barber was not an expert swimmer and the other man lay nearly in the deepest part of the pool. Twice he was forced to the surface, gasping and gagging; but finally he succeeded in pulling the body to a place where his feet touched the bottom. After one more slip that submerged him and his burden again, he reached the steps and dragged the inert mass to the floor beyond.

He had to rest a few seconds, then he grasped the lean body by the hips and held it head downwards while a spreading pool of water dripped from himself and the other. He then lowered him and turning the body on its back, stood up, gasping from his exertions. The barber gazed without satisfaction at the clean-cut features of the man below, now tinged a ghastly blue-grey. He knelt and felt for the heart; there was not a movement in the quiet chest.

A barber on a transcontinental train is unlikely to be acquainted with methods of resuscitation and this one certainly was not. He rose again to his feet and shook himself like a dog, thinking rapidly. After a minute he moved to the front door of the car and locked it. Avoiding the body on the floor, he jumped over the pile of clothes untidily heaped in the passageway and a few seconds later had secured the rear door from the outside.

An incongruous figure with his pale face bleeding from a cut he had received against the side of the pool and his clothes still streaming water that left a moist trail in the thick carpet behind him, the barber ran down the aisle of the stateroom car to the rear.

BUFFALO
Sunday, 6.12 *a.m.*

Titus Nutt had risen early. The plain fact was that he was still too exhilarated to sleep. He stood now on the Buffalo platform beside "The Transcontinental" as the monster locomotive that had brought it through the night pulled away and another, just as huge, came backing down the track. There was the little bump, the sigh of the air brakes, and a thunderous roar of steam as a white plume shot upward from the new engine's escape valve.

Beside the conductor the station-master was grinning broadly. "Right on time, I see."

"Yes, sir," Nutt gloated. "One minute ahead. There'll be no delay this trip, if I can help it." Behind him the dishevelled figure of the barber-valet clambered, almost fell, down the steps.

The conductor's mouth dropped open with surprise. "Wha—what——" he stammered.

Rapidly the man gasped out his news. He was a trifle incoherent from shock and it was a minute or so before Nutt realised its import. When he did, he came to a quick decision; Titus Nutt was a harmless-looking little man, grey in the service of the railroad, but he was resourceful and competent, which was just why he had been selected for the post of honour he now held.

"Pulmotor!" he cried to the astonished station-master.

The locomotive ahead gave two short, impatient blasts. But Nutt signalled "Wait," and ran after the other toward the baggage room. He was still thinking at top speed.

Some young fool, he considered, who got up early for a swim. Hit his head, maybe; maybe drunk. . . Grunting, he helped the others pull the heavy machine from its rack in the emergency cabinet. . . . Nice thing to have happen the very first day. The less that's known about this the better; we'll soon have him around with the pulmotor. Thank God it's so early. Maybe no one will find out at all. . . They were carrying the bulky instrument with difficulty along the empty platform.

Doubt assailed the conductor as they reached the steps he had left a few minutes before. But no, it *must* be all right. The last thing he wanted to do was hold his train fifteen or twenty minutes for a hospital call. And what could an ambulance interne accomplish that he couldn't? He knew all about resuscitation, every conductor did, and he was perfectly acquainted with the operation of the railroad pulmotor. True, it was mostly used for reviving those overcome by smoke or gas; but what was the difference? Clear the lungs and start them breathing again, that was the point at issue.

With a final heave he pushed the pulmotor onto the car's vestibule and, turning, signalled the engineer who was leaning from his cab. The roar of escaping steam ceased abruptly and with a series of explosive snorts the great wheels began to turn.

He swung aboard, as the station-master jumped past him to the ground. "Not a word of this!" Nutt shouted after him, and the other nodded violently in affirmation.

Almost three minutes late, "The Transcontinental" dwindled down the track, the locomotive straining to accelerate the heavy tons behind it. Ten minutes later the speedometer needle at the engineer's shoulder was trembling above seventy-eight miles and in the swimming pool car Nutt, the barber and a shaken porter were bending over the still body.

PART TWO

DR. MABON RAQUETTE: DEATH INSTINCTS

TOLEDO

Sunday, 10.33 *a.m.*

AT SEVEN-THIRTY Dr. Mabon Raquette awoke in his twin bed with the sunlight falling directly across his face. He turned away from the window, onto his side, and a slight frown appeared on his brow. He had just experienced a vivid dream in which brightness and huge flames had been prominent and his professional attitude was at once aroused. Before doing anything else he must interpret these recent apparitions.*

Failing at first to apply successfully the archetypal significance of flame symbolism to his own case, he relaxed and entered upon the free association method.† Almost at once there swam among his images that of a tall, gloomy house. . . "*Bien*," Raquette muttered, "*chez ma tante à Dijon. J'avais une jalousie extrême pour mon oncle dedans. J'avais trois ans. . .*" Having thus, to his entire sat-

---

* Psychoanalytic therapy, like certain systems of even longer standing, relies in large measure upon the interpretation of dreams.

† In using the free association method one permits one's mind to wander without conscious control, merely noting by introspection (or otherwise) whatever pops in and out. The idea is that eventually something worth talking about will appear, something too horrid to raise its head unless stalked in this crafty manner.

isfaction, put his finger upon the lurking childhood experience for which his dream must be serving as a disguised release, he stretched his legs comfortably down between the sheets and turned to more pleasant matters.

This stateroom in which he found himself was pleasant, to begin with. Across the other (unoccupied) twin bed the psychoanalyst watched the countryside moving steadily past through the clear polished glass of the windows. Opposite the foot of his bed the hand of an electric wall clock jerked to seven-thirty-five; and below the clock a large and comfortable arm-chair supported the inextricable mess in which a Frenchman throws his clothes upon retiring, unless watched. By contrast the other easy-chair looked inviting indeed.

Dr. Raquette sighed with content as he reflected upon the trip ahead of him. Never before had he been west of Chicago; to go at all was excellent, and to go in this luxury, transcendent. For the first time in his life, moreover, the worthy doctor found himself without pressing future worries. He had always charged his patients such fees as, in his opinion, the traffic would bear; sometimes, when the patients were few, he had reluctantly reduced these fees through anxiety lest their numbers dwindle still further, but such occasions had not been many, since, for a number of years now, he had dealt successfully with a growing and fashionable practice.

But naturally his patients had been a set of most unstable persons—how, otherwise, should they have come to him at all? Not a few had gone so far as to repress into the unconscious all recollection of the sums they owed him; they apparently could not even recognise the repeated statements he always continued to send them for at least a year after they had quitted his parlours.

And, of course, with the sort of practice he was building up, the scandal of law suits was out of the question.

All this was now happily a matter of the past. Recently he had been retained by Sabot Hodges to delve into the hidden recesses of that gentleman's mind. Hodges, who for stretches at a time worked furiously hard and was, during these periods, precluded from ordinary recreations, had thought it would prove a relaxation to be analysed. He expected little else from it; but then, he knew that entertainment was very necessary to a hard worker and he hoped that Raquette could succeed in making him entertaining to himself.

It had been explained to Hodges at once that no few weeks could be of any avail. A complete analysis consumed many months. Dr. Raquette, after looking up the banker very carefully indeed, had appeared with a three years' contract in his pocket and Hodges, who did things thoroughly if at all, had signed it without hesitation. At the worst he was shrewdly confident that an advance payment would free him of Raquette's presence, if desired. He had hired experts before and the fee that the analyst had seen fit to postulate did not impress him as peculiar. Dr. Raquette was a little disappointed; still, the papers were executed, he would live in luxury for three years at least and if, at the end of them, he had not laid away a tidy sum, he was no *Bordelais*.

The analyst reflected that in all probability he had in no way exaggerated the necessity for a three years' course. Judging from the progress already made, at least that much time would be consumed before Hodges could be brought to take the treatment seriously. The banker made no concealment of the fact that much of the psychoanalytic viewpoint appealed to his sense of humour. It was not an unheard-of form of resistance, but it was a form with which Raquette, building up a list of clients from among the neurotic women of New York, had had little experience. He was working against it with considerable deftness but no victory could be expected for some time. There was certainly no hint whatsoever of any transference* as yet. The analyst sighed again, altogether contented with the prospect of a lengthy analysis. An extraordinary fellow, that Sabot Hodges; masterful and successful, obviously well adapted, but with some serious, because so fundamental, conflicts, none the less. *Eh, bien. . .*

Dr. Raquette jumped out of bed and, compromising to the extent of a few drops of water across his face, sprang into his clothes. To the final, or outer, layer of these he gave his usual meticulous attention with the result that when, a few minutes later, he entered the dining car, he presented an excellently dressed appearance.

He was motioned to a table for four, already occupied by a red-headed young man engaged in reading the Buffalo morning paper while consuming shirred eggs and bacon. Noah Hall looked up at the new arrival, greeted him with an abrupt "Good-morning," and returned to the paper.

"Good-morning," the other responded. "I am Dr. Raquette. We shall have a pleasant day, I see."

The technocrat looked up again. "My name is Hall; glad to know you. You are a medical man?"

"I hold a medical degree," Raquette acknowledged. "But I am a psychologist; a psychoanalyst, to be exact. I am travelling professionally with one of my patients, a Mr. Hodges, who is taking the treatment."

---

* Transference: the phenomenon wherein the patient's Libido (or shall we say his affections?) becomes bound up with the analyst, thus rendering it somewhat simpler for the latter to persuade him that what he, the analyst, says and recommends, is said and recommended to some purpose.

"Hodges, the banker? Did you say he was a patient?"

"Well, perhaps not in the strict sense. There is nothing ostensibly the matter with him. In fact he is very well adjusted. But many of our leading men now realise that in bringing the subconscious to light they may greatly improve their efficiency and happiness. We all have our complexes, you know."

"Oh." Hall barked a short laugh. "Well, I wish you joy of trying to do anything with that antiquated dodo."

"Heh?" Dr. Raquette was plainly taken aback. "Do you mean Mr. Hodges? Do I understand that you know him?"

"I don't know whether you understand it or not, but I have certainly met him. I was talking to him last night. A more stupidly ignorant man I have seldom seen. He doesn't understand the first principles of scientific decision-arrival."

"He is not, of course, a scientist. But in his own sphere I believe he is a man of considerable authority. He is surely one of our most important financiers."

"Paugh! That's one of our main troubles. We let greedy ignoramuses usurp authority. If he has any now, he won't have it for long," said Hall darkly. "He is nothing but a public enemy, standing in the way of the next most probable social state. When the time comes, he will be brushed aside. The way things are going now, he has probably already been brushed aside."

"I gather the impression that you are a socialist, Mr. Hall."

"If you do, you're wrong. A socialist? Paugh! I'm a technocrat. Technocracy has smashed the price system, whether it happens to be capitalistic or communistic, and Technocracy must take control. You probably call yourself a scientist; don't you know what's happening in the world? Scientific Technocracy is happening!"

Mr. Noah Hall got abruptly to his feet and passed jerkily to-

ward the rear end of the car, leaving Dr. Raquette to his astonishment, his milk-and-coffee, his toast Melba and the Buffalo
paper (with the compliments of the New York Central).

•   •   •

At almost the same instant Michael Lord rose from his table farther up the car and turned toward the forward end of the
train. It was his intention to smoke a cigarette or so in the club
car and continue his observation of his fellow-passengers.

At the rear entrance to the swimming pool car, however, he
met with obstruction. The door was locked and, turn its knob as
he would, Lord could not open it. He reflected that, after all, a
guest of the train was hardly in a position to demand facilities
that for some reason appeared to be closed off for the time being
and was about to retrace his steps when Hans Summerladd burst
into the vestibule from the stateroom car behind.

Summerladd's face was a study of anxiety. He brushed past
Lord and rapped sharply on the closed door. Then, realising that
one of the passengers stood next to him, he turned and spoke in
a voice which he did his best to make casual.

"You can't go into the bath car now. It's—— Why, you're
Lord, aren't you? The detective I met at the station last night?
I'm afraid something serious has happened, Lord. Maybe you'd
better come with me."

"How? What's up?" Lord was instantly alert.

"A bad accident, I'm afraid. Some one drowned. Oh, it's an
accident, all right; but you'd better come along. My God, to have
a thing like that happen now!"

A porter opened the door in front of them, and re-locked it
after they had passed in. Together they hurried up the passage
between the shower compartments and, past the pool, came

upon the small group still bending over the body on the floor. Cushions from the chairs had been placed under it, but otherwise it lay just as the barber had first deposited it. The drone of the pulmotor continued steadily, as it had for the last hour and a half.

Summerladd bent over and a cry was forced from his lips. "Merciful God! It's Sabot Hodges!" Lord, too, was somehow more shocked than if the victim had been a passenger unknown to him.

Titus Nutt got up from his crouching position over the machine. "It's no use, Mr. Summerladd," he said. "I've been using the pulmotor ever since we left Buffalo and it won't work. He's dead."

"Had a doctor?"

"You know there aren't any doctors on board, Mr. Summerladd."

"You're right. All our doctors are Doctors of Philosophy. There certainly will be one on every trip from now on. That's no help now, though."

"I can't see what difference it would have made," the conductor pointed out. "The man is drowned. No one, doctor or not, can do any more than give him the pulmotor and try to bring him around. But it's too late; he'll never revive now." Nutt wiped the perspiration from his forehead, for the ventilators had been closed and, with the heat on, the car had become very warm. "I didn't send for you," he added, "until I was sure we had failed."

"How did this happen?" Lord interposed. "Who found Mr. Hodges? When?" He exhibited a small badge carried in his pocket and acquainted the conductor with his identity.

The barber, no longer breathless but with the cut still apparent on his cheek, related the circumstances of his discovery.

When he had finished his brief story Lord asked sharply, "And you locked both the doors of this car as soon as you had gotten the body out of the water? You're sure of that?"

"Yes, sir. I had to get my breath back. It wasn't a minute, though. Then, when I saw I couldn't do anything with him, I locked both the doors and went for the conductor. We had just stopped at Buffalo."

"How did you get that cut on your face?"

"I must have got it in the pool, when I was pulling him out." The man felt his injured cheek tenderly. "I ain't much of a swimmer. I slewed around some before I could get him."

"That's right," Nutt put in. "His face was bleeding when he found me. It must just have been cut. And I know he can hardly swim at all. It was a brave thing he did." The barber flushed.

"Summerladd," said Lord abruptly, "can Mr. Hodges' stateroom be locked from the outside?"

Summerladd, pale and shaken, had sunk down in a chair. He was mumbling "My God" over and over again. He seemed incapable of responding at all, and the detective looked at him in surprise. "Come on," he said, with some sharpness, "pull yourself together, man!"

Summerladd glanced up from the floor where his blank stare had been resting. His hands clenched and unclenched, and presently he got shakily to his feet.

"I know," the Publicity Director gritted in a low voice, "I know. This is more of a shock than you think. I'll be all right in a minute. . . . What did you say?"

Lord, still a little puzzled, repeated his question. "Can Mr. Hodges' stateroom be locked from the outside?"

"No, it can't. Only from the inside."

"I want it guarded at once. If there are any connecting doors, I want them locked from the side of Mr. Hodges' room. If there is any one in it, he is to be brought here. Anyhow, a man must be posted outside in the passage and no one at all is to enter until I come back."

"But—but what for? He was drowned in here, wasn't he?"

"Obviously. It looks simple enough. Just the same I want these precautions taken. I'm responsible in a matter like this, and I'm going to have no slips of any kind."

The detective's tone was serious and firm. Without further ado Titus Nutt set off on the errand. "Nothing in Mr. Hodges' room is to be touched in any way," Lord called after him.

"Just think what this will do to the train. And my God," Summerladd moaned, as a new thought struck him, "Edvanne. Some one has got to tell her."

Lord was busy writing notes on a slip of paper. He looked up as a frantic pounding was heard from the rear door, and walked down the car to see what caused this new disturbance. No sooner had he opened the door a crack than, as if in answer to Summerladd's thought, Edvanne pushed it violently into his face and ran into the car. Entwerk followed her, trying in vain to halt her progress.

"Where is he?" she cried, running forward. Before any one could stop her, she fell upon her knees beside her father's body. "Oh. . . OH! . . . *Dad!*" Edvanne's voice rose shrilly, she sobbed once and went into a high, hysterical laugh.

It was an exceedingly distressing scene. Lord, who in the excitement had again secured the rear door, approached. He walked firmly up to the shrieking girl and before any one grasped his intention, struck her a resounding slap directly in the face. She staggered back, gasped and would have fallen from her knees to the floor, had not Summerladd sprung forward and lifted her into a chair.

There was a dead silence.

"Sorry," said Lord quietly. "The only way to bring you around."

The girl, after a moment's relaxation, leaned forward. Her face crinkled up and she began to sob naturally. The secretary stepped to her side after looking carefully at the body on the floor. "I'm sorry," he said in a low voice. "He's been drowned. He's dead."

"B-but he c-can't b-be drowned," she stammered between sobs. "He can't be. He c-can't."

"Come," said Entwerk gently. "You can't do any more here. Let me take you back to your stateroom." He laid his hand on her shoulder.

The girl struck his hand away violently. "I won't," she cried coherently. "Go away. Don't touch me!"

"But Edvanne," Summerladd added his plea, "you can't do anything, really. We've done everything that is possible. Won't you go back? Please. Let me help you. We'll both go back with you."

She looked up at him, and her lower lip began to tremble. She was very appealing. "Oh, I know," she said, almost wearily. "There's nothing I can do. Yes, I'll go, Hans."

Summerladd took her hand and raised her to her feet. "Come on, Entwerk." Edvanne leaned against the publicity man and they started past the pool.

"I'll get Raquette," Entwerk proposed, as Edvanne broke out into fresh grief. "He's a doctor as well as a psychologist, I believe. He'll be able to do something for her."

Lord turned after them, as the barber followed them down

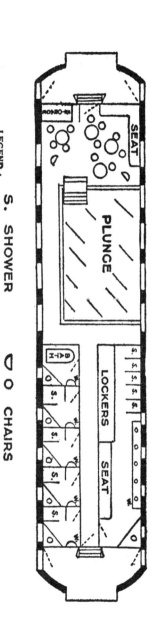

THE TRANSCONTINENTAL LIMITED

SWIMMING POOL CAR

forward.

PLUNGE

SEAT

LOCKERS

SEAT

LEGEND:

S. SHOWER

W. WASH BASIN

CHAIRS

TABLE

the car to lock the door after their departure. "If your man's a doctor, send him in here when he has finished with Miss Hodges," he called, and Entwerk nodded over his shoulder.

The detective was left alone above the corpse. He was scribbling furiously on his slip of paper.

Lord bent down and with some difficulty removed Hodges' bathing shirt and the trunks that were secured by a heavy belt with a large metal clasp. He laid them to one side and looked closely at the body thus exposed. Nothing appeared at all out of the way.

Slowly Lord went over the entire skin, almost inch by inch. There were no wounds and no bruises. He could find nothing until he came to the face. On one side of Hodges' nose he found a small wart, near the nostril, and this appeared to have recently suffered a very small cut; a little row of tiny red dots ran for no more than half an inch across it.

As he straightened up, the light fell somewhat differently across Hodges' trunk and the detective bent over again. Was there a slight, a very slight, discolouration in the region of the solar plexus? Lord could not be sure; if there was any at all, it was so little as to be nearly imperceptible. And even if there was, what then? He was well aware that people's complexions were not uniform all over their bodies; and it would take a long stretch of the imagination to call this extremely delicate discolouration the mark of a bruise, even if it actually existed. What if it were a bruise? The man might have hit himself two or three days ago; it could scarcely have anything to do with this.

Lord shrugged, and turned the body over on its face. The back, however, was smooth and unmarked. Last of all he felt carefully over the head, but here, too, no sign of injury was to be found; no cuts, no bump, no swelling. "I guess he was drowned all right," Lord murmured, getting to his feet for the last time.

"Sure he was drowned," confirmed the barber, who had now returned to Lord's side. "He was on the bottom of the pool when I found him."

The detective added to his notes and then turned to the other man. "Come with me," he directed.

There followed a complete examination of the car, commencing from the forward door. Lord looked over the walls, floor and ceiling carefully; he tried all the windows and found them all locked. The barber trailed after him in bewilderment.

"What are you looking for?" he finally asked.

"Nothing in particular; everything in general. This car has been locked ever since you found him. Nothing has been changed. There will never be a better chance to find out how this happened."

"Why, the poor man came in for a swim and got drowned. What is there to find out? Don't you think so?"

"Pretty early for a swim, don't *you* think? Still, that's certainly what it looks like. It's my job to find out just exactly how it happened, though. But as far as I can see, your idea is right."

They had now progressed beyond the pool, into which Lord had also gazed with attention, and were entering the narrow passage dividing the men's and the women's shower compartments. Here all the doors were fastened on both sides of them.

"Do you keep these locked?"

The barber grinned. "I lock 'em at night. The car is open but these places are full of bath towels and face towels. Soap, too. If any of those black porters lose some of their own supplies, it's an easy place to get more. And I'm responsible for these. So I just lock 'em up," he finished.

"I see. Well, we're through, I guess. Not a damn thing." They went back to the forward end of the car.

"Now see here," said Lord, when they had arrived. "Is everything *exactly* as it was when you came in here about six o'clock and found this body?"

"You mean literally?"

"Exactly and literally."

"Well, no, it isn't, of course."

"Is that so?" Lord's interest appeared in his voice. "What's different?"

"We closed the ventilators when we started to work on him with the pulmotor. Thought it would be better to keep the car warm."

"Yes?"

"And of course we got the cushions from those chairs and put them underneath him. I left him just on the floor when I went for the conductor."

"But the cushions were all on the chairs and the ventilators open—everything was just as it should have been—when you first came in?"

"Yep. That's right . . . Then there's one more thing.

"Go on, man."

"Well, the clothes on that chair over there. When I first saw him in the pool, I was carrying them back through the train, and I just dropped them in the aisle and jumped in after him. Later I took them up and put them where they are now." The barber grinned at Lord's crestfallen look.

"You win," the latter acknowledged. "There's nothing in those things to help us. Just the same, it's funny. You're sure *nothing whatever* has been moved? Except what you have just said?"

"Sure I'm sure. Nothing else at all. But what do you mean? Have you seen something that ain't right?"

"It isn't what I've seen," Lord replied. "It's something else I——" He stopped abruptly. No reason to put ideas into this fellow's head, he thought. "You've seen just what I have," he concluded. "And you know just as much about it as I do or any one else that might have gone over the car with us. There *is* something that seems peculiar to me, but it probably has no bearing on the matter."

"I don't know what you mean. Everything seems O.K. to me. What is it?"

"Oh, it's not so much. Figure it out for yourself," the detective invited. "And, by the way, open the door, would you? Some one's trying to get in."

It proved to be Summerladd and Dr. Raquette. "She'll be all right," the latter was assuring his companion as they came up the car. "I gave her a mild sedative, but the trouble now is psychic. A severe shock, naturally. But she is young and healthy. I shall charge myself with seeing that no trauma develops."

The doctor knelt beside Hodges and turned him on his back again.

"Are you a medical man, doctor?" Lord asked him.

"I hold a medical degree," was the response, "but I do not practice medicine. I believe it better, however, for my treatments that I should be qualified. I am quite competent to deal with a case of hysteria and prescribe and administer sedatives."

"Can you perform an autopsy?"

"No, I cannot. I have no instruments, and if I had, I am not a surgeon."

"That's too bad."

"But my dear man, how does the question of an autopsy arise? This man has been drowned."

"It's the usual procedure in all cases of death by violence. Still, if you can't you can't. He's been drowned, hasn't he? That's the opinion I wanted you here for."

Raquette looked somewhat astonished. He bent down once more and turned back the eyelids of the corpse. When he rose, his tone was decided.

"Yes," he said, "it is certainly my opinion that Mr. Hodges has met his death by suffocation due to drowning I would be prepared to give a certificate to that effect. Furthermore," he added, "it is much too late now to do anything for him."

Lord said, "Thank you, doctor. Well, I guess that settles it. Death by drowning." He added a final note to those already covering his paper.

•   •   •

"The Transcontinental" slipped swiftly through a deep cut and out into the sunlight again. Houses sprang up alongside the tracks; they grew thicker and the train clipped over switches leading to spurs beside factories. The whistle screamed once, the brakes were applied with gently increasing force and "The Transcontinental" slid into the Toledo station exactly on time.

Hans Summerladd knocked softly on the door to Edvanne's stateroom, directly behind her father's, and quietly opened it. In one of the chairs sat a maid from the recreation car, a coloured girl of large proportions and very sympathetic face. Edvanne lay in one of the beds. She was clad in a negligee; her eyes were closed and her lips were still trembling slightly. A single tear rolled down one of her cheeks.

Summerladd entered. "Will you wait outside a moment or

so?" he asked the maid. She got up without a word and went out into the passage, closing the door behind her.

Summerladd, who had read somewhere that women do not appreciate the supertactfulness that refuses to "take advantage" of their weaknesses or griefs, went directly to the bed and gathered Edvanne into his arms.

"Darling," he said, "I'm terribly sorry. It's awful."

She buried her head in his shoulder and sobbed quietly. He patted her arm . . . Presently he asked softly, "What do you want done, Edvanne?"

She looked up. "Done?" she asked, blankly.

"Yes. Do you want your father taken off the train? At Chicago?"

"Oh." Her face was lowered again and she spoke into the tweed of his lapel. "Oh, I don't know, Hans. I just can't think."

Suddenly she sat up. "I know I'm being an awful baby," she cried, shaking her head so that a brown curl fell down over the bridge of her nose. "I'll try to get together."

"All right, darling."

"But Hans!" The thought struck her for the first time. "Won't this be simply terrible for your train?"

"I'm afraid so," he admitted. "It will be pretty bad to take him off at Chicago . . . But that's not the point. What do you want? I don't have to tell you that you're more important than a train, do I?"

"Oh, Hans, I don't know. I don't know any one in Chicago, now. And the Lees in San Francisco are sort of cousins, or something. We were going to stay with them. . . . Can't we go on to San Francisco, Hans?"

"I'll see, dear. I'll do my damnedest, if that's what you want."

"Yes, I—I think so, Hans."

For some minutes there was silence. Then Summerladd laid her gently back on the bed. "Please try to rest a little. I'll come back later and tell you what I've arranged." He stepped to the door and summoned the maid, who was standing just outside.

"Good-bye, Edvanne." She tried to smile at him from across the room. He closed the door and passed a hand that shook a little across his forehead. It had been a trying interview for more reasons than one.

Out in the country beyond Toledo "The Transcontinental" was again driving swiftly ahead, eating up the track.

·   ·   ·

Behind the locked door between Edvanne's and her father's staterooms Michael Lord lit a cigarette and leaned back in one of Hodges' easy chairs. On the edge of the other chair, opposite him, sat Hopping, obviously ill at ease.

"Now suppose you tell me everything you know about this affair, Hopping." The detective's voice was casual, but underneath half-closed lids his eyes were taking close note of the other man.

The valet shifted his glance. "I don't know a thing about it, sir." The man's look was almost furtive, but Lord's experience had taught him that under the present circumstances the most innocent present a pseudo-guilty appearance. Actually, although a trifle surprised, he was not impressed one way or the other by Hopping's manner. What he was after was information; he entertained no notion that the valet had been involved in his master's death.

"Come now, Hopping. Mr. Entwerk sent you up here when Mr. Hodges was going to bed last night. I am assuming that that was the last time any one saw him alive. What happened?"

"Nothing happened."

"Will you stop that, Hopping?" Lord's voice took on a certain sharpness. "Just what happened when you went to Mr. Hodges last night?"

"I mean nothing out of the ordinary, sir. I helped him out of his dinner jacket. I had already unpacked his toilet things, and I got out his pyjamas, his bathrobe and his slippers, put them on the bed, took his boots to polish them, and left. That's all."

"What did Mr. Hodges say during this time? Did he make any unusual remarks? Was his manner at all peculiar?"

"Not at all. He said almost nothing to me. Just told me to call him in the morning. And then he said good-night."

"Ah. At what time were you to call him?"

The valet's gaze shifted again and he hesitated. Finally he said, "The usual time."

"What time was that? See here, my man, you're keeping something back. I'm only asking you for necessary information, but I can take a different line, I assure you. Now make up your mind to come clean, and do it; you'll avoid plenty of trouble."

The detective had made his tone purposely menacing. Hopping swallowed; he swallowed again and looked up with a new appearance of frankness. "He told me to call him at six o'clock," he admitted. "But—well, I overslept."

"Oh, you overslept?" Lord looked more closely and now observed that the other's eyes seemed somewhat bleary. "Probably you had a few more drinks when you got back to your own room?" he hazarded, recalling the smell of whisky he had encountered outside Hopping's door the previous evening.

"I had a nightcap," said the man, a little sullenly. "No harm in that."

"Not much. I don't doubt you had more than one, however. Well, when did you come to wake him up?"

"It was nearly eight o'clock."

"So that's it. And you found him gone, of course. What did you do then?"

"I knocked at Miss Hodges' door; and I inquired of Mr. Entwerk."

"Why?" Lord sat up with an access of attention.

The valet looked blank.

"I said why did you make these immediate inquiries? Surely the obvious conclusion was that Mr. Hodges had gotten up of his own accord and was probably having his breakfast in the dining car."

Hopping's face cleared. "No, sir. You see, I saw at once that he had not put on his clothes. His suits were all hanging in the closet there. But he wasn't in his suite. I couldn't think where he could be except with Miss Edvanne or Mr. Entwerk, and I thought I had better ask if he wanted anything, I being so late already. So I told them and then they went up ahead. Mr. Entwerk seemed to feel at once that something might be wrong."

"I see. Now about his clothes. I want you to look over everything and tell me if anything is missing or out of place. Go ahead, do it now."

They both rose and, while the valet went about his task, Lord subjected the bedroom, the lavatory and the baggage compartment to the same thorough examination he had made of the pool car. He could find, however, nothing at all unusual in the condition of the suite.

"Well?" he asked, as the valet finished.

"Everything's here, sir," Hopping answered. "Here's the boots I brought back this morning and there are his others. All his suits are just as I left them. And there's his pyjamas and bathrobe on the bed and the slippers underneath."

"You've looked in his trunks, of course?'

"Yes, sir. Everything's all right there, too. There's a drawer in the big one that he always kept locked. I don't know what's in that."

"All right. Let's see the trunk." They went into the baggage compartment. "Yes, I see. All right, Hopping, lock up that trunk with the drawer in it and I'll take the key . . . Thanks. I'll look into that later."

Back in the stateroom once more, Lord dismissed Hopping with an injunction to send in the porter. The latter appeared almost immediately.

"What's your name, porter?"

"Ma name Sam, suh." His face broke into an expansive grin; then, suddenly remembering where he was, abruptly changed to an expression of extreme solemnity. "This yea's a terrible thing, suh."

"That's right, Sam, it is. Now Sam, while I'm making a few notes, I want you to look around this suite and see if all the equipment is here that should be, and if everything is in its right place. You know, towels, pillows, sheets, ash trays, anything at all. Chair cushions, soap, footrests. The whole works. Do you get me?"

"Yassuh."

"Carefully, now. I want a real check-up."

"Yassuh, yassuh." Sam began moving about, commencing with the bedroom in which they stood. Lord watched him for some moments, then seated himself and became occupied with the notebook he now carried.

Some ten minutes later he heard the porter's step from the baggage room beyond. "Ah done finish, suh," Sam informed him.

"And so, what?"

"They jes' one thing ain' hyeh, suh. Yassuh, jes' one little thing. Everything else puffickly O.K."

"And what's that?"

"They jes' one bath towel ain' hyeh. Hit's missin'."

"You've looked all over for it, I suppose? It's not in here, in this room? And you've counted both the clean and used ones?"

"Yessuh, she ain' hyeh."

"How do you know it ought to be?"

"Ought to be six bath towels, suh. They's only five."

"Sure you put six in, to begin with?"

"Yassuh. Ah allus puts in de right numbeh."

"And when did you put the towels in this stateroom, Sam?"

"Ah'd say long about yestiddy noon I put 'em in."

"But surely you can't definitely remember putting just six in this particular room? You couldn't have taken any special note at the time."

Sam shook his head doubtfully. "Nosuh, that's right. I didn't take no special notice. But ah allus puts in de right numbeh, jes' the same."

"Hmm. And you haven't been in since, I suppose, to take any out? You gather them up every so often, don't you?"

"Yassah. Nosuh. Ah'd got 'em this mo'nin' but Ah couldn't git in. They was a trainman in the aisle wouldn' let me come in fo' 'em."

"I see. All right, Sam, that's enough, I guess. I don't want you to stand outside all the time, but I wish you'd keep your eye out and let me know who comes in here from now on."

"Yassuh, Ah'll do that. Ah keeps ma eye on this yea' room from now on. Yassuh."

The porter backed through the door, closing it behind him. Lord stood regarding the one neat and the one tumbled bed, abstractedly tapping his pencil against this notebook. "Hmm," he considered, "yes, it looks like an accident, all right. I've done everything I can think of and nothing has turned up at all."

He sat down and lit another cigarette. "Can't make much out of a missing towel. Ten to one he didn't put in the right number, anyhow. Wouldn't admit it, of course. That's the obvious thing; and the chances are a hundred to one for it." He exhaled a long streamer of smoke. "No, I can't see anything but accident. Just that one point, about the pool car. But hell, that has a perfectly natural explanation, too. It's silly to imagine far-fetched ones. Guess it's accident."

Lord drew in on his cigarette and exhaled again. He looked through the window at the countryside streaming swiftly past, then glanced at the closed door connecting with the stateroom behind. Poor kid, he thought; poor, pretty kid.

He got to his feet, extinguished the cigarette, and went out.

•   •   •

A moment later he knocked at Edvanne's door and found her sitting up in bed, calmer, apparently quite collected. Summerladd's call had, perhaps, been beneficial.

"I'm very sorry to intrude on you right now, Miss Hodges," Lord began. "But there are a few questions I want to get answered. And the sooner the better." He explained his position and who he was.

"It's perfectly all right," the girl assured him, unconsciously patting her hair into place. "I'm not really as silly as I've been acting. I'm going to get up in a few minutes; it's ridiculous for me to lie here in bed. What is it you want to know?"

"Well, your stateroom is right next to your father's. Did you hear him get up and go out this morning?"

"No, I didn't. I didn't wake up this morning until Hopping knocked on my door. That must have been a little after eight."

"And did you hear anything last night? Or during the night?"

"Let me see. After I left you in the club car, Mr. Lord, I came right back here and got undressed. I think some one came into dad's room just as I was getting into bed; and then a few minutes later, I think some one else went in. I can't be sure, though; it was just an impression, above the noise of the train. Why? Is it important?"

"I don't believe it is," Lord acknowledged. "The first person must have been Mr. Hodges and I know that Hopping went in to him a little later. . . . And, after that, I suppose, you went to sleep?"

"As a matter of fact, I didn't. I tried to read a magazine for a while and then I tried to go to sleep, and then I read some more. It must have been quite late when I finally fell asleep. That's why I woke up so late this morning."

"And you heard nothing at all during the night?"

Edvanne shook her head. "Really, Mr. Lord, I didn't hear a thing."

"I don't suppose there was anything to hear," he admitted. "Now tell me, Miss Hodges, does your father usually get up so very early in the morning?"

"Yes, he does. He sleeps very little compared to most people. About five hours, as an average, I'd say; sometimes less. And he often takes a swim when he gets up. He is a fine swimmer; that's why I can't understand his—anything happening to him in the water."

"It does sometimes, you know," Lord said gently. "Even to the very best swimmers."

He got up from where he had been sitting on the foot of the

bed. "There's just one more thing. I want to get some idea of the relationships between your father and the people immediately surrounding him. Can you tell me, for example, how Mr. Entwerk stood with him?"

Edvanne said, "He had a great admiration for Mr. Entwerk; I have often heard him praising his work." As she was speaking Lord wondered whether he was imagining it or whether her manner was faintly reminiscent of what he had noticed in the club car the night before. "He trusted Mr. Entwerk implicitly. I guess he was fond of him, too. Well, I know he was," she admitted, "really."

"And Hopping?"

"Oh, he has had Hopping for years. There is only one thing the matter with Hopping. He gets drunk every once in a while, and it's usually just when he shouldn't. . . He had a breath this morning when he knocked on my door . . . But he knew all dad's whims and nothing could have induced dad to get rid of him."

"I see. Your father knew Mr. Summerladd, too, I think? Was he equally friendly with him?"

"He really liked Hans well enough. He only disliked one thing about him; that was Hans liking me. Sometimes he got peevish, like a little boy; but men are funny about things like that. Poor dad. I'm glad we never really fought about it."

For the life of him Lord could not be certain whether Edvanne had blushed ever so slightly when she mentioned the publicity man. "I won't bother you any more now, Miss Hodges," he said, extending his hand. "You know, I'm sure, that you have my very sincere sympathy."

She took his hand and pressed it with gratitude. "You're very kind," she said. "Thank you."

Lord found himself once more in the aisle of the first stateroom car.

· · ·

In Hans Summerladd's stateroom the Publicity Director and Titus Nutt took counsel.

"You have the final authority," the latter pointed out. "For this first run my instructions were to follow your directions if any emergency arose, especially regarding the passengers."

"I know." Summerladd passed a hand across his forehead. "Well, we can do it, can't we?"

The conductor's assurances were definite. "It's perfectly feasible. We can clear one of the sections in the refrigeration car and carry him there. It will be entirely closed off from the rest of the car and we can lower the temperature as much as we need."

"Well," Summerladd concluded, after further consideration, "I think it's the best thing we can do. It would be an awful blow for the train to have his death leak out right when we were making the first run. Of course we can't keep it from the passengers, and some others will undoubtedly have to be notified, too. But we don't need to have it front page news quite yet." He thought of Edvanne, and his face cleared of all indecision. "Yes, we'll do it," he said firmly. "Miss Hodges wants it if possible, I know."

Nutt said, "That's settled, then." They both looked up as the door opened and Michael Lord came in.

"Hello, Lord," said the publicity man. "We have just decided to take Mr. Hodges' body through with us to San Francisco." He explained the arrangements and the reasons that had led to the decision. "Do you want us for anything?"

"Just what I came to find out," Lord replied. "I thought something like that might be arranged. In that case," he took a folded paper from his pocket and handed it to the conductor, "can you have this message sent for me?"

"Can I see it?" Summerladd asked, and, receiving permission, spread it out before him and read:

On board Transcontinental   Official Message: RUSH
    Chas
    Chicago
"r t q o s d m a D o l t X p m s n, m n e s t 2 3, u n s r u t
                                   Asny."

"What in heavens' name is that?" Summerladd was astonished and Nutt, peering over his shoulder, hardly less so. "I was afraid you might be going to give us some bad publicity, but this is cryptic enough for me. Whatever is the idea, though?"

"Just a report to the Department," Lord smiled. "I thought you might want it in cypher. It's a simple one; I'll explain it to you some time but I have some things I want to do now. How soon can you get it off, conductor?"

Nutt glanced through the window, then up at the electric clock on the wall. "One-ten," he said. "We'll be in Elkhart at twelve-eighteen. Change to Central Time there. That's only a few minutes; I'll put it off then."

"Rush," said Lord.

"I'll put it through myself," he was assured.

"All right then. Thanks." The detective left them and, at the door, turned back through the train. Just as he crossed the vestibule into the recreation car on the end, he felt the brake pressure against the wheels below. Three minutes ahead of time, "The Transcontinental" was running into Elkhart.

As "The Transcontinental" pulled out of the station and wound through the outskirts of the town, again picking up its headlong speed as the crossings grew fewer and fewer, Lord, for the first time enjoying the observation platform, felt a tap on his shoulder. He looked up to find Dr. Raquette bending over him with a most serious expression.

Raquette leaned still lower and, "Can I see you a few minutes, Mr. Lord?" he almost whispered.

Lord pushed himself around in his chair and indicated the one next him. "Sit down," he invited. "What's on your mind?"

"Not here," the doctor objected. He presented the dark appearance of conspiracy. He leaned confidentially closer. "I have certain information in regard to Mr. Hodges' death which I deem it my duty to place before you. Can we not seclude ourselves, Mr. Lord?"

The detective jumped to his feet without further delay. "Is that so? You have done well to come to me, doctor. We can go to Summerladd's stateroom, if you wish. If your information has nothing to do with him? He may be there, and the conductor, too; you won't mind?"

Raquette hesitated. "This is extremely confidential," he considered. "But Summerladd is a close friend of the family and the conductor, of course, has an official position . . . Yes, perhaps it would be better so."

In the stateroom they found Titus Nutt alone, but Summerladd returned almost as they entered. He had been to see Edvanne, but finding her about to get up and dressed, had merely acquainted her with the decision to take her father's body through with the train. To this she had again agreed.

"Dr. Raquette has certain information that he wishes to lay before us," Lord stated without preliminaries. "I understand it bears upon Mr. Hodges' death."

"Yes," said the analyst, "it does. As I have told Mr. Lord, it is very confidential. Ordinarily it would be unethical for me to disclose what I am about to say. But in the circumstances I can see no other course. It is much better, I am sure, for me to confide in Mr. Lord, who I believe is in some sort of official charge, than to offer my evidence at a public inquest, which I should have to do. There will be an inquest, I presume?"

"In San Francisco, probably."

"Ah, I thought there would be one somewhere . . . Now first, Mr. Lord, let me be clear. You look upon Mr. Hodges' death as an ordinary, or perhaps an extraordinary, accident, do you not?"

"So far as I have been able, up to now, I have examined into all the circumstances surrounding the affair; and I have found nothing to suggest any other explanation."

The analyst nodded. "Of course you know, Mr. Lord, that in the psychoanalytic treatment the relations between doctor and patient become extremely intimate. I have been engaged for nearly a month in analysing Mr. Hodges and, as a result, I am convinced that I can throw further light upon the manner of his death."

They all looked surprised and Lord demanded, "What are you leading up to, doctor? I gather that you entertain doubts as to the accident; are you suggesting there was foul play?"

"I am."

"What!" Summerladd's exclamation was incredulous. "You mean he was murdered? I don't believe it!" Titus Nutt's expression, too, was one of amazement, and Lord leaned forward intently, his eyes going from one to the other.

"That is just what I mean," Raquette said firmly. "But his murderer was himself; and the foul play that I am convinced took place, is called—suicide."

A curious sense of relaxation pervaded the room. It was not missed by Lord, who waited a moment before remarking, "I see, doctor. That is a serious statement. You must have solid reasons for putting forward such a theory?"

"I have, of course," Raquette acquiesced. "They derive from my analysis of Mr. Hodges' psyche. I can explain them in some detail if you wish; but I fear you will scarcely be acquainted with the technical terms I shall have to use. Can you accept my assurance that Mr. Hodges was fundamentally a suicidal type? You may believe that this is no hasty judgment. Or shall I go into further detail?"

"I think," said Lord drily, "that for so serious a charge I should like to hear all the details you can muster."

Dr. Raquette shrugged. It was plain that he hardly considered his hearers qualified to pass judgment upon his conclusions.

"I will do my best, gentlemen."

"Don't be bashful, doctor," Lord urged him. "I have met your colleague, Dr. Plechs. In fact, I met four very eminent psychologists on the *Meganaut*, and I became so interested in their theories that I have since read considerably in that field. I will understand your terms."

"Ah, I forgot. But it is a surprising accomplishment, if you will pardon the observation, in a detective."

"Yes? Yes, I guess it is. But then, I'm an unusual detective. I was destined originally for the ministry, you know. At that time it was still considered a learned profession."

Dr. Raquette regarded the speaker curiously. He appeared to ponder on weighty themes. Finally he spoke. "I think you did well, Mr. Lord."

"Thank you, I'm sure of it. And now, doctor, your reasons for thinking that Mr. Hodges committed suicide?"

"Very well." Raquette's voice took on a slightly didactic tone. "I must tell you that since its beginning psychoanalysis has been forced into several re-orientations of viewpoint. At first we endeavoured to divine the unconscious of the patient, his suppressed wishes and complexes,* especially as revealed in dream symbolism, and to expose the situation to him at the proper time. Thus our work was chiefly that of interpretation.

"We soon found, however, that this form of therapy was not successful; and we were forced to concern ourselves with unveiling the resistances of the patient, to the end that he might confirm our findings through his own memory. But we found that here, too, the unconscious was not fully brought into consciousness by this method. Too often the patient, though striving manfully, is literally unable to convince himself that our reconstructions of his past experiences are absolutely correct.

"How, then, is he to be convinced that we are right, for that,

---

* Complex: a series of related ideas, together with their emotional tones, assumed to be living, for the most part comfortably, in their specially furnished and "logic-tight" compartments in the "mind."

of course, is an essential item of his cure? Since his own memory cannot serve, it is necessary that he *repeat* the experiences we have discovered in his past and thus become persuaded of their reality. When he does so, there always appears with unwelcome fidelity some fragment of his infantile sex-life with its repressions, maladjustments and frustrations.

"The point I wish to make is that there exists a repetition compulsion upon which we may rely in the treatment. It exists in every one, but it is plainly exemplified in the shock dreams of traumatic* patients, in the play impulses of children and in the phenomena of transference.† Such repetition compulsions are obviously regressive in character, since they seek to repeat what has happened *before*. In normal cases the child thus obtains a mastery over his previous experiences, through playacting them over again."

Dr. Raquette paused a moment and glanced about. He was being heard attentively, however. He appeared to reflect, then continued.

"From our many observations of the repetition compulsion we have discovered that the nature of instinct in general is this: an instinct is an innate tendency in living, organic matter impelling it toward the reinstatement of an earlier condition; it is a sort of organic elasticity or organic inertia. But—the inanimate precedes the animate, and the earliest possible condition is that of conscious nonexistence, or death. Toward this goal all instincts directly or indirectly strive."

Again he paused, but no one disputed his claims. Lord, indeed, was watching him with fascination.

"In this sense we may say that the goal of all life is death and its phenomena are but circuitous ways to death. The pleasure

* Traumatic: adjectival form of "trauma"; "Trauma" is Greek shock.

† Transference: previously defined, once and for all.

principle and the reality principle both, though independent, seem directly to subserve the death instincts.

"Are you following me, gentlemen?" asked Dr. Raquette, who seemed a little nettled that no one commented upon the progress of his argument. "I wish to bring out that, though the sex instincts are life instincts, the ego instincts, which are of even earlier origin, are powerfully and ultimately directed toward reinstating the organism's death."*

"I have had no difficulty yet," Lord averred, "although I must confess the theory seems a trifle fine-spun."

"Fine-spun?" cried Summerladd. "Why, it's ridiculous! I've no intention at all of committing suicide, I can assure you. And as for Mr. Hodges, no one ever lived who was fonder of life. Really, Raquette, you don't expect us to swallow this?"

Titus Nutt looked on in helpless bewilderment.

The analyst shrugged, raising his shoulders in a Gallic gesture. "Nevertheless, gentlemen, I assure you it is so. Your resistances, dictated by the pleasure principle because the theory is repugnant to you, do not alter the reality of the death instincts."

Lord smiled good-humouredly. "Even so, doctor," he pointed out, "even if we should allow all you say, you have only established the presence of certain generalised death instincts, which may or may not exist, for all I know. You have not established that they were unusually strong in Mr. Hodges' case and, in fact, we know otherwise. Surely you do not maintain that all accidental deaths are due to these instincts? I could scarcely believe that."

* Dr. Raquette was undoubtedly referring to the "death instinct" theory worked out by Freud some time ago. For those who like this sort of thing, reference is made to *Beyond the Pleasure Principle*, Sigmund Freud, International Psycho-Analytical Library, No. 4, International Psycho-Analytical Press, London & Berlin, 1922, where they will find the viewpoint comprehensively set forth.

"No, no," Raquette was emphatic. "That is not what I mean, although many so-called 'accidents' are unconsciously brought about. But in this case I am sure the action was fully conscious. Shall I continue?"

Summerladd snorted, but Lord said, "Please do."

"Very well. Now first of all, in Mr. Hodges' case we find a very successful and well adapted man. The reality principle dominated superficially, ultimately subserving the pleasure principle, however; his pleasures were postponed until their gratification could be complete and this was achieved by the shrewd operation of the reality principle in acquiring money. Such an attitude betrays a high degree of intelligence.

"But now this man, intelligent as he is, finds himself in contact with psychoanalysis and undergoing the treatment. I may say that his resistances were violent, but after all, no one can be analysed and fully escape the consequences. Slowly but surely his unconscious was beginning to come to light, and remember that the death instincts were a powerful element in his unconscious, since he had never allowed himself to become aware of them at all but, as Mr. Summerladd says, had adopted a conscious attitude sternly repressive of them. I have no hesitation in believing that the death instincts, although by no means conscious as yet, had already entered the preconscious.* Under the treatment they were forcing their way upward and beginning obscurely to affect the ego.

"Now of course an instinct is unconscious. It is a mechanism acting unconsciously, which is one reason why there has been so much confusion of thought about the death instincts. Their goal is not only to bring the organism to death, but to bring it to

---

* The preconscious: a most peculiar and Janus-like region. It lies between the conscious and the unconscious, but, so spies report, somewhat closer to the former.

death *in its own especial way.* Thus they will operate to preserve the organism up to and including its normal life span, being really directed toward bringing about the organism's death at the end of this time in the manner usual to that type of organism. For a long or short period they can be confused with preservation instincts; this, however, is a deception, for their final aim is always death. But it is death in their own way; they operate, in fact, against any short cuts, for short cuts derive from intelligence and intelligence is the opposite of instinct.

"You will not forget, though, that Mr. Hodges was extraordinarily intelligent. When the death instincts, rising from the unconscious, began to affect his ego at all, there were two results. First, he reacted as exuberantly to them as he had previously reacted to the sex or life instincts. We may see in this a possible repetition compulsion, not so much to any definite previous experience as to the manner in which his reacting tendencies had been built up.

"And secondly, we see the entrance of intelligence, with its typical shortcut method. Obscurely feeling the death drive (which, to be sure, had no immediate death for its goal), his superficial, conscious intelligence took matters in its own hands and rapidly and efficiently shortcut the tendency.

"I do not for a moment believe," concluded Dr. Raquette, "that Mr. Hodges had conscious reasons for his act. But I do believe that he very deliberately adopted the means and carried them through, which resulted in his death. His reasons were not conscious, but his method was. I feel certain that he drowned himself on purpose."

A silence fell which Lord broke by asking, "Well, Summerladd, what do you say to that?"

"I still say it's nonsense. He couldn't possibly have meant to kill himself. Especially without any reasons for it; why, he had reasons for everything he did."

"No one," Dr. Raquette stated, "carries rationalisation* into everything."

"I suppose, doctor, there would be no way of proving your theory one way or the other?" It was Lord who asked the question.

"It is somewhat more than a theory, Mr. Lord. It is the evidence of Mr. Hodges' private consultant. Still," the analyst conceded, "I am not surprised at Mr. Summerladd's resistance. By the way, sir, may I ask you what is the name of the melody which we have heard Mr. Hodges humming and whistling of late?"

Summerladd, surprised, answered, "I think the name of it is something like 'I Hear You Calling Me.'"

"So I believe. Mr. Hodges was a widower. I can easily believe that, under the preconscious influence of the rising death instincts, he projected† the instinct and perhaps came to believe that his wife was summoning him from beyond the grave. *There* is psychological evidence, Mr. Lord. It cannot be denied that Mr. Hodges has recently manifested an obsession for this song. Of course, he said nothing of his reasons, either. They were not conscious, remember; they were still preconscious."

"Preconscious or not," the detective confessed, "I find myself still able to consider possible alternatives to your theory, doctor."

"Well here, then," Raquette replied triumphantly, "is a proof that will appeal to you."

"What is it?"

"Mr. Hodges was a fine swimmer. And he was drowned in a

---

* Rationalisation: the universal phenomenon of doing it first and finding excuses for it afterwards; difficult in the case of suicide.

† Projection: attribution of what is inside to what is outside; also universal.

tank so small that one stroke would have brought him to either side from any point in it. I submit that his drowning was not accidental, but intentional."

"Hmm." Lord sat back in his chair, considerably more impressed than he had yet been. "That is certainly a point, Dr. Raquette. Hmm. Well, Summerladd, you seem to be supporting the negative. What about it?"

The publicity man flushed uncomfortably and for a moment said nothing. Finally he brought forth, "I can't deny that Mr. Hodges was a fine swimmer, because I know he was. Just the same I don't believe he committed suicide. I knew him too well to believe that. Maybe—perhaps he had a cramp and sank before he could reach the side," he finished a little lamely.

"It's unlikely," Lord had to admit. "Was he really as excellent in the water as I am told?"

"Yes," Summerladd answered. "He was one of the best swimmers I've ever known."

The analyst rose from his seat. "Mr. Lord," he announced magnanimously, "I do not insist that you accept my theory, although I am convinced that it is the correct one. I have felt it my duty to put the facts before you but, after all, it is for you to judge. That is your responsibility. Mine is ended; but I trust for the sake of the family, whom I have contracted to assist for some time in the future, that you will do your best to avoid unpleasant notoriety. Suicide is the proper verdict, and the authorities should know it. Publicly, perhaps, I should advise adopting Mr. Summerladd's attitude."

With a parting offer of further assistance, if desired, the analyst left them. Lord looked quizzically across the room as Titus Nutt, as if suddenly and happily unleashed, got to his feet and made for the door without so much as a word.

Summerladd asserted stubbornly, "It's the bunk, Lord. It's nuttsy, I tell you."

Lord said, "Don't be too sure, my boy. There's no getting away from the fact that there are only three alternatives. There's accident, there's suicide; and there's murder. I've not found the slightest real evidence for murder, and I've looked pretty carefully in spite of having had no reason to. It's a damn funny accident for a good swimmer to drown in a pool as narrow as that one. And sometime before six in the morning is sort of early to get up for an ordinary swim, even for Mr. Hodges. . . . I'm not quite through yet, I'll admit, and some of the analytical theories seem pretty thin to me. But the last point impressed me; I'd say the suicide idea is definitely ahead at the moment. . . . And if I can't prove it, I can at least disprove it, if it's wrong."

Summerladd grunted. Lord lit a cigarette and lay back in his chair. He closed his eyes and began carefully going over the case Dr. Raquette had built.

ENGLEWOOD
Sunday, 2.05 p.m.

It was twenty minutes later when Lord, entering Hodges' stateroom and closing the door, found Entwerk rummaging through the banker's clothes in the closet. The secretary seemed in no way disconcerted by his discovery.

"Hello," he said, looking around, "I'm just going through Mr. Hodges' suits for any papers or correspondence. No objection, have you?"

"None at all," Lord responded. "You were his confidential secretary, I believe. I'd like a word with you and now's a good time."

"At your service." Entwerk closed the closet door and produced cigarettes. "Have one?"

"Thanks, I will. I take it you were in Mr. Hodges' complete confidence?"

"So far as any one was, yes. He was a hard man to be intimate with, personally, but I'm sure he was fond of me and, as I told you last night, I had the greatest admiration and affection for him. With his business affairs, of course, I am completely familiar."

"Just what was his position?"

81

"How?"

"I mean what actual positions did he hold in the business world?"

"Well, he was Chairman of International Cities; you know that, of course. Then he was a director in about twenty other enterprises, banks, large business houses, steel. Lately he has been serving on a semi-official commission for the government, emergency depression work. His loss will be felt very much."

"You've taken care of the necessary notifications, I presume? Summerladd, I understand, wants it hushed up as much as possible."

"I have," Entwerk said with some irritation. "As for Summerladd, it's just too bad. He and his toy train aren't so important as he seems to think at the moment."

"Tell me, Mr. Entwerk, has Mr. Hodges said or done anything recently that would give any hint of what has happened? Please think carefully."

The secretary was genuinely surprised. "Why, how could he? How could any one give a hint of a totally unforseen accident?"

"You are convinced it was an accident, Mr. Entwerk?"

"Aren't you?"

"What would you say to the idea that Mr. Hodges committed suicide?"

"Oh, I see." The secretary looked down at the floor and fingered his cigarette. "To tell you the truth, that hadn't occurred to me. . . . Why, I suppose it *is* just possible."

"Ah. Now that you hear the theory, have you any special reason to think it likely?"

Entwerk looked up. "No," he said frankly, "I haven't any special reason. But there are plenty of general ones. Nervous exhaustion, principally. Mr. Hodges has been working terrifically hard and he was pretty nearly worn out when we started on this trip. He's had great responsibilities, of course; men in his position have been bearing heavy burdens the last year or so."

"How about his private fortune?"

"Well, he's been hard hit, naturally. But he hasn't been ruined, by any means. The other is the more important factor, I'd say; the work that has nearly worn him out. He hasn't been himself for some time. Nervous and upset; it wasn't like him at all."

"You can't think of anything special he did or said yesterday, for example, that would have pointed to it, though?"

"No, I can't think of anything special."

"Well, really, what do you think of the suicide notion?"

Entwerk thought a moment before answering. Then, "I'd say it was definitely possible," he pronounced. "But I would still believe that accident was the more probable explanation. That's about the best I can do."

Lord got up purposefully from the bed where he had been lounging. "Thank you, Mr. Entwerk. I'll call on you again, if there is any way in which you can help me."

The secretary took his obvious dismissal in good part. He said, "I wish you would. I've some things to tend to; I'll see you again." He nodded and left.

Lord waited some minutes, then quietly crossed the room and locked the door to the aisle. He proceeded at once to the baggage compartment and, producing the key he had taken from Hopping, unfastened the large trunk. Two minutes later, working with a stout screw driver, he had broken the flimsy wood of the locked drawer and pulled it out.

Before him lay a handsome flat leather case, about four inches by five, and a large envelope apparently addressed to one of the partners of a law firm on Wall Street.

Lord examined the leather case first. When opened, it disclosed a photograph on gold of a very beautiful woman, resembling Edvanne but obviously older. On top of this picture lay a small folded sheet of paper covered by handwriting. The writing was a verse, entitled "Good-bye"; it was sentimental in the extreme, almost maudlin. With an unavoidable sense of having intruded upon another's privacy, Lord refolded the paper and shut the case. As he did so, he was forcibly reminded of Dr. Raquette's projection hypothesis.

With less compunction he opened the sealed envelope. A legal document, named "Last Will and Testament of Sabot Hodges—Copy," fell out; also a short, handwritten note.

Lord first examined the will. It was relatively simple; after a number of minor but substantial bequests to servants and associates (Entwerk was down for twenty-five thousand dollars) there followed the bequest of one million dollars to a well-known university for its general fund; the residue of the estate was left to Edvanne in trust until she reached thirty, when it became hers unconditionally. The bequest to the university had been deleted by a large cross in ink that blocked off that paragraph.

The note was much more startling. It was dated the previous evening and read:

"DEAR JACK,—You may not agree with me but I have made up my mind to finish it for good.

"If it is not too late when you receive this, will you have the change made in my will, as indicated?

"Yours always,

S. H."

Although it was so short, Lord read this epistle through carefully no less than three times. "Well," he considered finally, drawing a deep breath, "that seems to be that. I'll be damned; it certainly looks as if Raquette had been right, after all."

Suddenly he became conscious that the train had stopped and, looking through the window, caught a glimpse of a station platform. He sprang into activity. Quickly he put the letter into his inside pocket, closed the broken drawer, locked the trunk and slipped the key into his trousers. As if in some haste he crossed the stateroom, unfastened the door into the aisle and disappeared.

CHICAGO (ar.)
Sunday, 2.30 p.m.

For twenty-five minutes "The Transcontinental" had been rolling slowly through the immense yards that stretch between Englewood and Chicago. Since it took on no passengers during its entire journey, it did not enter any of the chief terminals of the city but was trundled across interminable switches over the belt line to a junction where it came finally to the tracks of the Union Pacific.

Sometimes it could make thirty miles an hour, sometimes only twenty, once it had even to stop for a minute while its whistle roared protestingly. At last, however, it rumbled over the last switch and pulled down a short stretch of track into the junction station, still on its schedule.

Titus Nutt was on the platform conferring with the agent almost before it had come to rest. Several of the passengers also descended to promenade along the deserted Sunday footboard during the seven minute change of locomotives.

The new engine, a tremendous oil burner, was just being coupled to the first car when a short little man walked up to the conductor and addressed him, indicating at the same time a pile of luggage that reposed further along the platform. In the pile were a large valise, an equally large leather case, a small bag and what looked like a collapsible table of generous proportions.

Nutt regarded the man with surprise. "We take no passengers from any point but New York," he stated emphatically. The small man drew him to one side and appeared to present a card; he also produced and unfolded what seemed to be a telegraph blank. Nutt inspected these papers with attention.

"I guess it's all right," the conductor conceded finally. "Here, porter," he called. "Get those things into the vestibule of the club car for the present . . . No, I don't know," he added to the man at his side. "Just go into the club car forward, and I'll see what I can do when we start."

The short man clambered into the train. Nutt blew his whistle and strode down the platform, looking for tardy passengers. But the platform was empty; the conductor raised his arm, signalling the engineer. Almost imperceptibly "The Transcontinental" began to move. Nutt looked once more up and down the platform, and swung aboard.

CHICAGO (lv.)
Sunday, 2.37 p.m.

Lord found Nutt and the little man in the club car just after the train had pulled out. "I'm terribly sorry," he apologised. "I should have met you. Actually, I was busy with the investigation and didn't realise we had gotten in."

"Don't worry about it," grunted the newcomer. "I'm on all right. We got your message," he went on. "I'm Dr. Black, Dr. Loress Black. What's up? I'm entirely in the dark, you know."

"Lieutenant Michael Lord of the New York Department." The detective introduced himself. "Let's go forward and I'll explain things. All right, Nutt, we won't need you now. Thanks for taking care of this chap. My fault, I'm sorry."

The conductor moved away and the other two stepped onto the forward vestibule of the car, where they were alone. Lord briefly explained what had happened and the course his investigation had followed up to the moment. "I'm afraid," he concluded, "that I've gotten you on for nothing. There were a couple of things that looked funny to me at first, but this latest evidence seems to make it pretty clear that Hodges committed suicide."

"You've still some checking up to do."

"Yes, as far as that sort of thing can be checked. Anyhow, now that you are here, we may as well have you confirm Dr. Raquette and give the final verdict."

"But there's no doubt about his drowning, is there?" Black asked, puzzled.

"Not in my mind now," Lord admitted. "Raquette struck me as fairly casual, though. I'd just as soon have you examine him and then everything will be tied up tight."

"Suppose I ought to do some work for the trip, at that. Where is he?"

"In a closed-off section of the refrigeration car, just ahead."

"And you say he's been dead since early this morning. Only one way to be sure now."

Lord looked his question.

"The knife."

"That's all right," said the detective. "Go ahead. It's funny; everything seems to be plain now and yet I want to be absolutely sure. I don't know why. Perhaps it's just because his daughter is so damn good-looking."

"You'll want him on my table anyhow, from here to San Francisco," the medical man put in. "If we can get my stuff up forward, I'll be through with my job in fifteen minutes. . . . By the way, is it cold enough where he is?"

"Plenty," Lord assured him. "Well, let's get started."

They turned back into the car and secured the assistance of the attendant and the barber.

•   •   •

It was exactly fifteen minutes later when Dr. Black, still in his white gown, beckoned Lord into the passage running along the side of the refrigeration car.

"Not drowned," said Black laconically.

"What!"

"I said the man wasn't drowned."

"But are you sure, man?" Lord looked at the doctor blankly, for, despite all his precautions, he had really been convinced. "I'm sure he was found at the bottom of the pool."

"Maybe he was." Black shrugged. "I don't care where he was found, he wasn't drowned."

"Why not?"

"Because drowning is caused by suffocation due to suffusion of the lungs."

"Well?"

"Well, there isn't enough water in the man's lungs to drown a fly. There isn't any."

"It couldn't have evaporated, could it?"

"Now don't be silly," Black was emphatic. "Whatever it does to your theories, you can take it for certain that this man was not drowned."

"Well." Lord drew a long breath. "That certainly opens it up again. What did kill him?"

"That," answered Black hesitantly, "I don't know for sure yet. He bears no real bruises, no contusions and no wounds. In private practice it would undoubtedly be called heart failure. I believe that's what it was myself. The man probably had a weak heart, and it just stopped."

"I'm really astonished," the detective admitted. "I am, for a fact. I suppose, though, you can establish that it was heart failure, without any question?"

"I can, if you'll give me time. I'll have to examine the heart, of course. Glad to, if you want it. Actually I haven't much doubt about it."

"All right," said Lord, "all right. Want to do it now?"

"Might as well. You'll find I'm correct, though."

The medical examiner went forward in the passageway and Lord stood for some minutes looking out the small window beside him. "Hell," he muttered. "And hell." He peered gloomily upon the speeding landscape. "And I thought it was all sewed up."

"The Transcontinental" thundered across a culvert and swept into a rising grade. Puff-puff-puff-puff, puff-puff, puff-puff.

PART THREE

PROF. DR. GOTTLIEB IRRTUM : PATTERNS

OMAHA (ar.)
Monday, 2.07 a.m.

Sunday afternoon.

Dr. Pons, who heartily disliked Christianity and all its works and who had not been inside a religious edifice for years, always found himself exceedingly somnolent as the Sabbath progressed. This may have been a curse called forth by his lack of piety but more probably was due to the enormous meal he was wont to absorb at noon. At home he combated sleep by writing or by reading up on some special branch of his multifarious profession. He had indeed made a similar attempt on "The Transcontinental," but the purring of the wheels and the lulling rumble of its passage had soon succeeded in undermining his research.

Now he lolled in one of the easy chairs in his stateroom, joggling slightly with the motion of the train. It was somewhat past three-thirty and after an hour's snooze he was hovering once more between dreams and waking. "Ugh . . . ugh!" He awoke with a start and assumed a more upright position.

Dr. Pons rubbed his sleepy eyes and considered that he was

wasting time. He glanced at his copy of the *Psychological Review**
which had fallen to the floor at his feet, but was overcome by the
fear that it might anaesthetise him again. No, he thought, I'll
look up that man, Irrtum; this is an excellent opportunity to hear
what he has to say.

He found the professor in the observation car, gazing stol-
idly out one of the side windows. Without hesitation Dr. Pons
introduced himself and took a chair next his quarry. After a few
remarks he found it easy to draw out the latter; they were soon
in a discussion of the professor's particular "school."

Acquainted with the appearance of the modern German professor (on sight indistinguishable from a smooth-shaven American business executive) Pons had been surprised when a fel-
low-passenger had pointed out Irrtum. This professor was a big
man, ponderous and dignified in the extreme; he wore, moreover, a sizeable, curly beard which seemed never to have known
trimming and which spread over his swelling waistcoat in generous waves. A gentleman of the old school, he might just have
stepped out of Wundt's† first psychological laboratory at Leipzig
in 1879.

"The Transcontinental" was still rolling across the Illinois
fields. Outside, the day, so brightly begun, was commencing to
be overcast and through the broad windows of the observation
car the sunlight shone wanly on highways and barns. Clickity-clickity-click came the sound of the wheels passing over the
rail joinings; clickity-clickity-click.

---

* *Psychological Review*: a bi-monthly publication of the American Psychological Association; contains original contributions of a technical nature.

† Wundt: together with Fechner one of the founders of modern experimental psychology. His endeavour was to equate physiological and mental occurrences. There are some who continue to think him better advised than certain of his successors.

Whatever Prof. Irrtum's appearance, his vocabulary and ideas were far from those of Wundt. "Psychology," he was saying, "must escape from the cramping cell of mere conscious phenomena. From the totality of experience it should start, but beyond the immediate experience sometimes it should look, to search for that complex of psycho-dispositional conditions that is the true symphony of inner life. Mere consciousness psychology is inadequate to the three problems of mental development, emotional experience and personality."

"I should hardly have thought so," said Pons. "I would be glad to hear in what sense you believe consciousness to be inappropriate to these questions."

Prof. Irrtum drew a deep and rumbling breath. "This in the field of perception, the stronghold of the external stimulus school, to be demonstrated is . . . *Ach!* sometimes with difficulty *englisch* I speak . . . Destructive analysis only could find the disconnected 'elements,' before supposed to compose our experiences. Partial or subordinate wholes can be distinguished but always they stand in relation to a greater structural organisation. The structure that happens to be most evident at one time only a part is of a state of mind."

"Structure?" asked Pons. "Structure?" Already he was becoming drowsy again.

"This word technically we use. The emotive totality-properties underlying perception we 'structures' call. They are not configurations, *gestalts*. Between structures and *gestalts* we make a difference. This to be remembered must.

"Our perceptions are not determined just by physical causes; the organisational dispositions *der Seele* here enter." He leaned over and tapped Pons, who sat up smartly. "When we small tachistoscopic* presentations of irregular figures make, they are as organised figures perceived. When enlarged, these constructs have much mobility, as the stimuli are regulated in order the soul's fundamental preference for form to overcome.

"So we find that for the soul certain optimal forms exist. The near-square it strives as a square to see; in this striving emotional stress we can plainly feel. *Die Seele* dynamic is. Also we see this in children's non-imitative building, in the non-objective ornamentation of savages, in the formalised designs in telephone booths scribbled. The crooked picture on the wall, it screams to be straightened; great discomfort it causes until we do this. Sounds, too, we strive to rhythmise, even though objectively regular. We shall to the sound of the wheels one moment listen . . . Ah, 1-2-3 . . . 1-2-3 . . . 1; 1-2-3 . . . 1-2-3 . . . 1; you hear this?"

"Ha." The example proved an unfortunate one. Once called to Pons' attention, he found it impossible to dismiss or avoid the monotonous rhythm. Clickity-clickity-click. The day outside the observation car was darkening long before evening; grey clouds had hidden the sun and the passing scenery was becoming less and less distinct. Inside, the lights had not yet been turned on. The professor was continuing his exposition but Dr. Pons' soul was fascinated beyond redemption by the rhythm of the wheels. Sometimes this rhythm seemed even to enter and become part of Dr. Irrtum's words.

"Configure . . . perceptual field." Clickity-clickity-click. "Dispositional interest transcends immediate present . . . Other unit properties . . . Contexts of meanings . . . structural totality."

---

* Tachistoscope: a device for the presentation of cards or other objects to the experimental subject's gaze. The time of presentation and its period (usually in fractions of seconds) is thus regulated mechanically. Many entertaining games can be played with it.

Clickity-clickity-click . . . "a transphenomenal effective psychic reality, a complex of psychodispositional conditions."

"Ugh," grunted Pons, momentarily unrhythmized.

"The personality as the sum-total of substructures . . . experienced configurations . . ." Clickity-clickity-click. ". . . transphenomenal structural totality . . . rounds itself . . . rests in the living and dynamic centre, the soul . . ." Clickity-clickity-click, clickity-clickity-click.*

Pons' head dropped forward.

Clickity-clickity-click.

Pons slept.

•   •   •

Michael Lord was looking for Dr. Black. After leaving the medical examiner to confirm his heart diagnosis, he had returned to his own stateroom; while there he had listed, among other matters, certain questions of a medical nature on which he was confused, and now he wanted the answers.

He finally found Black through appealing to Titus Nutt. There were three vacant suites in the train, two in the first state-

* The reader who is *seriously* interested in *Gestalt* Psychology is referred to the *gestalt* literature, the writings of such men as Koffka, Köhler, Wertheimer, Sander, Wohlfahrt, Schneider and others.

Two of Köhler's books, *The Mentality of Apes*, Harcourt, Brace & Co., N.Y., 1927, and *Gestalt Psychology*, Horace Liveright, N.Y., 1929, deal with the early experimental work and are readily accessible.

Both Koffka and Köhler have articles in *Psychologies of* 1925, Clark University Press, Worcester, Mass., 1925.

In *Psychologies of* 1930, *ibid.*, 1930, there are three articles: "Some Tasks of Gestalt Psychology" by Köhler, "Some Problems of Space Perception" by Koffka and "Structure, Totality of Experience and Gestalt" by Sander. It would appear that Prof. Irrtum had read the last of these articles; in fact, it would almost seem as if he had written it, although actually he had not.

For anything like a proper index of the *Gestalt* literature the reader is referred to the Psychological Section of any university library. There is plenty beside the above.

room car and one in the last. It was in the last one that Nutt had put the Chicago man, who had finished his examination and was now engaged in unpacking his valises.

Having located him, Lord sat down on one of his beds and lit the inevitable Piedmont. Dr. Black, who seemed somewhat taciturn, went on with his unpacking.

Said Lord at last, "I've been thinking over what you told me and there are a few points I'd like to have cleared up."

"Huh," said Black. "Go ahead; what are they?"

"In the first place, if Hodges wasn't drowned and there was no water in his lungs, how could he have been found on the *bottom* of the pool? His body would float, if his lungs were full of air, wouldn't it?"

"And maybe it was floating. How do you know? You said you didn't find it."

"I didn't find it," Lord admitted, "but I can't grant that. I've checked up on the barber, the man who discovered the body, with the conductor; asked him again about the fellow just now. He says he has known him for years and will absolutely vouch that he is an honest and reliable man. If he has lied about what he found, it can only mean that in some way he is implicated in Hodges' death. That's too far-fetched for me. I must assume, unless something very surprising turns up later, that the body had sunk."

"Well," said the doctor, "it's perfectly possible."

"Is it really? I didn't know it could happen."

"It's unusual, I'll admit, but it can certainly happen, There are several factors, of course. You know that a fat man will float more easily than a thin one at any time. A man who has been drowned sinks at first because of the single factor of the water in his lungs, but if he hasn't been drowned, other elements decide it. In the case of this man Hodges we have a lean body with rather unusually large bones. Fat has a specific gravity less than water but the boney structure is just the opposite. In this case the body is almost entirely lean muscle, internal organs and a heavy skeleton. Even with the lungs full of air, as they were, it would sink, and any weight, even an inconsiderable one, would surely take it to the bottom at first. Had he been fully dressed with his shoes on, there could have been no doubt about it."

"He had on a wool trunk and flannel shorts," Lord considered. "And yes," he added, "I remember he was wearing quite a heavy belt with a large metal, maybe silver, clasp. Did you notice it up forward? I believe it was taken into the car with the body."

"Now you mention it, I did. Rather an extraordinary belt, I thought. And it's quite enough to have taken the body to the bottom. So there you are; and your barber's evidence is still O K , so far as that goes."

Lord shifted on the bed and blew a long streamer of smoke across the room. "All right, then we can get on to the next point. You said there was no water at all in the lungs. Now even if Hodges died of heart failure while taking his early swim, it seems to me he must have gasped once or twice and therefore that there would be a certain amount of water in him, even if not enough to drown him. What about it?"

"You're right about his drawing a few breaths. But he might have done his gasping with his head above water. However, you needn't worry about it. He didn't die of heart failure."

"Aha. Here we have some news! You seemed so certain when I left you, that I was pretty much taking it for granted."

The medical examiner had finished his unpacking. He now drew a large, dark cigar from his pocket and crossed over to one of the easy chairs.

"Yes"—puff, puff—"that's"—puff—"what it looked like from the outside. But not from the inside. The man had a perfectly good heart, one of the strongest I've ever come across."

"So then?"

"So then, he didn't die of heart failure. When I say that, of course, I don't mean that his heart didn't stop beating. It did; but *why* it did, is another question. It certainly didn't stop because it was a weak heart, over-strained."

"You know," Lord stated, "this seems rather important to me. What did kill him, then? Any signs of poison?"

"Not a sign that I could find, as far as I went . . . No, here's the situation, lieutenant. I'm in the dark myself as to what caused the man's death. As you know, there are no wounds or other marks of external violence. And there are none of the more common symptoms of any poisoning. So it looks like a natural death. It's not heart failure, however. It might be a cerebral haemorrhage, but I looked at an artery or so, and there's no hardening apparent. The fact is that I've found no more to account for a natural death than I have to account for a violent one. And from a medical point of view I'm very interested to know what he did die from."

"But you can't leave it that way. Have you made a complete examination?"

"Of course not; by no means. When I have, I'll tell you the cause of death. I can't make a complete autopsy yet because of the lights. There are no windows in the compartment where I have to work and two little bulbs in the ceiling are no good to me. This looks more and more like a delicate job. Fortunately I've brought everything I need, but I can't work in the dark. I've spoken to the conductor about it and he has telegraphed ahead for a real light from a hospital in Omaha. When I get it, he tells me we can rig it up over the table. Then, I'll tell you something."

"I see." Lord's tone was disappointed. "Then we can't do anything more along that line until to-morrow. At present you don't know how Hodges died, but it looks as if no violence, or even poison, were mixed up in it. All right, then, there's just one more thing I want from you."

"What's that?"

"Time of death."

"Afraid I can't give you much on that. Think what happened; first the body is in the pool and that's relatively chilly; then it lies for some hours in an over-heated car; finally it's taken into a refrigeration car. And it's been there for some time before I see it. Temperature has a good deal to do with *rigor mortis*, and *rigor mortis* is an important factor in estimates such as you want. There are others, of course, but I can't investigate them yet on account of the light; and when I can, it will be too late . . ."

"Well, what is the best you can do, as things are?"

Dr. Black considered carefully, holding his cigar away from him and contemplating it appraisingly. Finally he said, "I really can't do much more than guess. I'd say anytime between one in the morning and six."

"But that's no good at all," Lord expostulated. "I saw Mr. Hodges myself considerably after one, and he was found dead at six or a few minutes after. I know that already. Can't you cut that down a little bit at either end?"

"Well . . . I don't know. If anything, I'd cut it down on the near end. Cut the six down to five. Yes, I think you can take it that he almost surely died at five o'clock in the morning or before."

"Hmm, that's something. Six o'clock is early enough for a swim, but five is *damn* early.

"Well, don't take it too seriously," Black admonished him. "It's really little more than a guess. I can't give you anything I'd stick to, on the stand."

"Just how am I to take that?"

"Take it for what it's worth," Black answered, almost brusquely. "It's my guess. It's not accurate medical evidence. Under the circumstances it can't be."

"Right." Lord relaxed and, turning on his side, looked out the window at the darkening day. As he looked, the rumble of the train rose more hollowly in his ears. The cars rolled out over a long span and underneath the window appeared the murky waters of the Mississippi. "The Transcontinental," even as he watched, rushed across the bridge and into Iowa. A raindrop splashed against the glass.

Lord stretched, and dropped his cigarette into an ash tray. "I think I'll wash up and go in to dinner," he proposed. "Will you join me?"

•   •   •

Outside the observation car a complete blackness held sway. It was raining steadily and the platform behind the rear door was damp and dismal. Inside, the car was bright with lights and a trifle stuffy. At the rear end two bridge tables, as yet unoccupied, had been set up, with cards, scores and pencils on a nearby chair; even duplicate boards were provided. The centre of the car had been cleared and a hardwood dancing space exposed. Beside the imposing radio-victrola one of the maids from the hairdressing compartment was idly turning the dials.

Lord and Entwerk entered the car from the forward vestibule and sought out chairs for an after-dinner smoke. Hardly had they settled into their seats when Pons and Prof. Irrtum, who had dined together, followed them into the car. For the moment they had the place to themselves, as they sat down nearly opposite each other at the forward end.

Dr. Pons in his anxiety lest the professor had become incensed as a result of his impromptu nap, had not only entered into long explanations concerning his fatigue but had stuck to the professor's side like a leech ever since. He had insisted upon inviting the *Gestaltist* to dinner; had they not both been guests of the train, undoubtedly he would have paid for it.

The two psychologists continued a desultory conversation for some time but at last all resources had been exhausted. Short of returning to the subject of psychodispositional conditions, nothing remained. And Dr. Pons did not desire to make this return.

Presently he got up and dragged his own and his companion's chairs across to Lord, who still remained opposite in company with the secretary. "I hear," he remarked, after the introductions were over, "that you're in it again. Some kind of mysterious accident aboard."

"Well, I don't know how mysterious it is," Lord answered. "It's serious enough, though; but probably just a death from natural causes. Still, there are one or two peculiar things about it on which I'm not entirely satisfied."

"If you care to discuss it, I'm a good listener," Pons offered. "I think I can guarantee Prof. Irrtum's discretion."

"I've no objection." The detective explained to Entwerk the circumstances of his acquaintance with Dr. Pons a year ago and in what ways they had both worked upon the same case. "Just the same," he continued, "although I don't object to discussing it with you gentlemen, I think we had better adjourn to my stateroom. There is no reason why it should be public property."

Entwerk glanced round and saw that the detective's point

was well taken. The evening had advanced and a number of passengers had drifted into the observation car during the interim. Both of the bridge tables were now occupied and two girls, accompanied by a young man in a dinner jacket, were endeavouring to select the best music on the radio-victrola. Still others sat or lounged about, awaiting their success. Even as Entwerk looked, Noah Hall strode into the car and gazing straight ahead, passed to a seat further down. His face was strained; doubtless he had been engaging in more argument.

"Why not go to my stateroom?" Pons invited. "They're all the same size. Come ahead."

The professor, whose interests were not those of his companion, appeared on the point of demurring; but Pons, still intent upon hospitality, pressed the invitation upon him and, no excuse immediately presenting itself, he also got up from his chair. Entwerk seemed to take it for granted that he was included; he held open the vestibule door for Irrtum and followed him into the next car.

In Pons' stateroom the rain, driving down from the northwest, splashed steadily against the windows. The doctor switched on the lights and closed the door; Lord and the secretary sat on the beds while the two psychologists, because of their bulk, were granted the easy chairs.

"Well, what's it all about?" Pons asked, as soon as they were settled.

"Actually," Lord began, stretching out comfortably on the bed, "there isn't much to tell. Mr. Hodges, the banker—you must have heard of him—left New York with us, accompanied by his daughter and his secretary, Mr. Entwerk here. Oh, yes, he had his valet with him, too; a man named Hopping. Early this morning the barber found Hodges' body at the bottom of the swimming pool. Apparently he had been drowned.

"The man pulled him out at once. Fortunately the train had just reached Buffalo; a pulmotor was taken aboard (it was then thought he could be revived) and they worked over him for an hour and a half or more, but without success."

Lord paused, and Pons put in, "Well, I don't see anything very peculiar about that. It's too bad, of course. But I gathered you weren't entirely satisfied. You must be looking for trouble; people do drown, you know."

"Don't you find it strange that an excellent swimmer should be drowned in such a small pool? He could almost reach across it."

"Was he an excellent swimmer?"

"According to competent testimony he was."

"Even so," Pons persisted, "I've known cases of very fine swimmers drowning."

Lord smiled to himself. "And isn't five o'clock in the morning rather early for a swim, doctor?"

"I don't know. That depends on the man's habits. Had he never done such a thing before?"

"Apparently he had. At any rate he had indulged in swimming at early hours."

"But then why try to make a mystery of it?" Pons was puzzled by the detective's attitude. "It seems to have been an unfortunate accident."

"Let me tell you the rest. The barber, who found Mr. Hodges' body, had had presence of mind enough to lock up the pool car, and I made a careful examination of it before it was opened to the passengers again. I then wired to Chicago for a police department medical examiner to board us there——"

"Why?" asked Entwerk suddenly. "What did you find in the pool car that made you dissatisfied?"

"On my word," Lord answered, "I went through that car with

a microscope, and I didn't find a thing. That is, I didn't find anything that wasn't part of the car and just where it should be."

"Well?"

"Well, I just didn't like the set-up as I found it, that's all. So I wired."

"But I don't see," Entwerk began. Then he paused, as if struck by an idea. "All right, go ahead, Lord."

"In the meantime Dr. Raquette, Mr. Hodges' psychoanalyst, informed me that in his opinion Mr. Hodges had committed suicide."

Pons looked up, surprised. "Drowned himself? A successful banker? Why should a man like that drown himself?"

"According to Dr. Raquette, because his death instincts were emerging into his consciousness and, influenced by these feelings, his intelligence took a short cut to the result."

"No?" Pons cried. He gave vent to a loud guffaw. "What a theory! Death instincts, did you say? What are death instincts? . . . Seriously," he went on, "an instinct is simply a name for certain motor patterns in the organism. No one could possibly commit suicide without knowing it. On purpose, I mean."

"Surely. That was one of his points. His idea was that the motive was unconscious, but that the means were consciously intelligent. He claimed that Hodges deliberately drowned himself on an impulse, as it were."

"I don't believe it at all," Pons asserted. "Was there other evidence of suicide?"

"As a matter of fact I did find some rather striking evidence. By the way, Entwerk," Lord tossed across the note he had found in the banker's trunk, "what do you make of that? I've been meaning to ask you."

The secretary's eyes opened widely as he read through the

short letter. "That's certainly peculiar," he acknowledged. "Do you mind if I read it out?"

Lord nodded acquiescence and Entwerk read:

"DEAR JACK,—You may not agree with me but I have made up my mind to finish it for good.

"If it is not too late when you receive this, will you have the change made in my will, as indicated?

"Yours always,

S. H."

"Yes," he said as he finished and handed the note back to Lord, "that does look bad. What do you think of it?"

"That's not the point," the detective smiled. "What do *you* think of it? What does it mean?"

"Looks to me as if it meant suicide," Entwerk admitted. "Do you happen to know what change is referred to, in the will? I don't know."

"Well, let's see now." The detective avoided the last question. "Mr. Hodges was graduated from Princeton, wasn't he? . . . Yes? What were his later relations with his college? Was he influential in its affairs?"

The secretary looked somewhat bewildered by the turn of the conversation but replied that the banker had for a time been a large factor in the counsels of the university. "With the recent change in administration down there, however," he continued, "Mr. Hodges has been taking less interest. As I understand it, he has had a distinct falling out on a matter of policy."

"Then it is conceivable that Mr. Hodges might have left a large bequest to Princeton in his will at some earlier period?"

"If he did, I knew nothing about it. I doubt it."

"And that since his estrangement, there may have been a period of reconsideration, followed by the decision to change his will in this respect and cut out the bequest?'

"All this," stated Entwerk, "seems to me to be one assumption on top of another. I doubt whether his note referred to any such subject. While I wouldn't call it conclusive proof, I'd say it was pretty strong evidence of an intention to do away with himself. You know, I told you he had been terrifically overworked and was very different from his usual self."

"Yes?" Lord sat up abruptly. "Well, Mr. Entwerk, you're mistaken. I have seen a copy of Mr. Hodges' will, accompanying this note, from which a large bequest to the university has been deleted. I merely wanted to confirm what it meant. And you are also wrong in supposing that this note is evidence that Mr. Hodges drowned himself. He didn't drown himself because, as a matter of fact, he wasn't drowned."

The information took all Lord's hearers by surprise. "But you said he was drowned," Dr. Pons protested.

The secretary's face became a study in expression, closely observed by Lord. From a blank stare it presented in turn complete amazement, and finally incredulity. When he had at last found his voice, he expostulated, "Don't be absurd. This isn't a joke."

"It certainly isn't," Lord agreed. He turned to Pons. "No, I didn't say Mr. Hodges was drowned. I said his body was found in the pool, and every one naturally assumed he had been drowned, of course. But actually my medical examiner found no water in his lungs and so he can't possibly have been drowned. That puts an end to the suicide theory once and for all."

"Well," Pons considered, "that does put a different face on it, for a fact. Was he poisoned? How did he die?"

"Apparently Dr. Black—that's the Chicago man's name—can

find no reason as yet to suspect poisoning. He is waiting for some lights which he will get at Omaha, in order to make a complete examination, but he tells me he can find no poison symptoms. His first diagnosis was heart failure."

"Oh," Pons' interest subsided. "I can't see anything against that. People die of heart failure in their bathtubs; no reason why they shouldn't in a swimming pool. More reason, in fact; they exert themselves more when swimming. I guess that's your answer."

"Unfortunately it isn't. Mr. Hodges didn't die of heart failure, either. Black has now examined the heart and found it to be exceptionally strong. As I told you, he cannot make a detailed autopsy until to-morrow, but as far as he has gone, he has been unable to account for death at all. There are no apparent bruises or wounds of any kind and no symptoms of disease or other cause of natural death."

Pons' interest returned. "Now that's more interesting, isn't it?" he said, feeling wider awake than at any time since noon. "You have a dead man at the bottom of a swimming pool; and he hasn't been drowned or wounded or bruised, nor is he unhealthy or suffering from any disease. Then why is he dead? . . . What are you going to do next?"

"I don't know," Lord admitted frankly. "The plain fact is that there is nothing for me to follow up. The reason the doctor is holding me up is just that, except for possible medical findings, I have no point of departure. I have been very carefully over Hodges' quarters and also the pool car where he met his death, and there isn't any real ground for viewing his death as suspicious. Except the false appearance of drowning; that *is* peculiar."

"That's it," Pons went on. "What seems most peculiar to me is that a man who has not been drowned should be found in the swimming pool. You will have to account for that before you are through."

"That seems to be the crux of the whole thing, don't you agree?" Entwerk put in.

"Of course," assented Lord. "If it weren't for that, it would seem to be only a question of waiting until the cause of death had been established. Ninety-nine chances out of a hundred it could be expected to be a perfectly natural one. It's the remarkable location of the corpse that makes it imperative to go into every detail with complete finality."

Prof. Irrtum stirred in his chair and entered the discussion for the first time since he had come into Pons' stateroom. There was a deep rumble within his beard, and, "Let me ask, *Herr* Lord," he proposed; "it is true that you have all examinations made and all usual inquiries put forward? Only the unusual position of the body it is that for you some doubt gives?"

Lord said, "Yes," doubtfully. "Well, yes, that *is* about the size of it . . . But it's a pretty big factor at that, don't you think?"

"*Nein, Herr* Lord," Irrtum spoke earnestly. "This is bad thinking. One factor only this is, but there are many others. One factor does not the whole situation make, but this whole situation you now wish to judge only by the one unusual factor. The part signifies not the whole; the part its own significance has, only in relation to the total organisation of the whole situation."

Lord looked a trifle confused, but the professor, once launched, was not to be stopped. "In everything we configuration find. In experience we find it; life also a configuration is. In chemistry not different is it the anode or the cathode to be; each only is determined by the total chemical situation. This it is which makes one the anode and the other the cathode, a relationship inherent in the whole, not in the parts . . . *Also* . . . Everywhere the same we find. Not at the part one must look, neither at the parts. Only by the total organisation of the whole situation envisaging, can we the real significance grasp. When we do this, then fall all the parts into a true meaningfulness."

"I gather that you would disregard this peculiar factor, then?"

"*Ach*, it is not disregarded to be but in the true perspective to be seen. What does this strange element mean, is the question. This only we shall see when in relationship to the whole situation that element we put. What is the whole situation, then? It is that a man has died and his body is found. How old, may I ask, was this *Herr* Hodges?"

Lord considered. "Around fifty, I guess," he hazarded.

"Fifty-six," Entwerk corrected him. "Fifty-seven next month. He looked younger because he kept himself up physically."

"So." The professor beamed. "The *Herr* has early gone for a swim, and this often before he has done. Later his body is found. We a careful investigation make but no signs can we find that he a companion had or that any one was with him when he died. That he himself could have killed, is disproven. He bears no bruises or wounds; no symptoms of poison can we discover. Therefore it is plain that a natural death comes. And this all the more is so when we find him far from young."

Pons felt constrained to point out, "But there are no symptoms of disease, professor."

"*Ach*, what is this? It was not heart failure. But many other things could it have been. Perhaps a stroke. Perhaps some hidden weakness. At that age the body no longer with impunity exercises as here is done. For a murder or violence some marks will easily be seen and they are not. But for a natural death the causes perhaps will lie deep. This we can leave to the physician. Soon he will find it."

Prof. Irrtum paused and Lord commented, "It still seems to me you are disregarding the fact that a man with plenty of air in his lungs was found at the bottom of a pool."

"So. We come now to this. But differently we come. Already we decide what is the whole situation and now we try this part in relation to the whole situation to explain. Not do we try the whole situation by one part to explain. It becomes now plain that the *Herr* Hodges, when by the fatal seizure attacked, close to the swimming pool was standing. He fell therein. This can we deduce, that when dying he perhaps is to the side of the pool clinging. *Legitimat* is this. But not the whole situation upside down we can turn, in order one part artificially to accommodate. You see what by this I mean, *Herr* Lord?"

"Yes," Lord conceded. "I get the idea. You bring to our attention that in the entire situation all the elements, except one, point to a single conclusion. You object to forcing all the other elements into a peculiar interpretation in order to satisfy the single peculiar element. You believe the single element should be interpreted in the light of all the others."

"Into the pattern of the whole the part must fit. Yes, certainly."

"You would force one factor into this pattern rather than many?"

"*Jawohl.* If this way you put it."

"But I don't really see," Entwerk contributed, "that there is much forcing to be done. If I seriously thought that there was a possibility of foul play, I should spare no effort or expense to clear it up. But after all, we know that Mr. Hodges died and he must have died somewhere in the pool car. It seems natural to me that, if his body was found in the pool, he must, as the professor says, have been seized close by it and fallen in. Evidently he was dead before he struck the water, for you say there was none in his lungs."

"It sounds reasonably enough." Lord's tone seemed close to conviction. "Perhaps in my work I'm over-suspicious, though heaven knows I have little enough reason to be in this case. Still, I'll be happier when Black finally tells us just why Hodges died." He looked at his watch. "I wonder; we ought to be getting into Omaha presently, where he gets those lights of his."

The others, following his suggestion, glanced involuntarily at the electric wall clock, and Entwerk jumped up in surprise. "My word," he ejaculated, "I'd no idea it was getting so late; it's nearly two o'clock! I'm off to bed, gentlemen, I've plenty to do to-mor-row."

Prof. Irrtum took a more formal departure and Pons and Lord were left alone. They walked together along the aisle of the car to the forward vestibule, where they stood talking for some time longer and occasionally trying to catch a glimpse of the surrounding country through the drenched windows. The rain, far from abating, seemed to be getting heavier.

Lord once more consulted his watch. "We ought to be getting into Omaha," he began, when, as he spoke, the train sped out on a high trestle. Cupping his hands about his eyes, he pressed his face to the glass. As he did so, a distant flickering of light gave him a momentary glimpse of dark waters swirling far below. "The Missouri," he announced. "We're almost in now."

Already the speed of the train was diminishing; "The Transcontinental" was rolling into the Omaha yards.

OMAHA (lv.)
Monday, 2.14 a.m.

As LORD and Dr. Pons, stretching their legs, walked down the empty platform beside the train, thunder reverberated through the wide cut in which the tracks lay. The sides of the cars glistened darkly in the dim lights of the station and up by the club car a small group stood about Dr. Black as he was checking over his delivered apparatus and signing for it.

"What do you think of the secretary?" Pons asked. "It seems to me he went pretty strongly for the suicide theory."

Lord answered smilingly, "I wouldn't blame him too much for that. Even with the copy of the will in front of me, that note looked very suspicious to me at first . . . No, I wasn't trying to trip him up; I just wanted to get the business about the bequest finally straightened out in my mind."

"What about other bequests, by the way? Money is a prime appetitive motive always, you know. Were there unusual beneficiaries? What did Entwerk get, for example?"

The detective regarded his companion quizzically. "You don't seem impressed with Prof. Irrtum's idea of natural death. I'm afraid you won't find much meat on Entwerk, though. What he gets isn't much for a man like Hodges to give. Merely an evidence of friendship, I'd say. Of course, I'll make a routine check-up on the secretary's circumstances; find out what salary he gets and so on. I doubt however, if he would have injured any one for the amount he receives under the will."

"Any one else?"

"No; his daughter gets practically all of it."

Hardly had Dr. Black, up forward, gotten his apparatus on the club car when a trainman down the platform began his cry of "All aboard!" With the usual dispatch another great locomotive had been coupled to the head of the train and, as the two friends hastened to an open doorway, "The Transcontinental" commenced moving slowly out of the station. Out ahead, more frequent flashes of lightning gleamed through the rain.

In the aisle of his own stateroom car Pons was saying, "No, I can't say I have any reason to disagree with Irrtum. His is certainly the simplest explanation of the whole thing. I was just seeing if there were any loose ends about."

"Oh, then you agree with him? In spite of the peculiarity, you think the natural death explanation to be correct?"

"Well, man, what else is there?" Pons demanded. "From what you say, I judge you have made a careful inquiry and turned up nothing at all. It's just too bad, but I'm afraid your case is an ordinary death, this time. . . . Here I am. I think I'll turn in now. See you to-morrow, Lord."

With a friendly gesture Pons entered his stateroom and Lord proceeded thoughtfully down the dim corridor. Actually, he mused, it looks as if they were right. . . . Trying to twist the whole thing to suit its one peculiarity. . . . Good point, that . . . I hope so; God knows it's less trouble for me. Well, Black will have it settled to-morrow, anyhow.

To-morrow, however, is always another day. And Lord, for all his ability, foresaw neither what clearing nor what further complexity the case would have taken by then.

FREMONT
Monday, 3.06 *a.m.*

THE DETECTIVE strolled slowly back in the car as the train rushed through the black night. He did not feel at all sleepy. Try as he would, the circumstances of the banker's death continued to obtrude themselves, and an unformed suspicion clung in the back of his mind.

Could the secretary have had anything to do with it? Twenty-five thousand dollars. No, that couldn't be a motive for a man in his position. He recalled Hodges' friendly attitude and words about his assistant. Nevertheless, he made an entry in his note-book—"Entwerk's salary." But always the cogency of the professor's argument came back to plague him. Why attempt the foolish labour of constructing mountains from molehills? Everything had a natural explanation except his own persistent desire to make it unnatural. Lord shrugged and entered the observation car.

In its empty expanse he sat down and lit a cigarette. In his mind he went over and over the same ground, the same *gestalt* argument. How long he sat there he had no idea; he was vaguely conscious of their passing through some fair-sized town. Finally he rose, stretched, lit another cigarette.

The car was brightly lit but despite this the electric flashes outside made a considerable display. The storm had gotten worse and "The Transcontinental" seemed to be running through the heart of it.

He stood for some time looking through the rear windows. The whistle, hooting over the Nebraska prairies, came faintly to his ears; half a minute later a few dismal and scattered lights sprang up about the track and the clickety-clack of switchpoints clipped up from beneath the car. What a place to live, thought Lord, the New Yorker. Then the lights were whirled backwards and vanished into the blackness.

He ground out his cigarette and turned away, with a vague intention of going forward. As he started, the intention became firmer. I'll just take a last look around Hodges' suite, he thought. Nothing in it probably, but I should be vastly amused to find Hopping or the secretary poking around there at this time of night. . . . Or any one else.

The train seemed to be running faster now. As he approached the first stateroom car, it swayed round a curve and he was thrown with some force against the wall of the vestibule. There was a blinding glare and a terrific crash of thunder. Wonder if that hit us, he thought. He had been thrown off balance and as he regained his feet there came to his ears, still ringing with the preceding din, a whole series of muffled reports.

Lord stood stock still and listened intently. The train was still running at high speed, so the sounds could not have been track torpedoes. As he was hesitating, uncertain as to the direction of the sounds, he heard three further reports. Two of them seemed quite close at hand, beyond the closed door of the car ahead.

"That's no thunder!"

In one motion Lord's automatic came into his hand and he leaped through the door of the stateroom car before him.

●   ●   ●

In the cab of "The Transcontinental" the wildness of the night was more apparent than in the comfortable quarters behind it. The rain, driving down in sheets, lashed against the windows and the engineer, a grizzled man of fifty, crouched on his seat, his face pressed close to the forward glass. This pane was equipped with a wiper but it was making little headway against the blurred and streaming surface. Occasionally the engineer opened a section of the window at his side and thrust his head into the tempest, only to withdraw it a few moments later and shake the water out of his eyes.

He knew the run perfectly and could have driven it blindfolded; in fact, that was what he was very nearly doing. But he had never seen a worse night, nor had he ever had so fast a schedule to maintain. He had run through Fremont at 3.04, two minutes ahead of time, and now, on the plains beyond, he notched up the throttle gradually higher. No telling whether some delay might occur later on.

The fireman leaned across the perilously jumping platform. "A swell night," he yelled. "Hope they's no washouts."

"They'll have the section crews out for us to-night," the engineer yelled back over the clangour of the clashing rods and whistling pistons. "Have to watch it for ourselves, though. Want you on the seat for that culvert past Schuyler."

The fireman grinned. "Oke." He turned back to the glaring, unappeasable maw of the boiler.

Out along the great side of the locomotive the engineer

peered forward. A lightning flash showed him the empty track ahead, and a green light winked suddenly out of the blackness and rushed past. He reached for the whistle and sent its blast echoing down the rails. The lights of the little town of Schuyler sprang up ahead, to the side, were gone.

Out in the gloom of the prairies again the headlight, bright as it was, made little impression through the swamped windows, as "The Transcontinental" tore ahead into the darkness. Again a green light flickered by and the train struck a sharp curve to the right. Crash! came a lightning stroke almost beside the track.

Momentarily blinded, the engineer looked around his shoulder for the fireman. The culvert, bridging a stream swollen by two days' heavy rain, was a mile ahead at the foot of the straight sloping stretch they were just entering. The fireman released his hold on the rail of the tender, nodded and climbed into his own seat across the cab from the engineer. To accustom his eyes to the darkness the latter glanced at the dim speedometer dial next him; the pointer was trembling between 72 and 73; in less than a minute they would reach it.

He opened the window beside him and thrust his head again into the storm. Immediately it was drenched and he raised one hand to shield his eyes and try to get a glimpse ahead. Below him and scarcely clear of the track there suddenly appeared the frantic dancing of a red light.

As he twisted his head to look back along the spurting wheels behind, it was gone. And the fireman was springing across the cab and seizing his arm. "Red——!"

"Hold!" yelled the engineer. He braced his knee against the wall in front of him as he closed off the throttle. Then, releasing the handle, he grasped the emergency lever with one hand while reaching the other to the sand control. The fireman, clinging to the seat, opened the whistle and its hoarse scream fled out over the plain. With a spasmodic jerk the engineer pulled the levers.

Irresistibly he was slewed around on his seat and, with his back jammed against the forward window, watched the speedometer needle fall. Sixty-eight . . . sixty-five . . . fifty-nine . . . fifty. In great streams the sand poured out over the rails, the brakes bit into the grinding wheels and along the sides of "The Transcontinental" a whispering hiss rose to the thin screech of sliding metal.

They were holding. Forty-five . . . thirty-five . . . Thirty . . .

      ·   ·   ·

As Lord came into the corridor of the first stateroom car, the engineer in the cab was just crying, "Hold!" But Lord did not hear him. Down at the forward end of the car he saw a vague figure flit around the corner of the aisle and vanish; the figure seemed a familiar one but the detective had only time to note that it carried a revolver in the right hand. He fired and his shot crashed out in the confined space of the passageway.

Running down the corridor he had passed the first two closed doors when, suddenly, "The Transcontinental" seemed to hesitate and gather itself as for a leap. A mighty force assailed Lord's back; he was hurled forward, grasped at a window rail, stumbled, was thrown.

A series of great lurches continued to propel him along the floor. Immediately he was rolled completely over, then began to slide backwards down the car on both knees and one elbow. During his passage he was conscious of an opened stateroom door, within which another man lay prone on the carpet in the darkness.

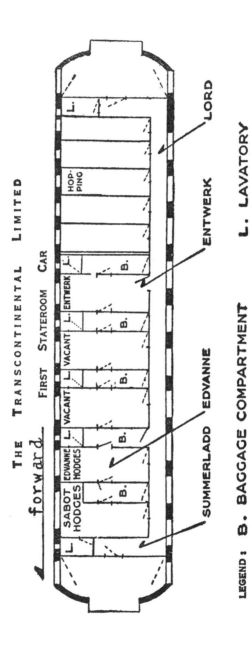

THE TRANSCONTINENTAL LIMITED
FIRST STATEROOM CAR

forward

LORD

HOP-PING

ENTWERK

SABOT HODGES
EDVANNE HODGES
L. VACANT
L. VACANT
L. ENTWERK
L.

B.

SUMMERLADD EDVANNE

LEGEND: B. BAGGAGE COMPARTMENT   L. LAVATORY

Somewhat further along a second door was open, the entrance from the aisle to one of the baggage compartments. Subconsciously his brain registered that this compartment belonged to Edvanne's suite; he tried to seize the frame as he went past, but missed it, since at all costs he desired to retain his automatic.

He was approaching the end of the corridor where the aisle made a right-angled turn to the forward door. With a final tremendous lurch he was rolled over again; his head came into violent contact with the wall. Bump! Nonentity . . .

.   .   .

Lord came to and sat up groggily. He was dizzy and for the moment attempted no more. The train had stopped and complete silence reigned in the car.

It was broken by the distant roar of steam as the escape valve of the locomotive functioned; a deep groan came from somewhere up the car. Lord got to his feet; his head was beginning to throb with pain, but his senses were clearing.

Disregarding the groans behind him, he made his way through the door to the forward vestibule, gun in hand. On the floor of the pool car platform sat Summerladd, holding his head in both hands. He was fully dressed; beside him lay a revolver.

"What's this?" demanded Lord.

Summerladd looked up. "Hit head." A moment later he had sprung to his feet and stood holding to the door of the car. "Some one shot at Edvanne," he gasped. "I was after him when something hit me. Are we wrecked?"

"I don't think so. These cars are all right. Do you mean to say that some one tried to shoot Miss Hodges? Was she hit?"

"Not hit, thank God. Come on, I think he went ahead." Summerladd looked about, still a little dazedly; it was evident that he was searching for his gun.

Lord retrieved it and, before straightening up again, clicked open the chamber. One shell had been fired. He handed it back to the publicity man.

"Were you hit?" he asked suddenly.

"No."

The detective smiled grimly, and for the first time in his life congratulated himself on a miss.

In the pool car the bathing compartment doors were all locked. Summerladd knew where the main light switch was and turned it on. The car was entirely empty. The space beyond the tank was wet where the water had splashed over, but now the surface of the pool was calm and unruffled again.

At the club car they came upon the first evidence of another's presence. Its left rear door stood open and the trap was raised. Lord went down the steps and flashed his torch on the ground beneath them. Footprints were visible but the rain had washed away any trace even of their direction from this point. As he stood in the downpour, a trainman came out of the gloom ahead.

Evidently he recognised Summerladd in the light of the vestibule, for without being asked, he said, "Dangerous culvert ahead; almost submerged. The section crew only found it ten minutes ago and had to flag us. Too late for anything except the emergency. They want to try the locomotive on it first."

Lord looked forward and through the rain glimpsed the engine slowly moving away from the stationary cars. "Did you open this door?" he asked the man at his side.

"Yes. Well, no. I mean the door was open when I got to it, but I raised the trap."

"When was that?"

"As soon as we stopped. I was in this car," indicating the club car, "but I had to hold on while we were stopping. Then I came out on the track to see what was wrong."

Lord climbed back into the train and motioned the trainman to follow him. "A couple of questions more. Could that door have opened by itself?"

The man scratched his head. "That's funny," he answered. "I didn't notice it much at the time. I wouldn't have thought it could. But," he finished, "it did; so I guess it could, after all."

"Look at the latch, will you?"

The man investigated. "It's bent now," he disclosed. "As it is now, it could open. But I think it got knocked that way when we stopped, if it was already open then. I don't know."

Summerladd was growing impatient. "Come on," he said, "we're wasting time. We've got to look forward anyhow."

Lord dissented. "Just a minute. We can do better." He turned back to the trainman. "Did any one come into the club car just before we stopped?"

"Nary a one."

"You're sure now? Not even one of the train crew?"

"No, *sir*. Since we left Omaha and that man stowed his lights away and went to bed, there hasn't been a soul in this car but me."

"There you are," said Lord, turning back to his companion. "Here's where he went. He could probably have gotten on again at several places behind us by now."

"But maybe he was in the pool car when we stopped. Maybe he went ahead after this man got off," Summerladd insisted.

"All right," the detective acquiesced. "You take a look while I stay here and see that no one gets on again."

The other departed and the trainman descended once more to

the roadbed. Lord felt in his pocket for a cigarette; just as he lit it, he felt the slight bump announcing the return of the engine. Series of five short blasts on the whistle came to his ears. He thought, I'd better get back and see what damage was done behind.

Summerladd returned almost immediately. He had found no one; even the barber-valet apparently had followed his colleague out on to the tracks. As they hurried back through the pool car, "The Transcontinental" commenced creeping slowly forward.

They found Edvanne dressed and calmly smoking. Her door was locked and Lord noticed that the baggage compartment door had also been closed. He wondered if he had been right about its having been hers that was open earlier. In the stateroom door were three neat bullet holes.

She came to the door as soon as Summerladd called to her; but as they were about to enter, Lord remembered the man whom he had seen prostrate further along the car. "I'll be back in a minute," he said. "Please wait for me."

Proceeding down the aisle, he found one of the stateroom doors still open, as he remembered it. It was dark inside, but as he came nearer, he thought he heard a faint groan. Stepping into the room without hesitation he switched on the lights.

On the floor against the forward wall of the room where he had rolled, lay Entwerk, white and unconscious. He was bleeding slowly from a wound above the heart.

Lord sprang to his side. The wound looked serious but Entwerk was certainly still breathing. He lifted him gingerly and placed him on the nearest bed. He rang the porter's bell furiously and called loudly for Summerladd.

Summerladd arrived first, on the run. "Get Dr. Black, last stateroom car," snapped the detective. "Hurry up!"

The publicity man's mouth dropped open foolishly as he took in the scene. Then, without a word, he turned and disappeared.

Left to himself, Lord looked more closely around the room. The place was in considerable disarray, both chairs overturned; but that was probably due to the sudden stoppage of the train. The wet blood stains on the carpet led from the spot by the wall where Entwerk to a position just in front of the door, and thence a foot or so across the room. For the first time he noticed the windows. One of them was broken and a fair-sized piece of glass had fallen out. The rain was rapidly making a small pool beneath it.

Then he saw the gun. It lay under the edge of the bed nearest the door to aisle, a heavy automatic of .45 calibre. Lord picked it up carefully by the barrel and wrapping his handkerchief around the grip, slipped it into his pocket. The cartridge clip had shown him that one bullet had been fired.

He addressed himself to the task of finding the bullet. He had not noticed whether it had passed through Entwerk's body and now he hesitated further to disturb the wounded man who had begun to breathe stertorously. He began going meticulously over the walls and floor of the stateroom. But he found nothing, despite his careful search. He straightened up and glanced at the broken window. Might have gone through there.

As he finished his search, Dr. Black came in, a bathrobe over his pyjamas. Black asked no questions. Stripping off his bathrobe, he opened up his bag and got to work.

"I think the bullet went through the window," Lord informed him. "I doubt if you'll have to probe for it."

Probe in hand, the doctor did not even glance around. "Huh."

"Will he live?"

"Don't know. Looks nasty."

Black worked on . . .

At the end of ten minutes he addressed the detective ever his shoulder. "He'll live all right. Bullet went straight through him; you were right. A poor shot, though, way above the heart. I can't be sure yet that it didn't puncture the lung, but if it didn't, he'll be O.K. If it did, he has better than an even chance, unless pneumonia develops."

"Shot with a .45?"

"Looks like it," the doctor admitted. "I'd rather see the bullet, though."

"I'm afraid you won't; it's probably out on the prairie somewhere. When can I talk with him?"

"When he comes to," snapped Black. "Unless there are symptoms of lung puncture. Then you can't talk to him at all. Until he is out of danger; might be weeks."

"But if it's not a lung puncture, when can I?"

"Give him a chance, will you? It's no joke to be hit by one of those sledge-hammers. He'll come out of it fairly soon. Then I want him to rest a bit; and then, if it's all right, you can see him. No use waiting now; I'll call you when you can talk with him."

"This doesn't look like an accident to you, does it, Black?"

"Accident? Oh, you mean the old gun-cleaning racket? Is the gun around?"

"There was a gun in here, with one cartridge fired. But there were plenty of other shots. I heard 'em."

"Who's looney now?" said the doctor. "Accident, hell! With plenty bullets and a guy damn near popped out? Don't kid me!"

Lord smiled at the other's vehemence. "O.K. I'll be just ahead here, in Miss Hodges' stateroom, when you want me."

In the doorway stood the porter, goggling into the room.

"Sam," said Lord, "see if you can rig up a sheet or something over that broken window."

Sam stared across the room. "Is all theseyea' windows broken?" he demanded. He pointed behind him to the one just across the aisle from the door.

Lord looked and now he saw that this window, too, had been pierced. There was a small hole near its centre, from which long splinters and deep cracks spread in all directions. He motioned the porter aside and, standing in the doorway, found that a line could pass through it from one broken window to the other. He noted that a shot, fired across the train, could have done it.

"Some of them are broken, that's a fact," the detective conceded. "Never mind, get the one in the stateroom fixed first; the man in there is badly wounded. When you get that done, stick around here; Dr. Black may want you for something."

"Yassuh." Sam turned away and went off in search of repairs, his eyes rolling wildly.

Black was bending over his patient, as Lord went forward toward Edvanne's suite. Thought Lord, there's the end of the Irrtum theory. Hodges is found strangely dead, and the next night his secretary is murderously attacked. Not to mention his daughter. Too much of a coincidence for me. No more "natural death" stuff. Now I've got something to bite on, too. Why do they always make the mistake of trying it on twice in a row? Criminals are dumb.

PART FOUR

DR. IVA POPPAS: HORMIC URGES

COLUMBUS
Monday, 3.48 *a.m.*

IT WAS ten minutes before four o'clock when Lord opened the door to Edvanne's stateroom, and "The Transcontinental" was rolling along as rapidly, apparently, as before its involuntary halt. About twelve minutes behind its schedule now, the engineer still hoped to pass through Columbus on the hour and regain at least some of the lost time before his run was ended at North Platte in the morning.

Nature, previously hostile, seemed trying to atone. The violent thunderstorm had cleared the air; probably it had put a period to the rainy weather of the last few days. At any rate the downpour was slackening, while behind the train the thunder rolled off eastward toward Omaha. A freshening wind from the west was tattering the heavy clouds and far ahead, near the prairie horizon, a single bright star peeped occasionally through a rip in the veil of the sky. Moreover, there would be no more dangerous culverts to pass until after daylight. Through the clearer glass of the cab window the headlight was once again becoming more than an ornament and the engineer of "The Transcontinental" sent his train hurtling down the track ahead.

Summerladd opened the door at Lord's knock and the detective, walking in, observed Edvanne with some curiosity. She
was sitting quietly in one of the easy chairs, just lighting a cigarette. She was not in the least pale; in her black evening dress,
which set off her own dark beauty to advantage, she looked as
if she might just have returned from a fashionable ball. If her
continual smoking was sign of nervousness, it was the only one
she showed. In the face of personal danger she was entirely unruffled, even exhilarated, and Lord marvelled that a girl whose
life had been so recently attempted should take the situation so
calmly. Her attitude was in complete contrast to her behaviour
on the discovery of her father's death.

Summerladd, from behind her chair, noticed the detective's
appraisal. As he looked across the room at Lord, his glance said
plainly, "Isn't she wonderful!"

"Well, Miss Hodges, I am certainly delighted that I find you
uninjured. I'm afraid you won't think much of the protection my
profession has afforded you."

"I don't see just what you could have done, Mr. Lord. It was
totally unexpected; my own feelings are still complete astonishment. But I'm not uninjured, I can assure you." She smiled
and held out for his inspection a tanned arm already blackening
above the elbow. "I got that when Hans' train did its little stopping act."

"That looks painful. You're sure it isn't broken?"

"I'll say it hurts. But no, it's not broken, thank goodness. I
imagine I was lucky to get no more than this, however. I'll bet
there are some sore heads in the rest of the train."

Lord felt the swelling on the back of his own and grinned
ruefully. But when he spoke his voice took on a new seriousness.
"Now, Miss Hodges," he begged, "please tell me as accurately as

possible exactly what happened. I mean the shooting. I'm not responsible for the operation of the train."

"I can tell you in a few words," Edvanne answered him. "I wasn't really very frightened; I remember everything that happened perfectly and I have my story all ready for you.

"I had not gone to bed," the girl continued. "The storm for one thing and I suppose I'm still pretty much upset about—everything. This dress is almost the only black one I own; I don't believe in mourning, but most of the clothes I have with me are rather gay, too much so for the circumstances. Just before the firing started, I was in my baggage compartment going through my things to see just what I did have that would be suitable for the rest of the trip. Fortunately I wasn't in here at all. My stateroom door happened to be locked, also fortunately.

"I heard some one knock on It fairly loudly; probably the knocking had been going on for some time before I did hear it. I had a reasonably heavy suitcase in my hand when I came into the stateroom to see who was at the door. I threw the suitcase on the bed as I went past and then the shooting began. Three shots came right through the door in succession. I think now that my dropping the suitcase must have made the bed creak as if some one were getting up. We have found where the shots went and you can see that they would have struck any one in that position. One of them is actually in the bed. Let me show you."

Edvanne got up and pointed out to Lord where the bullets had gone. Two of them had hit the outer wall, just behind the window. The third had penetrated the mattress; a small tear in the coverlet and, underneath it, in the mattress covering, demonstrated its course.

"And what happened then?" Lord demanded, when they were seated again.

"Well, I—— guess I screamed," the girl admitted. "Then I heard somebody running in the aisle outside and there were a number of other shots. I don't know how many. I haven't any idea what I would have done next, but just then the train began to have fits. The emergency brakes went on and I had enough to do to keep myself from being banged to pieces.

"After that was over, I sat down for a few minutes, and then I started trying to find out how many bones were broken. I bathed my arm in Pond's Extract and, when I had finished that, you and Hans were calling to me from outside . . . And I guess that's all."

"Thanks; that's well told, Miss Hodges. And now Summerladd, let's hear how you came to be in this. Oh, a minute; wasn't the aisle door of your baggage compartment open at the time of the shooting, Miss Hodges? Why do you suppose your attacker didn't go right in through it instead of firing through the other door?"

"Why, no," said Edvanne positively. "It couldn't have been open. Why, of course, I'm sure of that; I was in there just before, as I told you. What makes you think that, Mr. Lord?"

"Never mind for the moment. All right, Summerladd, go ahead."

"I was in my stateroom, reading," the publicity director took up the story. "I intended to stay up most of the night; to tell you the truth, I was a little afraid we might have something like we did. I mean a washout or some other delay; it's reported to have been bad along this stretch for some days.

"Not long after three I got bored and decided I'd go up to the club car and have some conversation with the trainman who was on duty. I didn't think any one else would be up. As I opened the door into this car I heard a regular fusillade of shots being fired. I was so surprised I just stood still for some sounds. Then I thought I heard a girl scream.

"There are no women in this car except Edvanne, so I knew it must be she. I ran into the passage just in time to see a man back away from her door and start running forward. I yelled at him, but he paid no attention and I took a shot at him, but I must have missed him. I called to Edvanne when I reached her door and she called back that she was all right . . . Don't you remember that, Edvanne? You didn't mention it."

Lord looked across questioningly and she said, "Yes, you did. I remember now. It must have slipped my mind when I was talking. He is right, Mr. Lord."

"O.K. Go on."

"There's not much more," Summerladd proceeded. "I chased after the fellow and I had only reached the vestibule when the brakes went on. I must have fallen and hit my head, because the next thing I knew, you were there in front of me. You know the rest yourself. If it hadn't been for the stop, I'd have gotten him, sure."

"Think back to when you ran down the aisle of this car; after you first heard the shots. Were any of the doors open? Can you recall noticing Miss Hodges' baggage compartment door?"

"I'm positive that wasn't open. I would surely have noticed it. Any of the others I can't be sure of."

"Hmph. That's funny. Well, it might have been the one behind, I suppose. I went past rather fast."

Lord considered the statements in silence for some minutes. Finally he said, "There seems a remarkable lot of coincidence about all this to me. First of all, that you should come along at the very moment all this happened. And then that the train should have stopped so damned conveniently to let the shooter jump off when he was practically cornered . . . You're sure you have both been perfectly accurate?" He glanced from one to the other.

Edvanne nodded decisively. Summerladd said, "I can't help it. As far as I'm concerned, that's exactly what happened. Coincidence or not, I can't change it."

"All right, let it go. By the way, "turning to the last speaker," do you always carry a gun? Have you a permit?"

"As a matter of fact I have, in New York. I hardly ever carry it, but on this trip both the conductor and I are armed. You know why. With all our publicity we might very well be troubled with cranks on this run."

"Let me see it again, will you?"

Summerladd handed it over. It was a revolver, .38 calibre. After a moment the detective returned it and the other slipped it again into his hip pocket.

"You didn't recognise the man you shot at." It was a statement rather than a question.

"No. I only saw his back for a few seconds, you know. He was a passenger; that is, I'm certain he wasn't in uniform, and he was fairly tall. That's honestly all I can say about him."

"Then the next thing to do is to check up on the shots," the detective decided. He crossed the room and with his pocket knife began to enlarge one of the bullet holes in the wall. Presently he managed to dislodge the buried missile. "You say these came all at once, in succession?" he asked the girl over his shoulder. "I mean, there was no perceptible interval between them?"

"Bang-bang-bang; just like that," she assured him.

"Then they must have come from the same gun. This one is a .45. I think we can take it the others are, too. Incidentally, Entwerk was shot with a .45. Let's see, Summerladd, you must have heard the shot that hit Entwerk. You say, though, that the man was already at Miss Hodges' door when you came into the car?"

"Yes. He must have shot Entwerk before I got here. I didn't hear that; in fact I had no idea he had been shot until you found him and called me."

"But you must have heard it, man. You were ahead of me and I distinctly remember two series of shots. I should have said the second series were nearer the rear end of the car than the first. In other words that Entwerk had been shot *after* Miss Hodges was fired at."

"Couldn't have been," Summerladd insisted. "I haven't any idea how many shots I heard, and it's no good guessing. I'd have said I only heard the ones at Edvanne's door, but I'm not claiming I can really remember. You must have heard my shot, if you were close behind me, you know."

"Did you actually see the man fire through Miss Hodges' door, Summerladd?"

"Well . . . No, I didn't see the actual shots, if that's what you mean. But I saw him backing away and reaching into his back pocket as if replacing a gun. My impression was very plain that he had just shot and was making off."

"You're *sure* about this? That the second shooting was at this door and that the man then immediately ran forward? It may be important."

"Of course I'm sure." Summerladd's tone seemed a little sullen at Lord's insistence. "I saw him. What more do you want?"

"Excuse me a moment; I'll be right back." Lord went out into the passageway and it was several minutes before he returned. As he came in, he announced, "I think I've found all the bullet marks in the passage. There are two at this end, and that's all. Those will be yours and mine. You know I took a shot at you as you went around the corner. Lucky you didn't hesitate or I would have winged you."

"I didn't know that, either," Summerladd admitted. His customary good humour had entirely returned. "I guess I was too excited to hear all the shots there seem to have been."

"Those are ours at the end outside," Lord repeated. "You have a .38 and mine happens to be a .45. I haven't dug the bullets out, but the holes apparently correspond. Now these three in here——— You're positive there were only three, Miss Hodges?"

"Oh, I'm sure. I can't possibly be mistaken," asserted Edvanne.

"Well, we know where those three went. That seems to have been all at this end. Now I'm certain I heard three shots first; from what you tell me those must have been at Entwerk's stateroom. One of them hit Entwerk. I've found none of the bullets, but two windows are broken down there and they may all have gone through. I'll know more about that when Entwerk can talk.

"After the first three, what I think I heard is two more, with a third closely after them. However, I suppose it's possible I heard three, followed by a fourth. The last, of course, was yours, Summerladd. Then there was actually one more, my own shot at you . . . So that's eight at most; and we have accounted for five, three in this room and two at the end of the aisle. That leaves three for me to find out about from Entwerk."

Summerladd asserted, "I don't see how you can be so sure. For all I'd say there may have been a dozen You don't count them on your fingers at a time like that."

"I do," Lord told him. "Not on my fingers, perhaps, but I have a knack of subconscious counting, especially for shots. No, I'm satisfied there were no more than eight; what surprises me is that I can only remember seven. Still, it might have been eight."

Edvanne asked, "Can I have a light, Mr. Lord? I seem to have used up all my matches."

The detective crossed over and lit her cigarette, then walked back to the door. "Of course," he remarked, "I haven't asked you the most important question of all yet, Miss Hodges. I'm sure you would already have told me if you knew. But, as a matter of form, have you any idea who would want to injure, possibly kill, both you and your father's confidential secretary? Is there any such enemy of whom you have knowledge, even the slightest?"

Edvanne said slowly, "I've been trying to think ever since, Mr. Lord. I haven't the faintest idea."

·   ·   ·

Through the train went Lord and Titus Nutt. It was high time to check up on that open door to the roadbed and its implication of a missing passenger. Lord, indeed, put a different interpretation on it; whoever had gone out, he believed, had climbed back at some other point, but he could afford no longer to overlook the alternative. A close check-up of those aboard was indicated, and overdue.

The conductor had the official list of passengers. Summerladd, who stated positively that he did not intend to leave Edvanne until she was protected from stealthy approach by the daily life of the train, had given his private up-to-the-minute list to the detective.

"More disturbance to every one," Nutt had suggested mildly, when acquainted with the proposed search.

"Can't help it," Lord has responded. "This thing has gone beyond 'disturbance.' We have—or have had—a murderer aboard."

"What! Was Mr. Entwerk killed?"

"No. He'll probably recover. I was thinking of Hodges."

"But—— You think he was murdered?"

"I don't know yet." Lord was impatient to get started. "If he was, I don't know how it was done. But I do know that some one was trying damn hard to commit murder to-night, if not last night, too." He thought a moment, and added, "As long as we're going to be a disturbance anyhow, let's make this thorough."

"The Transcontinental," accordingly, was put through a complete search; a more complete one than Nutt envisaged for some time after it began.

They commenced with the locomotive, climbing the swaying ladder of the towering tender. Fortunately it was an oil burner; there was no mountain of coal to slide over. No one had boarded it, during the stop or afterward. As they climbed back with the gale tearing at their clothes, Lord shouted, "We'll leave the cow-catcher, the brake rods and the car roofs until we see if any one's missing."

Nutt grunted despondently.

In the mail and refrigeration car, nothing was found. The body of the man who Lord now suspected might have been murdered, was miraculously undisturbed on the table close beside the forward wall. They looked into all compartments, open or locked.

The club car and the pool car yielded nothing, also, although here too all compartments were inspected. Lord took occasion to remark that the crew, of course, were included in the check-up.

In the first stateroom car Sabot Hodges' suite came first, then Edvanne's, then the two empty suites, and Entwerk's last of all. Behind Entwerk's were the five smaller rooms for valets and maids, and of these only one, Hopping's, was occupied by a passenger. Waiters from the diner were in the others, since they could be thus accommodated for the present trip, at least.

Lord went through them all, even Edvanne's. However it may

have been earlier, her baggage door was now locked from the inside, but so were all the others in the car, The stateroom door of the suite behind hers was unlocked; this, obviously, might have been opened and slammed shut by the train itself in its abrupt stop. All communicating doors between suites were locked. Through Entwerk's stateroom the detective went on tiptoe; the wounded man was restless and barely conscious as yet and Dr. Black motioned him on, after he had looked through the lavatory and baggage compartment.

On the other cars it was much the same. Most of the passengers were in their suites but few had returned to sleep. Minor injuries from the manhandling stoppage were numerous and Titus Nutt had recourse to all his diplomacy in responding to the numerous complaints.

One lady, apparently about sixty years of age, was especially snappish. She sat alone in her stateroom, fully dressed in a costume whose style, if not workmanship, had been outmoded several decades since. "I might have known," she declared, "that you never get anything for nothing in this world. My sakes, I thought train robbers were on us!" She ground out her cigarette and dropped it into an ashtray.

Nutt, overcome by the combination of costume and cigarette, was speechless. He bowed awkwardly and backed out of the door without a word.

It was just after this encounter that they came to Dr. Poppas' quarters. She likewise was dressed and she greeted Lord with an enthusiasm that perplexed him at first, for he had not seen her since the evening of their departure from New York. She followed him about closely as he searched the suite and afterwards drew him confidentially to one side.

"I have been looking all over for you," she informed him, in a voice so low that he had difficulty in understanding her words. "I have found out who you are, Mr. Lord; you are a detective!"

"I am," he confessed. "But you needn't whisper; the conductor knows it too."

"Oh—I see. I have heard, naturally, of the death of the gentleman we were talking with the other night. Have you arrested any one yet?"

"Arrested any one? Why should I do that?"

"Now Mr. Lord," reproachfully, "please don't try to deceive me. I know he wasn't drowned. I had a few words with Dr. Pons late to-night, just after the wreck or whatever it was. I have been thinking ever since, and there is something I must see you about at once. Won't you sit down?"

"It's impossible now, really. I'm sorry. In the morning."

"But I *must* see you." She grasped his arm, then becoming conscious of the gesture, withdrew her hand quickly. "It's important; it's very important. I'm sure you don't understand——"

She was plainly agitated and Lord looked at her in surprise. Then, as he observed her more closely, he thought he recognised the type. "Later——" he began.

But she interrupted him. "I know who did it. I believe I do. *Please* let me tell you."

"Dr. Poppas," he said firmly, "at this moment I cannot stay. I must finish my search. As soon as I can, I shall be glad to have your information. At the earliest chance. You must excuse me now."

Finally they got away. Lord, as they continued down the car, did not take the incident very seriously. Another volunteer informer, he thought; funny how they spring up whenever there's a crime, kidnapping or anything else.

Dr. Pons, when Lord reached his suite and told him, grinned

widely. "Perhaps I shouldn't have spoken to her about it," he acknowledged. "But she said she knew him. . . . Are you going to hear what she has to say?"

"Oh, yes. I'll have to, sometime. If I don't go to her, she'll come to me; I know them."

Pons considered, running a hand through his tousled hair. "Mind if I come along? I'm interested in these things, you know. And I'm quite intrigued to know what she wants to tell you. I'll promise not to put in my theories unless you ask for them."

Lord, who had taken an immediate liking to the large psychologist from the first day of meeting him a year previously, conceded the point without argument.

At last he came, with Nutt, to the observation car. The dining-car staff and the crew of "The Transcontinental" had been accounted for, all except one brakeman whom they would find at the end of the train. Of the passengers all had been checked off but four.

These four were soon accounted for. They were two youthful couples who evidently had decided to stay up the remainder of the night, after the excitement. When Lord and the conductor entered, they were dancing together on the small floor. Somewhere on the dial they had found either a very late orchestra or a very early one whose music, by some atmospheric freak, was coming through perfectly. When they disliked a selection, they put on a record instead.

So the search ended uneventfully, with every one checked off. The only information turned up came from the crew who asserted that, so far as they knew, only the club car door had been open during the few minutes' halt of the train. After starting again, all doors had been examined and found closed. Even this, however, Lord accepted with reservations. He had noticed more than one pair of muddy slippers or shoes as he went through the state-rooms and he could readily believe that doors had been opened and brief descents into the rain made, unknown to the trainmen.

They accosted the last brakeman.

"Were you on duty when we stopped?"

"Yep."

"What happened back here?"

"Waal, nothin' happened. We stopped and I went back along the track with my light."

"Did any one get on here while we were stopped?"

"Yep."

"Some one did, eh? Speak up; who was it?"

"I dunno. Jest as we was startin' and I was running down the track to get on, I seen a bloke climbin' up the wrong side of the platform out here, the ninny. He come up over the rail and beat it inside. I'd ha' gone after him but I knew we wasn't no-where where any one but a cluck passenger would be gettin' on. Dragged a lot o' mud in with him, he did."

The brakeman pointed to the floor near the door and they could see several muddy marks still on the carpet. But Lord could make a distinct print out of none of them.

He felt a touch on his arm and glanced up. Sam stood beside him.

"Mist' Lawd, suh, they doctor say you wan' speak to that shot man, you-all come along now."

Lord's interview with Entwerk was brief. Dr. Black allowed him fifteen minutes only and at the end of that period insisted that he leave. The wounded man was fully conscious when Lord arrived, but he was very pale and undoubtedly still suffering severely from shock. Black, chiefly because of Entwerk's own pleading—as he told Lord afterward—had administered sufficient stimulants for a short conference. The detective did most of the talking, framing his questions in order to permit of the most concise answers.

Entwerk's account, pieced together from these answers, amounted to the following declaration. The secretary had gone directly to bed on leaving Dr. Pons' stateroom and was asleep before "The Transcontinental" had pulled out of Omaha. At some later time—he did not know when, but Lord reflected it must have been shortly after three in the morning—he was awakened suddenly. He believed it had been the thunder that woke him up, but as he lay in his bed listening, he distinctly heard a series of pistol shots.

Acting almost automatically he had jumped up and taken his

own gun, a .45, from his suitcase. He had gone to his door without even stopping to get into slippers. As he was just reaching his hand to the latch, his door was thrust open from outside and he was shot. He was not sure but he thought he had pulled his own trigger as the other gun flashed. He knew nothing from the time he was struck until he had come to in bed with Black bending over him.

He had not seen his assailant. Although hastening out to the scene of the firing he had heard, he had been completely surprised by the sudden opening of his own door, immediately followed by the shot that had struck him down. If he were to guess—"only a guess, mind you"—he would say that the firer had been rather tall, about his own height, perhaps.

As Hodges' secretary he had a permit to carry a gun and he always did carry one. The private secretaries of very wealthy men usually did, nowadays.

Dr. Black at this point began to show signs of terminating the interview and Lord glanced hastily into his notebook for a final important question he might have overlooked. He found none; everything he wanted seemed to have been furnished, but his eye fell upon an earlier scribble—"Entwerk's salary."

It seemed a foolish question under the new circumstances, but Lord was a stickler for detail. All the queries in his notebooks always carried their answering entries at the end of his cases. He said, "One last question, Entwerk. Nothing to do with the shooting; you needn't reply if you don't want to. I'd like to know what Hodges paid you, if you don't mind telling me."

"I don't. Sixty thousand a year. He was a generous man to his friends."

At the last moment Lord realised that he *had* almost forgotten a most important inquiry. "Have you any enemy whom you would suspect of having shot you, Entwerk?"

"Can't—think of any one."

"Could this have been done by some enemy of Mr. Hodges? Some crank on his trail, or some desperate business antagonist?"

"I——" The secretary suppressed a groan, for the conference was commencing to tell on his remaining strength.

"That's enough," Black interrupted. "Finish." He prodded Lord to his feet and they stepped out into the aisle.

"He looks bad," Lord commented. "You're sure he'll be all right?"

The physician was brusque, as usual. "Of course he looks bad. Loss of blood and shock. Got to have complete rest and quiet for a while. See the conductor about sending in a maid here to act as nurse. Needn't do anything, but I want some one here to keep every one out and call me if necessary."

"Is it as serious as that?"

"Not as serious as it looks. But he's *got* to have quiet. And you don't want him shot again, do you?"

"That's right." The detective realised this aspect for the first time. "I'll see that Sam keeps his eye on who comes into this car from now on, when I'm not here, no fooling. Have my own quarters moved up here, too."

Black left him and Lord set off to find the conductor. That story confirmed his own impression, he thought; that the shots at Entwerk's door were the second batch. Damned funny about Summerladd's evidence; might be inaccuracy due to the excitement. I wonder if there could have been three series? he went on. Summerladd couldn't have shot several rounds himself without marking them, for there was only one bullet from his revolver immediately afterward. Have to dig into that further. . . .

Man must have fired twice at Entwerk, hitting him the first time. Both bullets through the window behind him. Entwerk's, of course, broke the glass across the aisle. . . . Too bad he couldn't get even a glimpse of the fellow. . . .

At the head of the club car Lord spied Titus Nutt and hurried forward.

KEARNEY

Monday, 6.07 a.m.

Michael Lord knocked at Dr. Pons' door. The matter of Entwerk's emergency "nurse" had been attended to and Sam had
been sent to collect the detective's belongings and move them
into the vacant suite behind Edvanne's. Might as well finish
this up now, Lord thought, and then get some breakfast; I'm too
hungry to go to sleep for only an hour, anyhow.

Pons appeared in his bathrobe, yawning.

"I'm going to speak to Dr. Poppas now," he was informed.
"Get into something and come along, if you still want to."

Pons grunted. "Why not bring her in here?" he suggested.
"Then I won't have to get dressed. She won't mind, you'll see. I'd
like to hear it, if she's willing."

Dr. Poppas, it soon appeared, had no objection to the arrangement. She accompanied Lord eagerly to Pons' stateroom where
the latter, with face washed and hair combed, welcomed them in.
Neither of the psychologists were as yet acquainted with the fact
of the recent shooting, and Lord for the present did not enlight-
en them. First, he would listen to Poppas' views as to the death

of Hodges, which he could privately assess in relation to the later developments.

"You wish to place certain information before me?" he prompted when the party had settled.

"Yes, I do, Mr. Lord." Now that her opportunity to present her views had arrived, the agitation she had exhibited earlier had entirely vanished. Dr. Poppas now spoke calmly and without haste. "I know enough about the circumstance of Mr. Hodges' death yesterday morning to realise that even on the surface it presents features that distinguish it plainly from an ordinary accident."

"It's peculiar," Lord admitted. "Especially now, and also since medical opinion has not yet been able to confirm the actual cause. But as I have said before, though not to you, doctor, I have been carefully over the scene of—whatever it was, and I have not been able to turn up anything to give grounds for suspicion."

Dr. Poppas said a bit snappishly, "I don't see why you say there are no grounds for suspicion. I should say there were very definite grounds. Have you forgotten what happened in the club car after we left New York?"

"Oh—well. You mean the argument between Hodges and that fellow Hall? I hardly think as casual a thing as that could have had a serious aftermath." Lord recounted to Pons the circumstances of the previous night's economic dispute. (It was only last night that happened, he reflected, in surprise.) "Hall, of course, was violent enough verbally, but I don't believe him capable of plotting serious injury to his opponent."

"Well, I believe him quite capable of it," Dr. Poppas announced positively. "Psychology may not be a perfect science as yet but I can assure you that there are very good grounds for investigating the activities of Mr. Hall after he left us."

"You really think so?"

Dr. Poppas leaned forward and spoke as impressively as she could. "Mr. Lord, I am entirely in earnest. I have been told that you know something of modern psychology. Psychologically there is every reason to suspect Hall of implication in Mr. Hodges' death, serious implication. Whether he has been guilty of murder or only of manslaughter, I don't know. But I beg you to let me put my reasons to you and try to convince you that some attention should be paid him."

"It's my job, doctor, to follow up any leads I can find. Your suggestion seems remote to me now, but, of course, I'll be glad to hear what your idea is . . . But first, I don't know to what exact school of psychology you belong, Dr. Poppas. Would you mind telling me, so that I can form a better opinion of what your theory is when you explain it?" He grinned. "I am well acquainted with the fact that modern psychologists hold quite different views on what seem to me to be fundamental matters."

"I should prefer to. I can see," she said shrewdly, "that your first impression is that I am an excitable woman, the sort of person who rushes to the police with ill-founded suspicions. Actually I am not. . . . I am a Hormic psychologist, Mr. Lord," she went on seriously. "I don't want to take up your time with a long lecture, but I do want enough of it to explain our viewpoint. I can see that you are far from convinced and I am very anxious to convince you."

Lord waved a hand. "My time is entirely at your disposal for any matter that has a bearing on the problem."

"Thank you. Then first of all, to give you some idea of our position, I must say that we do not at all agree with Dr. Pons' belief about instincts. An instinct is a native hormic impulse, not merely a mechanical pattern in the motor system. We recognise not only instinctive action but also very definite instincts, both in human beings and in animals. The more highly developed the species the more instincts it possesses, man of course having by far the greatest number. We find characteristic emotions associated with these instincts.

"Dr. Pons, I know, is not a great admirer of psychoanalysis, but I am. The analysts, I believe, have almost the correct viewpoint; they recognise drives, tendencies, real psychic urges that are surely found in human experience. We think, though, that they have made rather a common error in postulating two or more minds, conscious and unconscious. Both, of course, are merely aspects of a single mind which is much more unitary than they suppose. In this respect we take a position closer to the *Gestalt* view, but otherwise we find the analytic school an admirable one, truly engaged in the investigation of psychic life.

"You will see that we are utterly opposed to the mechanistic, materialistic schools of the moment. We do not attempt to explain higher activities by lower ones. We begin at the top and insofar as we deal with the simpler functions we deal with them in the light of the more complex but more readily accessible ones which are far better understood by every one.

"In general, we find that those psychic activities that are at present to be described at all adequately, are unquestionably teleological; they are activities that people indulge in for the sake of some result that they foresee or in pursuit of some perfectly recognisable goal.

"That situation is true of all life. Where there is life, there is mind. And the fundamental characteristic of mind is a primal urge to live, to construct and organise, to be active. Out of this primal urge the striving capacities and hormic tendencies of each species have been differentiated during the processes of evolution; for any species the kinds of goals that are instinctively sought are characteristic and specific. Their innate tendency is always to seek those goals that are natural to them, and this seeking of the natural goal is the fundamental nature of the hormic impulse."

Lord, who had been endeavouring for some time to interrupt the lady and had nearly been reduced to the class-room expedient of raising his hand, at last succeeded. He asked, "Would you mind telling me just what that word, 'hormic,' means?"

She obliged him without delay. "Hormic comes from the Greek ὁρμη (hormé) and means drive or urge. Hormé is the basic factor that distinguishes living animal matter from inanimate matter. This inborn impulse in living matter constitutes its final, underlying source of motive power; and, of course, that holds also for human beings. What I am trying to point out is the very great, the fundamental importance, especially for human beings, of the underlying, goal-seeking activities. They are basic to everything; the appetite for food, for example, is a reflection of the instinctive hormic impulse to eat. And one of the most deeply rooted and powerful of the hormic impulses is the impulse of fear. You see how closely the emotions are tied to the hormic urges."

"Pardon me." It was Dr. Pons who interrupted this time. "I have no intention of starting a controversy, but it is evident that this primal urge or motive power that you postulate is a form of energy manifestation. I am asking simply for my own information; what type of energy do you consider to be expended when such manifestations occur?"

"Oh," Poppas answered a trifle airily, "we pay little attention to such questions. Naturally it is a matter of energy manifestation, but we do not presume to say what kind of energy it is or just what its transformations may be. We can leave all that to others who will undoubtedly explain it eventually."

"I see," said Pons. And Lord put in, taking advantage of the lull. "Then I gather that you belong to the Purposivist school, Dr. Poppas?"

"Yes, of course. But you must distinguish, Mr. Lord, between the two branches of the Purposivist school, the Hedonistic and the Hormic. I belong to the Hormic branch. And here we notice a further objection to psychoanalysis; Freud's psychology, especially, would be purely hormic except that it is spoiled by his undue emphasis of the 'pleasure principle.' It is true that we try to prolong pleasure and avoid pain, but very few of our activities can be explained solely by this. Our pursuits of pleasure are really activities sustained by some impulse or desire of other nature than a pure desire for pleasure, that is by some hormic impulse such as striving for food, a mate, power, revenge, knowledge. Hedonism has a subordinate place in the hormic psychology."

"I think I'm beginning to understand your background, doctor." Lord acknowledged. "But it still seems very general to me. Can't you describe one of these hormic impulses in more detail for us?"

"Naturally I've been speaking in this way in order to give you a general idea," Dr. Poppas retorted. "Any specific impulse must, of course, be considered as a special instance, but I can characterise the nature of any true hormic impulse in five definite ways. First, its energy flows in such channels that the organism approaches its goal; second, the flow is determined by a cognitive activity on the part of the organism, an awareness, even if very vague, of the present situation and of the goal; third, the goal-seeking activity, once initiated, tends to continue until the goal is reached; fourth, when the goal is reached, the activity ceases; fifth and last, progress toward the goal is pleasurable and any thwarting is felt as disagreeable.

"That is the nature of the true hormic impulse and in the case of any given person, of course, many of them are operating simultaneously all the time. Because many of them are present at once, the result is some sort of compromise between incompatible goals. Thus in real circumstances this fundamental characteristic of psychic life is somewhat obscured, but to any reflective person it becomes apparent as soon as it is pointed out."[*]

Dr. Pons grunted and stretched. "It's stuffy in here, don't you think?" he demanded, and yawned openly. In fact, with the door and all the windows tightly closed against the storm the atmosphere had become too warm for comfort. He got up and clicked over the switch of the electric fan to its highest speed. The hum, rising from a low pitch, quickly attained its highest point and, mingling with the rumble of the speeding train, filtered through the subsequent conversation.

As an afterthought he raised one of the drawn shades and they were all astonished to see the early sunshine over the passing plains. Since the storm of the night the clouds had been rolled away and the sky was nearly clear. Pons pulled up the other shade, turned off the lights and raised one of the windows slightly. The air blew in fresh and vital through the permanent screen across the lower third of the window and, as always hap-

---

[*]   As good an account of the hormic apologetics as can be found is "The Hormic Psychology," William M'Dougall, in *Psychologies of* 1930, *op. cit.*

pens with the return of the sun, they felt the night's fatigue slough off and a new energy rising within them.

With an altered expression Lord turned back to Dr. Poppas. "I've been interested in your exposition, doctor. I think I understand your viewpoint and, so far at least, I'm not prepared to quibble with it. But now let's see just how you apply it to our quandary."

"I'm coming to that," the hormic psychologist answered. She straightened her skirt slightly and again leaned forward. "Mr. Lord," she continued, "I would ask you to consider seriously the nature of the argument between Hall and Hodges and especially the violence with which it was terminated by both of them. Hall took exception to the whole banking profession; he as much as called Mr. Hodges a scalawag and a dunderhead. He may have used even stronger expressions, although I do not remember them. Mr. Hodges at last became so incensed that he got up to leave, but the other man jumped up first and went away. He was very angry and just as he was going, I am almost sure I heard him mutter something about meeting Mr. Hodges again that night."

Neither the detective nor Pons seemed greatly impressed; the latter continued to maintain the air of an entirely passive listener which he had assumed from the time his visitors first arrived.

"Do you mind if I smoke, Dr. Poppas?" Lord asked; and receiving permission, went on, "Of course, there's no question about the fact that both men were good and angry at each other at the end. The whole argument seemed rather exaggerated to me, though. And, after all, there is a big difference between an angry dispute and a murder; nine men out of ten would have gone to bed and forgotten all about it. At most they would have regretted their words the next morning."

"No." Dr. Poppas, far from being convinced, pressed her point with renewed energy. "I agree about the nine men out of ten, but Mr. Lord, in Hall you have the tenth one. A well-balanced person would not have argued with so much heat in the first place; really it was an unrestrained, fanatical exhibition. The man *is* a fanatic, with a terrific drive toward this particular reform of his.

"The history of reform," she went on, "is the history of just such individuals. People who are motivated by such powerful drives that they lose themselves completely in the goals toward which they strive. Sometimes they make martyrs; and not a few of them have furnished us with the self-justifying type of assassin. I am not saying that this is natural, for it is an obvious abnormality. But it is simply the abnormal over-exaggeration of the fundamental goal-seeking activity of human life. It is the tremendous inflation of one goal to the virtual exclusion of all the others, so that the subject becomes heedless even of his own personal danger in striving furiously after the single object of his desire.

"In itself, of course, the ideal of economic betterment is a natural and even a praiseworthy one. I am sure," pronounced Dr. Poppas primly, "that we all wish to make the world we live in a better place. Some people give themselves wholeheartedly to such movements and have accomplished a great deal for civilisation.

"But in Mr. Hall's case there appear two stigmata that disclose the abnormal nature of the example. In the first place there is the exclusive aspect of his urge. Any one can see that he eats, sleeps, talks and lives this technology of his; and even a serious, major interest cannot so drastically shut out all other natural goals without showing itself to have reached a stage of definite abnormality.

"But this is not all. We must take the personality as well as the drive into consideration; we must consider what type of personality it is that has become subject to this series of powerful impulses which, for him, constitute a motive as strong as that of religion did for the Crusaders . . ."

Dr. Poppas paused for breath, and Pons put in, "I have gathered that he is scarcely troubled with tactfulness. But then, none of the reformers I've met have been."

"A rude mug, no doubt about it," Lord said unequivocally.

Poppas, with a fresh supply of breath, began again. "Among the many hormic impulses of the human being we recognise clearly a definite self-assertive impulse. This impulse can readily become a strong desire for fame or power. Now even admitting the brief opportunity I have had to observe the Hall man, I have no hesitation in saying that he is an extraordinarily self-assertive type. I think there can be no question but that, aside from the usual fanatical impulses of the reform itself, he is personally ambitious with regard to the working out of this technocracy. He is plainly out for publicity for himself as well as for his movement.

"Here, then, we have the two elements that show us the undoubted abnormality with which we are met. First, we have Hall's remarkable over-exaggeration of the cause itself; and not only this, but second, we have the fact that he strives for a personal triumph as well as a social one. These two goals are not only extremely powerful incentives separately, but, when combined as we find them here, they are certainly so strong as to produce a frame of mind that will literally stop at nothing.

"We find this fanatical crusader engaged in a bitter argument on his pet obsession with a powerful opponent. We see him leave in a rage, actually threatening his opponent; and in the morning we find his opponent dead. I certainly believe, Mr. Lord, that you should use every means to exhaust this possibility before looking elsewhere for an explanation that is plain to me at least. I think, in fact, that as a witness to the affair night before last, I would be entirely justified in demanding the arrest and questioning of Hall in connection with Mr. Hodges' death."

Dr. Poppas' voice ceased abruptly and she stared at the detective, her eyes dark behind her glasses and her plain face lit up with the intentness of her regard. The latter still half reclined upon the bed in a position of comfortable ease, but he had been following her closely, none the less. Now he dropped his cigarette into the ash tray with which he had provided himself and, swinging his legs to the floor, sat up.

"You have built up a stronger case than I would have expected, doctor," he admitted. "But you must see for yourself that there is nothing there on which I could arrest any one. As you put it, though, the presupposition is quite enough to point to an investigation. If I had any evidence pointing to Hall as being implicated, I should summon him for questioning, of course. But actually I haven't a shred of evidence to show that he had anything to do with it."

"That's not the point, Mr. Lord," the lady insisted. "The point is that you have a mysterious death, one that is not accounted for; and you have the very strong probability that, if there is anything peculiar about it, this man Hall is undoubtedly involved. The reason you have no evidence against him is because, by your own admission, you hadn't thought of him seriously in connection with the case. How do you know what he may have been up to after he left us?"

"There, I'm afraid, we shall have a hard nut to crack. The ordinary assumption would be that he went to bed and slept off his anger. And if he has quarters alone like most of us, an alibi would be impossible to ask for. On the other hand, I have no doubt that, if he didn't go to bed, he could have wandered from one end of the train to the other, night before last, without being seen by a single person. Especially if he had desired to remain unobserved. These porters, once they get their jobs done, snooze away the rest of the night, you know. . . . Anyhow, I'll be glad to check up on it, as far as I can."

"By the way." It was Pons who stirred in his seat and addressed no one in particular. "Where does this desperate Hall live? I mean, where is his stateroom?"

It became apparent that none of those present could answer his question. But after some minutes of searching, one of the passenger lists was brought to light and it was ascertained that Noah Hall's quarters were in the rear stateroom car, not far from those of Dr. Pons himself.

"So he would have had to go through five cars, four stateroom cars and the diner, in order to reach the pool car," was Lord's comment. "Not impossible, because the dining-car staff are accommodated elsewhere this trip. . . . And what do you think he did when he got there, Dr. Poppas? Don't forget that Mr. Hodges had not been shot or stabbed or apparently injured in any way at all. If Hall killed him, as you imply, he must have done so by some means."

Dr. Poppas was silent for some minutes; and Pons finally hazarded, "Poison?"

"There are no signs of his having been poisoned."

"Still," said Pons, "there are obscure poisons whose traces would not yet have been revealed by your examination."

Lord objected. "No, I can't see it. All this supposes premeditation and planning. I don't believe Hall had ever met Hodges before last night. I can't really believe that he had provided himself with an obscure poison against a chance meeting that he couldn't possibly foresee."

Poppas had been thinking and now she advanced a more reasonable suggestion. "Naturally I don't know what happened, but what I believe is something like this. Mr. Hodges got up to take his early swim and Hall met him in the swimming pool car. There they continued their row and finally Hall struck the other man down, knocking him into the pool."

"Just a minute now. How would Hall have happened to meet him there so early in the morning?"

"It may have been chance, but I think not. Hall probably had been brooding over the quarrel and didn't go to sleep at all. He could easily have found out somewhere that Mr. Hodges would get up early and go for a swim. Maybe he heard it mentioned without having to inquire. At the right time he also went to the pool to continue the argument. You yourself just said that he could go and return without being seen."

"All right. I think that's possible. But how did he kill him? There was no evidence of a fight."

"But there wouldn't need to be, would there? I—it seems to me I have heard of prize fighters being killed with a single blow. If the point of the jaw is struck with enough force, the consequences are serious, I'm sure."

"I've never heard of it," said Lord. "A broken neck, or a fractured skull, if they are knocked down hard enough. But his neck wasn't broken."

Dr. Poppas said slowly, evidently pursuing an elusive memory, "I think I remember something like that. I read about a fight in France, if I'm right. It was some time ago and it seems to me that one of the fighters was killed by a blow on the jaw."

"Hm. Dr. Pons, what do you say? Do you think it's possible?"

Thus appealed to, the masculine psychologist agreed that by a chance in some millions it might be possible. "It would depend somewhat on the configuration of the jaw and on delivering the full force against the nerve there. The paralysis might be sufficient to cause death, as a matter of theory. You saw the body shortly afterwards, Lord. Was the jaw swollen at all?"

"Not that I could see. I looked at the face carefully and it was unmarked. Except for a tiny little scratch against the nose. But that was much too small to have come from a blow."

"A little scratch on his nose, eh?" Dr. Pons looked interested, but came back to the previous point. "Well, there would be very little swelling on the jaw, you know, if such a blow were to be fatal, because the circulation and so on would cease before it could take place. Still, I imagine your medical fellow could find some trace, if he were to look."

"I'll have him look, of course." The detective still seemed doubtful but his doubt was lessening. "Your theory, then, Dr. Poppas, is that Hall met him by the pool and that in the rumpus that ensued he struck Hodges a terrific blow on the chin which actually killed him and caused his body to fall into the water. . . . Well, it does account for Hodges having died in the pool car and for his being found in the pool, although he wasn't drowned. Yes, you know there really may be something in it. I shall get hold of Black; we'll see if he can find anything to substantiate it."

"Meantime," Lord pulled out his watch, "I don't think it would be such a bad idea if we had some breakfast. My word, yes! It's nearly eight o'clock, do you know it?"

The others looked up at the clock and Dr. Poppas nearly squeaked in surprise. "My gracious," she cried, "I had no idea. I'm really famished." She gathered up a purse and a small scarf from her chair. "I'm going right now. You *will* do something about that Hall man, won't you, Mr. Lord?"

Lord assured her that he would give his immediate attention to her theory and she bustled out of the room. "I'll see Black," he told Pons. "Get into your clothes and I'll come back for you. We'll have breakfast together, if you like."

Dr. Pons was delighted.

NORTH PLATTE (ar.)
Monday, 8.04 a.m.

LORD HAD not been able to find Dr. Black quickly. He had, however, entrusted a note to Sam who would presently deliver it. Now, as he returned, he felt a sudden retardation of the train. Only three minutes late, "The Transcontinental" was rushing into the division head at North Platte.

He was still turning over in his mind the discussion just past. Not so slender, that case. Hall was a belligerent fellow, heaven knew. There was nothing far-fetched in the idea that he might have struck out at Hodges in a sudden burst of uncontrollable anger. But the fatal result of such a blow, that was harder to believe. Still, there were further considerations now. The idea of a crank tracking down the millionaire merged imperceptibly with the concept of an economic fanatic striking blindly not only at the banker himself but at his entourage.

He had now come into the last stateroom car and half-way down its length he noticed an open door. Pons must be ready, he surmised.

He turned in at the door, to find that he had made a mistake. It was Dr. Raquette who emerged from the lavatory to greet him in a gorgeous lavender dressing-gown. It was apparent that the analyst had for the moment dispensed with all other raiment; his bare legs and feet protruded from beneath the hem of the garment, as he crossed over and closed the door.

"I beg your pardon," said Lord. "I thought this was Dr. Pons' stateroom."

"Not at all; don't apologise. Sit down and have a cigarette with me, if you will, while I dress. I have hardly slept at all all night and now it is too late, although I feel quite done up. A little conversation will be a pleasant awakener."

Lord accepted the invitation and the proffered cigarette. "For a few minutes," he stipulated. "I have an appointment with Dr. Pons. I'm afraid," he added, leaning over to dispose of his match, "that your suicide theory is out. Perhaps you have heard that Mr. Hodges was not drowned?"

"I have heard this, yes. It is an astounding information. Is it possible that he may have taken a poison? I still fear that he has done away with himself; but perhaps by a means calculated to deceive us. Mr. Hodges was a most intelligent man."

Lord, who had now crossed the suicide theory entirely off his list, refused to be drawn. He asked rather abruptly. "By the way, Dr. Raquette, do you happen to know a man named Hall?"

"Hall? Hall? No, I do not think so. Is this man a psychologist?"

"By no means. A technocrat. He is on the train with us; a tall, red-headed man, lanky. Loud spoken."

"Ah, you say a technocrat? Is it possible that I have had breakfast with him? Such a man I met at the table yesterday morning.

He seemed under some great strain, very excitable. He has also an obsession; I would consider him somewhat abnormal."

"That's the fellow, all right. So you would say he was abnormal, eh? Dr. Poppas believes him to be abnormal, too."

"I am not acquainted with Dr. Poppas, but any psychologist can easily see that this man is not normal. He is perhaps not always as overwrought as he was when I talked with him, but he stands badly in need of an analysis. His libido is seriously thwarted."

"Did Hall know Mr. Hodges? I mean before this trip. Did Mr. Hodges ever speak of him or mention him in any way?"

"No, I do not think they were acquainted previously. I had never heard his name until you asked me of him just now. But Hall did mention that he had talked with Mr. Hodges the evening before I met him; he was abusive about it and became more excited than ever when he was telling me of their conversation."

"Do you mean to say he was still angry at breakfast? I should think he would have gotten over it by then."

"No, he seemed very angry. He abused Mr. Hodges vehemently, called him an enemy of the public and spoke of brushing him aside. In fact, I think he said he had already been brushed aside." The analyst stopped abruptly and almost caught his breath. "What a strange coincidence! For Mr. Hodges was of course dead, when he was speaking."

"Very strange," said Lord drily. "Did he use that actual expression, 'brushed aside'? This may be important. And can you recall just when you saw him yesterday morning?"

"Let me see, I believe I can recall. It must have been about eight o'clock, just about the time we have now. This man was already at the table when I came in and the waiter put me opposite him. Yes, those were the words he used. The psyche is a strange thing, Mr. Lord; we might even suppose that he had some sub-conscious intimation of what had happened."

"Perhaps he had more than a subconscious intimation. You can swear to those words?"

"I can. But is it so important?"

"I don't know. We have yet to see. But I'm glad I stopped to talk with you." Lord got up from his chair and turned toward the door. "I'm afraid I'll have to leave now. Pons will be waiting for me. Thanks for your hospitality."

At the door he glanced back. There was a whirring sound from the wall; they looked up and saw that the hands of the electric clock, regulated by the porter at the end of the car, now pointed to seven-ten, Mountain Time instead of Central.

"I thank you," declared Raquette with Gallic politeness. "I now feel myself once more." As Lord left, the psychoanalyst was adjusting his cravat.

NORTH PLATTE (lv.)
Monday, 7.11 a.m.

"IF YOU don't mind, let's have breakfast brought in here," Lord had just come in to the now attired Pons. "I've something to tell you, and I'd like to go over the whole case against Hall."

"All right with me, if you don't mind the unmade bed." Pons pressed the porter's button. "To tell you the truth, Lord, I'm not sold at all on our friend's notion."

Lord smiled. "Not professional jealousy, I hope. Seriously, though, there is more to it than she realises. Maybe you will think so too, when you have the rest."

"Ha." There was a knock at the door. "Let's order some food first." The porter came in and they made their selection from the card he drew from his pocket. As he was leaving, "The Transcontinental" slowly resumed its interrupted motion; the yards at North Platte were gliding past the window.

"There is quite a bit you don't know," the detective told his host. "Do you know that Hodges' daughter was shot at last night and that Entwerk, the secretary, was badly wounded?" He recounted the events of the night and also his chance conversation with Dr. Raquette. By the time he had ended, their breakfasts had been brought in; indeed they had almost finished them.

"So what is your opinion now?" Lord concluded. "You will have to admit that the general situation, as the professor calls it, is considerably changed, I think."

Pons wiped his mouth and leaned back from the small table between them. "You're inclined to think that the whole thing is connected? That Hodges' death and the shootings last night are to be attributed to the same source?"

"Well, just a bit," Lord answered with a smile. "What we call coincidence undoubtedly exists and I'm willing to grant some of it. My talk with Raquette, for instance. But not as much as this. Think of the number of coincidences we have now. Summerladd's arrival just when this last attack was going on, my own arrival on the scene at almost the same moment, the emergency stop of the train just in time to let the attacker escape, and finally the fact that a man is found dead one night and on the very next his daughter and his closest confidant are both assaulted with intent to kill. It's obviously impossible that all these occurrences, centring about one small group, should not have a connection."

"How about your own presence at the last rumpus? I gathered that that, at any rate, was due to chance."

"I'll have to concede that, for of course I know it was. I'm willing to do the same for Summerladd, too. But the rest of it— no, I can't look at everything that way. I have Nutt's word for it that the train's stoppage was unquestionably bona fide; and I can't see how anything could have been timed to coincide with it in advance. That is, I can't see it yet. But as to the first death and the following attempted murders, I'm perfectly sure that they have a common factor."

"And that is?"

"Obviously the influence that brought them about. That influence must just as obviously be a person."

Lord got up and took a turn around the room. He lit a cigarette and offered one to Pons. The latter pushed his chair farther back from the remains of their meal and asked, "And Hall is the person, eh?"

"He is the only one I have anything against," Lord reminded him. "And I have a good deal against him now. Motive, to begin with; that's a little weak, you will say, but you haven't seen the fellow in action. He's a firebrand, I can tell you. Then opportunity; there was plenty of that for him in both cases. Means, I don't know for sure yet, but that can be demonstrated by search probably. His remark about Hodges having been 'brushed aside' is a very funny-looking coincidence to me, too. First, however, I must go over the whole thing and organise the various elements that point to him as the man behind it."

"Go ahead; I'd like to hear you."

"Not quite so fast. Let me work this out a little first." Lord removed the trays from the table and sat down before it with his notebook and pencil. "You know," he added to the psychologist, "I haven't had a minute to get anything in shape since this thing began to break yesterday morning."

"Make yourself at home," Pons invited him. "I'll take a shave while you're convicting him, and then you can try it out on me first."

He rummaged around in a large and tumbled valise and presently disappeared into the lavatory with his shaving kit. At the small table Lord worked steadily on with his notebook, occasionally sitting back to ponder, then bending forward to add to his growing synopsis. The fan still hummed above his head and through the now closed window beside him the prairies flowed rapidly past. . . .

When Pons re-entered his stateroom, he was surprised to find it empty. Hardly had he arranged his collar and struggled into his coat, however, than the door opened and Lord came in, with a decidedly exultant gleam in his eye.

"Where have you been now?" Pons demanded. "And whose canary have you gobbled?"

Lord, it appeared, had made a hasty visit to Hall's quarters. The suspected passenger had not been at home; doubtless he was in the dining-car ahead. Lord had entered and made a rapid search. In a locked suitcase, which had nevertheless yielded to his practised manipulation, he had discovered a fully loaded automatic. .45 calibre, of course.

Pons asked, "Had it been fired?"

"It's clean now. But now is too late to tell. Naturally he would have cleaned it and thrown away whatever he used for the purpose, as soon as he got back to his stateroom."

"Well, if that's all you found, it's not much. Any one might have an automatic in his luggage." The psychologist had not yet relinquished his scepticism.

"Ah, but that wasn't all I found. In his baggage compartment, thrown into a dark corner behind his trunk, there was a pair of shoes plastered over with fresh mud and a coat and trousers still wringing wet! What do you say to that?"

Pons thought a moment and then replied, "I say Hall had been out in the rain."

"Another coincidence?"

"Well——"

"There's no 'well' about it, Pons. This man has got a lot to explain. I won't say I'm prepared to arrest him this minute and charge him with the murder of Hodges, but I'm certainly going in there and put him through an interrogation as soon as he gets back. Do you want to come? I'd as soon have a witness."

"Oh, I'll come," grinned Dr. Pons. "But I still advise you to go slow with this. If you object to coincidence, I must warn you solemnly of the remarkable coincidence of Poppas hitting it off correctly on her first guess."

Lord grinned back. "Mere jealousy, doctor. I hadn't expected it of you. There's really no reason why she shouldn't be right, you know. She accused Hall because she saw his motives plainly displayed and took them seriously. All the rest of her reasons were what Raquette would call rationalisations; if you happen to share her viewpoint, correct rationalisation, and if you don't share it, then incorrect. I'm not going into court with a hormic case, but that doesn't signify that she hasn't turned up something important."

"That's just what I mentioned. If she is right, in spite of dragging a good deal of pseudo-religion and a lot of loose, literary terms into what is supposed to be a science, what can you call that except a striking coincidence?"

"All right, that's one kind I can put up with."

"All right, you can. But before we go to beard the lion, can I see how you have organised this case?"

"Sure thing. Just a minute." Lord sat down again and added a few words to his notebook. Then, folding back the page, handed it to Dr. Pons. "For brevity I've called Hodges' death the 'first crime' and the shooting affair last night the 'second crime.'"

The psychologist took the book and holding the indicated page up to the light, for he was slightly near-sighted, saw that it was entirely covered with headings and subheadings:

Case vs. Hall

Causes of suspicion: 1. Dr. Poppas' account of Hall's motivation.

2. Some threat about "meeting" Hodges "at night," made by Hall at close of argument.

Motive: 1st crime—economic fanaticism aroused by bitter argument with Hodges.

2nd crime—fanaticism projected against Hodges' party.

Opportunity: 1st crime—possibility of passage to pool car and return unobserved (5 a.m. or before).

2nd crime—same possibility of entrance to first stateroom car (c. 3 a.m.); train stop after shooting allows descent from club car and entrance over rear observation platform.

Means: 1st crime—blow to jaw, resulting from renewed argument.

2nd crime—.45 automatic.

Supporting circumstances: 1. Conversation with Dr. Raquette in which Hall spoke of Hodges as a "public enemy."

2. Hall spoke of Hodges as having been "brushed aside" a few hours after his death and before he could have known of Hodges' death, if innocent.

3. Possession of .45 automatic.

4. Evidence of clothes shows Hall to have been outside train for some time.

Pons returned the document with the remark, "A couple of points occur to me."

"Yes?"

"You said that the shots fired at Miss Hodges went through her door and struck the bed. In the first place how could any one fire through the closed door and know what he was going to hit, anyhow?"

"With a little attention that can be calculated. I'm certain I could hit anything you like in this room through the door if you give me half an hour to figure it out and time to memorise the door's dimensions and panelling. Anything within range, of course; I can't hit something on the wall, right beside the door."

"All right, granting that. Then it must have been some one familiar with her stateroom, some one who had a chance to do all this figuring you talk about. How does Hall fit in there?"

Lord smiled. "You're still trying, aren't you? But that doesn't follow. Each of these staterooms is exactly alike. Even the door panelling is the same throughout the train, and the beds are all fastened to the floor in just the same relative places. A chair might be a different proposition, but the beds can't change their location. The calculation I spoke of can be done for any stateroom and will fit all the others."

"Hu—huh. Yes, you're right about that. . . . Here's the last point, then. Why fire through the door at all and take a chance of missing—which happened, by the way—when all you have to do is wait until the door is opened? Surely the girl could have been hit as easily as Entwerk was. That doesn't make sense to me."

"It doesn't at first. There is only one explanation, though, so it must be the right one. Undoubtedly the plan was to shoot when the door was opened, just as was done with Entwerk. If the door wasn't opened, then the alternative of firing by calculation would be chosen. But, with the girl, there wasn't time to wait for the opening of the door. Remember, Summerladd is sure that the secretary was fired on first. If we take his version then the firer ran down the aisle to Miss Hodges' stateroom. There had already been three shots, enough to arouse the car in spite of the thunderstorm. Imagine standing there right in the open, with one killing behind you, waiting to accomplish the next before you were discovered. There wasn't much time to waste.

"And some certainly was wasted. Hodges' daughter was actually in the baggage compartment and did not answer the knocking immediately. There was no response and he was probably just getting ready to shoot into the bed, anyhow. Then he may have heard Summerladd open the rear door of the car. Or he may have seen him down at the far end. Summerladd says he didn't see the actual shooting, but he seems a little mixed up on the details of what occurred; I don't think his testimony can be trusted to be entirely accurate. At any rate the man was really hurried, or imagined he was; he heard the bed creak and couldn't stand another second of delay. He fired at the sound, and ran."

Pons grunted non-committally. "Sounds plausible that way. You're probably right." There was a rapping on the door and the porter stuck his head in, announcing that Hall had returned to his stateroom.

"Let's get started," Lord proposed, rising.

"I point out three things," he added, as they prepared to confront the technocrat. "First, the theory accounts for the undrowned body in the pool.

"Second, the firing was done with a .45 and Hall has one. Everybody on this train can't be carrying along that very calibre of weapon. And I have accounted for all the shots from two other .45's, mine and Entwerk's, that I have already found.

"Third, a man was actually seen climbing up the rear observation platform just as the train was starting after the emergency stop."

•   •   •

"What do you want?" Hall opened his door a grudging crack and peered out.

"I want to come in. I have something to say to you."

"Well, you can't."

The door was almost closed when Lord, with a sudden motion, flung his weight against it. Hall, on his side, pushed back and the barrier remained stationary. Dr. Pons somewhat reluctantly placed his shoulder next to his friend's; he sincerely hoped that the .45 was still snugly locked in Hall's suitcase. His two hundred and eighty pounds immediately and easily swung back the hinges.

They entered.

"What the hell do you mean by this!" Hall blazed from the centre of the stateroom, whither he had been pushed. His sandy red hair seemed to grow more ruddy with his anger and his fists were clenched.

"I want to see you, and I mean to." Lord exhibited his police badge and extended a card to the infuriated man across the room. The latter reached forward and took it, apparently in astonishment.

The card was small and very plain. In the centre it bore merely—Lieutenant Michael Lord; and in the lower left-hand corner were the words—Police Department of New York City. There were also three tiny dots in appropriate places, spots that were changed every thirty days. These dots Hall did not even see.

"A dick, hey?" he sneered. "Who's your fat friend? Another dick?"

Lord remained unruffled. "Permit me," he said. "My friend, Dr. L. Rees Pons. . . . Mr. Noah Hall, doctor. In a pet . . . Dr. Pons is a well-known psychologist."

Pons, unaware of any etiquette covering the circumstances, said nothing. Hall was not amused.

"Well, now that you've come in, suppose you get out."

"We will leave here," said Lord levelly, "just as soon as you have given me satisfactory answers to the questions I intend putting to you. Not before."

"Questions be damned. I don't know what you're talking about and I don't care. You can ask all the questions you want; you'll be talking to yourself." Hall crossed the room and sat down in one of his chairs, turning his back on the intruders.

Pons looked inquiringly at his companion, who motioned him to the other chair. The psychologist sank into it while Lord closed the door and remained leaning negligently against it as he lit a cigarette.

"No use in your being pigheaded, Hall," he remarked. "I have the necessary authority and you are simply trying to obstruct justice. It won't pay. I could arrest you now for that, if I wished."

Silence. Hall stared sulkily out the window and made no move.

"What have you got a .45 with you for?" Lord demanded suddenly.

"None of your damned business!"

"How did you get your clothes wet last night?"

Silence.

"What were you doing in the pool car when Mr. Hodges died?"

Silence again.

"Very well," said Lord. He crossed over to one of the beds and sat down on it. "If you won't answer these questions, I'm going to tell you something. . . . I'm going to tell you, Hall, how you killed Mr. Hodges and how you tried last night to kill his secretary and his daughter. I'm going to tell you how you did it and why you did it. When I finish, I think you'll realise that you're in a pretty bad mess and that you had better come across with anything you can think of in your own favour."

Hall jerked around in his seat and his expression was sufficiently surprised, at all events. "You've gone off your nut!" he cried. "The old fool was drowned, I heard. I didn't drown him; I can't even swim. A damned good job if some one else did, though."

"You know perfectly well he wasn't drowned, and so do I. Or maybe you don't; maybe you didn't wait to see."

"You're looney! This fat boy must be your keeper." Hall turned contemptuously back to his window.

"Are you ready to answer my questions now?"

"Oh, go to hell."

The detective, still recalling Pons' caution, kept his temper. Pons, for his part, was observing the situation with considerable interest, not unmixed with amusement, despite the reflections upon his personal appearance.

Lord returned to his task. "What about it, Hall? Ready now?"

He was met, however, simply with further silence; and after some moments he decided to carry out his earlier intention. Settling back on one elbow, he commenced the recital of his case in an unemotional voice.

"You're a fanatic, Hall, an extremist and a fanatic. You are not only against the banking system as such but you bear an active hatred toward bankers. That's what gives you away; sincere reformers are out to change a system and they don't really care who runs it or who will run the new one they hope to substitute. But you do care; *you* want to run the next system and in the last analysis your hatred of the men who run this one is no more than envy.

"You hate their guts, and when you had that argument with Hodges the other night, you concentrated all your malevolence on him. You went back to your stateroom and brooded on your wrongs, which you managed to blow up and inflate until you saw Hodges not merely as your own enemy but as the enemy of all civilisation. That's a regular dodge of envious fanatics.

"Finally you reached the point where you became completely abnormal. You had heard that Hodges intended to swim very early the next morning and after working yourself up for hours, you decided to proceed to the swimming pool and express your enmity further. I don't need to say that you formed the definite intention of killing him; that came afterward.

"You found him there, as you expected. But Hodges had probably had enough of you by that time and told you to go about your business. The words that followed put you into a blind rage. You struck out at him with all your force and hit him a terrific blow on the point of the jaw. Such a blow can be fatal and your blow actually did kill him.

"He fell back into the pool, but he was really dead before he struck the water. Now comes the part you'll be executed for. Instead of being shocked and dismayed at the result of your out-burst, as would any normal man, instead of doing your best to pull him out of the water and prevent his drowning, you stood there and gloated. Presently, when you had calmed down enough to consider practical matters, you reflected that no one had seen you going forward in the train at that hour in the morning. I don't know whether you made your way back again unobserved with ease or with difficulty, but I'm pretty sure you succeeded.

"That brings us to yesterday morning. Your abnormal anger continued, and you actually had the effrontery to go in to break-fast and boast of your deed in veiled phrases to Hodges' private consultant, Dr. Raquette, whom you met in the dining-car. And not so veiled, either; you told him contemptuously that Mr. Hodges had been 'brushed aside.'"

Lord paused and Dr. Pons stirred in his chair. Hall remained perfectly still, not once looking around. The psychologist glanced questioningly at the detective, wondering if his idea was to en-rage his victim beyond control. Lord's next words lent probabil-ity to the notion.

His quiet voice went on, "You're really homicidal, Hall. Yes-terday you were like some wolf that has tasted blood and thirsts for more of it. Not content with the crime you had already com-mitted, you continued to brood. Why not clean out the whole nest of them, the daughter and the secretary, too? The more you thought of it, the more it appealed to your twisted brain. You be-gan to make your plans.

"You had a .45 automatic and you decided on gunning them. You calculated on your own stateroom door how to fire through it and strike the beds, in case they refused to open to you. You were acquainted with the possibility of going through the train at night without being seen and you chose three o'clock in the morning for your enterprise. You knew also that your victims would be alone in their staterooms and the passenger list easily located them for you.

"A little before three you set out, sneaking through the train. By the way, Hall, how did you time it so as to coincide with the emergency stop?"

Lord waited some seconds for an answer but none was forthcoming and he proceeded. "Which of them you shot at first, I don't know yet. Outside of Miss Hodges' stateroom you had to wait and I think your nerve failed you because the door wasn't opened for you immediately. Finally you heard the bed creak and you fired three shots at it through the closed door. She wasn't on the bed, though, Hall; you didn't hit her!

"At Entwerk's door you were luckier. It was not fastened and you pulled it open yourself just as he was coming out. You fired at him twice and the first time you hit him. He also fired at you but missed, unfortunately. You left him there dying, as you hoped; but, as a matter of fact, he will recover.

"Now you had to get back to your own stateroom. But you couldn't because Summerladd was coming forward and was already at the rear door of the car. You had to run forward, trusting to find a hiding-place. He called to you but you only ran faster. He fired, but he missed you too. You ran into the pool car.

"Then you either had a most astounding piece of luck or else you knew something that no one else on the train knew. There was a dangerous culvert ahead and the engineer threw on the emergency brakes. Both you and your pursuers, for I was after you too, were thrown down with a good deal of violence and for the moment the chase ended. That's when you got that cut I can see on your face.

"When you managed to get up again, the train had stopped. What a break! You had either reached the forward end of the pool car or rolled there. You opened the platform door of the club car just ahead and jumped out on the tracks before even the trainman had a chance to get out.

"After that it was easy. All you had to do was to run back along the train and get on at the rear end. You did, but you were seen. The rear brakeman saw you climbing the observation railing just before the train started again. But you ran through the car and got back to your own stateroom all right.

"That's nearly all, except, of course, that you immediately cleaned your automatic and reloaded it. Then you threw away the cleaning materials somewhere along the road bed, as the train went along. You took off your wet clothes and put them behind the trunk in your baggage compartment where you thought they would not be seen until they had dried out.

"And then you probably went quietly to bed for some more first-class gloating. A swell night's work! But you can't get away with it, you homicidal hound."

For some minutes there was a complete silence in the stateroom as Lord completed his indictment. The accused man had shifted around in his chair; his breathing was noticeable and his eyes gleamed angrily. When he finally spoke, his tone was strained and menacing.

"Why, you damn fool. What do you come in here with that fairy tale for? I am a representative of technocracy——"

"Like hell you are!" Lord bit off the words, raising his voice for the first time. "You're a representative of the gas-house gang, a homicidal, low-born, lousy, envious degenerate!"

Hall jumped to his feet, eyes flaming. "You're a Goddamned

liar!" he shouted and flung himself upon the detective's reclining form on the bed, reaching wildly for his throat.

Pons, surprised by the suddenness of the attack, pulled himself out of his seat with remarkable rapidity for so big a man. Lord, with a swift twist, had jerked himself from beneath his opponent and they rolled to the floor together. Dr. Pons had played varsity football in his college days; he now dove across the room and a tremendous thud, announcing his arrival on top of the struggling men, knocked most of the wind out of both of them. There was a distinct clap as the psychologist's elbow drove forward, colliding abruptly with Hall's face and the side of his jaw.

Pons rolled off Lord and a moment later came the click of handcuffs on the technocrat's wrists. Lord and Pons scrambled to their feet, the latter grunting heavily. He was now thoroughly aroused and drew back his foot to deliver a powerful kick against the body of the prostrate man.

"Hey!" cried Lord. "We've got him now. Don't kick him; save him for the gallows."

Pons was halted in time. He pulled himself together and helped Lord assist his erstwhile attacker to an upright position. Hall was still gasping inarticulately and they deposited him in one of the chairs. Lord rang the porter's bell and sent the man, when he appeared, to summon Titus Nutt.

For what seemed a long time the three men sat in an awkward stillness. After one snarling "I'll get you both for this," Hall had relapsed into his former silence and the other two were content to sit and recover from their brief but exhausting struggle.

Finally the conductor appeared. His mouth dropped open as he spied the manacled passenger. He stood hesitating in the entrance.

"Please get that brakeman we talked to in the observation car last night," Lord requested him. "I want him here as soon as we can have him." Nutt nodded and withdrew, closing the door after him. He had spoken no word.

This time the wait was even longer; apparently the man Lord wanted was not immediately to be found. The low noises of the train's passage reasserted themselves in the quiet of the room as "The Transcontinental" rushed steadily across the upland western prairies. Already the Nebraska line had been passed and some time ago they had clicked across the junction of the branch track to Yoder and Scott's Bluff National Monument. They flashed past a weather-beaten little station so fast that it was impossible to make more than a fleeting blur of its designation. It was Archer, in Wyoming.

At last Nutt returned, bringing with him the brakeman, who had been sleeping soundly after his night's duty. Lord met them at the door and stepped out into the passage.

"That man you told us climbed on the end of the train last night, do you know who he was?"

"Nope."

"Can you describe him for us?"

"Tall, skinny fella, I'd say he was. I ain't much good at describin' people, mister."

"Well, would you recognise him if you saw him again?"

"Reckon I would. Yep."

Without more ado Lord opened the door. Hall looked up at their entrance.

"Is that the man you told us about? Do you recognise him?"

"Yep, that's him."

"You're sure? You would be willing to swear to it?"

"That's the fella, mister, sure 'nough. I'd swear to it on all the Good Books in this state."

"Thank you. That's all, then. I'm sorry we had to disturb you." The brakeman was dismissed and departed to his interrupted slumbers without delay.

Lord said quietly, "I guess that settles it, Hall. We've got you now. I wouldn't want a better witness than that brakeman."

As he spoke, a familiar grinding came from below their feet. The speed of the train was lessening. Titus Nutt pulled out his watch.

To THE west lay Laramie, Ogden, Reno, Portland, San Francisco; to the south lay Denver; behind them, Omaha and the east. "The Transcontinental" stood in the station at the busy junction point.

In the transient stillness of the stateroom Hall spoke reasonably for the first time since his door had been forced by Lord and Pons.

"Do you really mean to say I'm under arrest?" he demanded incredulously. "For murder?"

"You certainly are," Lord assured him. "You might as well come across now as later. There are two things I want to know. How could you figure that the train was going to stop just after three, or didn't you? And which did you shoot at first, Entwerk or Miss Hodges?"

"Bah!" Some of Hall's earlier manner returned. "I'd like nothing better than to make a fool out of you in court but I'd even rather save myself the inconvenience. So I'll take the trouble to put it through your thick skull that I couldn't possibly have done anything you're talking about. Whatever else a nincompoop like you thinks, can hardly matter to technocracy." He turned to the conductor who still remained standing in a bewildered fashion in the middle of the floor.

"Tell them about these doors," Hall commanded sharply.

"Heh?" said Nutt, with a perceptible start.

"Don't be an old fool. Snap out of it and tell this smart dick here about my doors."

"What about his doors, Nutt?" Lord added, as the conductor still hesitated.

"They got jammed," said Nutt plaintively. "He slammed them both when he went to bed about twelve o'clock the first night out; he slammed them so hard that we couldn't even get this one open until eight this morning, and the baggage door is still stuck tight."

Lord jumped up and Nutt's mournful voice followed him as he went to confirm the startling information. "They are brand new doors; it's no way to treat them."

The detective could be plainly heard rattling and straining the entrance to the baggage compartment from the aisle. Soon he was back again and, "This one was that way, too, from twelve o'clock night before last until eight o'clock this morning?" he inquired. "Can you be sure of those times?"

Nutt nodded in affirmation. "Yes, those are the times. He made an awful fuss as soon as he found it out. I had to come back here. And I saw the stateroom door opened myself this morning."

"But I saw you in the observation car yesterday afternoon," Lord addressed Hall once more. "You weren't in here all that time. How did you get out?"

"There's only one other way out, you simpleton. This is the last stateroom in the car but it has a connecting door to the stateroom ahead. I had to go through there."

"So how does that change anything, Hall?" Lord asked softly.

"Because there's an old ass in there who can give me an excellent alibi. Probably the only use he's been to the world since he was born."

The statement was quickly checked. In response to Lord's loud rapping an elderly gentleman opened the connecting door reluctantly, then stepped back in astonishment as he saw the number of men in the stateroom. "How did you get in?" he quavered to the detective.

"The regular door is open now," Lord told him. "Do you know the man in this stateroom, may I ask?"

"I do now," came the shaking accents. "To my sorrow, sir. A most impertinent young man. But I was forced to give him access. I have never seen him before I got on this train and I hope I never see him again."

"Did he leave this room at all last night?"

"Yes, he did. Just after that terrible shaking-up when we stopped. He had flung on a coat and trousers and he came rushing through as if the devil was after him. No consideration at all. He almost knocked me over. At such a——"

"And the night before, sir. Do you recollect exactly during what hours he occupied his room that night? I'm sorry to trouble you, but this is extremely important information."

"Then fortunately," the old gentleman assured them, "there is no doubt about it. I was awakened just after midnight by the disturbance about his doors and the arrangement was then made that he should use my means of exit until his own was repaired.

He did not use it then, however. He apparently went to bed and did not go out until seven in the morning."

"How can you be sure he didn't go out and return while you slept?"

"I sleep very poorly and lightly," the newcomer complained tremblingly. "It would have been quite impossible, but in any case I kept the door bolted on my side and required him to knock when he wished it opened. After all, I do not know who he may be and his manner is not reassuring. He awoke me rudely at seven yesterday morning, just as I was falling into a doze."

"Thank you, sir," Lord acknowledged. "You have been very helpful." His manner as the witness withdrew, however, was decidedly crestfallen. He walked directly across to Hall and silently removed the handcuffs, returning them to his own belt beneath his coat.

"I apologise," said Lord simply. "I cannot possibly hold you now. . . . But why in heaven's name, man, didn't you tell me all this at once?"

"Because it's none of your business," Hall retorted. "Of course I went out to see what was the matter last night. I got off at the forward end of this car, but I hadn't raised the trap and the wind blew the door shut. This ought to teach you a lesson about meddling in other people's affairs, flatfoot. If I have time from more important matters, I'll make it hot for you, I promise. I hope you'll get out now."

Lord said in a conciliating tone, "I'm sorry it happened as it did. But you brought it on yourself, you know, through your own obstinacy and——"

"Oh, get to hell out of here, will you?"

Pons, as they passed out of the stateroom, could not repress a chuckle. He placed his hand friendlily on Lord's shoulder. "Go get some sleep, lad," he advised. "You must be done up. Haven't had any since night before last, have you?"

The reaction of anticlimax had already settled over Michael Lord. "What a fiasco," he murmured . . . "I'm done up, all right. I'm turning in." His figure receded up the aisle, making its way forward on dragging feet.

PART FIVE

DR. L. REES PONS: APPETITE AS LOVE

LARAMIE
Monday, 2.04 *p.m.*

Dr. Pons was to be numbered among those who have given anthropologists the notion that the human race is gregarious. He liked people, he liked their company and their conversation, he was even anxious to be of assistance to them when they stood in need of his experience or his specialized knowledge. It was this characteristic of his which had drawn him into professional psychology. To his mind psychology was, or should be, a very practical science with immediate application to the various personality types into which men are divided and to the situations in which they find themselves in everyday life. Despite the fact that his own contributions had been mainly in the field of basic theory, involving complex and delicate laboratory research, he remained personally the consultant type.

But he possessed a peculiar characteristic; he found it impossible to charge proper fees to those who did frequently consult him regarding their difficulties and private disasters. Thus he treated them gratis; and in the circumstances of the social order in which he found himself, he was prevented from making his aptitude more than an avocation, since the current economic system precluded the free use of his very special ability.

However, when not engaged in remunerative—or, as he would call it, appetitive—pursuits, he rode his hobby energetically, its generalised form taking the shape of a vivid interest in the underlying causes of human behaviour. Obviously such a conundrum as the one confronting Michael Lord would appeal to him strongly. Here was not only a puzzle similar to the more technical problems of research but, beyond coldly theoretical considerations, a group of human beings was involved. A real man lay dead, another had been shot down, a real girl had luckily escaped—so far. And some other real human being, sinister and deadly, held unknown menace still.

For the moment, however, he was concerned with other matters. He had left Lord outside his new quarters just behind Edvanne Hodges'; the detective weary and at least temporarily discouraged, had gone in and by now was doubtless deep in fatigued sleep. Dr. Pons, loath to return to the solitude of his own stateroom, decided to see who might be lounging in the club car ahead.

But the swimming pool car, when he entered it on his way forward, proved so entertaining that he abandoned his first idea and took an empty chair beside a small table in the open space beyond the tank. Quite a number of the passengers were taking advantage of the novel facilities of the car. A diminutive blonde, in what Pons felt at sight was a most fetching outfit, was diving beautifully into the deeper end of the pool, and several other girls and young men splashed in and out of the water.

In the space where Pons sat, older guests of "The Transcontinental" had taken chairs to watch the antics of the bathers and converse among themselves. For all this scene exhibited, there might never have been a tragedy aboard; and, in fact, of those present only the psychologist had heard more than vague rumours. Of course some report of the banker's death had spread through the train and those who had heard of it, considered it without question an unpropitious christening for the swimming pool. It was clear, however, that rumour was not proving a severe deterrant to those inclined to swim. And as a matter of fact, no one except the persons actually involved knew anything about the attempted murders of the previous night, masked as they had been by the excitement of "The Transcontinental's" emergency stop.

Bright sunlight streamed in through the broad windows and intermittant shouts and laughter rose from the pool. An older man in a sombre blue bathing suit appeared at the end of the rear corridor; he hung up his bathrobe on a peg in the wall by his side, kicked off his slippers and dove cleanly into the water. An attendant approached Dr. Pons.

"Can I get you something, sir?"

"Ha." Pons turned with a start; then bent over and scanned the list of cigars, cigarettes, mineral waters, tea and sandwiches which the man presented. Prohibition was not yet repealed in all states, although progress in that direction was happy, so the train served no spirits; but a decade of moral legislation had accustomed the doctor to carry a flask, and one even now reposed in his hip pocket.

He glanced about and wondered if the idea which presently occurred to him were feasible. He need not have worried; despite the previous errands of the waiter who still stood beside him, there was not a soft drink in the car.

"A bottle of ginger ale," decided Dr. Pons.

It was soon placed at his elbow, accompanied by a large, ice-

200 · C. DALY KING

filled glass. He reached into his pocket to pay for it but the attendant demurred.

"There is no charge, sir, on this trip. With the compliments of the train."

"Oh, ha, thank you—uh, thank you." Instead of the change he had sought, Pons brought forth his flask and as the waiter withdrew, quietly mixed himself a drink.

He took a long and satisfactory pull at his glass and settled back comfortably, continuing his observation of his fellow-travellers. No one joined him and he saw no one with whom, for the pleasant moment, he desired to strike up an acquaintance. The little blonde climbed out of the water and ran off toward one of the dressing-rooms, calling a laughing retort back over her plump shoulder. Dr. Pons thoughts began to wander; it occurred to him, with the effect of sudden shock, that here in this pleasant car Sabot Hodges' death had taken place, that in the very tank now before his eyes the banker's body had laid for an indeterminate time while the heat and warmth of life had ebbed away. Little more than twenty-four hours ago, while Pons himself was slumbering peacefully in bed.

No change was apparent in Dr. Pons' easy attitude, but certain electrical tensions were abruptly released in his brain. This brain, by its miraculous possession of the ability of imagery, now began to reconstruct the fatal scene. The current noise and chatter died away, the sunlight faded out to the pale hint of a coming dawn and two dim lights in the ceiling filtered down on the deserted and chilly pool. Dr. Pons had set the stage.

Onto it walked Hodges' simulacrum. And hesitated beside the tank's low barrier. Its hand went up to its throat—clutched; and a strangled expression appeared on the face. The figure swayed, gasped, leaned sideways over the edge of the pool. Disappeared.

Dr. Pons shook himself mentally. Something was lacking in the otherwise complete picture. What was it? He went through it again, this time forcing his images along the pathway already laid down. He was left again with an importuning sense of incompleteness. Something.

But of course! Another figure should have accompanied Hodges'. That was it . . . Was it? . . . Certainly, it must be; after the happenings of the past night no doubt could remain that the financier's death had been, well, facilitated. To such an extent at all events one must agree with Lord's reading of the case . . . And yet . . . ?

Pons dismissed a persistently lingering doubt and concentrated on visioning the missing figure. There it was, vaguely, very vaguely. Following Hodges along the narrow passage and into the car proper. They stood beside the pool; Hodges, in fact, sat upon its raised side. And the hand of the second figure came up. But not to Hodges' throat! How was this? Remembering his first picture, Pons strove in vain to arrest that reaching hand at the throat. But he could not; no, it went higher, to the face. And Hodges stiffened, slumped, fell backwards into the water behind him.

"Hah," said Dr. Pons. "I'm not in the state for 'seeing'; and I know it perfectly well. As for the rest, eight drinks couldn't do it for me, let alone half of one drink. Let's get after this thing."

Well, seriously, what was the situation? That Hodges had been murdered, here, in this car. But the location of the deed was scarcely important in comparison with the question of its perpetrator. Pons realised now that his first imagery had been based on Irrtum's theory of a sudden seizure. That was out. Who, then, had harboured in his heart the most abnormal of all possible responses, to its fruition?

First, could it have been some crank, driven beyond control by the possessor of great wealth? Dr. Pons had no illusions about wealthy men; he knew too well by what dominantly appetitive means they came by their fortunes. But greed is relatively simple-minded, hardly as intelligent as Raquette imagined; beside the envy that can be aroused to murder, it pales into insignificance. He had no illusions, either, about the abnormality of fanatical cranks. "Reformers," as they were sentimentally called by pastors who wrote columns for the tabloids. Some of these pastors, by the way—— He came back to the point at hand.

On the whole he thought not. Why seek the far-fetched solution of some unknown lunatic? Without a doubt both Summerladd and Lord had checked up on the passengers aboard "The Transcontinental," entirely apart from the presentation of credentials that had admitted every one to the train on its departure. Surely the very purpose of Lord's presence would demand that. No, such an explanation would not satisfy Pons at all; it would take the affair completely out of the realm of calculable psychology and put it into the field of unaccountable chance. Unquestionably, thought Dr. Pons, this murder had been committed by one of the bona fide passengers and, moreover, by one of those already in some association with the principals of Hodges' small cast. . . . Summerladd and Lord . . . But Lord was certainly out; his rôle was known from the past.

What of Summerladd, then? In spite of an acquaintance with the publicity director, Pons knew really very little of him. An assured young man who had made his way from small beginnings to a post of some responsibility and whom Pons had met casually through a literary agent. So far as he knew, Summerladd had never shown any ability outside the field of his own occupation, publicity.

Let me think about publicity for a moment, Dr. Pons proposed to himself. What is publicity, actually? It is the business of making people admire or respond to one by suggestion, of suggesting them into the idea that one is noteworthy or superlative in some way or other. So that by emulation or even by indirect contact they themselves can reflect some part of this superiority. A proper enough response, inducement, really.

But the publicity agent? Let me see now; he puts over the Inducement-mechanism, publicity, by means of further Inducement behaviour. Still all right. But it's a business with him, which is certainly appetitive; furthermore, as he does it professionally, it follows that his Inducement abilities are at the disposal of the highest bidder. The successful publicity agent will publicise anything, a screen star, a shady investment house, a munitions factory. Even so abnormal a procedure as war itself. In fact, now that I think of it, paid publicity men had a considerable importance in the last war.

So then, their publicity Inducement is for sale; in other words, it is directed toward an appetitive result and thus is under the final guidance and domination of the appetitive interests. An abnormal pattern, without a doubt, in dealing, as publicity does, with human personalities.

Well, to get back to Summerladd. Probably, since he did his work so well, his personality type was appetitive. No, probably not; the Inducement responses were too well organised. Duplex, almost surely, with the love response organisation only sometimes controlled by the appetitive organisation. Yes, that was it; duplex, with appetitive interests occasionally in control.

Now how about the rest of the situation? A millionaire, his secretary, his daughter—and a publicity man. By Jove, his daughter! Pons wondered if Summerladd had any interest in the daughter. Pretty crude motivation, though, for a well-organised personality, if he should have gone to such lengths simply for the money. Still, Pons had never seen the girl; maybe she was attractive. Possibly he had an appetitive "love" interest in her, as well. But what about Entwerk? How did the attack on him fit in? For certainly whoever killed Hodges had had an equally good reason to dispose of the secretary; the fact that the attempt had failed was no more than a piece of good luck. A rival, perhaps? I must look into the situation between the four of them, the psychologist considered . . . See what relationships did exist . . . On the surface there's a possibility of dynamite. . . .

Splash! A stout gentleman struck the surface of the pool a resounding whack and Dr. Pons came out of his reverie abruptly. He looked up to find the car much as he had left it when departing on his mental excursion. The swimmers were still numerous and the spectators still sat and talked and watched. Yes, he must check up on some of these ideas when Lord awoke.

Dr. Pons took another refreshing drink from his glass.

RAWLINS
Monday, 4.31 p.m.

It was pleasant sitting in the sunny pool car as the train bore its invited passengers ever westward. Pleasant and warmly comfortable. The great Nebraska plains now lay behind them and ever since noon "The Transcontinental," with two monster locomotives straining at its head instead of one, had been pushing through the Rocky Mountain division. Outside the windows the sun, still high above the prairie horizon, but already sinking closer to the summits of the towering peaks that dominated the Wyoming landscape, painted purple, blue, brown, even scarlet splashes in the distance. The grandeur and dignity of aloof mass met those eyes that gazed from the broad windows of "The Transcontinental."

So very pleasant was this part of the train in which he found himself that Dr. Pons lingered on and on. Presently he ordered himself another drink, mixed it, let it rest beside him for minutes at a time with only an occasional sip from its frosty rim. His thoughts wandered here and there, lazily released from any definite control . . . His profession . . . The lectures he had arranged to give at Leland Stanford, as some excuse for his trip west. . . .

His family still at home in the continually receding east. . . . For the time being all speculation concerning the dark mystery that travelled with him toward California, was dismissed.

In such fashion Pons must have lounged in the swimming pool car for two full hours. But at length the gradual exodus, first of the bathers and then of the spectators and conversationalists, reminded him that the day was drawing on. He looked about, to find himself the sole remaining passenger in the car; the attendant was puttering around, clearing the little tables of their glasses and tea cups, gathering up bathtowels that the bathers had abandoned here and there. The man walked to the end of the car, closed a switch, and the soft light of the ceiling fixtures flooded down. They emphasized the preceding dusk, which had grown so gradually as to be almost imperceptible until underlined by the change to electricity.

Pons rose, took a last drink and prepared to return to his stateroom to make ready for a leisurely dinner. But as he let himself out to the vestibule, the thought occurred to him of making a brief inspection of the passageway of the first stateroom car. Although he had passed through it several times, he had not, on any of these occasions, stopped to view it as the scene of the attempted murders. No one would be about now, he reflected, trying to push past him in the aisle or observing his movements with undue curiosity; every one would be in their own quarters sprucing up for the evening. He would have the place to himself.

And so, indeed, he found it. The aisle stretched deserted from one end of the car to the other, a line of blankly closed doors on the left and wide but darkening windows to the right. The plentiful lights above had been turned on, however, and the passage was as brightly illuminated as at noon, possibly more brightly.

First he listened at the closed door of Lord's stateroom. The train was pulling up a long grade and the chug-puff, chug-puff of the two engines was plainly audible; a wheel keened as they rounded a curve and echoes from a cut they were entering rose about the car. Pons could detect no sound from behind the door and passed down the corridor to the rear.

A paper patch over one of the aisle windows showed him the location of the room where Entwerk lay wounded. Pons halted and looked up and down the car. The position, he noted, was about one-third forward from the rear entrance. Here the would-be assassin had stood, opened Entwerk's door and fired.

Pons speculated on how loud the three shots that had been fired here would have been. They must, he thought, have been very loud indeed in this narrow space. And then the man, according to Summerladd, had run ahead to the stateroom of the Hodges girl and waited there, for some time at least, before he fired again? No, even if the train had been making all the noise of which it was capable, that was hardly possible. Pons remembered that Entwerk's story had contradicted Summerladd's; according to him the shots at the forward end had come first and had brought him out of bed, gun in hand. That was certainly more credible from every point of view.

The psychologist now measured the distance from Entwerk's door to the rear end of the car. It was not very far. Had the criminal heard some one open that rear door, Summerladd (or Lord?), just after he had shot down the secretary? Or had he run forward according to an original plan? And why should he have paused at Edvanne Hodges' door? To look through one of the bullet holes in it, hoping to see the girl's body on the bed he had fired at? If so, he had not then known that some one was close on his heels. At that moment, perhaps, he had seen his pursuer and dashed on . . . Hmm, thought Pons, I guess there's no more to be found here. He started forward.

Edvanne's door was easily identified by the bullet holes, even had he not known that her stateroom was just ahead of Lord's. There they were, three round little perforations running in a diagonal line across the centre of the entrance. Dr. Pons bent forward to look at them, then realised that peeping into the young lady's stateroom was possibly unjustified.

Before he could draw back, however, he had one of those pieces of pure luck that occasionally come the way of investigators and researchers alike. "The Transcontinental" had now breasted the slope up which it had been labouring and with throttle eased off was sliding down its reverse side. In the quiet that followed, a series of words came, very distinctly, to Pons' ears through the apertures just in front of him. They were few, but significant.

A man's voice . . . "Why wait?" . . . a murmur ". . . get married as soon as we reach San Francisco . . . Edvanne, dear, please . . ."

Summerladd, thought Pons; that's his voice for anything you like. The psychologist smiled rather grimly. And felt his right arm suddenly clutched with considerable force from behind.

"What you-all doin' creeping roun' thisyea' ca'! What yo' bizness heah, mistah! Who is you-all?"

Dr. Pons, astonished beyond reply, gaped foolishly at Sam's dark face and equally dark expression.

"Don' you-all make no move! Don' you go' way. Ah'm a-goin' to call Mistah Lawd." The porter's shout, somewhat frightened but sufficiently loud, rose in the corridor. "Mistah Lawd, suh, *Mistah Lawd!*"

Beside them Lord's door jerked open and the detective jumped into the aisle.

ROCK SPRINGS
Monday, 7.00 p.m.

"I EXPECT to stay up all night and see that there is no more shooting up this car. If I catch any one trying it, I'll have our man. But if anything's doing, it won't be until later; so I'd like to lie around comfortably for the next few hours. . . . What about having Sam get a waiter to bring our dinner in here for us? I'm famished. . . . Unless you have other plans."

Lord sprawled in one of his chairs, shoes and trousers on but without shirt, collar or tie; an ancient smoking jacket, spotted and worn, covered his undershirt and displayed his strong throat and neck muscles.

Dr. Pons agreed with alacrity. He always felt cramped at the small tables in dining cars and the evening ahead of him, offering no special activity, had seemed barren enough. Moreover, he liked Lord's company. The detective had a quick and intelligent mind; conversation points did not have to be explained to him in detail. And finally, Pons now considered himself involved in "The Transcontinental's" mystery, with all the rights appertaining thereto. Having cast himself headlong to Lord's rescue he felt himself definitely part of the forces of law and order.

The detective got up and, bringing forth a telegraph blank from the pocket of his smoking jacket, handed it to his friend. "Here," he said, "while I'm washing up a bit, see if you can figure that out. I remember explaining that code to you once. This is the telegram that produced Black."

Pons spread it out:

On board Transcontinental   Official message: RUSH
    Chas
    Chicago
"r t q o s d m a D o l t X p m s n,   m n e s t 2 3,   u n s r u t
                                        Asny."

I ought to remember that, thought Pons; now let me see. . . . Aloud he called, "I know that the '2' means to take every second letter for transposition, but I've forgotten what the '3' means."

Muffled tones came from the lavatory, "Drop off the last three letters until your transposition is made."

Pons got to work—

r t q o s d m a D o l t X p m s n,   m n e s t,   u n s/r u t

then,

  r q s m D l X m n m e t u s
      t o d a o t p s, n s, n /r u t

next,   r q s m D l X m n m e t u s t o d a o t p s, n s, n r u t

and finally,   rqs mDl Xmn met us toda otps, ns, n rut

Dr. Pons read it off: "Request medical examiner meet us to-day. Autopsy necessary en route."

Lord came into the room, wiping his dripping face, towel in hand. "Get it?"

"Got the message part of it. I remembered that code better than I thought I had. But what is the rest? Who is Charles, or Chas?"

"Oh, that's just a code word; we use it to designate a message asking for help. 'Ch'—Chicago; 'as'—assistance; 'As' for assistance again, and 'ny' for New York. If the situation had been reversed and Chicago had wanted help from us, it would have been addressed 'Nyas' with a signature 'Asch.' Pretty?"

"Too pretty for words." Pons grunted, handed back the blank to the detective.

The waiter came in, summoned by Sam who was still beaming because of the commendation Lord had given him for his alertness in seizing upon Dr. Pons. For some minutes they were busy making plentiful selections from the dinner menu; Lord, having eaten nothing since his breakfast in the psychologist's stateroom, was really hungry and the psychologist's capacity was always extraordinary.

When the man had left, after marking most of the dishes on his card, Pons sighed and asked, "By the way, I suppose, after the outcome of the case against Hall, no swelling was found on Hodges' jaw by your man, Black?"

"No," Lord's manner seemed a little despondent. "Black shoved a note under my door sometime while I was asleep; not a mark of any kind on the jaw. . . . Let's give this case a pass for a while, until after dinner at any rate. Do you mind?"

"All right with me, old man." Pons realised that the detective was still smarting under the mistake he had made in the matter of the technocrat and although Pons' own feeling was primarily one of amusement, he had no desire to rub it in. His endeavour to change the subject, however, was only partially successful. He said, "What was the argument you got involved in, the evening we left New York?"

"Oh, economics. By George, that seems a long while ago. . . . Banking capitalism versus technocracy. You know the technocractic racket, don't you?"

"Ugh; yes, I know something of it. Thought it had folded up now. I've heard of Hall, too; from what I know of him, I'd say he was the Mike Romanoff of economics."*

Lord smiled. "Not bad, that. I guess you're not so far off the mark, either. Well, you can imagine what it was like. Ergs, decision-arrivals, all the rest of it. Are you interested in economics?"

"Not so much. All the economics I've ever read or heard of was just so much theoretical twaddle. The basis of economics, Lord, happens to be the Inducement mechanisms whereby men exchange and deal in goods. Ever hear of an economist who even knew that his real subject matter was human responses?"

"Probably you're right, fundamentally. Still, you'll have to admit there has to be some mere credit mechanism to facilitate exchange so that the responses can function. Primarily, it's a question of instrumenting consumption in order that our product can be used instead of sabotaged, as plenty of it is now. There's certainly——"

Lord's discourse was interrupted by the entrance of the waiter. He came in bearing two trays piled high with tureens, covered plates, side dishes; in the aisle outside his assistant

---

* Dr. Pons' reference was to one Harry Gergusson, who for years lived in sumptuous style and was entertained from one end of the country to the other, on the claim that he was Michael Romanoff, a scion of the Russian Imperial House. His success was apparently attributable to the large number of occasions on which his imposture was exposed.

waited with a large portable heater which presently appeared also. The setting of the table and the distribution of all this food consumed some time.

"Go ahead," Pons invited, when the waiter had at last departed. "You were telling me what is the trouble with our economic system."

Lord, already engaged with his dinner, glanced sceptically at his companion; then, perceiving that he was in earnest and apparently interested, said, "All right, I'll tell you." He continued to attend to the food before him and the remarks that followed were interspersed through the meal.

"I'm—not an expert. Some of what I tell you may be inaccurate, but I can give you an idea. . .

"We'll suppose for a moment that you own a business. Now, under a capitalistic system, there is one essential condition that you must fulfill in order to remain in business; although you can break even for a while, even suffer temporary losses, in the long run you must make a profit or else quit. Right?"

"Uh-huh."

"You have something for sale, either goods or services. Into the price that you must charge for these go several items. Cost of raw materials, rent, salaries, wages of employees, bank interest perhaps or interest on your funded debt if you are a large corporation, insurance charges, taxes, light, heat and power rates, and also that essential profit. If you add all these up correctly for a year and if you receive their sum for the goods you provide, you can stay in business . . .

"So that is what you take in, in purchasing power. Now what do you distribute, as an economic unit? Wages, salaries and dividends, including your own profit; and that's all. But the sum distributed is a part only of the sum charged. Therefore it is obvious that if society consists of your business alone, there is not enough distributed, in the form of purchasing power, to buy what is produced.

"But under our present system every other business is equally in your own situation. They, too, must distribute less than they receive or eventually go bankrupt. The sums your business pays to its own suppliers do not constitute a distribution of purchasing power, because they merely reimburse that whose use and effect society has *already* experienced, when the supplier previously paid out the costs of the goods and services with which he *later* supplies you. Therefore the costs of your supplies do not furnish purchasing power, since *this* transaction is only a cancellation arrangement. All other businesses are in like case with you here, too; and purchasing power relative to production grows continually less as time goes on."

"Ha." Pons' eyes twinkled. "Then why haven't we collapsed long ago? Instead of that, we have bigger factories now than ever."

"Are you serious? . . . Yes? Well, here are a batch of reasons for you. In the first place we have had a continent to develop here in America; that has taken up some of the slack. Then whole civilisations, so far as I know, have never lived by commerce except during the very brief past; in previous societies large numbers lived by appropriating goods by force or other non-commercial right. Now we are organised so that every one is really part of the commercial system. It has only lasted a short time and that time is just about up, unless the fallacy I mention is cured.

"We have developed some temporary expedients—bankruptcy, sabotage, the creation of a pyramiding debt structure. The refusal to operate existing plant, by the way, is sabotage in exactly the same sense that operating it and then destroying the product is. But all these are temporary and all of them are about played out."

"So what? . . . This is damn good duckling, Lord. . . . So we're washed up, eh? What would you do about it?"

"I propose a system based on the following considerations. One: the purpose of production is consumption. Two: the prime purpose of any monetary system is to facilitate the production-consumption process. Three: any monetary system should be based on the Real Wealth of the community it serves. Four: the Real Wealth of the community consists of the goods and services it can deliver where and when desired.

"So I'm against a gold standard or any other similar standard. A gold standard is fictitious and artificial; its only use is in connection with transactions that treat money as a commodity instead of as a medium of exchange. Treating money as a commodity should be outlawed in any capitalistic society because, in the last analysis, it is a crime against every member of the society, including those members who have been dealing in money, buying and selling it. The only base for a workable monetary system, currency and credit, is Real Wealth. There should always be enough credit in the community to purchase the community's entire product (so long as its product is desired); otherwise producing plant goes bankrupt and the community does without. I'm for keeping dollars, but I'm for basing dollars on real things, not on a transitory pile of useless metal; I'm for basing them on our real wheat, our millions of shoes, tables, automobiles, insurance organisations, everything that we really possess and now prevent ourselves from using."

"Could it be done?"

"Certainly. It's a matter of statistics and accounting. We have the means and we have plenty of men capable of handling them. The first means is an accurate National Capital Account and the further means, of course, are periodic National Dividends."

"National Dividends? Sounds socialistic, doesn't it?"

"Damnation! Why do people think that National Dividends are socialistic? They're capitalistic, and the only thing that will save our system of individual enterprise. Come on; pull yourself together, Pons. You know we *can* produce around a hundred million dollars' worth of goods annually; we have the plant and we have the men to operate it. Our national income this year is probably somewhere between thirty and forty millions. That leaves sixty billions to be sabotaged, either by destruction or by omission of production. Why shouldn't we instrument ourselves to use that sixty millions through our own monetary system? After all, it's our system; it doesn't belong to a few bankers who can make personal profits in disrupting our credit and preventing our money from functioning as a medium of exchange because they want to deal in it like wheat."

Lord cleared away his dinner plates and procured a salad from the container near the door. He tasted it, smacked his lips, and proceeded more calmly.

"The mechanism seems simple to me. National Dividends would be issued for a period, say three or six months, and would have to be used during that period; they would be issued again in different amount during the next succeeding period, depending upon the change in productivity or Real Wealth. Your fifty thousand dollar a year man would still have his fifty thousand, and the two thousand dollar man would have his two thousand. But they would each share in the dividend, in addition. In other words, their rewards would still be maintained in relation to their different abilities, as at present.

"Even if we distributed the dividends equally (and I don't see that we would have to), the change would simply be that we could feed and clothe everybody in America easily and have a lot left over, we could put our men and our plants to work. Why not?"

Dr. Pons appeared to have been listening and considering the proposal in all seriousness. Now he put in, "Just where is all this new money coming from, that you intend to issue in the form of dividends?"

"That's what every one wants to know," Lord replied, smiling. "They all imagine that money is something real in itself. But it isn't; money is a social device for economic use, and our increasing troubles can largely be traced back to the illusion that it is not a device but a commodity. The illusion, of course, is fostered by those to whose personal advantage it is to use money outside its real function.

"But you want to know where the extra money for National Dividends is coming from. Such dividends will naturally be in the form of credit rather than currency. And where does credit come from now? It is issued by private citizens in their private capacities as bankers. Most of them are under some form of restriction, true; but within these restrictions, they inflate or deflate our credit structure in accordance with their private judgment and without any relation to objective, *national*, commercial realities. Also, of course, they never issue as much credit as is objectively demanded, because, as private owners of money-right, it is to their advantage to keep their special commodity scarce. The point is that credit issue belongs by right to the government, the organised community itself, no member of which can possibly be justified in making a personal profit from this essential device of the nation's life.

"So credit issue now arises from private judgment concerning the future, a risky business at best. What is proposed is that it arise by reason of scientific computation in a central bureau that compiles the actual facts concerning the various amounts necessary in order that the production-consumption mechanism of society should function to its fullest extent. Such issue depends on no one's prophecy about the future but derives from figures that refer to real happenings that have *already* taken place. Among other advantages, therefore, it is far less risky than the present system."

"But how could you manage all these intricate dividend payments? It would take half of us to pay out the dividends all the time."

"Not at all. A general retail discount would do it just as well as the actual issuance of dividends, in connection with price control over the period in question, of course. All costs are collected in the retail price, therefore that's the point of application. The retail merchant sells his article, we'll say, for two dollars, as before; he is prevented from raising this price, but as it is the price he himself previously set, it is hard to see how he can properly object. The customer pays only a dollar and a half, however, because of the discount in force. The merchant deposits his money and his bank credits his account, in addition to the deposit itself, with the extra half dollar. This deficit is made up to the bank through the Federal Reserve system which receives its own credit from the Treasury, by monetary issue that is not fiat in any sense but is solidly based on the current productivity of the nation. So long as credit issue does not exceed Real Wealth, there simply cannot be inflation in the injurious sense; until it equals Real Wealth, there will continue to be deflation in a very injurious sense indeed."

"What do you call this ingenious arrangement? I've never heard of it before."

"To tell you the truth, I'm not quite sure. I think it's called the Douglas System of Social Credit.* I heard of it last year in London and for a time I was quite interested. I think now that if we don't adopt this scheme or a similar one, we are certainly going to collapse into some form of draft labour as an alternative to starvation. Or else we'll have to have a war; probably it will be that. . . ."

Dr. Pons pushed back his chair, stretched, yawned, dawdled with his coffee cup. "Hmm. Well, Lord, that's quite a dissertation. You get around a bit, don't you, for a detective?"

"I have sort of a snap job," Lord admitted. "When I'm on a case, there's plenty to do, but they don't keep me very busy. I'm on the Commissioner's personal staff, you know. My father, when he was alive, was a close friend of Oliver Darrow, the present Commissioner. I went into police work for fun; then I got really interested and now I'm trying to make a profession of it. I'm fairly well off, too; don't have to rely on the salary. So you see I have no axe to grind about National Dividends. I'm lucky, that's all, economically speaking."

"Hmm. I'm glad to hear it. . . . I suppose you'd be surprised to

---

* There is already a considerable Social Credit literature: Major C. H. Douglas' books, *Economic Democracy, Credit Power and Democracy, The Control and Distribution of Production, Social Credit, The Monopoly of Credit, Warning Democracy*, can be obtained through the New Economics Group, 425 Fourth Ave., New York City. Major Douglas is the originator of the system. *Unemployment or War*, Maurice Colbourne, was published by Coward-M'Cann, N.Y. *The New English Weekly*, a London periodical of public affairs, literature and art, reviews current events in the light of Major Douglas' system, which it endorses—emphatically. It publishes a good many American contributions but, even so, is far and away the most entertaining of the English weeklies.

So there is little excuse for Dr. Pons' ignorance, although his subsequent criticism should not, perhaps, be taken too lightly by neophytic inquirers.

find that this new system of yours is even more dangerous than if, like most of them, it were absolutely unworkable?"

"I really would, rather."

"Like to hear why?"

"You bet." Lord, secure in his several months' investigation of Social Credit, smiled tolerantly. "Shoot."

"I won't say anything about stumbling blocks in the system itself. I don't know enough about it, and from what you say, I judge it's quite possible to work it out practically, once it's adopted. Economic techniques are not very abstruse, really, although most economists are adepts at smoke screening. No, I'll take it for granted that your system can be worked, and worked as you propose.

"And what then? You know, Lord, you've done just what all economists do. You have conveniently forgotten that your system is applicable to human beings and not to anything else. Most of them take human beings in a ridiculously naive way as 'economic units,' usually production machines. You take them as production-consumption machines, but *your* doubled unit has very little more to do with reality than *their* monorail model has.

"What would you think of an engineer who selected the materials for a bridge on the single basis of colour? He picks out nice, solid-looking colours; but the colours happen to be on cardboard and the 'bridge' folds up. That's just the sort of thing you do when you devise an economic system for production-consumption units—and apply it to men. Men never were, are not now, and never will be production-consumption units. Those aspects, superficially so impressive, are basically almost unimportant in comparison with what you have overlooked. Don't you know that men have starved, that under very usual motivation they have chosen death to survival millions of times?"

"But there is no reason for them to starve now. Why should they? That belongs to a time of scarcity and the fact is that we now possess plenty. Why not use it?"

"Of course. But you'll have to devise a practical way to use it. A mere mechanism of distribution will bring worse than it solves. Until economists wake up to the fact that they are dealing with human beings and take the trouble to find out something about them, economics, except in the sense of rationalisation after the fact, will be more dangerous than any posible *laissez-faire*. You disregard fundamental factors in the struggle to obtain an age of luxury that will be out of the question for centuries to come, at the very least."

"Why so? We can easily produce the luxuries and easily distribute them."

"But you can't enjoy them, my plausible reformer. . . . See here; I shall give you just one reason out of a good many why your credit scheme would create far more misery than it would alleviate. It will work, we'll say, and every one will increasingly get what he wants. Invention will flourish, of course, and presently machines will displace the greatest part of human labour. You admit that, I suppose?"

"Certainly. And why not? If all of us can make use of the products provided by the machines. If unemployment is leisure instead of starvation, it would seem to be an improvement. It is certainly an aim of Social Credit."

"So it looks just like Utopia. But it's much nearer hell than we are to-day. Human beings, Lord, are subject to three fundamental drives, the erotic, the procreative and the appetitive. These drives result from bodily mechanisms, appetitive drive from the hunger mechanisms. An abundance of goods and a complete economic freedom do not in any way diminish appetitive drive;

if you imagine they do, you will have to explain how a multimillionaire can be appetitive and also how a National Dividend can cause the stomach to vanish. But our present economic struggle, based, as I must agree with you, on a purely artificial scarcity, provides an outlet and a buffer for this socially dangerous drive. To destroy a competitor's business, even to take away his house through bankruptcy proceedings, is relatively harmless compared to what Dominance, one of the components of appetitive drive, can do when really unleashed.

"And that's just what will happen as soon as your Utopian abundance is really established. Without any economic scarcity as a shock absorber for the tremendous volume of appetitive drive continually being manufactured in the bodies of the citizens, your social credit nation will become the arena of bitterness, hatreds, private feuds and mob killings that would make war itself look civilised. . . .

"Don't forget that that's just one objection out of a half dozen equally sound psychological ones. Man cannot enjoy abundance without work, through employing machines or in any other way. Not because it's immoral or because work is holy, but because his body physiologically is the way it is. . . ."

GREEN RIVER
Monday, 7.45 p.m.

LORD LIT a Piedmont and leaned back in his chair, extending his legs out in front of him beside the table. He was not a profound disciple of Social Credit and he was replete with food after his previous hunger; his face expressed a contented satisfaction as he inhaled the cigarette smoke deeply. So accustomed had the undertones of the train's progress now become that, when the doctor ceased speaking, the room seemed silent.

"Let's get rid of this mess," Lord proposed presently. He crossed to the push-button and rang.

"That's all very well," he continued, re-seating himself. "But I still suspect Social Credit of having value, although I'll admit you have me on some of this psychological stuff. I don't know how to answer you because I don't know enough about it."

"How's that?" Pons demanded. "I thought the *Meganaut* business had gotten you interested in psychology and that you had read up on it; taken quite a course, in fact. You don't mean to tell me that you skipped my special brand, do you?"

Lord grinned widely. "No, I didn't exactly skip it, doctor. But I found yours somewhat more difficult than most of them. Based on too many facts, if you know what I mean. Now most of them are pretty easy reading, if you don't mind long words; it's obvious that what's behind them is nine-tenths speculation and their experiments, when they bother with them, appear to me to be set up in advance to prove what they do prove. . . . Well, it's a cinch to follow some other fellow's speculation, but it's a bit different to have to master a whole lot of data from other sciences."

"Uh, so you did pass it up."

"No. I tried *Emotions of Normal People*,* for example. But that's just what I say; so much about the eighth nerve and the activation of the autonomic system that I couldn't follow it very well. I don't know the first thing about physiology."

"Just too bad, my boy, if you really want to learn something about psychology. Because if you can't accept unfounded philosophical speculations as scientific explanations (and *I* certainly cannot), you will find that experience and behaviour are both based on physiology in the last analysis. You might try *Integrative Psychology*,† if the emotions book was too much for you. It's not so technical; give you a better idea of the whole thing, too."

Lord crossed the room and rummaged in one of his suitcases for the cigarette cartons he always carried with him. "What is your idea about psychology as a whole? To tell you the truth, doctor, a year's reading has left me with the impression that it isn't a science at all yet, in the sense that chemistry is, or even botany. I've run across the most contradictory statements and

---

* *Emotions of Normal People*, W. M. Marston, International Library Series, Harcourt, Brace & Co., N. Y., and Kegan, Paul, Trench, Trubner & Co., Ltd., London, 1928. A bit technical, perhaps; unless one is really interested in emotions.

† *Integrative Psychology*, Marston, King & Marston, *ibid.*, 1931. An *expose* of the entire field of modern psychology; also a complete outline of the Integrative system. Entertaining and instructive, with many practical hints.

theories. No one seems able to refute the other fellow or definitely to establish his own views."

"I think your criticism is well justified," Pons answered him. "Psychology hasn't settled down yet. My own system is an attempt to organise the whole field and to lay the foundations for psychology as a separate science in its own right and a complete one, in outline at least. For years, you know, psychologists have been trying to duck out of their first big problem and to go ahead on easier jobs before it is solved. So long as the most important factor in human experience and behaviour—I mean consciousness—is an enigma and almost taboo to research the rest of psychology will be haphazard and uncoordinated because it has no base. Even a standard of evaluation for other problems is lacking. Half the psychologists of the world are scared to death of the consciousness problem and offer silly denials of its existence, and the other half, well, burble about it in circles. As Irrtum does, if you'll pardon me. He uses the word every five minutes and hasn't the slightest idea what it means. I don't think that is the scientific method."

"Neither do I. . . . So you begin with consciousness. Have you found out anything about it?"

"Yes, by using only verified data and by proceeding experimentally. I believe I know what consciousness is, scientifically."

"And what is it?"

"It is a highly concentrated form of energy. Like other forms of energy that are real and not imaginary, it exists in definite places and at definite times. Here is where you have to go to physiology for a moment, because physiology can show us the equipment of the body that actually manufactures the consciousness which the body manifests. The body has a nervous system whose prime function is to integrate the thousands of activities it carries on, to co-ordinate them and thus to permit the body to live and function as a unit.

"In the nervous system there are millions of what physiologists call synapses, places where one nerve ends and another begins, junction points. Almost all of them are in the central nervous system, the head brain and the spinal cord. It is just at these places that the intergrations of various nerve impulses take place; and it is just here that a subtle and powerful type of energy is built up when the impulse crosses the synapse and joins or is joined by others. The synapse lies like a sheet electrode or a tungsten filament in the path of the nerve impulse, and only by manifesting a more intense degree of energy than else-where in the circuit, can the impulse pass. That energy corresponds in all ten fundamental ways with what we mean by the word consciousness, subjectively. I call the portion of the synapse that is energised a psychon; I call the energy psychonic energy; and psychonic energy *is* consciousness. You probably don't want all the proofs now, but there are plenty. That's just the statement.

"Now there are three different kinds of psychons in the body, the sensory psychons, the correlation ones and the motor ones. These centres are all in the head brain. And there are also three kinds of consciousness—sensation, thought process and emotion. The psychonic energy of the correlation psychons is the thought process you experience and that of the motor psychons is the emotion. You see, the solution of the consciousness problem now permits us to go ahead on either of the two main paths, the explanation of subjective experience or, just as easily, the explanation of objective behaviour. Because psychonic energy is both conscious experience and physical behaviour at once. Of course the name, psychonic energy, is only my label, but the thing itself, whatever it may eventually be called, exists and it does possess this double characteristic."

"You know, I think you have gotten hold of the right starting point for psychology, doctor." Lord raised his arm and glanced at his wrist watch. "I don't have to get dressed quite yet; I wish you'd give me a brief notion of the rest of your system. Not your proofs and experiments; I will read up more on that later, but just the general conclusions. Do you mind?"

"Not a bit. Conclusions aren't very impressive without their proofs, but I'll give you a general idea. . . . The behaviour of the body as a whole is fundamentally the behaviour of its integrating mechanisms, what I call the hidden machinery. Among other things, physiology investigates this machinery, but not, of course, from the psychological standpoint. Psychology's task is to take such data and interpret it further, to explain what the unit responses of bodies are as units and then to prove its explanations by experiment. When this is done, remember, we have an account of both experience and behaviour.

"Take the hunger mechanisms as an example. When the stomach is empty, a series of rhythmical contractions is initiated which sends impulses to the sensory centres of the head brain—hunger pangs. These impulses, spreading through the correlation centres to the motor centres at the base of the brain, result, in the infant, in restlessness and random movements; in the adult, because of the correlation functions that have now become organised, they cause a direct seeking for food.

"Now consider the human organism for a moment in relation to environment. The organism manufactures its own internal stimuli and it is also continuously being stimulated by energy from outside in the form of various physical wave-lengths that affect its sensory organs. Its behaviour results from the integration of these two sets of forces. You will see that there are only four type relationships that these forces can bear to each other; the energies of the organism can be in opposition to the outside stimulation and either stronger or weaker than it, or they can be in alliance with the outside stimulation and again either stronger or weaker. We name these four fundamental types of response respectively Dominance, Compliance, Inducement and Submission.

"Now when the organism obtains and eats the food which the hunger pang mechanism causes it to seek, it responds to the food with a combination of Dominance and Compliance. It has to comply with certain characteristics of the food; the food may have to be cooked and certainly it has to be obtained, if only in the dining-room; but the Dominance component of the response is obviously the most powerful at this stage. The organism has a more powerful effect on the food than vice versa. We call the combination of such active Dominance with passive Compliance, Desire.

"During the digestive process, however, the foods itself exerts a more and more powerful effect on the organism. It brings about drastic changes in the energy balance of the organism, effects that can easily be seen in gross behaviour. As hunger is satisfied, the man or animal becomes contented, lethargic, sleepy." (That's what happened to me with Irrtun, Pons reflected, simultaneously.) "The motor discharge is no longer primarily to the muscles of the skeletal system but to the internal systems. Thus the situation now becomes reversed and the organism is responding to the food with passive Dominance combined with active Compliance. A good name for such a combination is Satisfaction. And this recurrent activation of responses passing from

Desire to Satisfaction builds up a spontaneous drive of the organism called Hunger Drive.

"Then comes a further complexity. Hunger Drive affects the motor centres during its operation and there initiates similar integrations of the Desire and Satisfaction types. You will remember that motor centre activation produces subjective emotion as well as motor impulse discharge. Thus an appetitive mechanism is built up in the motor centres themselves; and due, finally, to the function of the correlation centres, this now generalised Appetitive Drive becomes associated with anything in the world, with academic honours, with automobiles, with power in the stock market and even, abnormally, with other human beings. Appetitive Drive, a definite physical mechanism, is the basis of all the self-seeking, egoistic behaviour of men which is necessary for their survival. As I said, it won't evaporate because you give people goods. In fact, every time they eat, and thus pass through Desire to Satisfaction, Appetitive Drive is reinforced.

"In a similar fashion Erotic Drive is built up, the initial impulses coming in this case, however, not from the stomach but from the genital systems. Here we have the Primary Responses of Inducement and Submission, combining into the Compound Responses of Passion and Captivation, with a similar recurrent merging from the former into the latter as the whole love response cycle is completed. The corresponding emotions, of course, are identical in both men and women, although women experience brief Passion and long Captivation, while with men it is the opposite. But there is no doubt that Erotic Drive is stronger in women than in men, since their bodies possess a periodically operating mechanism whereby erotic stimulation constantly recurs. That is one reason why women should be the captivatresses and leaders in all erotic relationships.

"There is one more drive, the Procreative. It is more complicated than the other two and less well understood. It appears to be initiated by the female reproductive mechanisms but it also seems to be more often and strongly manifested by the male organism than by the female. Its simplest units are the already Compound Responses of Origination and Transformation. A good deal more work remains to be done on it before we understand it as well as the simpler drives. . . .

"Our account of motivation, I suppose, is the most practical thing in this system for you, Lord. By motivation I mean simply the internal initiation of behaviour and in this sense almost all gross behaviour is motivated behaviour. Motivation referrable to the three drives I have been mentioning, is obvious. Then there is unit response motivation in addition. The primary unit responses of the organism I've told you are Dominance, Compliance, Inducement and Submission; the first two appetitive type responses and the last two love type. Scores, if not hundreds, of compound responses are constructed from them; we have already seen six examples—Desire and Satisfaction, appetitive type, Passion and Captivation, love type, and Origination and Transformation. There are many others, Grasping and Knowing, for instance, correlation centre responses still constructed from the four primaries. All of these, apparently, can serve as motivations without having been built into organised drive patterns.

"Finally, we have the question of personality types, depending upon the observed patterns into which the typical behaviour of the individual is organised. Here we find both Appetitive Type and Love Type personalities, dependent upon which kind of response has become most strongly organised and thus governs the behaviour as a whole. Also there is a large class of Duplex Type, in which both appetitive and love responses are strongly developed but kept pretty well separated and manifested separately in the typical behaviour pattern.

"That's about as brief as I can make it, Lord; probably too brief to have much meaning . . ."

Lord said, "No, that's not bad at all, doctor. As you were talking I began to remember some more of it for myself, anyhow. But straighten me out on one thing again, will you? Just what is your difference between Compliance and Submission? I have a job to get that right."

"Yes." Pons scratched his arm and frowned. "Every one finds it so. Probably Submission is not a good word, but we haven't been able to get a better one. It still carries associations of compulsion, almost violent compulsion; and of course the idea is just the opposite. It is meant to indicate wholehearted and willing Submission, Submission because that is the inner wish of the one who submits . . . Always add the adjective, willing, to it in your mind and you won't be far off."

"I see. Yes. And what about things like will and attention in your system? They're words that used to be employed considerably in psychology."

"Attention is what happens when a good deal of psychonic energy is concentrated in one series of brain centres and absence of attention is what happens when there are no especially intense concentrations. That will give you a notion about how we deal with it. As to will, I think that has pretty well vanished from modern psychology. The Integrative system treats of it as a Conative Attitude, an 'Attitude' being a relationship between groups of sensory and motor impulses which are integrating in the correlation arcs connecting those two regions. Will, as a *deus ex machina* or unpredictable, arbitrary force of a supernatural order, we do not credit at all. The subjective feeling of will arises under the conditions I mentioned, but, as regards its former guise in the old religious psychology, it constitutes no more than a delusion."

"You may be right, at that. I incline to the scientific viewpoint on such questions, myself. I imagine, though, that you still find resistances, as Raquette calls them, to——"

There came a succession of loud raps on the door behind Dr. Pons. Before either Lord or his guest could answer the summons, the door opened and Dr. Black walked in.

EVANSTON
Monday, 9.48 p.m.

"GLAD TO know you." Black acknowledged his introduction to Dr. Pons and extended toward Lord a long, white envelope. With the physician's entrance the atmosphere of the stateroom had undergone an abrupt change from the scholarly to the practical.

"Here's your copy of the autopsy report. I finished it late this afternoon, but I've been waiting for the steno. to get through with it. Fairly long; you don't need to go through it all now. Full of negative findings. I stopped in to let you know anything you want immediately, but I haven't got much for you."

"Sit down," Lord invited. "Take the weight off your feet. We've got something definite now, have we?"

The medical examiner grunted, dropped a cigar ash on the floor and sat down on the edge of a bed, chewing on the black end of his cheroot. "Can't stay long; got to get back to my patient."

"How is Entwerk getting on? Mending up O.K.?"

"Not so good," Black growled. "He's got a lung puncture, all right, I guess. Probably pull through, though. He's pretty sick now; hard to keep him quiet. He insisted on writing something or other this afternoon; all right as long as he stays on his back. If he keeps moving around, he'll get a sweet little haemorrhage."

"I'm sorry to hear it," Lord asserted. "In that case I won't keep you long. Just let us hear what the upshot of the autopsy is. In a word."

"It's natural death."

"What?" Both Black's hearers evidenced their astonishment. "I'm certainly surprised," Lord added. "I don't know just what I was expecting, but it wasn't that. I can't get it out of my head that Hodges was done in. Especially after the attack on Entwerk. It's impossible that those two events are disconnected."

Black shrugged. "There's the report. Nothing doing on any evidence of attack. There's not a wound of any serious kind on the body and none of the organs contain any poison at all. That puts the lid on death by violence. Unless you believe in the evil eye, or black magic. I don't."

"I don't, either," the detective admitted. "Well, what was it, then? A stroke or something like that?"

Black cleared his throat twice and looked a little uncomfortable. "It's not always possible to establish the exact cause of natural death, especially a couple of days after it has occurred and in the case of a man approaching sixty. They can have dozens of things the matter with them. Machine beginning to wear out; may be a little thing but a vital one that goes first. These fellows that throw medicine balls and swim and hunt as if they were still twenty, are plenty liable to that. Might have been a stroke, but if it was, there is no sign of it now."

"In other words the cause of death has not been finally established?"

"That's right; can't help it. But don't make anything very mysterious out of it. There are plenty of perfectly good reasons for what I've found. Your main question is answered, anyway; no violence."

"That is certain, is it?"

"Say," Black spoke somewhat impatiently, "you saw the body yourself, didn't you? I've examined it more carefully than you did, but I can't produce a gunshot wound or a stab perforation that doesn't exist. Now take it from top to bottom. The eyes are bloodshot, sure enough, and they probably convinced your Racket man that death was due to drowning. But there are thousands of people with bloodshot eyes, especially early in the morning, who haven't been drowned. Next, there's a little scratch on the nose; not enough to hurt a fly. Could have been done with his own fingernail if he had scratched at the wart it runs across.

"Next, the teeth. I had a look at them, of course. They seemed to be in pretty good shape; some expensive bridge work, but most of them are still there and still good. There is a shred of lint stuck in between the left canine and the tooth in front of it. He probably used dental floss between his teeth after meals, but I don't think that will help you.

"Not even the suggestion of a bruise on the jaw, as I told you. That was a phoney idea anyway, but I examined for it just the same. There *is* a slight discolouration of the coeliac plexus, and you can call that a minor bruise if you want to. And that's the works. That's all there is on the outside and there's no sign of attack on the inside either. So the answer is natural death."

"About that solar plexus bruise," Lord ventured. "Wouldn't the same consideration apply to that as to the jaw swelling? Some one, I think it was Pons here, told me that if death followed immediately, the swelling would be very small because the usual physiological reactions would not have had time to take place. Why not the same for the solar plexus?"

"Sure," grunted Black, "theoretically." He cast a glance of sour asperity across the stateroom at the psychologist. "But it's too much theory. To have the effect you speak of, the coeliac, or solar plexus, would have had to be struck fatally, and that's out of the question."

"Absolutely?"

"This is what happens when a blow strikes the coeliac plexus," Black explained, in the tone of one who instructs a backward child. "First of all the coeliac plexus is paralyzed and through it the autonomic system is paralyzed. If the blow is hard enough, the whole sympathetic can share in the paralysis, with the result that the basal motor constrictors temporarily cease to function. The dilators then work without any counterbalancing, there is an immediate fall in blood pressure and the blood congregates in the vessels controlled by the autonomic. This 'laking' of blood in the vascular system produces cerebral anaemia and resulting unconsciousness.

"There is also partial respiratory paralysis, but certainly not enough to be fatal. The harder the blow the more the paralysis, but also the quicker the onset of unconsciousness. And with unconsciousness comes the normal resumption of respiration, because then the head-brain dominance is withdrawn. The idea that the man might have been struck on the coeliac plexus with a fatal result is out. The blood distribution, I'll admit, might indicate that there was a slight blow just preceding death, but it certainly didn't cause death. I'd say the plexus was probably struck as he fell."

"There aren't any marks of a fist there, or anything like that, are there?"

"Get it out of your head, Lord. There is nothing but a very slight general discolouration; he may have been struck harder than the discolouration indicates, due to the special condition you spoke of, but I don't care how hard it was, *it didn't cause his death*. That's final. Say, I've got to get out of here; it's half-past ten. I've got a job on my hands."

"All right," the detective conceded. His voice was still unwilling. "I don't want to keep you away from Entwerk. But surely you didn't leave the cause of death as vague as you've told us?"

Black, at the door, waved a hand in the direction of the envelope in Lord's grasp. "You'll find it in there. Thrombosis is my diagnosis, on general grounds. Plugging of a vein by a blood clot," he added, seeing the blank expression on Lord's face. "Expected I'd find the clot in the heart, but it wasn't there. Men of his age very liable to thrombosis. It will be in the veinous system somewhere, not a doubt. Or on the brain. Can't examine every cell in the body in one afternoon."

Black was gone. Dr. Pons, who had been an attentive listener to the conversation without entering it, suddenly jumped up and ran into the corridor after the physician, slamming the door shut behind him.

•　　　　•　　　　•

"What did you want of Black?" Lord demanded. He had thrown off his smoking jacket and gotten into his shirt. Now he was arranging collar and tie before the mirror in the lavatory. Pons had just lumbered back to the stateroom.

"I'll tell you in a minute," the psychologist assured him. "Look here, Lord, I have a fairly definite idea about Hodges' death; want me to tell you?"

"Sure thing. Oh, hell," sighed the detective, "it's time I got back on it, I guess. At the moment I haven't many ideas that are definite enough to lead anywhere, I'll grant. I can't get rid of the notion, though, that that man didn't die from accidental or natural causes. Trouble is, all my reasons are either too minor or too vague and general."

Pons said quietly, "I agree with you that it was murder. I believe I know who did it."

"Go right ahead . . . Go right ahead."

"Let me set the thing up for a few minutes . . . Here we have a mysterious death which you and I are convinced for various general or specific reasons, was engineered—murder. Where are we to look for the murderer? A man like Hodges, from what I gather, must have had enemies, undoubtedly. He was also subject to the impersonal hatreds of reformers and other persons who oppose the system for which he stood and which he symbolised, as it were. And he had opponents within his own system, too.

"I don't believe any of these directions a likely one to investigate. The unknown crank theory went out for me with the assault on his secretary. Not because a crank would not attack a millionaire's secretary, but because no one could fail to see that this attack was a crime; and it therefore disclosed that Hodges' death was a crime. But Hodges' death was *not* a crank attack or anything like one; consequently neither of them were, since both were connected.

"Hodges' death was cleverly brought about; so cleverly that your own medical examiner still insists that it was a natural occurence. It was no mere Dominance phenomenon, that murder, but a subtly managed affair, and there is a subtle, complicated personality behind it. A Duplex personality, not a straight-forward Appetitive one, I'll wager. I'll also wager that the springs of this crime are in the relationships between people rather than in some confused theorising about economic abstractions.

"My man is Summerladd," stated Dr. Pons, leaning forward and staring intently at Lord. "I'll tell you why. I know him only slightly, but my diagnosis is duplex; it goes with his activities and his ordinary behaviour pattern. Obviously he's clever, or he wouldn't be publicity director for a big railroad; and he is clever in regard to other people's personalities, for he successfully judges and affects them.

"Now consider for a moment the other characters who are involved. The father, the daughter, the secretary. I happen to know that Summerladd wants to marry the daughter; I overheard him begging her consent to an immediate marriage only a short time ago. By the way, you've seen her; is Miss Hodges a captivating girl?"

"She's damn pretty," said Lord without hesitation. He recalled his first sight of Edvanne in the pool car not long after "The Transcontinental" had left the Grand Central. "And ordinarily she isn't very bashful; she spoke to me right off the bat, before there had been any introductions."

"She probably has plenty of Inducement then, the active element in Captivation," Pons surmised. "In that case Summerladd may have some real love response toward her. At the same time he is almost certain to have appetitive Desire responses, too; Duplex types sometimes have both kinds of response toward the same person, if they are complex personalities as well as Duplex. His love responses lead him to submit to whatever he believes will be to her benefit, but his Desire is simply a wish to possess her for his own gratification. If he had only love responses, he would be inclined to wait until she made him propose, and he certainly wasn't doing that. I heard him distinctly and it is my opinion that there is a lot of appetite in his love.

"Moreover, if the girl is really captivating, Entwerk is very probably in love with her, too. There you have a serious rivalry and plenty of appetitive motivation for the second crime."

"You think Summerladd shot Entwerk?"

"I have been thinking about that and I have examined the passage out here where the shooting happened. I was doing it when your porter caught me. Summerladd's story of what occurred, as you told it to me, is just impossible. And why should he have a peculiar story unless he couldn't tell the real one?"

"Of course you're right about his story being inaccurate." Lord stirred in his chair and brushed some ashes from where they had fallen on his coat. "But why couldn't that be due to the excitement? It's my experience that testimony under such conditions usually is confused."

"It is. But not on every point. And Summerladd's tale sounds suspicious to me from beginning to end. Why did he just happen to be there in the first place? When you say that your arrival was coincidence, I already have good reason to believe you; but I have no similar reason to credit his statement. And two arrivals at such a crucial moment bring the improbabilities up incredibly high, when we know to begin with that one of them really was by chance.

"Then the train's emergency stop. That also happened at the very moment when the alleged assailant wanted to escape. Much too much, all this convenient arrangement, I don't believe there ever was an assailant who got beyond the forward platform of this car, and I think your open door was just a matter of a broken latch and that's all. The only luck in it was the opportunity it gave Summerladd; and, of course, he knew it would be open, even if he didn't know about the broken latch. He knew that there was a forward trainman who would be out on the track. Originally he never expected that you, of all people, would come upon him so soon after the crime. His leading you forward to find that open door was the typical trick of a clever opportunist."

Dr. Pons paused and was seen to be feeling through his pockets. Finally he brought forth a rumpled and dirty envelope. "I made some notes," he informed his hearer. "Yes. Now according to what you told me, you heard the shots when you were standing on the rear platform of this car and immediately ran in. Summerladd's tale is that he heard them from approximately the same place you did, and that then he did the same thing you did. That is impossible, as you must know, for you were there and didn't see him where he said he was when the firing began. And I submit that it is something on which he could not possibly be confused. He hasn't forgotten where he was when he heard the shots, and he most certainly has not told you the truth about it.

"Consider the bearing of Entwerk's story on this. Entwerk didn't make his story up; he's got a bullet through him to prove it wasn't imaginary. And what does he say?" Dr. Pons voice rose portentously. "He says that he was awakened by shots somewhere else in the car and that later he was shot himself. That is obviously true. But Summerladd says that Entwerk was shot first, which cannot be true. On the other hand it is plain why he has to say so; he must account for his own presence at the front end of the car where you told him you had seen him. Therefore he invents an imaginary assailant whom he claims to be chasing and after this invention he finds that the assailant has to run forward. Because he, Summerladd, has to go forward, since you are in his rear. Ergo, the assailant's progress must be from the rear to the front of the car for Summerladd's purposes. And that is just where he badly over-reached himself."

"But if Summerladd shot Entwerk, as you are trying to establish, why should he have tried to kill Edvanne Hodges. I thought your idea was that he was in love with her and getting rid of a rival?"

"I'm sure he wanted her. But that is very different from being really in love with her. My point about him is that in this situation his appetitive responses govern and dominate his love responses, at least for the time being. He tried to kill her (which of course is complete proof that his relation toward her was ultimately appetitive), because she was the one witness to his crime. To preserve his own neck he had to get her out of the way."

"But," Lord seemed plainly puzzled, "then you are now supporting the very story of Summerladd's that you were just objecting to. In other words, that Entwerk was shot first."

"No . . . Real things don't happen so simply, just one, two, three. I will admit that this is imagination on my part, for I wasn't there, but I believe that what happened was as follows. First Summerladd went to Entwerk's door and was probably trying it or even attempting to get it unlocked without awakening the man asleep inside, when the girl looked out of her own door and saw him. She made some noise, perhaps cried out in surprise; anyhow, he looked around and saw her——"

"By George, her baggage compartment door *was* open," the detective interrupted with his first show of agreement. "I know it was open when I went past. Yes, I see your notion. For some reason she opened it, looked down the corridor and saw Summerladd unmistakably about to attack the secretary."

"Whereupon," the psychologist took up the narration, "Summerladd ran back and, in his excitement, did not follow her through the baggage door that was still open, but tried the state-room door. She was frightened and wouldn't let him in. He shot through the door and ran back to finish the job with Entwerk. Then he went back *again* to the girl's stateroom to see if he had been successful there. And that's where you caught him." Dr. Pons concluded and wiped off his forehead, which already was beginning to perspire.

Lord leaned his head back, considering the resumé. Presently he asked, "If you are right about it, how do you explain the fact that Edvanne Hodges has not accused him to me? She has had an opportunity, and after all she couldn't be under any doubt as to the situation. If Summerladd tried to get her once, he will try again; why not have him arrested before it's too late? Why deny, as she did, that she knew who had attacked her?"

"Hah, you haven't forgotten Coralie Reake-Lyons, have you? She wouldn't give a criminal away, either, although her life was certainly in danger. She was afraid to give him away, feeling sure that no one would believe her. Actually she was very foolish and almost died as a result; I, for one, would have supported her to the limit until proof could have been obtained one way or the other, no matter what that fellow Mansfield had done. But people don't act logically, Lord; they act on motor energy and motor energy goes through the motor centres first.

"People act for emotional reasons, primarily. This girl may not be afraid, or she may be. She may have any of a number of reasons that keeps her silent. That's what human beings are like, as distinct from conventional units, and the only way you can account for their behaviour is not by syllogistic but by emotional knowledge. The present case is a good example; if you proceed by merely logical stages, you will inevitably say that she cannot have been a witness to this crime, because, although she has had a chance, she had not denounced it. I don't believe that at all. If you don't watch your step, my friend, she will be attacked again, and this time, perhaps, with more forethought."

"I agree with this much, anyhow," said Lord, his face serious. "Whatever was the cause of her being attacked, that cause is almost surely still operative. There will be another attempt by some one; that's why I'm here next door to her and why I intend to stay up all night to-night.

The echoes from another cut clamoured about "The Transcontintinental" and Pons raised his voice to supersede them. "But, man, you don't expect he's going to parade in here with a gun again to-night and merely repeat the performance, a clever man such as you have to do with? He won't strike when you are looking; it will be when you aren't." Abruptly the psychologist pulled out his handkerchief again "He's in there with her right now! Or was, when I came in here."

He broke off and stared at the closed door in Lord's wall leading to Edvanne's baggage compartment and beyond it to her stateroom, as if trying to see through it the drama of terror that might even now be occurring within a few feet of him . . . The girl, keeping a tight hold on her courage, knowing her companion's intention, trying to fence . . . the man, waiting his chance . . . or maybe that chance had already——

Pons sprang out of his chair. "Look here, we've got to do something!"

"Hold everything, doctor." Lord's voice, perfectly calm, cut across the disturbing picture in his friend's mind. "You have a good way to go yet before the case against Summerladd is clear enough for worry."

"Don't wait!" Pons adjured him, almost hoarsely. "Can't you see what it may mean!"

Still without visible symptoms of excitement, Lord crossed the room and rapped sharply on the connecting door. "Miss Hodges," he called. "Lord."

After what seemed to Pons an interminable delay there were light footsteps on the other side and a muffled voice said, "Yes? What is it?"

"Is Mr. Summerladd with you?"

They could hear the bolt being drawn back, and the door opened. Edvanne, in her same black evening dress, looked through and Dr. Pons realised that her appearance, certainly, was captivating enough. Her cheeks, even under the electric light, were remarkably rosy and she appeared at the moment in no way terror-stricken. "Yes, he's here," she said. "Do you want him?"

"Not just now, thanks. I may want him a little later, though. Sorry to have bothered you. Will you tell him?"

"Surely." Edvanne was gone, closing the door again but not bolting it. Dr. Pons slumped back in his chair, sighing with relief, and it was as if a school of porpoises had given tongue announcing their presence.

"You needn't worry now, doctor. He knows that we know he is there. That will stop him for the time being, supposing your case will really hold water."

"Oh, it will." Pons' own self-possession had now entirely returned. "Probably this isn't the time for him to try anything, at that. He may still hope to persuade her to marry him, which destroys her testimony as surely as any other way. . . . Now that I've seen her, I haven't any doubt that he wants her, too. Much the best solution to his way of thinking."

"Pretty, isn't she?"

"Hah," said Pons, "she's lovely."

"I can't see your case against Summerladd yet, though," Lord went on. "Don't forget that whoever did one of these things did the other, too. Accepting your own reasoning, which I do, up to the point where you decided that Hodges was murdered, how does Summerladd fit in there? That must be explained before any case is valid."

The psychologist had moved his chair as far away from the connecting door as possible. Now he continued, in a voice so low as to be nearly inaudible and with one eye on the alert toward the next suite.

"Why, that's obvious. Summerladd wants the Hodges girl, partly on account of her own attractions, partly because of her father's wealth. That's where the two parts of the duplex response get mixed up together since they're both directed toward the same object. Entwerk also wants her. And Entwerk has all the advantages; he sees her more often than Summerladd possibly can, since he lives in the same menage, and being a trusted confidant of her father, he can make use of innumerable opportunities to advance his own cause with the parent and undermine his rival's. With the result that the father supports Entwerk and may even have gone so far as to forbid any marriage between his daughter and her other suitor."

"As a matter of fact, Pons, you're right about that. The girl as much as admitted your general situation to me last Sunday morning when I had my first interview with her. Your point, for what it's worth."

"You see." Pons' eyes blinked triumphantly. "You'll find that this kind of motivation is underneath both crimes. We know Hodges wasn't killed for robbery and motives like revenge or fanaticism are definitely far-fetched when right under our noses is a violent emotional tangle revolving around the chief actors. Balked of any possibility of marrying the girl while her father was alive, Summerladd waited his chance, planned his action carefully in advance and overcame the obstacle in his way by means of Hodges' death. On his own ground, too. He has had more to do with planning this train and arranging the passengers' quarters than any one else. He probably assigned Hodges to the suite next the pool car himself."

"But how did he do it? You'll have to show more than motive, you know. You'll have to show means. With Black's testimony as it stands now, I could be sure I knew the murderer and still I wouldn't have a show of proving it."

"Black," said Pons confidently, "is getting the evidence for you now. I told him what to look for a little while ago, when I went out of here after him."

"You don't say so?" Lord was now distinctly surprised. "What did you tell him to look for?"

"Hydrocyanic acid. In the blood, not in the organs. I'm taking it for granted there is none in the stomach, for example. But it may be in the blood. In fact, it *must* be in the blood. That, or some other poison; I'm sure of it. Because I'm sure Hodges was killed and I can't see any other possibility now than poison in the blood stream. It's the only thing the autopsy hasn't ruled out."

"Well, well, doctor. This is rather worth thinking about. I wonder if you can be right about that. You have had this poison notion in the back of your head all along, haven't you? . . . But let's see now; it must have gotten into the blood stream somehow. And there aren't any hypo. marks on the body that Black hasn't seen, I'll stake my word on that. Oh, I—— But no; you wouldn't give me such a Sunday Supplement theory as that it was somehow put on the dental floss he used, which was found between his teeth?"

"Good heavens, no." Pons was emphatic. "The dental floss is

just one of those things that mix you up if you take it too seriously. It hasn't anything to do with the crime; it's just there because he used it and a little bit got broken off and stuck. We don't need anything nearly as involved as that, especially when the mark is right on the body in full view."

"But what mark?"

"Why, the scratch on the nose, of course. Where could you find a less suspicious place to make a little scratch on a man's skin than on his face? On any other part of him, except his hands, it could hardly be accidental, but on the ordinarily exposed surface of the skin it has all the appearance of accident and, nine times out of ten, won't even be noticed. There's another instance of the murderer's cleverness."

"By damn, doctor, if it turns out that you're right, I'll feel pretty small." Lord looked more than a little chagrined. "I should have thought of that and I missed it completely."

Pons nodded his acknowledgement and went ahead. "Here's why I think it was probably hydrocyanic acid. In the first place its action is almost instantaneous, as you know. In the second place a drop of it in the blood is fatal, and the blood absorbs it in a moment, even through the stomach tissue. And in the third place it can be introduced directly into the blood by means of a scratch with any ordinary, sharp object, a toothpick for instance, or a pin. You don't need a hypodermic needle or other special equipment.

"Then all the symptoms are of relatively short duration. The body is unusually cold immediately after death, but in this case the body was thrown into the pool and would have been cold in any event by the time it was found. The dilation of the eye pupils tells nothing by itself, unless it is extraordinary, and there is no reason why it should be. And the water would wash any trace of the chemical off the nose. There would be none of the distinctive bitter almond odour, of course, because the poison wasn't swallowed or introduced into the mouth cavity at all, but went directly into the blood. The result is that a medical examination, if put off for only a short time, is thrown off the track, unless it knows ahead of time just what to look for, and is reduced to nothing better than a general guess as to the cause of death. Just what happened to the examination you procured.

"I'm fairly sure," Pons concluded with some satisfaction, "that Black's blood analysis will show not only poison, but hydrocyanic acid poisoning."

Hands clasped behind his head, Lord leaned back and tilted his face to the ceiling. "Give me a few minutes, doctor, to think this over."

Pons replied by settling back in his own chair and lighting a cigarette, Pall Mall Specials; he was extremely fond of them, but they came high these days. The New York Central, however, was lavish in its hospitality and the Union Pacific no less so. Dr. Pons had carried two packs in his pocket continuously since boarding "The Transcontinental" . . . The train rumbled on through the night. For a full twenty minutes no word was spoken in the quarters of the detective.

At last Lord opened eyes that for some time had been mere slits as he gazed at the ceiling. "All right, Pons," he said, "you have built a good theoretical case. I'm willing to admit that. There's almost no evidence, though. Of course, if Black's test bears you out, your case will be much stronger. . . . Meantime, I have a couple of items for consideration.

"Dr. Raquette proposed his theory of Hodges' death in Summerladd's presence, but at first Raquette merely hinted around the subject of foul play. I was watching fairly closely and there is no doubt that Summerladd was taken aback by the suggestion and expressed himself as incredulous. When it came out that Raquette's meaning was suicide, Summerladd appeared undoubtedly relieved.

"But now mark this, I was not greatly impressed with the suicide hypothesis, but Summerladd opposed it far more strongly than I did. He fought it tooth and nail, ridiculed it and would have none of it. Why so, if he were guilty? A verdict of suicide, even if hushed up for the sake of the daughter, would let him out nicely."

"Only one reason that I can see off-hand," Pons answered. "He felt that sooner or later the suicide theory was bound to be blown up and he was clever enough not to let himself be compromisingly associated with it. *Damn* clever, that, too."

"All right," Lord shrugged. "Let it go. Here is something you'll have to get around, though, and I don't see how you're going to do it. You say Summerladd started to attack Entwerk, was interrupted, attacked the girl, went back and shot Entwerk, then returned to the girl's stateroom door, was seen by me, and ran forward. Right?"

"That's my guess," Pons conceded. "I may not be right in every detail, but the main sequence must be correct."

"Then what about—— Now who can that be?" A slight but insistent knocking was coming from the closed door to the aisle. Lord got up in leisurely fashion, crossed, opened the stateroom entrance. A young woman in a white silk blouse and dark, short-length skirt stood outside. He recognised the semi-uniform of "The Transcontinental's" women employees.

"Come in. Are you looking for me?"

"I want Mr. Lord," said the girl questioningly. She glanced in hesitation from one of the men to the other, as she strolled in languidly. She was a rather dazzling blonde and even the single ceiling light in the stateroom made brilliant yellow glints in her marcelled hair. Dr. Pons noted her trim figure with approval.

"I'm Lord. Haven't I seen you somewhere before, young lady?"

"I guess you have," smiling directly into his eyes. "I've seen you, although I didn't know your name. I'm a manicurist and I used to be in the Terminal Shop at the Grand Central. I applied for a position on this train, and got it."

Yes, thought Pons, I'll bet you did. And a break for the train, too. There was nothing more dismal, he was convinced, than a non-alluring manicurist; but "The Transcontinental" appeared to have solved this question satisfactorily.

"Of course. I remember you, perfectly. I shall come back and visit your booth in the recreation car the first chance I get," declared Lord gallantly.

"I have a note for you, Mr. Lord," the girl drawled, her demeanour changing slightly.

"A note? From whom?"

"Oh, I haven't told you, I guess. I've had a little nursing experience and I have been helping Dr. Black to-day. The note is from Mr. Entwerk, the poor gentleman who was shot last night. I'm sorry; I was supposed to give it to you hours ago. But I knocked on your door about two-thirty this afternoon and there was no answer, and the porter said he couldn't find you anywhere. And when I went off for dinner, I forgot all about it. I'm fraightfully sorry."

She held out the note, then raised a slim hand and touched, very faintly, the back of her hair, exposing through the thin blouse the lovely profile curves of her torso.

"I guess there's nothing to worry about," Lord smiled. "It can't make a whole lot of difference. I was asleep all this afternoon, anyhow. Won't you have a seat, Miss, ah, Miss——?"

"Miss Delacroix." Her hand had now accomplished its mission at the back of her neck and returned to a more decorous position. "Therese Delacroix." She gave full value to all the letters, even the "ex"; —Delakroycks. "I'm fraightfully sorry, but I must be getting back. I dare not leave the poor man for more than a minute . . . Another time." With an arch smile she swayed through the door, which closed, ever so gently, behind her shapely, silken legs.

Pons' mouth dropped partly open. "My God," he proclaimed, "I hope the French psychoanalyst who's aboard, hasn't seen *that* duchess yet. He'll be complexing all——"

The detective had opened his note; and all trace of amused gallantry vanished abruptly from his features. Without a word he handed it across.

Pons took it. There was no address, no signature, only one sentence, in a sprawling but legible hand—

> "I think it may have been Summeria
>
> d
>
> d——"

OGDEN (ar.)
Tuesday, 12.24 *a.m.*

RAPIDLY "THE Transcontinental" was drawing near to Ogden. It was running faster now, its giant engine pulling it smoothly along the rails. In the recreation car there was dancing, as usual, to cheerful syncopation. In the diner a reduced staff was preparing the midnight supper, served every evening in the last car and to any who might desire the little sandwiches and *canapes* in their own quarters. The travellers were still up and about, and few of the occupied suites were dark.

But fast as "The Transcontinental" was running, its speed was not great enough. There was one of its passengers who would never see the small city of Ogden, its lights sloping upward from the station against the backdrop of the mountain behind it. The peak of the mountain still held snow; through the high, clear air it gleamed mistily in the bright moonlight, as if distantly watching over the clustered buildings far below. That, too, would not be seen by one.

Summerladd still lingered in Edvanne's stateroom, but not for Lord's possible summons which now had slipped his mind. Lord himself had just given Dr. Pons a note. Pons was staring at it intently. Into the dim suite where Entwerk lay, came the manicurist-nurse. She glanced at his face, pale against the pillow, but he was lying still and breathing evenly. She took up her novel from the chair beneath the bracketed reading-lamp, the room's only illumination. The train rumbled on . . .

The man on the bed gave a sudden cough. A rasping noise, ending in a sound like bubbles. The girl looked up and saw his hand grasp convulsively at the side of the bedclothes. She sprang to her feet and switched on the main light. His face was deadly white; he raised himself partly on one elbow and, as he coughed again, a little trickle of red ran down his chin.

Human personalities, as Dr. Pons had often found occasion to inform his classes, are complicated and not to be judged too hastily. Miss Delakroycks was across the room in one leap and opened the aisle door, pressing the button beside it with all her might. By a lucky chance Sam appeared around the corner nearly instantly.

"Quick!" she cried to him down the passage. "Quick! Get the doctor! Run!" Her voice snapped like a precise whip. Sam ran.

In another second she was across the stateroom and put a steady but gentle arm around Entwerk's shoulders. He was coughing violently now and the blood bubbled from between his shaking lips; it splattered the front of her white blouse and one of her arms.

"Easy, boy," she said with quiet force. "Easy does it. The doctor will be here in a minute."

A gasp tore down Entwerk's throat. "Hakch—hakch! . . . note . . . letter . . . note . . . you . . . hakch! . . . promised . . ."

"I did. Take it easy, boy." She was holding his retching body with both strong arms. Almost unconsciously she heard the brakes grinding beneath her as the train drew into Ogden.

"Hakch! Hakch! . . . promised . . ."

"I'll do it. Oh, easy, *please.*" With a final convulsion he almost writhed loose. Then his body straightened stiffly and a rattling sound, drowned wetly, came to her ears from his throat. . . . Very easily she laid him back on the bed.

She knew he had died.

When Black came running into the stateroom, Miss Delacroix, her head in two red, dripping hands, was sobbing violently where she had collapsed in one of the chairs.

A light, whirring noise whispered through the room. The pointers of the wall clock slid back to eleven-twenty-five.

OGDEN (lv.)
Monday, 11.31 *p.m.*

DEATH AND "The Transcontinental" stood in the Ogden station. Far above the city's lights a white peak towered, ghostly and distant. Death had come to Ogden, but just seven minutes after it had come, "The Transcontinental" left, on time. It carried death with it; double death now. The observation platform dwindled down the track; its plaque, like a flashing jewel in the night with the two red safety lights above and to either side, receded westward. Fainter . . . fainter.

"What more do you want than this note?" Pons was urging in Lord's stateroom. "Why, it's as good as an accusation, that's what it is. It's high time we got after that Summerladd fellow."

"Maybe. That piece of paper won't help much, though. 'May have been' is far from an accusation where I have to take it. I'd better see Entwerk as soon as I can and find out just what he means."

There had been no sound, but both men looked around simultaneously. Dr. Black stood in the doorway. The corners of his usually taciturn mouth were drawn sharply downward, forming an exaggerated bow.

"Hello," Lord greeted him. "That's some nurse you've got. How is the Queen of Sheba now?"

Pons noticed that, when Black spoke, only the middle of his mouth moved; the sharp, downward angles at the corners remained immobile. His voice was utterly expressionless as he said, "Don't be any more of a God-damned fool than you need to be. That girl's worth all the cheap cops in the country. . . . Entwerk's dead."

Clickety-click, clickety-clickety-click rose the voices of the wheels through the silence. Clank-brom—a shackling. It could not have been a minute that the shocked quiet lasted. It seemed without end. Clickety-clickety-click. But it did end, and Lord passed a hand decisively across his eyes, as if to wipe vision clear.

He spoke in a low, firm voice. "That's murder. We don't need any autopsy this time."

"Will you get him now?" Pons cried in the broken silence. "Surely this is enough, without waiting for more."

"I don't know." The detective's hand, suddenly weary, passed again across his forehead. "There's more in Summerladd's favour than you think, Pons."

Black's voice, still expressionless, interrupted. "I'm going to do that blood test—now." He turned to the psychologist. "You got anything on this?" jerking his thumb toward the car's rear.

"I certainly have," spoke Pons grimly. "I've got him." Lord was looking questioningly toward the medical examiner. "Try it on. Whatever the other was, this one is the works." Black stalked out of the room and into the passage, turning forward.

"But Pons," Lord's tone was almost pleading, "what about that shot of his that went into the forward wall of the aisle? It won't fit in, it's right out of your picture. And his gun; it isn't right——"

"Stop worrying," said Dr. Pons briefly. "I've got all those things fitted in, too."

The connecting door to the forward stateroom opened. Summerladd came through alone and closed it behind him. "Hello," he said, "I just remembered you wanted to see me. I'm going to get undressed in a few minutes; put on a bathrobe and lie around, although I don't think I'll turn in to-night." He noticed something peculiar in the way the two men were regarding him. "What's up?"

"I don't think you'll go to bed to-night, either," said Lord slowly. "Entwerk died at Ogden."

"He did? I thought he was out of danger. Well!"

"You don't seem very disconsolate," the detective suggested, after a small pause during which no one spoke.

Summerladd assented cheerfully enough. "You're quite right. I shall not shed a single tear over him. I didn't like him; I don't intend to claim I did."

"Why not?" Lord's guest cut in. "It wasn't by any chance because you were both after Hodges' daughter and he had the inside track, was it?"

As Summerladd turned to stare at the new speaker, an unmistakable flush spread over his features. "My good Dr. Pons," he said coldly, "if you will permit me to point it out, that is none of your personal business."

"You're a cool customer, aren't you?" Pons' dander (or Dominance) was rising rapidly as he observed the calm, unruffled attitude with which the man who had obviously shot Entwerk received the news of his victim's death. "You think you've got everything so well covered up that you can be as brazen as you please. Well, you haven't. Murder is beyond even your remarkable abilities." The psychologist broke off suddenly, with the feeling that he had sprung his mine too soon.

Curiously enough, Summerladd, realising Pons' hostility, but unaware of the careful foundation on which it rested, felt his own animosity fade. It was with something very close to amusement in his voice that he asked, "What the dickens are you getting at, Pons? Are you trying to suggest that *I* shot Entwerk?"

"I'll do more than suggest it," the doctor replied grimly. "I'll prove it."

The publicity man did not smile now. "Go ahead." He turned to Lord. "Do I understand that you think I shot him, too?"

Lord said shortly, "I don't know. It depends a good deal on what you do. Are you willing to stay and answer the points of Pons' case?"

"It looks as if I'd better, doesn't it? What kind of a brainstorm this 'case' is, though, I can't imagine. You certainly ought to know better, even if he doesn't. You were there."

"What do you mean by that?" Pons demanded. "He wasn't there until after the shooting had occurred."

"Neither was I."

"Where is the proof of that?"

"Why, I was——" Summerladd left his sentence hanging in the air and bit his lip. "Well, there is just as much proof for my statement as for his."

"Nonsense. You know Lord is a police officer as well as I do. He has no proof as to how he came on the scene, but he doesn't need any. You do."

"O.K." The accused man shrugged nonchalantly. "You say I need it, but that doesn't make it so. At any rate you're not going to get it. So what?"

"So you're going to be tried for Entwerk's murder."

"Oh, grow up. What nonsense!" Summerladd laughed, to every appearance sincerely.

"Look here," the detective interposed, a certain sternness in his tone, "stop trying to laugh this off, Summerladd. There's nothing funny about it. Dr. Pons is perfectly serious in his charge, I assure you."

"But you're not?"

"I told you once I hadn't made my mind up yet. If you keep on bluffing instead of answering, I'll take it a good deal more seriously than I have up to this moment."

"But man alive!" Summerladd expostulated, "you saw me fire the only shot I did fire and it didn't hit any one."

Lord said, "No, I didn't see you fire it. When I first reached the aisle you were already at the forward end, running. I got only a glimpse of you, not enough even to recognise you. You had fired before that."

"Well, anyhow, you checked up on it. You know my revolver was a .38 with only one shot fired. And you found the bullet at the end of the aisle; you told me yourself it was the only .38 bullet in the whole fracas. The ones in Miss Hodges' stateroom are .45s and you said Entwerk had been hit with a .45, too. How can you try to make one .38 take the place of a whole covey of .45s? I tell you, this is the silliest thing I've ever heard of."

Lord made no reply. The point now raised by the publicity man was, in fact, exactly what had occurred to him when Pons' outline had been interrupted by Miss Delacroix' entrance. He still felt that this answer effectually disposed of the case against Summerladd. He therefore proposed to let Pons deal with it, if he could, and awaited the psychologist's next move with considerable curiosity.

He had not long to wait, for Pons immediately demanded, "How many shots do you say were fired during the whole affair, Summerladd?"

"I haven't the slightest idea. I didn't count them. There were a good many, that's all I can tell you."

The psychologist turned to Lord. "You discussed this with him," he pointed out. "How many did he say to you had been fired?"

"He told me there had been at least eight—three at Entwerk's door, three into the stateroom ahead here, his own into the end of the corridor, and mine."

"And how many do you say yourself?"

"I say seven."

"I think," said Pons with grim satisfaction, "that we can take your testimony on that point as correct. How many bullets, Lord, does a .45 automatic fire without reloading?"

"That depends on the model. Some clips hold six cartridges and some hold eight. When they have been fired, the clip must be removed and a fresh one inserted."

"And what has all this to do with me?" Summerladd's amused attitude showed signs of returning. "What difference does it make how many bullets a .45 holds, so far as I am concerned?"

"Why, because you had one," Pons asserted calmly. "It's perfectly obvious that you had two guns, a .38 *and* a .45. Lord will find it presently and I think we can take it now that it will be a six-clip model . . . You were never searched at the time of the crime, were you?" he added, suddenly.

Summerladd's expression, for some instants, was too astonished to admit of any reply, and it was plain to his accuser that the publicity man had, for some time at least, felt secure against such an interpretation.

At length Summerladd spoke. "Preposterous! I've never owned a .45 of any kind. You can search me, or my stateroom, or my luggage; you certainly won't find anything like one."

"Then you have thrown it off the train somewhere, that's all," he was told with assurance.

"But whatever gave you such an idea?"

"I'll tell you what gave it to me." Pons' tone was as confident as the other's was surprised. "The phoney story you gave about your part in the affair. You couldn't have been on the rear platform of this car when the firing began and then have gone in to investigate. Lord was on that platform at that time. Furthermore, there simply wasn't time between the moment when Lord first heard the shots and when he reached the corridor, a matter of about six or seven feet, for two different people, the imaginary criminal and you, to have been running up and down the aisle. *There could only have been one person, the criminal,* and you were the one person actually then in the passage. This alleged gunner is nothing but your own invention; can't be anything else."

"But some one got out of the train up forward; before the brakeman." Summerladd appealed to the detective. "You saw the open door."

"The door was open because it was broken," Pons insisted. "The door of the club car can have nothing to do with some one who went forward before you did, for the reason that there was no time for any one to have preceded you out of this car. How about it?" Pons also turned to the detective.

Lord was thinking rapidly. Up to the present he had felt fairly certain that Summerladd's inaccurate evidence was no more than the confusion of excitement; now for the first time he saw clearly the cogency of the psychologist's point concerning the temporal elements involved. There *had* been no opportunity for the events comprised in Summerladd's account of some man who fled before him.

"Your reasoning is quite correct," he told Pons. His voice became colder. "I fail to see how Summerladd's story can be further considered as due to mere confusion. It's not a matter of details here; it's a question of the entire course of events. But go ahead; what is your distinction about the number of shots that we disagreed on?"

"Since he has made so many deliberate mis-statements, I see no reason to imagine that his story about the shots is not one, too. Especially as you are sure there were only seven. Now what could have decided him to insist that more shots were fired than actually were? It would be foolish unless he had some definite reason, but there *is* a definite reason.

"I claim that he had two guns, a .45 automatic and a .38 revolver. He shot up the stateroom and he shot Entwerk with the .45. That's five shots in all, counting Entwerk's and disregarding the two in the end of the corridor which complete your seven. When he went back to Miss Hodges' stateroom, therefore, he had only two cartridges left in the automatic; and he produced his second gun, the .38, to use in the stateroom again, if necessary. His whole plan depended on quick action, and he had provided himself with two guns so that no reloading would be required.

"It was at this point that he heard you coming. He could do no more at the stateroom; he started forward and fired one of his .38 bullets into the front wall of the car for the purpose of supporting his story that he was pursuing the legendary criminal ahead of him. As I have already shown, however, there couldn't have been any one ahead of him.

"Now the fact that the glass in Entwerk's room had been broken, as had the window opposite, gave him the opportunity of asserting that more shots had been fired than was the case, since it was always possible that more bullets had passed out of the car than did pass out. Even when you got back to this car again, after your excursion forward, he still wasn't sure that you might not search him and discover the .45 with four bullets gone and only two left. Therefore he wanted you to believe that six shots instead of five had been fired in the main affair; even should you then find *his* .45, there would remain at least one shot to account for further, thus showing that some one beside himself had been present and fired. That, of course, is the basis of his whole tale.

"I believe I have now explained all the discrepancies in his story; the place where he falsely claimed to be at the beginning of the crime, the 'absence' of a .45 that was in his pocket all the time, and the fictitious number of shots to which he testifies."

Both his hearers had listened attentively to Pons' recital, and Lord was not the only one to be impressed with the closeness of its reasoning. Summerladd also perceived that he had made a mistake in taking the case against himself too lightly. His face was serious enough as he replied to it.

"What you have just explained, as you call it, is what you have made up in your own imagination; and I don't intend even to answer it, since there can never be any proof of it, anyhow. But I gathered that you accuse me not only of shooting Entwerk but also of trying to kill Miss Hodges. You must see yourself that that is absurd, even on your own grounds. If you suppose I killed Entwerk for jealousy, why in heavens' name should I try to injure Miss Hodges?"

"Your motive with Entwerk was jealousy, all right," the psychologist said, slowly and deliberately. "But you shot at the girl because your response to her is not a love response at all; you want her only for your own appetitive gratification. In most men (with the false education to which we now subject them) this masquerade exists—appetite as love; with you it goes to an abnormal degree, that's all . . . You tried to kill her because she actually witnessed the beginning of your later successful attempt on Entwerk. There is excellent evidence that her baggage compartment door was open, and it wasn't open for nothing. She had looked out of it and seen you."

At last the publicity director realised that there was no loophole in the case against him. Inexorably it held together, each detail fitting neatly into the general structure. He was in a grave position. His face assumed set lines as he heard the final items clicking into place.

For the first time in some minutes Lord spoke—sternly. "Summerladd, you have not told me the truth. I shall give you one more chance to explain, if you can explain, where you were when this shooting commenced and what your real connection with it was. Otherwise I must conclude that you cannot offer a satisfactory explanation . . ."

A silence fell in the stateroom, a silence in which the sound of light footsteps on the other side of the connecting door forward, escaped the attention of all three men.

"Come, Summerladd, for the last time."

Summerladd's face had grown very white. Staring straight ahead of him, he said evenly, "I have told you where I was. Not now, and not at any future time, will I change my evidence by one iota."

Lord stood up, as one who sees no alternative. "Then, Hans Summerladd, I arrest you on the charge of murdering——"

The connecting door flew open. And in it stood a figure that brought Summerladd also to his feet and caused Pons to stare in stunned confusion. Edvanne Hodges was grasping a pale green negligee about her slim waist; it fell open across her bosom, disclosing the lacy top of a delicately sheer black night-gown, beneath which her breasts rose and fell tumultuously. One small, bare foot, in a green and gold mule, stamped furiously on the threshhold.

"You fool!" she cried at Lord. "You *damn* fool! Hans was with me, alone with me in my stateroom, when Lew was wounded. That's why he's been lying like a—like a silly schoolboy! Because it was three o'clock in the morning instead of three in the afternoon. Oh, what *simpletons* you men can be!"

She included all three specimens before her in a comprehensive and flashing glance of scorn. "I wondered what you were wrangling about so long and I came to the other side of the door and listened. I would have come in sooner if I hadn't had to go back and get a negligee." Suddenly she grew conscious of the present insufficiency of that garment; without the slightest discomposure she drew it calmly together around her throat and walked over to where Dr. Pons speechlessly presented a chair.

Lord was the first to recover from the precipitate interruption. "I am sorry, Miss Hodges," he said with a certain amount of dignity, "but Mr. Summerladd's behaviour left me with no choice. Entwerk, you know, is dead; it's murder, nothing to be taken lightly, now."

Edvanne looked up sharply from where she had been regarding an indignantly swinging little foot. The news abruptly sobered her, and her expression underwent a curious mixture of change. "So he's dead," she murmured in a low tone. "I can scarcely believe it. . . . Who could possibly have killed him?" Her voice trailed off nearly to a whisper.

"I understand, Miss Hodges, that you give Summerladd an

alibi. Was he with you while all the shots were being fired? Will you please tell me now just what did happen?"

"I certainly will." She brought her attention back with an effort. "I would have told you in the first place, but before you came in to question us, Hans had said he was going to give you the story he had made up, whether I did so or not, and there was no use in our accounts being different. That would only mix you up and delay you. This serves him right," she added, looking over to where Summerladd leaned moodily against the wall but without to Dr. Pons' now observant eye, a very successful imitation of anger.

"As I said," she went on, "Hans was with me. He had come in about half-past two, seeing the light under my door. We talked for some time and then I went into the baggage space to look through my clothes as I did tell you. He was in the stateroom, smoking and waiting for me to come back; he knew I couldn't sleep and he was keeping me company, so I wouldn't get morbid all alone. Not that I would have"—Edvanne, Lord realised, was even lovelier when she smiled—"but you can see from what he did with you, that he is almost simple-minded.

"I had just come back into the stateroom and thrown a suitcase on the bed when, without the slightest warning, the shots came through the door. I told you before that there had been some knocking, I think, but that wasn't so. The thing was utterly unexpected. We do really think that the bed, creaking as it did, was the signal for it.

"Naturally we just stood there with our mouths open for some time. Then Hans pulled out his gun and dashed into the baggage compartment to go out that way and find who was attacking us. As he left the stateroom, I heard some more shots, two, I think; I don't know whether he actually heard them or not. But I heard them while he was still within my sight and I know he didn't fire them. After that, there were only two more; and these last two were yours and his. . . . So you see, Mr. Lord," Edvanne moved her hands gracefully, "Hans couldn't have shot any one. It's just his grandmother's impure conventions about three a.m. that got him into a mess."

Lord smiled in spite of himself. "Well, Summerladd," he addressed the youth across the stateroom, "do you agree at this late date with what Miss Hodges has just told us? Is that the real story?"

Summerladd nodded briefly, "It is. Of course." He still seemed a little disgruntled by the exposure that had rescued him. Of them all, only Pons, however, realised how foolish he must now appear in his own eyes. There is little more disconcerting than a gallant gesture (Compliance wholly governed by Submission) that doesn't come off.

"There's one more thing," Lord considered. "The second series of shots *must* have been to the rear of the car from you. Why did you shoot forward, when you reached the aisle? You didn't actually see any one up there, did you?"

"I didn't see a soul from beginning to end," Summerladd admitted. "Not even you, until after the stop. I heard the second series of shots as I was running out, but I couldn't place them. I had an idea they were aimed into Edvanne's room like the first, although, of course, they must have been further away. I didn't notice it at the time, though. I just came through the baggage room door and fired across the front of the stateroom door without waiting to see if any one was there or not. I was mad; and I came out to get whoever had done it. When I found no one was there, I don't know why I went forward instead of to the rear. Only because I had been so sure some one would be in that direction when I came out and fired, I guess. Anyhow, there was no one in sight, and I chased ahead, hoping to come up with him."

Pons said, "Summerladd, I have misjudged you and I apologise. Oh, not for the circumstantial case I built against you; that was a good case and you really built it against yourself, quite unnecessarily, as I agree with Miss Hodges. All I did was to fit it together, and you provided me with all the pieces. But it is plain to me now that I entirely miscalculated your response to her and probably your personality type, too. I had too few data; inexcusable, scientifically. Accept my apologies; I'm prepared to concede that your responses are certainly love type." He walked across, hand outstretched, and murmured, for Summerladd's ear alone, "I hope you get her, young fellow."

The youth was sadly embarrassed. He blushed a deep crimson, stammered, took Dr. Pons' hand limply. "All right—don't speak of it—silly of me—it's all right—hum——"

Edvanne laughed delightedly. "Oh, you crazy boy! Leave him alone, doctor; he'll *melt*."

The girl got up, again gathering the treacherous negligee about her. "Now that I've done my day's good deed," she remarked, "I'm going to bed. See if you can't arrange my good deed a little earlier to-morrow, please, I'm absolutely frazzled . . . Good-night." She included them all in her smile, and the connecting door closed behind her.

Summerladd seized his chance and escaped rapidly; any further discussion of his responses, even though complimentary, he felt to be superfluous. Black almost collided with him as he left.

"Nothing doing," the physician told the two still in the stateroom. "I've got a complete blood analysis and everything is within normal limits. No hydrocyanic acid reaction or any other poison reaction. Did you get your man for the Entwerk murder?"

Lord shook his head glumly. Pons acknowledged, "My mistake, I guess. He told us a phoney story and we broke it down. But instead of convicting him, that cleared him. I'm out of ideas now; going to bed and sleep it off. Maybe there will be new ones in the morning."

The psychologist took his departure and Black followed him shortly. At the door, the medical examiner jerked his head forward, "Girl all right? Better keep an eye on her . . . Night."

Lord paced up and down the confined space of his quarters for some minutes. The situation remained as before Pons' now exploded accusation. A killer rode with them; and the killer had missed Edvanne—once. Lord took off his outer clothing and put on a comfortable bathrobe, slipping his automatic into the pocket. He opened the connecting door a few inches and called softly into the darkness, "Miss Hodges?"

He heard a slight movement. Then a very sleepy voice. "Yes?"

"Are your doors locked, Miss Hodges? Your stateroom door, the baggage door, and the connecting door forward?"

"Yes, they are."

"You are sure the connecting door forward is locked, on your side?"

"Yes."

"Do you mind if I look through your suite? Into the closets?"

Flashlight in hand, the detective went rapidly through the girl's quarters. Nothing rewarded him except the momentary sight of innumerable feminine costumes. The blur of a tousled head against the dim whiteness of a pillow.

At the door again, he asked, "I'm sorry to bother you so much but will it be all right if I leave my connecting door open?"

"Perfectly all right." The drowsy voice was almost inaudible. "Good-night, Saint Michael."

Lord switched off his lights, drew a chair to the window and raised the shade. "The Transcontinental" was rolling smoothly and swiftly over the trestled cut-off across the centre of the Great Salt Lake. As far as his eyes could see, flat water stretched and across it a westering moon laid a narrow path, glinting brightly from the minute crest of an occasional ripple. His own aisle door was open and his right hand lay relaxed over his automatic. He was ready for action.

Michael Lord settled down for his silent vigil.

PART SIX

LIEUT. MICHAEL LORD: INTREXTROVERSION

RENO
Tuesday, 1.17 *p.m.*

Promptly at noon the porter's knock sounded on Michael Lord's door; within the minute the detective was out of his bed and laying out his shaving kit in the lavatory.

His surveillance of the previous night over Edvanne's stateroom and the car in general had gone unrewarded. The dark hours had passed slowly and, except for the sounds of the train itself, silently. There had been no disturbance and but a single man had passed down the aisle outside the watcher's door. Lord, slipping soundlessly across his room to the entrance, had seen the unmistakable back of a trainman proceeding rearward, lantern in hand. With dawn and, a little later, with the rising of the sun in clear sky, passengers, porters and waiters had commenced their daily migrations through the train, and any opportunities that solitude might have given the criminal were over. The detective, weary with his guarding, had lain down—he believed they were then somewhere between Palisade and Battle Mountain—to snatch a few hours sleep. His instructions to Sam regarding noon had been emphatic.

Having shaved, he threw a bathrobe over his bathing suit

and stepped into the car ahead for a dip. Much refreshed and ravenously hungry, he then returned to his suite, to find the porter, his dark face beaming, in the very act of chaperoning a substantial breakfast to the stateroom. He dressed quickly but, even so, by the time he had finished, his bed had been made and his meal set out appetisingly on a table beside the window. Sam had vanished.

Lord sat down and the initial phases of his attack upon the food before him were coloured by Desire rather than Satisfaction; but as the more strenuous hunger pangs subsided, other ideas began to emerge and it was borne in upon him that the situation he now faced was a serious one.

It was Nevada that was sliding past outside the window now. More than seven-eighths of "The Transcontinental's" journey had been completed. Through the industrial cities of the east, past the farms of Illinois and Iowa, over the barren and drea-ry western plains, even across the Rocky Mountains the train had sped in its flight toward sunset. He realised that the run had been a remarkable one; "The Transcontinental" in the flesh was living up to Summerladd's advance publicity.

And there was little cause to expect a change. That very night they would reach San Francisco, and Lord had no doubt that they would reach it at ten-thirty, as advertised. This was the last day and a good part of it had already passed. He had given Ti-tus Nutt the strictest injunction that his crew were to be on the alert at every stop so that no one might leave the train and he felt confident that no one had done so. But with the end of "The Transcontinental's" run, such precautions lapsed. The passengers would descend and scatter; among them, if not already captured, the man who had murdered Entwerk and—Lord even yet could not overrule his conviction—Hodges, also. From San Francisco access to half the world lay open.

The detective had a momentary doubt as to the morning behind him during which he had lain asleep. But no, he had been wise in that. Not only the solution of the case was yet before him, if time enough was available; but also there remained the matter of apprehending a violent and dangerous criminal, one, moreover, who would face the crisis, as disclosure became more imminent, with the courage of desperation. Lord would have need of all his wits and energy, if he were to reach a solution at all; and at the end he might have to shoot—very quickly and very straight. He was right to have rested.

He cleared away the tray with its dishes from the table, lit a cigarette and brought out his notebook. The first step was obvious; he must review the whole case from the beginning to its present stage. . . . The train rolled onward, as the stateroom gradually became blue with the smoke of one Piedmont after another. Once he glanced up, to note with surprise a large sign gliding past the window—"This is Reno. Come again." He looked at the wall clock; nearly one-twenty. And bent once more to his task.

It was the best part of an hour and a half before he had gone through all his memoranda on the main characters involved and his notes on conversations, the aspects of Hodges' and Entwerk's staterooms, and other details. Finally, from the miscellaneous mass of his notations, he selected and wrote down an abstract of what seemed to him the essential, although not as yet illuminating points.

He had divided it into two parts, and he now sat staring at it and considering every interdependence and implication that he could perceive:

Hodges

Medical evidence: death between 1 a.m. and 5 a.m. Sunday.

Eyes slightly bloodshot; small scratch, right side of nostril (over wart); small piece of lint (dental floss?) between right canine and next tooth forward; slight solar plexus bruise.

Not drowned (no water in lungs); no wounds; no poison, either in organs or blood.

Cause of death—thrombosis?

Investigation: body discovered by barber at bottom of pool, almost exactly 6 a.m.; body dressed in bathing shirt and flannel trunks; pool car examined and everything found to have been in proper place when barber entered; nothing missing and nothing superfluous found; shower compartment doors locked; stateroom suite undisturbed—all clothing found in proper places, including pyjamas, bathrobe, slippers (valet's testimony)—one towel missing? (porter's testimony).

Other Information: last saw Hodges alive about 1.15 a.m. Sunday; valet sent to him about 1.20 a.m. (last person known to have seen him alive).

Hodges' manner usual—asked to be called at 6 o'clock (valet's testimony).

Edvanne Hodges' fondness for Summerladd opposed by Hodges; objected to Summerladd's attentions (E. H.'s testimony).

Hodges admired and liked Entwerk (E. H.'s and Entwerk's testimony).

Entwerk reciprocated Hodges' feelings toward him (Entwerk's testimony).

Valet a periodical drunkard but liked by Hodges—long and satisfactory service (E. H.'s testimony).

Hodges a strong swimmer (E. H.'s and Summerladd's testimony).

Hodges overworked and nervous, not his usual self (Entwerk's testimony).

Entwerk

Medical evidence: shot below left shoulder with .45 bullet; bullet passed through body and through stateroom window; upper part of lung punctured; died from haemorrhage resulting from lung puncture.

Investigation: shooting occurred about 3 a.m. Monday.

Stages of crime:

1. Three shots into Edvanne Hodges' stateroom.
2. Two shots (one Entwerk's, one criminal's) at Entwerk's stateroom.
3. Summerladd comes through baggage door of E. H.'s suite and fires forward.
4. Lord comes into aisle, sees Summerladd disappearing around corner and fires.
5. Lord passes Entwerk's open door; body on floor; passes E. H.'s open baggage compartment door.
6. Lord finds Summerladd on forward platform.

Piece from Entwerk's stateroom window broken out; this piece fell outward (no glass on floor below window).

Bloodstains on carpet, leading from point before stateroom door several feet across stateroom toward window, also leading from point before door to forward wall of stateroom where Entwerk lay.

Bullet hole through aisle window opposite door.

Lord went back to the first part of his abstract, the part that concerned Hodges. Somehow he felt that here, rather than in the second more obvious crime, lay the essential secret. Three times he went over the data he had listed and each time was left with a feeling of insufficiency. Surely more facts, just plain facts, could have been determined under the head of "Investigation." Suddenly he grunted audibly. Well, *there* was something, at any rate, that had been skipped in the succession of psychological theories he had been called upon to probe. It would be skipped no longer. He rang the bell for Sam and sent him on an errand.

A few minutes later the valet, Hopping, answered his summons. He came in and stood rock-like in the centre of the stateroom; the odour of bootleg Scotch began spreading around him in the atmosphere as a pool of water spreads beneath a dripping dog. Lord observed him sharply but, despite the aroma, he was sober to all appearances.

"Hopping," the detective said, "you testified that you went to Mr. Hodges' stateroom at eight o'clock Sunday morning, and found it unoccupied. You then sought out Miss Hodges and Mr. Entwerk; when you explained the situation, Mr. Entwerk immediately felt uneasy and hurried forward. That's right?"

"Yes, sir."

"When you first went into Mr. Hodges' stateroom—I'm assuming that you were the first to enter after he had left it—the entrance door was unfastened, of course?"

"Yes, sir, of course it was. I couldn't get in if it hadn't been."

"He had left it that way when he went out, naturally. Now, Hopping, were the *other doors locked or unlocked?*" Lord leaned forward and his voice tingled with emphasis.

The valet, surprised by the emphasis and the suddenness of

the question, was taken aback. "I—I don't know. I didn't look to see . . . As I told you, I observed the master's clothes———"

Lord, disappointed, leaned back in his chair again and interrupted. "All right, Hopping, that's all. Find Sam, the porter, and send him in here at once, will you?"

Lord scribbled busily at a note and, when Sam appeared handed it to him in an envelope. "Find Titus Nutt," he directed, "and bring me back an answer to that as soon as you can."

As the porter left, Lord was knocking at the now closed connecting door to Edvanne's suite. A moment later he went in and found her alone. She was sitting by the window through which she had been gazing, dressed in a bright green sports dress with a tiny green hat tilted over the side of her dark hair. She looked around and welcomed him with a smile.

"I need some more information, Miss Hodges," he said, going directly to the point. "Last Saturday night, when you went to bed, was the connecting door to your father's stateroom locked or unlocked. If it was locked, on which side was it locked?"

Edvanne's face sobered instantly and she replied without hesitation. "It wasn't locked at all, on either side. We had opened it when we first came aboard, and I know it was still unlocked when I went to bed because I tried it when I came into my stateroom. We never kept our connecting doors locked. It was closed, though. I didn't lock it on my side until, oh, some time Sunday afternoon."

"And how would your father's aisle door have been during the night, locked or unlocked?"

"It would have been locked, I'm sure. He always did that when he went to bed."

"And yours?"

"My aisle door? Oh, I always lock that at night."

"Thank you, that's just what I wanted to know. With that out of the way," Lord smiled, "how are you to-day, after the circus Summerladd put you through last night?"

The girl's eyes twinkled at the recollection, but she remonstrated none the less. "You mustn't think Hans was quite as silly as I made out, Saint Michael," she reproved him. "Since you seem to have appointed yourself my guardian angel, I am going to tell you a secret; but it *is* a secret, I mean that. Hans and I were once caught in what passes for a compromising situation. And for a time it began to look as if some rather ugly blackmail was going to develop. That's why Hans was so determined to deny that he had been in my stateroom with me at three o'clock."

The detective's eyes narrowed slightly. "This—incident has nothing to do with anything that has happened on 'The Transcontinental,' has it?"

"No," Edvanne shook her head decidedly. "I don't see how it possibly could have. It was some time ago and it is all finished now, definitely finished. It *can't* be revived. I only told you about it because I don't want you to think Hans is really as foolish as he looked. He really isn't, you know."

"I can see," Lord assured her solemnly, "that the young man is not so retarded that we should be justified in refusing to allow him at large." Edvanne laughed and he added, "Excuse me now, please. I think I hear the porter looking for me."

In his own stateroom Lord spread out Nutt's answer to his questions. When the conductor had reached Hodges' suite on Sunday morning to place it under guard, he had found (a) the stateroom aisle door unlocked, closed; (b) the baggage compartment aisle door locked on the inside and (c) the connecting door to the suite next behind (Edvanne's suite) locked on Hodges' side.

Lord sat back and considered the bearing of the information. It hinged, of course, on the connecting door, unlocked in the evening, locked in the morning. There was the possibility, then, that some one had entered Hodges' stateroom after the banker had left. No, it was a probability, for it was surely improbable that Hodges himself had surreptitiously fastened the door between his own suite and his daughter's. But what could have been the purpose of such an intruder? So far as could be found, nothing had been taken; Entwerk, surely, would have reported any missing papers or valuables and Lord knew he had been through the suite on Sunday, since he had met him there. In addition, there had been no sign of ransacking when Lord had examined the place. He himself had caused the only violence, when he broke open the banker's trunk.

Could an unknown, then, have entered before Hodges left and have accompanied him forward to the pool car? But in that case the reason for locking the door seemed lacking. A secret conference in the middle of the night, to be guarded against any possible interference? Lord felt his ideas getting a little wild.

Still, no implication could now be abandoned without exploration. Was there any one, he asked himself, whom Hodges could have summoned to such a conference? Some important financial scheming, hidden from every one, even from the banker's own confidential secretary? The detective knew of no one on the train who could be remotely considered as the recipient of that invitation.

Then, alternatively, who could have gone to Hodges' stateroom at such an hour and gained admittance by waking him? Who had unquestionable access to him? Well, that was easier. No less than three persons had access to him at any time; his daughter, his secretary, and Hopping, his valet. No, there was a fourth, also. Undoubtedly Dr. Raquette, the private consultant who had taken up his domicile with Hodges and was occupied in so intimate a form of treatment, could have demanded and received admission at any hour.

To add up these names was to begin eliminating them. Preposterous as it was in any case to suspect Edvanne of implication in her father's death, the fact that she herself had subsequently been attacked effectually disposed of any question about her. The same argument might as easily be applied to Entwerk, or at any rate the last portion of it; it appeared that he had not only been attacked but murdered.

Which left Hopping and Raquette, the valet and the psychoanalyst. And by Hodges' death both of them had lost good jobs and gained nothing to offset the loss. Hopping, in fact, would find difficulty in holding a similar position in view of his addiction; and Raquette, for all his hopeful assumption, must know that the banker's executors would find reasons and to spare for dismissing a consultant whose services were no longer required.

Pshaw, thought Lord, suppose one of them had gone in to see him, even at four a.m. And whispered to him behind locked doors. What then? Why then, Hodges gets into his bathing suit and they go out and into the next car so that Hodges can have his swim. It's fantastic!

And, he continued, if the theory I'm working on is right, the next thing that happens is that Hodges is murdered. But *how,* that's what I'm up against. The locking of a connecting door couldn't have killed him. No, that isn't it; the locking of the door only shows that some one else was in his room, either before he left or afterwards. That some one, whoever he was, I believe was the murderer. But how did he do it—how *could* he have done it?

Hodges had been drowned, that was the first idea. What was drowning? Drowning was suffocation by water. But there hadn't been any water, so drowning was out. Then Irrtum's theory of a sudden seizure, natural death. That, really, was the official theory of Dr. Black, too, and the medical evidence certainly seemed to support it. Well, to go on. Poppas' notion of his having been killed by a blow and Pons' hypothesis of poison, cleverly as it had utilised the tiny scratch on the nose, had both been disproven. Nor could there have been poison on the scrap of lint between the teeth, to include all the minutiae, however absurd; for it, too, would have shown up in the blood test.

Lord sighed despondently, and proceeded to the second part of his abstract, the part dealing with Entwerk. As he drew it to him, darkness fell over the page and a deep gloom enshrouded the stateroom. He looked up and noticed that "The Transcontinental" was puffing in and out of long snow sheds, winding through precipitous passes whose ravined forests appeared intermittently as the train traversed the spaces between the wooden tunnels. Also, despite the brightness of the sunlight, the air was cold in the high Sierra Nevadas and its chill was penetrating the stateroom.

He got up and turned on both lights and heat. The steam hissed gently, filling the radiator pipes along the wall, as he sat down and drew his notes to him again.

From the first, Dr. Pons' contention about the time elements involved, was in his mind, and he went over most of the noted points carefully but hastily. He saw what looked like a slight discrepancy almost at the end of his items, but concentrated his attention on the numbered data he had called the "stages of the crime":

"1. Three shots into Edvanne Hodges' stateroom.
"2. Two shots (one Entwerk's, one criminal's) at Entwerk's stateroom.
"3. Summerladd comes through baggage door of E. H.'s suite and fires forward.
"4. Lord comes into aisle, sees Summerladd disappearing around forward corner and fires.
"5. Lord passes Entwerk's open door; body on floor; passes E. H.'s open baggage compartment door.
"6. Lord finds Summerladd on forward platform."

As he went over this schedule, certain considerations promptly began taking definite shape in the detective's reflections:

First: between stage 2 and stage 3 the criminal could not have had time to leave Entwerk's door and get ahead of Summerladd in the car.

Second: therefore the criminal was in the rear of Summerladd.

Third: between stage 3 and stage 4 the criminal could not have passed either Summerladd or himself.

Fourth: therefore, when he, Lord, reached the aisle, the criminal must have been still between him and Summerladd.

Fifth: the criminal was not in the aisle, so where could he have been? Only in one of the staterooms between Summerladd and Lord.

Sixth: the crucial staterooms were the two directly behind Edvanne's, now occupied by the detective and the publicity man but then vacant, Entwerk's, and the smaller quarters to the rear which were all occupied, since the dining-car staff was quartered there during the present trip.

Now could the criminal's position be narrowed down further? Lord thought a few minutes and decided it could be. Probably the two vacant staterooms could be counted out, in spite of their availability. Edvannes' evidence had established that Summerladd was actually going through her baggage compartment when the shots at Entwerk's door were fired. He must have come into the aisle and fired his own shot a second or so later, turning forward. Summerladd's emergence into the aisle ahead would have prevented any forward progress of the criminal. Accordingly, he would have jumped either into the stateroom of his victim, Entwerk, or into one of those in the back, for Lord had not yet come through the car's rear entrance.

He considered the question of Entwerk's stateroom; he had looked into that as he had tumbled past down the aisle. Well, he couldn't be sure, not absolutely sure; some one, of course, might have been flattened out next the aisle wall, inside. But he was reasonably sure, none the less, that the only occupant of that stateroom had been Entwerk, lying seriously wounded next the forward wall. But that left only the smaller staterooms behind Entwerk's. And they were all occupied; no one could have intruded there without being subsequently reported, he felt certain. Unless—

"My God!" cried Lord, springing to his feet. "Have I found him?"

Rapidly he went over the possibilities of the first crime, Hodges' death. For any perpetrator of the second crime must fit there, too. Well, he thought, that may be all right; after all, I just don't know what motive there may have been.

Then he sank back, and his face took on a baffled expression. The criminal must have had a gun, no doubt about that. And Lord's search of the car where the firing had occurred, had been even more thorough than his search of the rest of the train. Here he had looked not only for a missing passenger but also for a present weapon; and there had been no weapon in the car except his own, Summerladd's and Entwerk's.

But then, his search had taken place some time after the shooting. Yes, that might be it. As he came to this point in his reasoning, he felt the clear retardation of the train. He glanced out the window; they were slowing down. What was the next station? Truckee? And they were even then coming into it. He must hurry, if he wanted to get a message off there. Lord plumped down beside his table and began writing furiously on a blank sheet of paper. . . .

TRUCKEE
Tuesday, 2.32 p.m.

THE SEASON was early and there were few visitors as yet at the loveliest mountain lake in America—Tahoe—that lay in the high hills to the south of Truckee. The station platform was deserted and Titus Nutt stood alone beside "The Transcontinental," about to signal it forward, when Lord ran from the train, waving a slip of paper.

"Just half a minute," the detective cried. "Let me get this off; it's important."

Together they hurried into the agent's office and the message was placed before his telegraph instrument:

On board Transcontinental   Official message: RUSH
> Omas
> Omaha, Neb.

" r t n p a l l k o i n f B e f L T, t k f r—v e n o F—t T l m k s T—t m 3 9 n p s—m s l n h s d l e m w c o s S c h u y l e r .

Asny."

It was apparently the first of the kind that the western station agent had ever had to handle, for he shook his head dubiously when urged to send it. However, impressed with Lord's badge and also by his imperative manner, the telegrapher was already busy with his key as the detective and Nutt returned to the train. Nutt signalled the engineer and the wheels were resuming their revolutions when the two swung aboard. Slowly "The Transcontinental" moved forward on its long, winding drop down from the heights of the Sierras to the fertile plains of California.

As they turned into the first stateroom car, the conductor was saying, "It's cool up here in the mountains, isn't it? I'll bet it will be suffocating out on those prairies, though, on the summer trips. By the way, I understand, Mr. Lord, that the death of Mr. Hodges has been determined to have been natural. What was the idea of the doors that you wanted to know about a little while ago? They couldn't have affected it, could they?"

Lord grunted absently. Inaudibly he had been going over the very question of that death. Drowning, what was drowning? seizure; blow; poison. Drowning, seizure, blow—— Suddenly he halted and Nutt bumped sharply into him from behind. He turned and caught the surprised conductor by the shoulders.

"I've got it!" he exclaimed. "By damn, Nutt, I believe I've got it! . . . Yes, everything fits into place, every last little thing. So utterly simple. And no one has even had a hint of it."

"But, but what? What have you got?" Nutt stuttered, astonished by his companion's antics.

"Hodges' death. I see how it could have happened; why, it *must* have happened that way." The detective's face was transformed with his eagerness and he maintained his hold on Nutt's shoulder. "Look here, man, you can clear this car and keep it cleared for me for an hour or an hour and a half, can't you? There's something I've got to find, and I'll lay all the reputation I ever hope to have that it's still in this car to *be* found. But I must have the whole place to myself, without interruption, for a time. How about it?"

Titus Nutt, somewhat concerned for the detective's mental health, nodded hesitantly. "Of course, we *can* do it."

"Then come on. Let's get started." Lord hustled the bewildered conductor down the aisle and, almost before the latter realised that the extraordinary plan had been adopted, it had been executed. The first stateroom car was empty of all occupants, even of Edvanne Hodges, and for the third time since Sunday morning, Michael Lord was searching in it.

This time, however, he had some general idea of what he was looking for. He began at the very forward end and was prepared to continue minutely through the entire car until he reached the rear platform, if necessary. Hodges' suite, strangely, he seemed to go over almost superficially, as also Edvanne's. But with the quarters he himself now occupied, his search became painstaking and he continued thereafter to examine almost literally every square foot of the ground he traversed.

And eventually he discovered what he was hunting for. A little more than two-thirds of the way down the car he emerged into the aisle carrying a small bundle which he had carefully wrapped in a piece of paper; but his expression of triumph was mixed with at least as much serious perplexity. He had found what he expected, but not where he had expected it.

The heterogeneous expression was still in his face when, a few moments later, he released the guards whom Nutt had placed on the rear and forward platforms.

·   ·   ·

Lord found Dr. Black in the recreation car; on the observation platform, in fact, bundled in his overcoat and watching the curves unwind from beneath the slowly moving train. The brakes ground constantly now, as "The Transcontinental" gradually lost altitude sliding down the western slopes of the Sierras like a gigantic and undulating snake. The boarded snow sheds continued intermittent, shutting off what always seemed certain to be the best views outward or downward.

The medical examiner, in response to Lord's exigent summons, led the way to his own stateroom in the next to the last car. "Lock the door," the latter demanded, as they were entering. "We can't afford an interruption."

Black looked mildly surprised, but fulfilled the requirement. "What's it about?" he grunted, in his usual fashion.

The detective was busy unwrapping his parcel. He drew forth a small, metal object that gleamed dully in the light and took it over to the window. Black stood beside him, gazing at it curiously.

"You see," said Lord, pointing with his finger but being careful not to touch the surface indicated, "you see the discolouration along this edge? First of all, I want to know if that's blood. I think it is, but I'm not sure."

Black took the object gingerly by one of its corners, and peered at it closely. "Looks like it," he admitted. "Yeh, you're right. No doubt about it."

"Good. Then the next thing is this. I think, Black, you can tell me whose blood it is. If you can, and if I'm right about it, the hardest part of this case is solved. I mean the way Hodges was murdered."

"Huh. Still stuck on the murder notion, eh? . . . Well, I can analyse that blood, all right. But telling you whose it is, is another story. Might be some prints on that gadget, though, if it's something to do with the case."

"I didn't think there would be much chance of prints. The handles, or whatever you call 'em, are too narrow to take more than a small section across a finger. Still, try it. If you get anything from it, we can check up easily enough; the matching print is still aboard. But the blood is the important thing," Lord repeated. "And I think you will find that you can tell me whose it is."

"Oh." The examiner's face changed with a dawning idea. "*Yeah?*"

"Now this," Lord went on, unrolling the remainder of his bundle's contents, "I thought maybe this could be matched up, too. What do *you* think?"

Black regarded the new object before him, and especially the aperture near its centre, with something like stupefaction. Presently his eyebrows shot up nearly to the line of his hair, and he sat down weakly on the bed behind him.

"Well, for——; well, for—— *Jeez,* boy, you're right; you got it! The old bloke was done in, after all."

·   ·   ·

"The Transcontinental" paused for a few minutes on the curve of the bluff overlooking American River Canyon. A broad gravel platform reached to the very brink of the cliff, and through the single opened door that Nutt's precautions allowed, the passengers streamed out to inspect the impressive, closely forested chasm. At every other exit from the cars, even though closed, either a porter or a trainman stood; the rear brakeman guarded the observation platform and two others of the crew watched at either end of the outside walk, where the railings almost touched the sides of the cars. Its rear car out of sight to the left, "The Transcontinental" lay extended along the observatory stage beside it; far away at its head the steam pipes of the two locomotives that had brought it from Reno were whispering to each other of the steep grades still lying before them.

Lord and the conductor stood together against the outer railing of the look-out platform, gazing into the green depths below. The first breath of California touched them here, and it was balmy, softly warm and gentle after the chill of the Nevada uplands. Reason said it must have breathed of the surrounding forests, dense as they were, but the nostrils, sniffing delightedly after the formerly unremarked stuffiness of the train, already seemed to scent the hint of orange orchards scores of miles away.

The detective looked up from the scene below him and glanced around. All the passengers without exception appeared to have taken advantage of this opportunity. He noticed Raquette and Irrtum in the crowd, and Pons and Dr. Poppas. Edvanne Hodges and Summerladd were walking by themselves, up forward; and Lord noticed, with some amusement, a similar pair at the other end of the observatory—Miss Therese Delacroix and Dr. Loress Black. Yes, and there was Hopping, too, leaning over the rail not far from where Lord himself was standing. Of all his acquaintances only Noah Hall seemed missing, but he, likewise, was no doubt somewhere in the throng. Unless such a view as was magnificently spread before them had, in sober fact, no place among his ergs and joules.

A porter came up to Titus Nutt and beckoned him a little to one side. After a few words the conductor, in turn, beckoned to Lord.

As the detective strolled over, Nutt leaned confidentially toward him. "Have you any idea what BL 3F is? There is a call for it, or him, or whatever."

"That," said Lord, smiling, "happens to be your humble servant. But a call," he added more alertly, "what kind of a call do you mean? No one on this train ever knew that symbol; except Pons, and he must have forgotten it long ago."

"A telephone call," Nutt reassured him. "We're equipped with wireless telephones, you know."

"That's right; I had forgotten. I suppose I might have used those myself, instead of telegraphing both times. Still, I imagine it's a little public, speaking plain English over the air, isn't it?"

Nutt said, "Yes. Of course it depends what you're talking about. No one on the train, though, will get your message now, unless the second booth is tuned in. I'll come along with you and see to that; also help you with your own apparatus, if you need me."

They boarded the standing train and hurried through the temporarily deserted aisles to the recreation car. The second booth was empty; Nutt entered the first one and commenced making slight adjustments on the dialling arrangements beside the instrument.

"Hello," he spoke into the mouthpiece. "Hello." He made another small adjustment. "This is the conductor of 'The Transcontinental' speaking. At American River Canyon . . . Yes, he's here; just a minute." He turned the instrument over to Lord.

"BL 3F speaking." . . . "Right. Yes, hello, chief, how are you?" . . . "Oh, you did? Picked it up yesterday, eh? That's a break." . . . "How's that? Communicating through the railroad company to reach me at S.F.? Well, we needn't bother about that, now. Any identifying marks?"

On Lord's end of the conversation there ensued a relatively long silence. The Omaha authorities, the conductor supposed, were giving him some description or other.

"Yes," said Lord then . . . "Yes, four gone, that's right." . . . Suddenly he cried sharply, "What! What's that you say? And ex-what?" . . . "Repeat that, please." . . . "Thank you." . . . "No, I suppose there can't be any mistake in that case." . . . "All right, chief, thank you plenty. Hope I can reciprocate some day." . . . "Good-bye." He handed back the instrument to Nutt, who returned it to its place and reset the dials in their position receptive for being called.

Michael Lord came out of the booth, a sorely puzzled frown on his face.

"What's the matter?" the conductor asked, with justifiable curiosity. "Didn't you get the information you wanted?"

"Yes," Lord replied. "Oh, I got the information all right, but more than I bargained for . . . I've nearly collared the wrong man, according to this. My case is all thrown off; I'll have to go over the whole thing again and reconstruct it. I hope to God there's time."

The detective started forward toward his stateroom, head already bent in thought. As he did so, "The Transcontinental," its brakes only partially released, commenced sliding quietly ahead.

· · ·

"Now, how the devil," thought Lord, "can that gun *not* belong to the man I picked? Is it possible, then, that it doesn't belong to the criminal?"

He sat in his stateroom, lying back in his chair, head tilted up, narrowed eyes on the ceiling. He had turned off the heat and the lights, pulled down the shades of the windows against any distraction. Here he was at the crisis of the case, with his hardly won solution knocked clean from under him. He forced himself to a slow, cool, concentrated appraisal of the facts, as "The Transcontinental's" low sounds lulled the air of the stateroom and the cigarette smoke clouded more and more thickly.

Of course, this new information left his solution of the first crime intact; so much he was glad to admit. It might even be said to strengthen it, since it confirmed the results of his last search down to the last detail. But it threw his reading of the second murder miles off; and the second one was by far the easiest to decipher. Or so it had seemed up to now. And now, all at once, it became incredible that the same man could have done them both. Had he been wrong all along, then? Were they, well, reciprocal, or entirely separate? Lord's head began to whirl. "Good God," he muttered, "in another minute I'll have Hodges murdering Entwerk, although he himself was killed a day or more sooner."

For a long minute he relaxed and thought of nothing; then came back to the problem again. It was time to get back to first principles, obviously time. First principles in Lord's profession were simple; get the facts and interpret them in strict accord with reason. No matter where they led.

Well, he had the facts, or at any rate enough of them. And so far as concerned the first crime, they pointed inexorably to a single man as the criminal. They pointed pure logic alone considered—to the same man in the second crime, too. Did they truly? Yes; yes, even there, the indicated person fulfilled every logical qualification. Only common sense cried loudly against the incredible, common sense stoutly denying outrageous reason. And Lord, try as he would, was not the man to abandon common sense.

He returned once more to the attempted reconciliation. How

was it possible that the man who had committed the first murder, had also done the second? Were there any conceivable circumstances in which it might have happened? There was only one circumstance that Lord could imagine, and that circumstance had not occurred in the present case. Could the criminal have made such a mistake, could he have mistaken one circumstance for another? The detective tried desperately to remember every word, each phrase of a certain conversation, and it began to seem just possible to him that such a mistake might have been made. But one error would not cover the matter; two must have been made, a serious double error. Well, gasping and sorely pressed, common sense might be driven as far as that—a man could make two mistakes; even, just possibly, two like these.

But reason, since reason is exact if it is itself, could find nothing to yield. And so the reconciliation must stand as agreed by common sense. The man indicated by strict logic must be the criminal; the compromise could cover no more than the two just possible mistakes.

Some obscure operation at this moment caused Lord to think of a man he had met a year previously, a Dr. Hayvier, with his behaviouristic insistence that those conditioned to a certain course of reaction could not change their reflexes for a non-psychological author or a merely baffled detective. Reason, however, might be superior even to behaviourism, in the present case.

One thing remained—motive. Of course, for the second crime, the motive was now agreed; it was the first half of the double mistake. But for the first crime? The means were determined, and the criminal, but where was the motive? Lord thought long and hard. Finally he recalled a conversation with Dr. Pons, and one with Edvanne Hodges; but most of all he recalled a chance remark of not so long ago. That might, he took a long conjectural leap, be it; but how he could ever know, unless the criminal himself should kindly tell him, he could not guess. With Hodges' death, the last chance of corroboration appeared to have vanished.

Lord looked around quickly. Dr. Black had opened his door without announcement. The physician took one sniff of the atmosphere in the stateroom and grunted his disapproval. "What ventilation! You'll be dead in another ten minutes in a sty like this."

The detective got up, raised shades and windows and switched on the electric fan. As if by magic the room cleared itself and the fresh, spring air blew in.

His thoughts still revolving about "The Transcontinental's" duplex crime, Lord remarked almost absently, "I've got the solution, Black, at last. Just mopping up the last outskirt details. When you came in, I was remembering something that happened at Albany and happened again between Buffalo and Toledo. And something else that happened near Omaha and would have put me on the right track then, if I hadn't dismissed it as unimportant. It all fits now, perfectly."

"I hope it does," Black answered shortly. "Because I have the fellow myself, thanks to your material evidence. Proof. If you don't agree already with what I've found, you'll be out of luck again. It was his blood, all right, just whose you thought. And enough fingerprint came out, too, for identification. It was——"

Lord mentioned a name.

"Right," confirmed the physician. "That's the man."

"But how did you get a specimen to match? You couldn't have guessed it very well." Lord was a bit surprised.

"Moseyed through some of the staterooms that happened to be conveniently vacant at the moment, dusting them down.

The print from the gadget was too good to pass up. After that, I managed to get a direct print, too, just to check up on the stateroom ones." Black grinned, as at some cosmic joke. "He never knew I was getting it, either."

Lord returned his look, subtracting the grin. "Good for you; you're a smart fellow. He won't be trying to escape, then."

"Not because of the print I took, he won't." Black grinned more widely than ever.

· · ·

Dr. Pons clapped his friend on the back as he walked through the recreation car and followed him out on to the observation platform, which, for the moment, they had to themselves. "The Transcontinental" was running rapidly once more, as rapidly as it had at any part of its journey. Coming cautiously down out of the mountains, it had reached flat country again and was reeling off its seventy to eighty miles an hour as it had so often before. A cloud of dust swirled up around the rear platform, a single stroke of a crossing bell reached their ears, and a station was flying backwards from them. Lord caught a fleeting glimpse of its sign-board; it was Auburn.

"We're getting close to the end," Pons commented, as he drew a chair into the sheltered corner of the floor. "How is the case coming on? I have been thinking about it all day, and I must confess I'm no nearer to it than ever, now that Summerladd is eliminated."

"The case," Lord told him calmly, "is solved. It has been for the past half-hour."

"You don't say so? Do you really mean it? Who is the man behind these murders?"

"Now doctor, not so impatient. I have invited Miss Hodges and Summerladd, and Hopping and Black and Nutt—oh, yes, and Dr. Raquette, to meet me after we leave Sacramento. Of course you're included. I intend to expose the particulars of both the crimes that have occurred on the train at that time, including the name of the criminal. We shall have *all* the interested parties present at that meeting—except Hodges and Entwerk, of course—so for the next little while you can take your pick."

"You aren't worried, I suppose, about your acquiescent criminal turning up at the meeting? You don't think he might get off in the meantime? If you're so sure who he is, he may have some little notion himself about your idea."

"I assure you he has no notion of it, that has been taken care of. I haven't been near enough to him to speak to him since I found out for certain who it was and Black, the only other person who knows his identity and has been close to him, is sure the intention of his visit was unrecognised. So am I."

"Sublime confidence, my boy. I shall merely trust it isn't misplaced. You would look a little foolish, playing this last minute game, if your man should happen to get off before your time comes."

"He can't get off. I'll give you one very good reason; this train will not stop at Sacramento and it will run at least at half its present speed all the way from here to Oakland. No one will get off."

"All right; or I hope so." Pons' mind turned to other subjects. "That's a lot of people you have invited, to get into one of these staterooms."

"We shall be in the club car. I forgot to tell you. It will be closed from Sacramento on, anyhow, and the conductor has offered it to me for my meeting. . . . I really was forehanded about that. I arranged it while we were at the American Canyon and before I actually knew who the criminal was."

"You are a proud man, Michael Lord," said the psychologist with mock severity. "Probably too proud. But tell me this, if you still refuse to disclose the criminal. You have listened to several methods of approaching the desired solution, since these crimes took place. Which method have you followed so successfully? Mine, I trust."

"I'm afraid not, doctor," Lord confessed. "I am glad to welcome all the suggestions I have received, but obviously they involved methods I am not sufficiently acquainted with, myself, to follow. No, my own method is the only one I know well enough to use."

"Seriously, Lord, what is your method? Apparently it works out quite successfully for you."

"I'm perfectly willing to tell you how I work on a case," the detective answered candidly. "Even though I'm afraid you may find it rather simple, and perhaps not altogether scientific. My first stage is trying to get all the facts I can, about what has happened, connected facts, disconnected ones, any and every one I can collect. Without at first endeavouring to draw any conclusion at all. After that is done, I may begin to draw some conclusions, or I may go directly into the second stage of my method.

"The second stage is a little harder to describe. It consists in my trying to put myself in the criminal's boots, trying my best to get inside him, as it were, and to make up my mind just what I would have done and would now do in his place. Theoretically, of course, each of these systems would point to both criminal and means, even to motive, perhaps; but together they do so more quickly and by their combination they iron out—or so it seems to me—many errors that either alone is bound to possess."

"By George, that's interesting," Dr. Pons commented. "And not unscientific by any means. I believe," he went on, "yes, I do believe that in a moment or so I can supply you with a nice, brand new, scientific name for it, too. Let me see . . . You begin with extrovert activities, don't you? And you go further by introvert ones. Ahuh; well, extroversion-introversion, for a starter. And then following well-known authorities, we shall condense. So extro-introversion. Or, still more condensed, extrintroversion. . . . No, I don't quite like that yet. Ah, now I have it, the same thing really. Intrextroversion. There you are, my friend; the very name for your own especial method, in excellent, scientific Latin."

"'My friend' to you," said Lord, with a smiling bow that lost somewhat by reason of the fact that he was sitting down. "I'm obliged to you; I am indeed. As long as it continues to work, of course, I won't need the name so much. But when it doesn't, some fine day—— why, then, I shall be in your debt to no small degree."

Lord paused, and Pons chuckled, as at a fair hit. Then added, in a wheedling tone of voice, "After that, who *is* the criminal?"

"Doctor, you're a veritable magpie. . . . I'll tell you this much now, and only this much. It is the most unlikely person of any one aboard 'The Transcontinental.' History is up to its old trick of repetition. It is, I also repeat, the most unlikely person aboard 'The Transcontinental.'"

"Ugh . . . Huh . . . Of course, if the girl could be considered as an accomplice——"

"Back to your first love, are you, doctor?"

"Well, if you really want the most unlikely person on this train, I can make a reasonable guess."

"It is now your guess."

"I shall guess," said Pons slowly, "that your criminal died at—I think I remember this correctly—twelve-twenty-four Tuesday morning, approximately."

"Wel-l-ll." The psychologist had succeeded in surprising Lord, at all events. "That's a guess and a good one, doctor. It's so good that I am sorry I shall have to tell you this. My criminal did not die at twelve-twenty-four or at any other time Tuesday morning. I am quite certain that no one will announce his time of death, until after we have passed Sacramento, at least. . . . Before we reach Oakland, however, I venture to predict that I can tell it to you, approximately. . . ."

SACRAMENTO
Tuesday, 7.20 p.m.

"THE TRANSCONTINENTAL" whirled over the switches of California's capital and past its station as rapidly as Lord had said. The light was dimming as they roared out into the final stretch to Oakland, and the block signals ahead, like stars which the darkening heavens reveal, twinkled in the distance and then gleamed brightly as they rushed toward the train. A red glare hovered transiently above the locomotive's cab as the fireman opened the firebox and peered within.

In the club car the party was assembling. As each member came into the otherwise deserted carriage, a definite increment was added to the tension in the air. They all understood the purpose of their invitations but none knew just what to expect. None except Lord and Dr. Black. These two sat talking in low tones near the forward end of the two rows of chairs stretching up the car.

Pons sat down, puffing, toward the rear and Summerladd, coming in a few minutes later, joined him. Titus Nutt fidgeted about the rear door, admitting each one of the arrivals as they came and carefully locking the entrance as soon as they had passed within. There was a considerable wait; then the dead banker's valet entered and looked hesitantly about for a chair. Obviously he felt ill at ease, out of place in this company made up of those he was accustomed to serve. He seemed unable even to choose a seat from among the many empty ones before him.

Summerladd smiled. "Come over here, Hopping, and sit down with us. We're not all here yet. There may be some time to wait."

Hopping said, "Thank you, sir," and sat down directly opposite Dr. Pons. Immediately a bar-room odour was wafted across the aisle.

They waited . . .

And waited . . .

The psychologist's intermittent conversation with Summerladd at length evaporated. "Hey there, Lord," Dr. Pons called up the car, "where are the rest? Miss Hodges is coming, isn't she? It's nearly eight o'clock."

The detective, still talking with Black, looked at his watch in surprise. He gave a sudden exclamation and got to his feet. "We'll wait another five minutes," he called back. "Both Miss Hodges and Dr. Raquette ought to be here."

The minutes, now that there were five of them, passed interrminably. Pons sat back and stared through the dark window across from him, reflecting that the detective must have everything in hand. Summerladd, next him, was becoming restless and Hopping continued to emit vaporised whisky almost audibly. The conductor was still out of sight down the corridor at the car's rear end.

At the forward end Lord began pacing up and down; six steps down, six steps up. On an average of every twenty seconds now he glanced at his watch. "What the hell," he muttered to Black.

The frown of perplexity on his face deepened as the minutes passed. And his pacing became more nervous. Rapidly he went over his case for the dozenth time in his mind; yes, it was all there, method, clues, circumstantial evidence, the final conclusive proof of gun and fingerprints. There could be no mistake. And yet, irrationally, the undeniable facts that Edvanne Hodges had been attacked with intent to kill and that Edvanne Hodges was long overdue at the present meeting (at which her attacker was to be disclosed) kept forcing themselves into his attention.

Was it possible that his whole case rested on some monstrous error? *Could* it be possible that somehow he had made a fundamental miscalculation, mistaken the identity of the criminal? Try as he would, he could find no loophole in the close train of his reasoning. And yet? If anything should happen to Edvanne Hodges at this last moment——

Only four of the five minutes had elapsed when Lord turned and strode decisively down the length of the car. "I'll be back in a few minutes," he stated, as he passed the others. "Please don't come with me." As Nutt opened the door for him, however, Summerladd was on his heels. He had marked the detective's white face and the taut lines around his mouth.

And it was Summerladd who knocked on Edvanne's door, then tried it and found it locked. "Edvanne," he called sharply, "are you there? Let me in."

There was no immediate answer. The detective poked out one of the wads with which the previous holes in the door had been closed. It dropped to the carpet with a tiny thud and he bent forward, applying his eye to the aperture. His range of vision was circumscribed, but it was enough to show him the girl's figure lying back on one of the beds. Her eyes were closed and she did not move. Summerladd was now hammering on the panels of the door.

A moment later Dr. Raquette's professional tones came from within. "It is all right. Please do not disturb us. Miss Hodges is resting."

"Raquette," the detective called through the hole in front of him, "Lieutenant Lord speaking. Open this door immediately! If it is not open within thirty seconds, I shall shoot it open!" As he spoke, his automatic came into his hand and the double click of its slide threw the first of its eight bullets into the firing chamber.

Well within the stipulated half-minute, however, the psychoanalyst had admitted them. He stood aside from the unfastened door and drawing himself up in his most dignified manner, demanded, "What is the cause of this, gentlemen? My patient——"

"What do you mean, your patient?" Lord's voice was crisp and his weapon was still in his hand. "You're not a physician. What's wrong with Miss Hodges?"

The girl had not stirred, despite the wrangle proceeding so close to her and it was evident that she was unconscious. "Get Black at once!" Lord went on, without giving Dr. Raquette an opportunity to reply to his previous question.

Summerladd was out of the room on the instant.

Raquette said calmly, "I fail to understand, Mr. Lord, the meaning of all this excitement. Miss Hodges has been through a great deal in the last few days and she is in no condition to be overwrought and distressed further by a recital of the circumstances of her father's death. I advised her not to attend; even the prospect made her nervous and I gave her a harmless sedative to quiet her nerves. She is now sleeping and resting."

"By what authority did you embark upon this procedure?"

"I have been retained as the private consultant of the Hodges family. I must also remind you, Mr. Lord, that I hold a medical certificate."

"Hmph. We shall see about all this as soon as Dr. Black gets here. If anything—— Ah, here he is. Black, please examine Miss Hodges at once. This man claims to have administered a harmless sedative to put her to sleep. I'm not so sure."

"I protest——" began the psychoanalyst.

Lord interrupted sharply. "Protest all you like, Dr. Raquette. But don't try any interference." He glanced briefly and meaningly at his automatic. "I'm on a murder case."

"What j'you give her?" snapped Black.

Raquette, still the offended professional man, told him; and the medical examiner commenced taking Edvanne's pulse and listening to her heart and respiration.

In a short time he straightened up. "Looks all right. No symptoms except those of the drug he gave her."

Lord observed the analyst with a puzzled frown and slid his gun back into his pocket. "In that case," he said, "I'm inclined to believe his explanation of this. Provisionally. Can you bring her out of it, Black, without any danger?"

"Can. I'll have to get my bag."

"Go ahead . . . Forget it, Raquette! For the moment I'm willing to concede theoretically that you may not know how serious a business you're mixing yourself up in. You're through now, until this case is settled for good, and you're lucky you haven't got a bullet in you for your pains."

Black returned with his supplies and the detective explained to him Raquette's account of the circumstances. "If she doesn't corroborate that in every particular when she comes to," he added, "let me know right away. I want you to stay with her, in any case, until we have finished up forward. . . . You are to come with us, Dr. Raquette. Invitations for the kind of conference I'm having in the club car are not discretionary. When you're invited, it means you're to be there."

Lord conducted his companions to the car ahead, where the others who were waiting for him betrayed their curiosity plainly in their questioning looks. He vouchsafed them no information, however, beyond the fact that Edvanne Hodges would not attend the meeting. He led the way to the centre of the car, where he grouped his hearers in a semi-circle of chairs and took his place in front of them.

There was, however, to be one more interruption before Lord commenced his exposition. A knocking on the door, just as they were seating themselves, sent Nutt pattering down the car and through the rear corridor.

He opened the entrance and found Miss Delacroix confronting him. "I have a message," drawled the blonde manicurist, "for Mr. Lord. Is he in theah, please?"

The dried-up little conductor had unfortunately passed the age when blonde beauty produced any measurable effect on him. He said, "We're busy. You can see him later." And closed the door firmly.

"What was that?" Lord asked, when he had come back to the group in the club car.

"Nothing," Nutt assured him. "Nothing important."

"Good." Lord seemed anxious to get about the purpose of his delayed meeting. He hitched his chair a little more into the centre of the aisle and lit another of his cigarettes. "Now, gentlemen, I have called you together in order to expose to you the actual solution of the crimes that have taken place on board 'The Transcontinental.' If the affair results as I foresee that it may, it may still be possible to avoid the notoriety that would harm both this train and Mr. Hodges' surviving relatives, and to have the murder, so far as the public is concerned, considered as an accidental drowning. I do not say that this will be possible, but should it prove so, every one here is entitled to know the facts. I intend to tell you them now, in case later they should not be available."

Lord paused and Dr. Pons thought, what the dickens! Isn't the criminal here? Or does Lord know that he has the means to suicide with him and will use them when the game is up? Is he taking this way to advise such an outcome? He recalled, suddenly, Lord's statement that the criminal's time of death would be established before they reached Oakland.

The detective was continuing. "For Hodges' death was murder, first degree murder," he was saying, looking sternly around the circle but, so far as Pons could detect, singling out no special individual for his glance. "My first introduction to this case pointed so strongly to that conclusion that, although at times another explanation seemed almost to have been established, I have never been able to give up my first idea entirely.

"I must remind you that Mr. Hodges' body was found at the bottom of the swimming pool in the car behind us, apparently drowned. But even before we knew that he had not been drowned, I had come across a very suspicious circumstance. As events fell out, I had an opportunity to examine the pool car thoroughly, before there had been any chance of alteration in its condition, since the attendant who found the body had had sufficient presence of mind to lock both doors to the car when he left it to summon aid; and since then, and up to the time of my inspection, the criminal had had no chance to alter matters.

"What I found in that car was—nothing. And that was just the trouble, for something should very much have been there. I searched thoroughly every part of the car that had been accessible (its compartment doors were all locked), but I could not find a trace of what must be there if the appearances that met us were true appearances. If Hodges really went for an early morning swim, *where were his bathrobe, his slippers and, his bath towel?*"

"My God!" cried Pons, with sudden recollection, "that's right! I tried to reconstruct that scene and when I imagined Hodges walking into the car, I knew something was lacking. There was something vaguely unnatural about his coming into the car completely ready to jump into the water. I'd just seen another man come in and hang up his bathrobe, too." The psychologist grunted with some disgust.

"Of course," Lord proceeded, "he must have had these things, if he came for the ordinary purpose indicated. Even had he neglected bathrobe and towel, he would never have come without slippers; consider the fact that, near as his quarters were to the swimming pool, he had not only to walk barefooted along the aisles but also across the vestibule between the cars, which was covered with soot and cinders. The thing was much too peculiar to be dismissed easily.

"Had the record of the vestibule floor been clear, the matter could have been decided then and there. For the prints of his bare feet could have shown that, despite the improbabilities, he had gone forward without slippers. But by the time I knew what to look for, it was too late; too many feet had scuffled across the floor and what could confirm my suspicion was really the absence of his footprints. Such a negative could not be established then.

"However, the deduction from the absence of the slippers remained good. And it led in drastic directions. Because, if Hodges had not walked to the pool, he had been conveyed there; and if this were the case, the 'accident,' of which he had been the victim, had taken place not in the pool car but elsewhere. And if that were so, the 'accident' was not an accident, because then the removal of Hodges' body to the swimming pool would be incredible.

"Furthermore, if Hodges did not walk, some one carried him. Also pointing to the intervention of some unknown person was the set stage we found, the stage prepared to make every one jump to the conclusion of accidental drowning. But stages do not set themselves.

"From all of this I concluded that he had not died in the pool car. The next most likely place was his own stateroom, for I myself had seen him go into it to retire and I heard him request his valet to be sent in to him. I did not think it likely that he was producing some elaborate deceit for the benefit of myself whom he had just met casually. Accordingly, I concluded that he had gone to bed for the night; and at some time between the hour when he had retired and five o'clock in the morning, he had been murdered in his stateroom.

"I investigated his quarters very carefully indeed, but with little result. There were no indications of any struggle, and his pyjamas, bathrobe and slippers at the foot of his bed merely confirmed what their absence from the pool car had already disclosed. Only one anomaly could be found. It appeared that in his suite there was one less bath towel than should have been there; you will recall that this missing bath towel was not in the pool car, either. Its absence might, of course, have been due to an oversight, although the porter maintained the opposite tenaciously. At the time the fact was meaningless, but I noted it down and in the end it turned out to be a very vital one.

"Let me repeat the main point so far. Hodges had not walked

into the pool car. Therefore he had not died in the pool car. Therefore he had died in his stateroom. Had he died naturally, his body would have been found there in the morning; but his body had been removed. Therefore he had been murdered.

"Could he have been murdered in his sleep? If so, only one person could have done it. I ascertained the situation with regard to the doors of his and his daughter's suites, when he went to bed that night. All the doors leading to the aisle of the car were closed and locked; the connecting door between their suites was closed, but unlocked. These doors cannot be unlocked by duplicate keys for they are fastened by catches that can only be operated from the inside. Consequently, the only person who could reach him once he had retired was Miss Hodges, his dau——"

"What do you mean?" Summerladd began hotly. "Are you trying to put this, this damnable thing off onto——"

In turn Lord interrupted also. "No, Mr. Summerladd," he smiled, "I have never seriously considered that Miss Hodges was implicated in these crimes, except as an intended victim. Especially as she was herself the source of my information as to the doors. She would hardly have been stupid enough to build up the case against herself in that way, were she guilty.

"But," he went on, "this establishes another important point. It means that some one awoke Mr. Hodges in the middle of the night and was admitted to his stateroom by the victim himself. The only other possibility is that Miss Hodges admitted the murderer; and for the reason I have just mentioned, she could not be either principal or accomplice. So some one knocked and was let in—and there are very few people on this train who were in a position to do that.

"I will name them," said Lord quietly. As he did so, Pons noticed that the two whom he mentioned and who were before him, each manifested a distinct uneasiness in his own way. "They were his consultant, Dr. Raquette, his valet, Hopping, and Entwerk, his secretary." Hopping began to breathe heavily, to the increased pollution of the atmosphere, and the psychoanalyst's face paled perceptibly and assumed an uncomfortable expression.

"Each of these could have awakened Mr. Hodges and gained admittance. And such a qualification the murderer simply must have had, since it was impossible for him to come upon Hodges unawares in the circumstances that existed last Saturday night. Hopping, it is true, was perhaps scarcely in a position to disturb his master at such an hour, but Hopping was actually in the room with him during the period in question. This we know; but we also know that Hodges was not yet asleep when his valet was with him. So, in any case, it is established that Hodges was awake when he was killed.

"There is one more detail about the doors. In the evening the connecting door to Miss Hodges' suite was unlocked, as I said. In the morning, however, it was locked, and locked on her father's side. If you will consider this fact for a moment, I think you will agree that it is the last piece of evidence we need in order to be convinced that some one else beside the murdered man was certainly in his stateroom during the night. No one came forward to admit it and I thought it quite useless to inquire. It is plain that that visitor was the person who killed the banker.

"We have therefore decided that one of three people, Dr. Raquette, Mr. Entwerk, or Hopping, came into Hodges' room during the night, killed him and secured the door against interruption. The further steps are easy to construct; the victim's body was stripped of its pyjamas and dressed in bathing costume. It was then carried into the pool car ahead and dropped into the water in the hope that this circumstance would be accepted as an

explanation so obvious as to preclude further inquiry. If you believe that the plan was sure to fail and so a foolish one, I can only
remind you that it nearly succeeded. Very nearly indeed.

"And what caused it not to succeed was by no means any defect in the plan itself, but the mistakes made in carrying it out.
For the murderer to have left the connecting door still locked
when he departed was a serious error, but to have omitted taking
the dead man's bath robe and slippers with him was a fatal one.
Had he been just so little more careful, I really doubt whether I
would have insisted on the autopsy that made a complete and
final investigation necessary.

"But now see what a problem we have raised. Hodges was
murdered in his stateroom, he was awake when he was murdered
and there are no signs of any real struggle. His bed was mussed
up but no more so than any one else's that had been slept in.
These three considerations seem incompatible with any method
of murder except the administration of an exceedingly rapid poison. Dr. Pons contributed the poison explanation, but a complete
autopsy immediately showed that no poison of any kind, rapid
or otherwise, had been used.

"This brings, us, gentlemen, to the most difficult aspect of the
entire case, a more difficult one even than the identification of
the criminal. From the very first I have been sure that murder was
committed, but only this afternoon did I solve how it was done.
So far as my own experience goes, this is the first case I have
ever had to do with, in which a violent death has been brought
about without the necessity of leaving behind any physical trace
whatsoever on the victim's body. . . . It is true that this time some
few traces *were* left behind. Otherwise I fear the crime would
have remained unsolved. But they were so negligible as to mean
almost nothing. The fact is that they were also little mistakes of

the murderer. On the other hand, all little mistakes can never be avoided; let me assure you, gentlemen, that murder in real fact is very much more difficult than it sounds."

Dr. Pons sat staring intently at Lord as he carefully built up his reasoning. He could begin now to see, he believed, the intent that lay behind the exposition. It was not just melodramatics on the detective's part. He was engaged in convincing the criminal that every detail of his crime had been discovered, that no tiny loophole of escape remained. Lord wanted a confession; perhaps he actually wanted the suicide at which he might have been hinting earlier. Would that happen, Pons wondered; would one of the men in this car, sitting so quietly beside him as yet, presently be stretched at their feet, himself the executioner of the penalty for his own act? When would the tension become unendurable, and break? Dr. Pons drew an audible breath.

"Thank you, Summerladd." Lord accepted the lighter handed to him by the publicity man, and handed it back. "I will recall for you the medical evidence supplied by Dr. Black's examination. As I said, there was no trace of any poison at all in Hodges' body. Nor were there any wounds or any bruises that could have even a remotely fatal effect. His eyes were somewhat bloodshot, there was a little scratch on his nose, there was a little piece of lint between his teeth and there was what appeared to be a very slight bruise of the solar plexus. That was all, but, as it turned out, each of these small things was directly the result of the murder method employed."

Dr. Pons, as he continued to give his attention to the detective's recital, was becoming more and more convinced that Lord's leisurely approach to whatever disclosures he had in mind must be due to his desire to break down the morale of the criminal. He was speaking slowly, taking all the time he could to let the finality of his conclusions sink in. He *was* fishing for a suicide. Pons suddenly decided that, as far as he was concerned, it was a method to which he was opposed. The rules of the society in which he lived did not appeal to Dr. Pons as approximating perfection but, for the present, the best course was to live up to them. The criminal should be arrested and have his trial. Pons' decision was taken; he would prevent this suicide if he could, when the moment came. From this time on, while listening, he was closely observing those about him, especially the analyst and the valet, prepared to interfere at any second.

Meanwhile Lord's argument was pushing ahead. "The medical verdict was natural death. But it was not a satisfactory verdict for two reasons. In the first place the data I have already outlined pointed conclusively to murder; and in the second place, no actual cause of death of a natural order could be found and proven. Up to a short time ago the diagnosis was thrombosis, which I understand to be death from a wandering blood-clot in the veins. But the clot itself was not found. I was unable to accept that verdict and I kept thinking and puzzling over a solution that would accord with the other facts in the case.

"I came across it by luck, mainly. Titus Nutt remarked to me that during the summer the heat on the plains behind us would be suffocating," said Lord, with an abrupt change of tone from his easy narration. "That clicked; *Mr. Hodges was done to death by suffocation!*"

Hopping gasped and his face took on a mottled appearance; as Lord's words snapped out, there came a sound from Raquette's throat, too, as if a swallow had been reversed half-way down the esophagus.

After a short pause, during which the detective looked keenly from one to the other of those before him, he went on. "Drowning is suffocation due to suffusion of the lung by water. But there are other means of suffocation. I told you that Mr. Hodges' eyes were bloodshot, a symptom of suffocation, although it could also have come from many other causes. It is a method of attack that leaves no telltale marks behind and presents an autopsy with the fact of death, but nothing to account for it. Heart failure, or thrombosis, or any other diagnosis suggested by the general condition of the victim, is indicated.

"In the present case, moreover, it was unlikely to be hit upon as the real explanation because it had once been dismissed— when drowning was dismissed. Eliminate drowning and you come close to eliminating suffocation, also. Subconsciously, eh, Dr. Raquette? In fact, the device of suffocating a man and then placing him where he appears to have been suffocated different-ly—so that, if the deception is discovered, the original method is likewise dismissed from consideration—is almost as clever as the operations of the unconscious that we are told about."

Lord glanced at the psychoanalyst, who said, "Agh!" and looked away.

"Once we consider suffocation, however, everything fits in. Hodges was first struck on the solar plexus and then smothered. The solar plexus bruise was slight because he died almost immediately afterwards, but the blow was powerful. The effect of such a blow is to paralyse the person struck and to render him nearly helpless for a short time; and that accounts for the absence of any serious struggle. After he was struck, a bath towel was stuffed in his mouth and held there until he died from lack of oxygen; and it was a shred from that towel that remained between his teeth. The scratch on his nose I will tell you about in a minute.

"When I had gotten this far and realised that the towel missing from Hodges' stateroom was the one he had been strangled with, the question was whether that towel were still on the train. It could have been thrown out of a door or window, or it could have been burned up. I decided that probably neither of these things had happened. Nine chances out of ten a towel along the track would never be remarked, but what about the tenth chance? Why take any risk at all of calling attention to towels? And as for burning it up, that also, I imagine, is harder than it appears.

"Why not leave it in Hodges' suite, then; why take it away? Because it had a slight tear in it, made by the death struggles of the murdered man and because it was surely probable that some search of his quarters would be made. The risk was slight of suspicion being aroused even then, but the safest course would be to take the towel along. The criminal's suite would not be searched at all, if he succeeded in escaping suspicion."

If Dr. Pons had not been listening intently, he would have missed the little moaning sound that seemed to come from Raquette, who sat next him and just behind Summerladd.

"I made a search of the entire first stateroom car. And in one of the suites, at the bottom of the stack of fresh towels in the lavatory, I found a bath towel, neatly folded like the rest, but with a small tear near its centre. The suite where I found it surprised me very much because it did not at all fit in with my ideas about the second crime, the shooting of Entwerk. But after all, there is such a thing as the planting of incriminating evidence, just to be on the safe side.

"That brings us to the second crime, which I have never been able to think was unconnected with the first one. Now, when another crime follows upon an original one, it usually simplifies the search for the criminal, because there inevitably result further clues and more evidence, all eventually pointing in the same direction. But in this case the very opposite happened; the criminals indicated by the two crimes were two *different* persons; the evidence, instead of pointing to the same man, pointed to separate individuals, as you will see.

"Without going into all the reasons, I shall simply tell you that the crux of the second crime was this. The time factors involved show conclusively that the person who shot at Miss Hodges and who killed Entwerk, must have been between myself and Mr. Summerladd in the stateroom car at one point in the affair. But the criminal was not in the aisle (which I could see) and so he must have been in a stateroom and, moreover, in one of the occupied staterooms.

"From Entwerk's room to the rear end of the car, the crucial area, all the rooms were occupied. Therefore, since the criminal had not been given away by any one, the stateroom he had gone into *must have been his own!* But of all our suspects only Entwerk and Hopping had rooms in that space, and Entwerk had been the second vic——"

The blood drained out of the valet's face, leaving it still mottled, but livid, as he lurched to his feet. "I didn't," he shouted hoarsely. "I didn't do it!"

Pons, looking involuntarily in his direction, only by chance caught a glimpse, out of the corner of his eye, of Dr. Raquette's hand stealing toward Summerladd's hip pocket. For a moment Pons hesitated, while the hand came out, clutching the publicity man's revolver. Then he cast himself at the analyst, just as the latter, half rising from his chair, endeavoured to cock the weapon which he was turning against himself.

Pons reached vainly for the gun beyond his grasp. "Stop!" screamed Raquette shrilly. "Leave me alone! Let me——"

A chair crashed over as Lord leaped across the few feet intervening between him and the struggling men. He caught Raquette's wrist and twisted it sharply, sending the revolver clattering to the floor. He twisted some more, and the man was forced back into his chair, groaning through the flecks of saliva on his lips.

"Quiet!" thundered Lord, in the voice of a drill master. "Everybody keep quiet and stay still a minute! Entwerk is the man who murdered Hodges and killed himself. What the hell has gotten into you people?"

Summerladd, who also had jumped up in the excitement, said "What?" blankly.

The detective snapped, "Certainly. When I tell you this case is solved, it's solved. The criminal was Entwerk and I have full proof of it. I can understand Hopping getting excited as I was leading up to it, but what *you* think you were doing with that revolver," keeping a wary eye on the psychoanalyst, "I can't imagine. What is the idea, Dr. Raquette?"

Raquette was leaning sidewise in his chair, rubbing an arm that was already beginning to swell a little. Shockingly, two tears were running down one of his cheeks. "I don't know," he said in a strangled tone, "I don't——"

"Look here, now. There's been enough of this." Lord brought his own voice down to a calm measure. "It's not a matter of 'don't know.' Unless you were trying to shoot yourself with Summerladd's gun, I'm a katydid. Will you please tell us why?"

Raquette gulped plaintively. "I thought maybe I—maybe I *had* done it. I couldn't fa—face the evidence piling——"

"You thought you had killed Hodges? Why, you know damn well you didn't!" Lord stared incredulously at the man in front of him.

"But I could have. From what you told us——"

Dr. Pons said quietly, "Pull yourself together, Raquette. And tell us just what it is you have on your mind."

Under the persuasion of the other psychologist's voice the Frenchman was already becoming calmer. He continued to rub his arm as he spoke, but there was no longer any involuntary hesitation in his speech. "I have myself very strong death instincts. And I have ego-instincts, also very strong. Continually comes the battle between them, the ones seeking always to outwit the others. Very subtle strategems often they employ . . .

"Ah, and while you are building up the evidence about Mr. Hodges' death and showing that I am of those who come within suspicion, I begin to wonder. Could it be so? Could it be that I project my death instincts subconsciously upon him and finally bring about his death instead of my own? I might thus make him the actual surrogate for my subconscious wish. And afterwards, of course, I know nothing of what I have done, for it is a separate part of my unconscious personality that has done it; and when it is over and the wish released, this part sinks back into the unconscious again. Everything you said seemed to be building up to the *dénouement* I myself most feared. Especially when you spoke of the murder resembling the tricks of the subconscious. At the last I could stand it no longer; I must have done with my own accusation that I could not bear to hear plainly stated by another."

Dr. Raquette reached out and grasped Lord's coat firmly with his left hand. "You are sure that Entwerk has done this? That it cannot be I? How can you be so sure?" His voice pled horribly for certainty.

Lord looked at Dr. Pons, who nodded in a fashion the detective took to mean that the explanation could be accepted. "I'll tell you how I know," he assured them all, "how I can be entirely sure. You may dismiss your fears, Dr. Raquette.

"I have said already that the man who shot Entwerk must have gone into his own stateroom, and that the only two possibilities were Hopping and Entwerk. At this point I believed Hopping was the man. But I had searched his room on the night of the shooting and there was no gun in it. There must have been another gun somewhere, for we had accounted for only three of the seven shots fired, one each from my gun, Summerladd's, and the one that was found beside Entwerk and which he admitted was his. I telegraphed back to the Omaha department to inquire about a gun that might have been thrown from the train near the place where it made its emergency stop Sunday night, for that was where the shooting had occurred.

"A gun *had* been picked up there by the road crew, I was told over the wireless telephone, and was being forwarded to me at San Francisco by the railroad. But this gun bore the initials, X.L.E., on its grip; Entwerk's initials. When I tell you that I had found the towel with which Hodges had been suffocated, in Entwerk's quarters, you will see that the appearance of the gun which had been used in the second crime, with his initials on it, made a reconsideration of the whole case necessary.

"I had to examine seriously the question whether he could be not only the man who had killed Hodges but also the man who had shot Entwerk. So far as I could see, only one set of circumstances could account for that; *if* he were Hodges' murderer and *if* he believed himself discovered, he might have done it.

"Was it possible that he could have believed himself found out, when in fact I was still far from suspecting him? You will remember," Lord stated, turning to Dr. Pons, "that Entwerk was present in your stateroom on the occasion when we discussed the case with Prof. Irrtum. I cannot remember all that was said, but I do recall that I gave some hint that everything in the pool car on the morning of Hodges' death was not as it should have been. Entwerk noted this particularly; I think he even made some comment to the effect that he saw what I meant. Something like that, anyhow.

"I then said that there was now no possibility of dropping the case until it had been finally cleared up. He saw that I meant that, and he felt undoubtedly that the trail was leading to him and would reach him soon. That very night, and only long enough after our talk for him to have devised his new plan, he shot himself."

"That hound wouldn't have committed suicide at so early a stage," Summerladd protested. "To tell you the truth, I can't see him ever doing it. He was too yellow."

"Oh, he never intended to commit suicide, man. That was his second mistake; but not a hard one to make. All he wanted to do was to wound himself harmlessly through the shoulder, but he shot just a little bit too low. He knicked the tip of his lung and later he died of a haemorrhage from the puncture. His shot went much too far away from his heart to have been intended for it. No, he wanted to be the lucky victim of the second crime and so escape all suspicion for the first. There was a good chance that he could keep his freedom long enough, at any rate, to reach San Francisco and, once there, he would have escaped for good."

Dr. Pons grunted for attention. "But he still tried to kill Miss Hodges, too," he pointed out. "I can't see how that fits in with what you're saying."

"There's a personal mix-up there, something along the lines you yourself proposed," Lord suggested. "I don't know much about it myself yet, but I rather think Miss Hodges can tell me, when she learns who really did fire at her."

"I think she can," Summerladd said shortly.

"You know," the detective continued, "when you once begin thinking of Entwerk, there are a lot of things about him that would have added up to quite a sum, had there been any original reason to suspect him. For instance, Hopping says when he first told Entwerk and Miss Hodges that her father was not in his room on Sunday morning, that Entwerk seemed to feel right away that something might be wrong. What gave him that idea, unless he knew something *was* wrong? And how did he know just where to go to find it? He is said to have led the way right to the pool car, without any beating around the bush.

"In addition to the promptness with which the second crime followed his realisation that truly I believed Hodges' death to have been murder, I remember that he supported the suicide theory as strongly as he dared. Dr. Pons pointed that out once. He also supported the theory of natural death. And there is no question but that Entwerk must have known about Hodges' changing his bequest to Princeton. He simply could not have been in ignorance of that, as he claimed, in his position as confidential secretary. But I was so busy trying to avoid a false lead that I disregarded his mis-step, as well as Dr. Pons' rather weak suggestion of Entwerk as the criminal, just when Entwerk himself thought I was getting on to him.

"But to get back to the second crime. Entwerk decided to take this means of establishing his innocence of the murder and, while he was about it, decided to dispose of Edvanne Hodges at the same time, for reasons that, as I say, I do not know in detail. He shot through her door, possibly because he heard Summerladd inside and didn't dare show himself, then. After which he ran back to his own stateroom. He was the man who had two guns, of course, not Summerladd. He fired one of his guns through the window across the isle, in order to support the story of an attack on himself which he had prepared, and threw that gun through his own stateroom window, breaking the glass. Then he stood in the middle of his room, with his back to the broken window, and fired a shot from his second gun through his own shoulder. He wanted this bullet to go through the broken window behind him if possible, because it matched the calibre of the gun he intended to admit was his, the one that was to be found on the floor.

"The shot knocked him down in the middle of the stateroom; a .45 delivers a very powerful blow, aside from the penetrating effect. But he was able to crawl to the entrance (where his story demanded him), and didn't faint until the sudden stopping of the train rolled him across the floor and against the room's forward wall. That accounts for the blood trail from the centre of the room to the doorway, and then to the wall. I couldn't read the first half of that trail until I understood that Entwerk had shot himself and that his account was false. If he had really been shot at his own door and fallen there, as he claimed, there should have been no blood stains *behind* him.

"You see the train of reasoning that follows. Entwerk shot himself. He could only have done so because he wanted suspicion definitely diverted from him. If he needed that, then he must have been guilty of the murder."

Titus Nutt, who was staying cautiously on the outskirts of the group, put his watch back in his pocket and spoke up meekly. "We shall be in, in thirty-nine minutes," he told Lord, "and I must leave you now. But before I go, if you don't mind—just as a matter of figuring—why couldn't the other man, Mr. Hopping, have done the shooting with Mr. Entwerk's gun. Of course," he added hastily, "I don't mean that he did."

"A good point," said Lord. "As a matter of theory he could both have planted the towel in Entwerk's suite and have stolen one of Entwerk's guns. Fortunately the matter is proven beyond any doubt, however. When I found that towel, I searched Entwerk's effects thoroughly. Among other things, I turned out a portfolio of his and I discovered a paper clip on one of whose edges there seemed to be a few drops of blood. You know the sort of clips that hold together a whole sheaf of papers, the kind you open by pinching the handles together and that have two blades on the other end to clamp over the edges of the papers? This was quite a big one.

"I gave that clip to Dr. Black, who already had made an analysis of Mr. Hodges' blood and he was able to say that the blood on the clip was Hodges', also. That clip was pinched over Hodges' nose while the towel in his mouth suffocated him; it scratched his nose in one place, where a small wart made the skin weak, and the murderer probably never noticed afterwards that a little blood had gotten on it.

"But Black did even better than that. He found a fingerprint on the clip and the print was Entwerk's. He matched it not only with prints from Entwerk's stateroom but with one from Entwerk's body, which is being carried in the car ahead, with Hodges'. That clinched it."

"I see," said Nutt. "I see. Er, well, I must go back." He bobbed his head to the company in general and stepped down the car. As he did so, a thunderous banging resounded on the rear door; and shortly following Nutt's disappearance into the corridor leading to it, Dr. Black appeared, escorting Miss Delacroix.

The medical examiner came up the car belligerently. "This

lady has something important for you," he told Lord. "If she says it's important, it is. Why the hell didn't you let her in sooner?" He glared defiantly at the detective.

The other repressed a smile. "I didn't know she wanted to get in," he stated mildly. "Some one knocked earlier, but Nutt said it was nothing."

"That simp conductor," Black growled and handed across the envelope his blonde companion took from her dress.

Lord took it, opened it, glanced at the enclosure. He caught his breath sharply. "You're right, this is important. It's just Entwerk's confession! Why didn't I get this long ago, Miss Delacroix?"

The girl was standing with one slim hand on her hip. "The poor gentleman made me promise to give it to you after we left Sacramento," the silky voice drawled. "I tried to, but I couldn't get in until Dr. Black lent me his assistance." She smiled at the man next her, who was regarding her trig figure with a dog-like devotion plain on his face. It occurred to Dr. Pons that "The Transcontinental" had better watch out for its manicurist.

"I see," Lord was saying. "Well, no harm done, Miss Delacroix. Thank you. This certainly settles it completely, gentlemen."

Dr. Raquette murmured, "Thank God. *Merci à Dieu,*" under his breath.

As THEY walked back, "The Transcontinental" was rolling through the night with little diminishment of speed; Oakland was still twenty minutes down the track. In the empty pool car Dr. Pons drew Lord to one side and detained him in the small area where the tables stood before the swimming pool, until the others had passed.

"Look here," the psychologist demanded, when they were alone, "why did you tell me Entwerk wasn't the criminal, when I guessed him? That was a cheap trick, Lord. I wouldn't have expected it of you."

Lord grinned. "It was only a guess on your part. You hadn't any reasons for it at all; you were only trying to hit on some one unlikely. If you had given me one good reason, I wouldn't have denied that. And furthermore, I never told you that Entwerk didn't do it."

"Hah, you did so. I said it was Entwerk and you said it wasn't."

"No, doctor, you're wrong. What you said was that the criminal had died Tuesday morning at twelve-twenty-four or some such time. I told you that the man who had murdered Hodges

330

and killed Entwerk had not died at any time Tuesday. And he hadn't. Entwerk died at Ogden, within the city limits of Ogden. And it was eleven-twenty-four p.m. *on Monday* when he died. A clock can be wrong, you know; it can even be an hour fast. And the clocks on this train were exactly one hour fast when the train stopped in the Ogden station. They were set back before we left, but that doesn't alter the fact that the real time when we arrived was p.m., not a.m. That is where Entwerk died, and he died on Monday, not Tuesday. That's all I told you; if you were deceived, doctor, you've no idea how terribly, terribly sorry I am."

"Uh!" Pons snorted and shrugged. "Well, I suppose you're right, technically. But I think it's a trick just the same. A low trick, too."

Lord clapped him friendlily on the back and started to move away. "Come, come now. You won't hold a grudge just because you weren't on your guard. There are technical tricks in all trades, you know. . . . To make up for it, I'll take you in to see Miss Hodges for a minute, if she has recovered as much as Black says."

Edvanne had, in fact, recovered from the sedative which, she told them, she was sure Dr. Raquette had administered in good faith, despite her protests. She was still reclining on the bed and seemed a little drowsy, but otherwise she was the same as ever. Lord's first judgment on her vitality had not been mistaken.

Summerladd was with her when Pons and Lord came in, and he had already told her of the detective's solution of the case. "Yes," she answered Lord's question, "Entwerk was the man who had been blackmailing me . . . It's all right, Dr. Pons, you can stay . . . I would have told you, I could even have suspected him of killing father and trying to kill me, except that I thought he had been attacked, too, and so it couldn't be he. He was the only one on the train whom I could imagine as injuring me and so, when

I counted him out, I could only say that I hadn't any idea who *had* shot at me."

"Take a look at this, Miss Hodges," Lord proffered the sheet of paper that had recently been delivered to him by Miss Delacroix.

The girl spread out Entwerk's confession on the bed beside her. She bit her lip as she looked at it, but determinedly read it through:

"LORD,

"I am afraid I am going to die—afraid to die with this on me. I killed Hodges, shot myself. Had to get the girl; she knew why I had killed her father, but hadn't realised it yet. Only wanted to wound myself, you were getting too close. Too late now. Fool not to take bathrobe to pool but had to think too quick. If I die clear Summerladd. All I can do now. God help me.

X. L. E."

There was a silence when she finished. Then she said, almost inaudibly, "Why didn't I take him seriously? Why didn't I go to dad myself?"

Lord reached for the letter and put it back in his wallet. "You needn't say anything, Miss Hodges," he told her. "I think I can guess. Enough."

Edvanne brushed a hand across her eyes. "No," she said, succeeding in making her voice cease its trembling after the first few words. "I want to tell you. I want to say it, and maybe if another time comes, I won't do it again." Once more Dr. Pons made a move to leave, but she waved him back.

"Lew wanted to marry me and so did Hans. Lew got father on his side—I guess he was a good secretary—and then he found out that Hans and I had spent a week-end in the Adirondacks together, in spite of dad's objections to my seeing so much of Hans. The night we left New York, after you had gone past the pool, Mr. Lord, he told me he would take his proofs to father unless I promised to marry him. I told him to go ahead; I wouldn't marry him, no matter what he did. But I was afraid for Hans. Father could have ruined his chance of publicity work with any large company, easily."

"So that was what was the matter when you came into the club car at Albany? I thought something was wrong."

"Yes, that was it. I was angry all through, and I was frightened. I thought Lew might do it, but I had no idea he would do it that very night. I should have gone to father and told him myself; I wasn't afraid of him, but I was awfully afraid he would injure Hans, if he knew. So I didn't do it; I waited and thought maybe I could get my courage up later." Edvanne's voice faltered badly.

Lord interrupted gently. "Don't distress yourself too much, Miss Hodges. More experienced people than you would have made the same mistake. . . . I think I can see the rest as clearly as you can. Entwerk did awaken your father some time during the night and go to him with his dirty tale. But your father was not the man Entwerk took him for. Entwerk himself was the one that story ruined, not Summerladd. I can well believe that your father denounced him, discharged him and probably warned him out of America. Entwerk attacked him in desperation . . ."

Lord crossed the room and took her hand in his. Her control had broken now and she was sobbing. "My dear girl," he said, "you have been through a sad and terrible experience. Try to believe me that it has not been your fault. I hope very sincerely that the rest of your life will hold more than enough happiness to balance these last few days."

Pons found the words good and added no more. In the aisle outside, as they walked back to their quarters to make ready to leave the train, he asked, "Is that what you really think happened? Or were you just trying to put the best face on it?"

Lord answered, "No. We'll never know for sure, but that's my guess. Don't you agree? The murder was never premeditated, I'm certain. Too many mistakes in execution. The slippers would surely have been noticed, in any careful plan."

"I think you're right. Yes, I believe you are. Rage behaviour is always uncontrolled; always carries too far too quickly. Entwerk, cornered by his own misjudgment, went into bitter rage and killed before he knew what he was doing."

"Poor kid," said Lord irrelevantly. "It wasn't her fault, really. I hate to see a pretty girl cry."

·　　　　·　　　　·

Barrenness haunts the Oakland Terminal, as it haunts every structure part of whose design comprises an arching, windy shed. The preparations made for the reception of "The Transcontinental" succeeded in banishing this air somewhat, but not entirely.

As in the Grand Central, three thousand miles away, bunting and decorations lent a festive atmosphere and at least one long platform, stretching like an immense finger out towards the yards, gleamed brilliantly under the rows of extra lights strung down its length. Here a carpet lay unrolled; it led the full distance of the platform beside the rails, thence across the broad plaza where the tracks ended and out to the ferry slip where the shiny new "Twin Peaks" glittered in its own lights as they shone brightly over its proud, fresh paint.

An orchestra sat in the plaza, here also. "The Transcontinental" had been played out of New York; it would be played into Oakland, and its guests would be played across the Bay. Although the number of casual spectators was less than on its departure, a reception committee of officials and citizens awaited its arrival, nor was there any lack of the gentlemen of the press.

Nine-thirty-two. Over the wires to the station-master came the word that "The Transcontinental" was passing through Berkeley. The minutes passed, the orchestra played an anticipatory melody. Far away down the tracks, in the distant darkness beyond the limits of the covered shed, a pin-point of light twinkled where blackness had been before.

Rapidly the light grew brighter and larger; it was approaching. When it had reached the dimensions of a thumbnail, already it seemed to be penetrating the train shed and lighting the end of the track it had traversed so steadily for three days past. From beneath the light, as it came nearer, two gleaming threads, the rails, began to glisten; they stretched toward the platform, they reached it, then seemed to contract, drawing with them to its final berth the single spot of illumination that as yet was the train.

Suddenly it was upon them. Instead of a spot it became a glare, lighting up the faces of the spectators, playing over the brasses of the orchestra, filling the station with a dazzling brilliance. Then, as the great engine thrust its nose under the train shed, it was abruptly dimmed. From a flaming sun it sank to a glow, and the heavy cars became visible following the locomotive into the station.

A mighty and towering mass, the thousands of tons slid along the track, slowly, decelerating. Ten feet from the bumper's red light at the westward end came the final groan of the brakes. With steam hissing and whispering about it, the locomotive stopped, and stood panting; panting as a spent dog pants after a long, hard run. "The Transcontinental" was in.

Nine-forty-six.

SAN FRANCISCO
Tuesday, 10.30 *p.m.*

BEHIND THE city the Twin Peaks towered above the evening mist that still shrouded their namesake on the Bay. Around them clung the spiralled strings of lights along their observatory highways, as jewelled girdles cling to the breasts of a dancer. The great city stretched below them, throbbing under the foggy glow above its buildings, the tip of Telegraph Hill alone rising out of concealment.

On the water the gentle mist was blowing for a little longer through the Golden Gate, the fleeting mist that the Pacific sends with early evening to touch with cool fingers the brows of those who live beside it, to refresh and reinvigorate them for the pleasures of San Francisco nights. On the upper deck of the "Twin Peaks" it curled in tendrils around stanchions and canopy supports and licked lazily through the white webs of the guard-railings as the engines purred steadily beneath, pushing the boat over the smooth water. It softened the glare of the big cabin, it hid the farther reaches of the decks outside in dimness.

Almost all of the passengers were within, where the orchestra played music modulated to the cabin's confinement. By the forward rail two figures stood in solitude, breathing the fresh, damp air, hearing the low gurgle of the bows below against the diminutive waves. The girl was muffled to her small ears in a rough and dark-brown coat; then came a glimpse of dark hair, the curve of a cheek and the lines of a tight little felt hat. It is possible that the man was a publicity director.

Abreast of Goat Island the mist lifted for several minutes and, high above, bright stars peered down on the moving boat. It slipped quickly across the open space and once more was enshrouded in obscurity. The girl's hand was in the man's, as she leaned lightly against him. They rode in an intimate silence. From above them came a long, low, penetrating hoot from the "Twin Peaks" fog-horn; from behind came a snatch of melody as a door was opened and closed.

The man looked away from the gloom ahead and down at the girl beside him. He said softly, without special emphasis, as one who states a fact, "Edvanne, darling, I love you."

The girl said nothing. She raised her chin from its enfolding collar, she raised her lips and drew his head down to them. Very gently.

Ahead, the mist was thinning. The purring of the engines ceased, and the boat glided forward silently. A red light and a green light, on jutting piers. Beyond them the dark mass of the terminal, its clock tower rising high against the luminous glow of Market Street. The clang of a tramcar, the cry of a taxi, drifted out tenuously over the water.

Journey's end.

THE END

APPENDIX A
Bibliography of References

Colbourne, Maurice, *Unemployment or War,* Coward-McCann, N.Y.

Douglas, C. H., *Economic Democracy,* Cecil Palmer, Oakley House, London; *Credit Power and Democracy, ibid.,* 1921; *The Control and Distribution of Production, ibid.,* 1922; *Social Credit, ibid.,* 1924; *The Monopoly of Credit; Warning Democracy,* C. M. Grieve, London, 1931.

Freud, Sigmund, "Beyond the Pleasure Principle," *International Psycho-Analytical Library, No.* 4, International Psycho-Analytical Press, London and Berlin, 1922.

Koffka, K., "Mental Development," *Psychologies of* 1925, Clark University Press, Worcester, Mass., 1925. "Some Problems of Space Perception," *Psychologies of* 1930, Clark University Press, Worcester, Mass., 1930.

Köhler, W., "Intelligence of Apes," *Psychologies of* 1925, *op. cit.*; "An Aspect of Gestalt Psychology," *ibid.*; *The Mentality of Apes,* Harcourt, Brace & Co., N.Y., 1927; *Gestalt Psychology,* Horace Liveright, N.Y. 1929; "Some Tasks of Gestalt Psychology," *Psychologies of* 1930, *op. cit.*

Marston, W. M., *Emotions of Normal People,* International Library of Psychology, Philosophy and Scientific Method, Kegan Paul, Trench, Trubner & Co., London, 1928, and

Harcourt, Brace & Co., N.Y., 1928. *Integrative Psychology* (with King, C. D. and Marston, E. H.), *ibid.,* 1931.

M'Dougall, William, "The Hormic Psychology," *Psychologies of 1930, op. cit.*

Sander, F., "Structure, Totality of Experience and Gestalt," *Psychologies of 1930, op. cit.*

Periodicals: *New English Weekly,* London (weekly); *Psychological Abstracts,* The American Psychological Association, Lancaster, Pa. (monthly); *Psychological Review,* The American Psychological Association Lancaster, Pa. (bi-monthly).

APPENDIX B
The Clue Finder

Do not open until you have finished the story.*

* To cheat others is dishonourable; to cheat oneself is merely ridiculous.

At,

one might say, this last and final gasp, the author begs leave to insinuate (and hopes the reader, after just reflection, will agree) that the criminal hereinbefore was indicated—

As to His Ill-favour with One	Page	28,	par.	1	line	3
He seeks to Injure	”	52,	”	6.		
	”	67,	”	1,	”	3
	”	266,	”	4.		
As to His Ill-favour with a Friend of That Person	”	258,	”	6.		
As to His Method of Murder	”	58,	”	4,	”	2
	”	285,	”	1,	”	2
	”	290,	”	1,	”	3
As to the Weapon He Used	”	64,	”	3.		
	”	65,	”	1,	”	2
	”	293,	”	3.		
As to His Mistakes:						
Something Essential is Not where it Should Be	”	57,	”	2.		
	”	65,	”	1.		
	”	201,	”	1.		
	”	278,	”	5,	”	5
The Something is Mentioned	”	64,	”	3.		
	”	199,	”	1,	”	4
	”	206,	”	1,	”	7
	”	275,	”	3,	”	2
	”	278,	”	5,	”	8
The Criminal Realises One of His Mistakes	”	108,	”	3.		

And Endeavors to Deny His Realisation	Page	114,	par.	7,	line	5
A Bit of Knowledge He	"	81,	"	6,	"	4
must have had	"	109,	"	last.		
Another Bit He would have	"	62,	"	7,	"	6
done Well to Conceal	"	280,	"	3,	"	5
A Trail that was Longer	"	129,	"	2,	"	4
than it Should Be	"	150,	"		"	3
	"	286,	"	1,	"	4
As to the False Leads He	"	82,	"	last.		
Espoused	"	109,	"	6.		
	"	110,	"	2,	"	4
	"	114,	"	last.		
	"	116,	"	2.		
As to His Knowledge of a	"	110,	"	last.		
Coming Autopsy	"	111,	"	2,	"	4
As to His Knowledge that Disclosures could Not Be	"	112,	"		"	1
Avoided	"	115,	"	1,	"	4
As to a suspiciously Bad Shot	"	130,	"	2,	"	3
As to a Letter Written	"	243,	"		"	1
	"	254,	"	6.		
As to a Time of Death	"	69,	"	5,	"	3
	"	171,	"	4.		
	"	254,	"	last,	"	2
	"	255,	"	last.		
	"	304,	"	last.		
	"	330,	"	last.		

As to the Location of His   Page   29, par.   9.
   Stateroom   ”   207,   ”   1.
                                           ”   291,   ”   4, line   2
As to a Distinctive Initial,
   perhaps?   ”   296,   ”   1,   ”   3
As to His Motive for Both
   Crimes   ”   282,   ”   2.

DISCUSSION QUESTIONS

- Did any aspects of the plot date the story? If so, which?

- Would the story be different if it were set in the present day? If so, how?

- Did the social context of the time play a role in the narrative? If so, how?

- How did this compare with other train-bound mysteries you may have read?

- Did you find the maps and diagrams helpful for following the action of the story?

- How did the author's psychological insights add to the mystery plot?

- Did this remind you of any books or authors being published today? If so, which?

MORE GOLDEN AGE TRAIN MYSTERIES FROM

═══ AMERICAN MYSTERY CLASSICS ═══

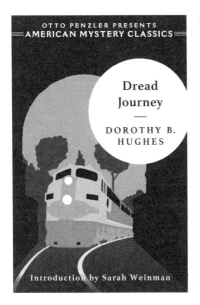

Dread
Journey
—
DOROTHY B.
HUGHES

Introduction by Sarah Weinman

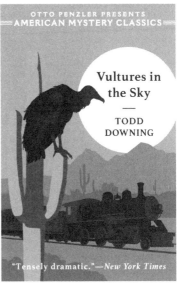

Vultures in
the Sky
—
TODD
DOWNING

"Tensely dramatic." —*New York Times*

All titles are available in hardcover and in trade paperback.

Order from your favorite bookstore or from
The Mysterious Bookshop, 58 Warren Street, New York, N.Y. 10007
(www.mysteriousbookshop.com).

Charlotte Armstrong, *The Chocolate Cobweb*. When Amanda Garth was born, a mix-up caused the hospital to briefly hand her over to the prestigious Garrison family instead of to her birth parents. The error was quickly fixed, Amanda was never told, and the secret was forgotten for twenty-three years ... until her aunt revealed it in casual conversation. But what if the initial switch never actually occurred? **Introduction by A. J. Finn.**

Charlotte Armstrong, *The Unsuspected*. First published in 1946, this suspenseful novel opens with a young woman who has ostensibly hanged herself, leaving a suicide note. Her friend doesn't believe it and begins an investigation that puts her own life in jeopardy. It was filmed in 1947 by Warner Brothers, starring Claude Rains and Joan Caulfield. **Introduction by Otto Penzler.**

Anthony Boucher, *The Case of the Baker Street Irregulars*. When a studio announces a new hard-boiled Sherlock Holmes film, the Baker Street Irregulars begin a campaign to discredit it. Attempting to mollify them, the producers invite members to the set, where threats are received, each referring to one of the original Holmes tales, followed by murder. Fortunately, the amateur sleuths use Holmesian lessons to solve the crime. **Introduction by Otto Penzler.**

Anthony Boucher, *Rocket to the Morgue*. Hilary Foulkes has made so many enemies that it is difficult to speculate who was responsible for stabbing him nearly to death in a room with only one door through which no one was seen entering or leaving. This classic locked room mystery is populated by such thinly disguised science fiction legends as Robert Heinlein, L. Ron Hubbard, and John W. Campbell. **Introduction by F. Paul Wilson.**

Fredric Brown, *The Fabulous Clipjoint*. Brown's outstanding mystery won an Edgar as the best first novel of the year (1947). When Wallace

Hunter is found dead in an alley after a long night of drinking, the police don't really care. But his teenage son Ed and his uncle Am, the carnival worker, are convinced that some things don't add up and the crime isn't what it seems to be. **Introduction by Lawrence Block.**

John Dickson Carr, *The Crooked Hinge*. Selected by a group of mystery experts as one of the 15 best impossible crime novels ever written, this is one of Gideon Fell's greatest challenges. Estranged from his family for 25 years, Sir John Farnleigh returns to England from America to claim his inheritance but another person turns up claiming that he can prove he is the real Sir John. Inevitably, one of them is murdered. **Introduction by Charles Todd.**

John Dickson Carr, *The Eight of Swords*. When Gideon Fell arrives at a crime scene, it appears to be straightforward enough. A man has been shot to death in an unlocked room and the likely perpetrator was a recent visitor. But Fell discovers inconsistencies and his investigations are complicated by an apparent poltergeist, some American gangsters, and two meddling amateur sleuths. **Introduction by Otto Penzler.**

John Dickson Carr, *The Mad Hatter Mystery*. A prankster has been stealing top hats all around London. Gideon Fell suspects that the same person may be responsible for the theft of a manuscript of a long-lost story by Edgar Allan Poe. The hats reappear in unexpected but conspicuous places but, when one is found on the head of a corpse by the Tower of London, it is evident that the thefts are more than pranks. **Introduction by Otto Penzler.**

John Dickson Carr, *The Plague Court Murders*. When murder occurs in a locked hut on Plague Court, an estate haunted by the ghost of a hangman's assistant who died a victim of the black death, Sir Henry Merrivale seeks a logical solution to a ghostly crime. A spiritual medium employed to rid the house of his spirit is found stabbed to death in a locked stone hut on the grounds, surrounded by an untouched circle of mud. **Introduction by Michael Dirda.**

John Dickson Carr, *The Red Widow Murders.* In a "haunted" mansion, the room known as the Red Widow's Chamber proves lethal to all who spend the night. Eight people investigate and the one who draws the ace of spades must sleep in it. The room is locked from the inside and watched all night by the others. When the door is unlocked, the victim has been poisoned. Enter Sir Henry Merrivale to solve the crime. **Introduction by Tom Mead.**

Frances Crane, *The Turquoise Shop.* In an arty little New Mexico town, Mona Brandon has arrived from the East and becomes the subject of gossip about her money, her influence, and the corpse in the nearby desert who may be her husband. Pat Holly, who runs the local gift shop, is as interested as anyone in the goings on—but even more in Pat Abbott, the detective investigating the possible murder. **Introduction by Anne Hillerman.**

Todd Downing, *Vultures in the Sky.* There is no end to the series of terrifying events that befall a luxury train bound for Mexico. First, a man dies when the train passes through a dark tunnel, then it comes to an abrupt stop in the middle of the desert. More deaths occur when night falls and the passengers panic when they realize they are trapped with a murderer on the loose. **Introduction by James Sallis.**

Mignon G. Eberhart, *Murder by an Aristocrat.* Nurse Keate is called to help a man who has been "accidentally" shot in the shoulder. When he is murdered while convalescing, it is clear that there was no accident. Although a killer is loose in the mansion, the family seems more concerned that news of the murder will leave their circle. *The New Yorker* wrote than "Eberhart can weave an almost flawless mystery." **Introduction by Nancy Pickard.**

Erle Stanley Gardner, *The Case of the Baited Hook.* Perry Mason gets a phone call in the middle of the night and his potential client says it's urgent, that he has two one-thousand-dollar bills that he will give him as a retainer, with an additional ten-thousand whenever he is called on to represent him. When

Mason takes the case, it is not for the caller but for a beautiful woman whose identity is hidden behind a mask. **Introduction by Otto Penzler.**

Erle Stanley Gardner, *The Case of the Borrowed Brunette.* A mysterious man named Mr. Hines has advertised a job for a woman who has to fulfill very specific physical requirements. Eva Martell, pretty but struggling in her career as a model, takes the job but her aunt smells a rat and hires Perry Mason to investigate. Her fears are realized when Hines turns up in the apartment with a bullet hole in his head. **Introduction by Otto Penzler.**

Erle Stanley Gardner, *The Case of the Careless Kitten.* Helen Kendal receives a mysterious phone call from her vanished uncle Franklin, long presumed dead, who urges her to contact Perry Mason. Soon, she finds herself the main suspect in the murder of an unfamiliar man. Her kitten has just survived a poisoning attempt—as has her aunt Matilda. What is the connection between Franklin's return and the murder attempts? **Introduction by Otto Penzler.**

Erle Stanley Gardner, *The Case of the Rolling Bones.* One of Gardner's most successful Perry Mason novels opens with a clear case of blackmail, though the person being blackmailed claims he isn't. It is not long before the police are searching for someone wanted for killing the same man in two different states—thirty-three years apart. The confounding puzzle of what happened to the dead man's toes is a challenge. **Introduction by Otto Penzler.**

Erle Stanley Gardner, *The Case of the Shoplifter's Shoe.* Most cases for Perry Mason involve murder but here he is hired because a young woman fears her aunt is a kleptomaniac. Sarah may not have been precisely the best guardian for a collection of valuable diamonds and, sure enough, they go missing. When the jeweler is found shot dead, Sarah is spotted leaving the murder scene with a bundle of gems stuffed in her purse. **Introduction by Otto Penzler.**

Erle Stanley Gardner, *The Bigger They Come.* Gardner's first novel using the pseudonym A.A. Fair starts off a series featuring the large and loud Bertha Cool and her employee, the small and meek Donald Lam. Given the job of delivering divorce papers to an evident crook,

Lam can't find him—but neither can the police. The *Los Angeles Times* called this book: "Breathlessly dramatic … an original." **Introduction by Otto Penzler.**

Frances Noyes Hart, *The Bellamy Trial*. Inspired by the real-life Hall-Mills case, the most sensational trial of its day, this is the story of Stephen Bellamy and Susan Ives, accused of murdering Bellamy's wife Madeleine. Eight days of dynamic testimony, some true, some not, make headlines for an enthralled public. Rex Stout called this historic courtroom thriller one of the ten best mysteries of all time. **Introduction by Hank Phillippi Ryan.**

H.F. Heard, *A Taste for Honey*. The elderly Mr. Mycroft quietly keeps bees in Sussex, where he is approached by the reclusive and somewhat misanthropic Mr. Silchester, whose honey supplier was found dead, stung to death by her bees. Mycroft, who shares many traits with Sherlock Holmes, sets out to find the vicious killer. Rex Stout described it as "sinister … a tale well and truly told." **Introduction by Otto Penzler.**

Dolores Hitchens, *The Alarm of the Black Cat*. Detective fiction aficionado Rachel Murdock has a peculiar meeting with a little girl and a dead toad, sparking her curiosity about a love triangle that has sparked anger. When the girl's great grandmother is found dead, Rachel and her cat Samantha work with a friend in the Los Angeles Police Department to get to the bottom of things. **Introduction by David Handler.**

Dolores Hitchens, *The Cat Saw Murder*. Miss Rachel Murdock, the highly intelligent 70-year-old amateur sleuth, is not entirely heartbroken when her slovenly, unattractive, bridge-cheating niece is murdered. Miss Rachel is happy to help the socially maladroit and somewhat bumbling Detective Lieutenant Stephen Mayhew, retaining her composure when a second brutal murder occurs. **Introduction by Joyce Carol Oates.**

Dorothy B. Hughes, *Dread Journey*. A big-shot Hollywood producer has worked on his magnum opus for years, hiring and firing one beautiful starlet after another. But Kitten Agnew's contract won't allow her to be fired, so she fears she might be terminated more permanently. Together with the producer on a train journey from Hollywood to Chicago, Kitten becomes more terrified with each passing mile. **Introduction by Sarah Weinman.**

Dorothy B. Hughes, *Ride the Pink Horse*. When Sailor met Willis Douglass, he was just a poor kid who Douglass groomed to work as a confidential secretary. As the senator became increasingly corrupt, he knew he could count on Sailor to clean up his messes. No longer a senator, Douglass flees Chicago for Santa Fe, leaving behind a murder rap and Sailor as the prime suspect. Seeking vengeance, Sailor follows. **Introduction by Sara Paretsky.**

Dorothy B. Hughes, *The So Blue Marble*. Set in the glamorous world of New York high society, this novel became a suspense classic as twins from Europe try to steal a rare and beautiful gem owned by an aristocrat whose sister is an even more menacing presence. *The New Yorker* called it "Extraordinary … [Hughes'] brilliant descriptive powers make and unmake reality." **Introduction by Otto Penzler.**

W. Bolingbroke Johnson, *The Widening Stain*. After a cocktail party, the attractive Lucie Coindreau, a "black-eyed, black-haired Frenchwoman" visits the rare books wing of the library and apparently takes a head-first fall from an upper gallery. Dismissed as a horrible accident, it seems dubious when Professor Hyett is strangled while reading a priceless 12th-century manuscript, which has gone missing. **Introduction by Nicholas A. Basbanes**

Baynard Kendrick, *Blind Man's Bluff*. Blinded in World War II, Duncan Maclain forms a successful private detective agency, aided by his two dogs. Here, he is called on to solve the case of a blind man who plummets from the top of an eight-story building, apparently with no one present except his dead-drunk son. **Introduction by Otto Penzler.**

Baynard Kendrick, *The Odor of Violets*. Duncan Maclain, a blind former intelligence officer, is asked to investigate the murder of an actor in his Greenwich Village apartment. This would cause a stir at any time but, when the actor possesses secret government plans that then go missing, it's enough to interest the local police as well as the American government and Maclain, who suspects a German spy plot. **Introduction by Otto Penzler.**

C. Daly King, *Obelists at Sea*. On a cruise ship traveling from New York to Paris, the lights of the smoking room briefly go out, a gunshot crashes through the night, and a man is dead. Two detectives are on board but so are four psychiatrists who believe their professional knowledge can solve the case by understanding the psyche of the killer—each with a different theory. **Introduction by Martin Edwards.**

Jonathan Latimer, *Headed for a Hearse*. Featuring Bill Crane, the booze-soaked Chicago private detective, this humorous hard-boiled novel was filmed as *The Westland Case* in 1937 starring Preston Foster. Robert Westland has been framed for the grisly murder of his wife in a room with doors and windows locked from the inside. As the day of his execution nears, he relies on Crane to find the real murderer. **Introduction by Max Allan Collins**

Lange Lewis, *The Birthday Murder*. Victoria is a successful novelist and screenwriter and her husband is a movie director so their marriage seems almost too good to be true. Then, on her birthday, her happy new life comes crashing down when her husband is murdered using a method of poisoning that was described in one of her books. She quickly becomes the leading suspect. **Introduction by Randal S. Brandt.**

Frances and Richard Lockridge, *Death on the Aisle*. In one of the most beloved books to feature Mr. and Mrs. North, the body of a wealthy backer of a play is found dead in a seat of the 45th Street Theater. Pam is thrilled to engage in her favorite pastime—playing amateur sleuth—much to the annoyance of Jerry, her publisher husband. The Norths inspired a stage play, a film, and long-running radio and TV series. **Introduction by Otto Penzler.**

John P. Marquand, *Your Turn, Mr. Moto*. The first novel about Mr. Moto, originally titled *No Hero*, is the story of a World War I hero pilot who finds himself jobless during the Depression. In Tokyo for a big opportunity that falls apart, he meets a Japanese agent and his Russian colleague and the pilot suddenly finds himself caught in a web of intrigue. Peter Lorre played Mr. Moto in a series of popular films. **Introduction by Lawrence Block.**

Stuart Palmer, *The Penguin Pool Murder*. The first adventure of schoolteacher and dedicated amateur sleuth Hildegarde Withers occurs at the New York Aquarium when she and her young students notice a corpse in one of the tanks. It was published in 1931 and filmed the next year, starring Edna May Oliver as the American Miss Marple—though much funnier than her English counterpart. **Introduction by Otto Penzler.**

Stuart Palmer, *The Puzzle of the Happy Hooligan*. New York City schoolteacher Hildegarde Withers cannot resist "assisting" homicide detective Oliver Piper. In this novel, she is on vacation in Hollywood and on the set of a movie about Lizzie Borden when the screenwriter is found dead. Six comic films about Withers appeared in the 1930s, most successfully starring Edna May Oliver. **Introduction by Otto Penzler.**

Otto Penzler, ed., *Golden Age Bibliomysteries*. Stories of murder, theft, and suspense occur with alarming regularity in the unlikely world of books and bibliophiles, including bookshops, libraries, and private rare book collections, written by such giants of the mystery genre as Ellery Queen, Cornell Woolrich, Lawrence G. Blochman, Vincent Starrett, and Anthony Boucher. **Introduction by Otto Penzler.**

Otto Penzler, ed., *Golden Age Detective Stories*. The history of American mystery fiction has its pantheon of authors who have influenced and entertained readers for nearly a century, reaching its peak during the Golden Age, and this collection pays homage to the work of the most acclaimed: Cornell Woolrich, Erle Stanley Gardner, Craig Rice, Ellery Queen, Dorothy B. Hughes, Mary Roberts Rinehart, and more. **Introduction by Otto Penzler.**

Otto Penzler, ed., *Golden Age Locked Room Mysteries*. The so-called impossible crime category reached its zenith during the 1920s, 1930s, and 1940s, and this volume includes the greatest of the great authors who mastered the form: John Dickson Carr, Ellery Queen, C. Daly King, Clayton Rawson, and Erle Stanley Gardner. Like great magicians, these literary conjurors will baffle and delight readers. **Introduction by Otto Penzler.**

Ellery Queen, *The Adventures of Ellery Queen*. These stories are the earliest short works to feature Queen as a detective and are among the best of the author's fair-play mysteries. So many of the elements that comprise the gestalt of Queen may be found in these tales: alternate solutions, the dying clue, a bizarre crime, and the author's ability to find fresh variations of works by other authors. **Introduction by Otto Penzler.**

Ellery Queen, *The American Gun Mystery.* A rodeo comes to New York City at the Colosseum. The headliner is Buck Horne, the once popular film cowboy who opens the show leading a charge of forty whooping cowboys until they pull out their guns and fire into the air. Buck falls to the ground, shot dead. The police instantly lock the doors to search everyone but the offending weapon has completely vanished. **Introduction by Otto Penzler.**

Ellery Queen, *The Chinese Orange Mystery.* The offices of publisher Donald Kirk have seen strange events but nothing like this. A strange man is found dead with two long spears alongside his back. And, though no one was seen entering or leaving the room, everything has been turned backwards or upside down: pictures face the wall, the victim's clothes are worn backwards, the rug upside down. Why in the world? **Introduction by Otto Penzler.**

Ellery Queen, *The Dutch Shoe Mystery.* Millionaire philanthropist Abagail Doorn falls into a coma and she is rushed to the hospital she funds for an emergency operation by one of the leading surgeons on the East Coast. When she is wheeled into the operating theater, the sheet covering her body is pulled back to reveal her garroted corpse—the first of a series of murders **Introduction by Otto Penzler.**

Ellery Queen, *The Egyptian Cross Mystery.* A small-town schoolteacher is found dead, headed, and tied to a T-shaped cross on December 25th, inspiring such sensational headlines as "Crucifixion on Christmas Day." Amateur sleuth Ellery Queen is so intrigued he travels to Virginia but fails to solve the crime. Then a similar murder takes place on New York's Long Island—and then another. **Introduction by Otto Penzler.**

Ellery Queen, *The Siamese Twin Mystery.* When Ellery and his father encounter a raging forest fire on a mountain, their only hope is to drive up to an isolated hillside manor

owned by a secretive surgeon and his strange guests. While playing solitaire in the middle of the night, the doctor is shot. The only clue is a torn playing card. Suspects include a society beauty, a valet, and conjoined twins. **Introduction by Otto Penzler.**

Ellery Queen, *The Spanish Cape Mystery.* Amateur detective Ellery Queen arrives in the resort town of Spanish Cape soon after a young woman and her uncle are abducted by a gun-toting, one-eyed giant. The next day, the woman's somewhat dicey boyfriend is found murdered—totally naked under a black fedora and opera cloak. **Introduction by Otto Penzler.**

Patrick Quentin, *A Puzzle for Fools.* Broadway producer Peter Duluth takes to the bottle when his wife dies but enters a sanitarium to dry out. Malevolent events plague the hospital, including when Peter hears his own voice intone, "There will be murder." And there is. He investigates, aided by a young woman who is also a patient. This is the first of nine mysteries featuring Peter and Iris Duluth. **Introduction by Otto Penzler.**

Clayton Rawson, *Death from a Top Hat.* When the New York City Police Department is baffled by an apparently impossible crime, they call on The Great Merlini, a retired stage magician who now runs a Times Square magic shop. In his first case, two occultists have been murdered in a room locked from the inside, their bodies positioned to form a pentagram. **Introduction by Otto Penzler.**

Craig Rice, *Eight Faces at Three.* Gin-soaked John J. Malone, defender of the guilty, is notorious for getting his culpable clients off. It's the innocent ones who are problems. Like Holly Inglehart, accused of piercing the black heart of her well-heeled aunt Alexandria with a lovely Florentine paper cutter. No one who knew the old battle-ax liked her, but Holly's prints were found on the murder weapon. **Introduction by Lisa Lutz.**

Craig Rice, *Home Sweet Homicide.* Known as the Dorothy Parker of mystery fiction for her memorable wit, Craig Rice was the first detective writer to appear on the cover of *Time* magazine. This comic mystery features two kids who are trying to find a husband for their widowed mother while she's engaged in sleuthing. Filmed with the same title in 1946 with Peggy Ann Garner and Randolph Scott. **Introduction by Otto Penzler.**

Mary Roberts Rinehart, *The Album*. Crescent Place is a quiet enclave of wealthy people in which nothing ever happens—until a bedridden old woman is attacked by an intruder with an ax. *The New York Times* stated: "All Mary Roberts Rinehart mystery stories are good, but this one is better." **Introduction by Otto Penzler.**

Mary Roberts Rinehart, *The Haunted Lady*. The arsenic in her sugar bowl was wealthy widow Eliza Fairbanks' first clue that somebody wanted her dead. Nightly visits of bats, birds, and rats, obviously aimed at scaring the dowager to death, was the second. Eliza calls the police, who send nurse Hilda Adams, the amateur sleuth they refer to as "Miss Pinkerton," to work undercover to discover the culprit. **Introduction by Otto Penzler.**

Mary Roberts Rinehart, *Miss Pinkerton*. Hilda Adams is a nurse, not a detective, but she is observant and smart and so it is common for Inspector Patton to call on her for help. Her success results in his calling her "Miss Pinkerton." *The New Republic* wrote: "From thousands of hearts and homes the cry will go up: Thank God for Mary Roberts Rinehart." **Introduction by Carolyn Hart.**

Mary Roberts Rinehart, *The Red Lamp*. Professor William Porter refuses to believe that the seaside manor he's just inherited is haunted but he has to convince his wife to move in. However, he soon sees evidence of the occult phenomena of which the townspeople speak. Whether it is a spirit or a human being, Porter accepts that there is a connection to the rash of murders that have terrorized the countryside. **Introduction by Otto Penzler.**

Mary Roberts Rinehart, *The Wall*. For two decades, Mary Roberts Rinehart was the second-best-selling author in America (only Sinclair Lewis outsold her) and was beloved for her tales of suspense. In a magnificent mansion, the ex-wife of one of the owners turns up making demands and is found dead the next day. And there are more dark secrets lying behind the walls of the estate. **Introduction by Otto Penzler.**

Joel Townsley Rogers, *The Red Right Hand*. This extraordinary whodunit that is as puzzling as it is terrifying was identified by crime fiction scholar Jack Adrian as "one of the dozen or so finest mystery novels of the 20th century." A deranged killer sends a doctor on a quest for the truth—deep into the recesses of his own mind—when he and his bride-to-be elope but pick up a terrifying sharp-toothed hitch-hiker. **Introduction by Joe R. Lansdale.**

Roger Scarlett, *Cat's Paw*. The family of the wealthy old bachelor Martin Greenough cares far more about his money than they do about him. For his birthday, he invites all his potential heirs to his mansion to tell them what they hope to hear. Before he can disburse funds, however, he is murdered, and the Boston Police Department's big problem is that there are too many suspects. **Introduction by Curtis Evans**

Vincent Starrett, *Dead Man Inside*. 1930s Chicago is a tough town but some crimes are more bizarre than others. Customers arrive at a haberdasher to find a corpse in the window and a sign on the door: *Dead Man Inside! I am Dead. The store will not open today*. This is just one of a series of odd murders that terrorizes the city. Reluctant detective Walter Ghost leaps into action to learn what is behind the plague. **Introduction by Otto Penzler.**

Vincent Starrett, *The Great Hotel Murder*. Theater critic and amateur sleuth Riley Blackwood investigates a murder in a Chicago hotel where the dead man had changed rooms with a stranger who had registered under a fake name. *The New York Times* described it as "an ingenious plot with enough complications to keep the reader guessing." **Introduction by Lyndsay Faye.**

Vincent Starrett, *Murder on 'B' Deck*. Walter Ghost, a psychologist, scientist, explorer, and former intelligence officer, is on a cruise ship and his friend novelist Dunsten Mollock, a Nigel Bruce-like Watson whose role is to offer occasional comic relief, accommodates when he fails to leave the ship before it takes off. Although they make mistakes along the way, the amateur sleuths solve the shipboard murders. **Introduction by Ray Betzner.**

Phoebe Atwood Taylor, *The Cape Cod Mystery*. Vacationers have flocked to Cape Cod to avoid the heat wave that hit the Northeast and find their holiday unpleasant when the area is flooded with police trying to find the murderer of a muckraking journalist who took a cottage for the season. Finding a solution falls to Asey Mayo, "the Cape Cod Sherlock," known for his worldly wisdom, folksy humor, and common sense. **Introduction by Otto Penzler.**

S. S. Van Dine, *The Benson Murder Case.* The first of 12 novels to feature Philo Vance, the most popular and influential detective character of the early part of the 20th century. When wealthy stockbroker Alvin Benson is found shot to death in a locked room in his mansion, the police are baffled until the erudite flaneur and art collector arrives on the scene. Paramount filmed it in 1930 with William Powell as Vance. **Introduction by Ragnar Jónasson.**

Cornell Woolrich, *The Bride Wore Black.* The first suspense novel by one of the greatest of all noir authors opens with a bride and her new husband walking out of the church. A car speeds by, shots ring out, and he falls dead at her feet. Determined to avenge his death, she tracks down everyone in the car, concluding with a shocking surprise. It was filmed by Francois Truffaut in 1968, starring Jeanne Moreau. **Introduction by Eddie Muller.**

Cornell Woolrich, *Deadline at Dawn.* Quinn is overcome with guilt about having robbed a stranger's home. He meets Bricky, a dime-a-dance girl, and they fall for each other. When they return to the crime scene, they discover a dead body. Knowing Quinn will be accused of the crime, they race to find the true killer before he's arrested. A 1946 film starring Susan Hayward was loosely based on the plot. **Introduction by David Gordon.**

Cornell Woolrich, *Waltz into Darkness.* A New Orleans businessman successfully courts a woman through the mail but he is shocked to find when she arrives that she is not the plain brunette whose picture he'd received but a radiant blond beauty. She soon absconds with his fortune. Wracked with disappointment and loneliness, he vows to track her down. When he finds her, the real nightmare begins. **Introduction by Wallace Stroby.**